THE TURN

BOOKS BY
CHRISTOPHER RANSOM

The Turn
Beneath the Lake
The Orphan
The Fading
The People Next Door
The Haunting of James Hastings
The Birthing House

THE TURN

A NOVEL

CHRISTOPHER RANSOM

INTERNATIONALLY BESTSELLING AUTHOR

BLACK
STONE
PUBLISHING

Copyright © 2025 by Christopher Ransom
Published in 2025 by Blackstone Publishing
Cover and book design by Kathryn Galloway English

Printed in the United States of America
Originally published in hardcover by Blackstone Publishing in 2025

First paperback edition: 2025
ISBN 979-8-228-00064-3
Fiction / Literary

Version 1

Blackstone Publishing
31 Mistletoe Rd.
Ashland, OR 97520

www.BlackstonePublishing.com

For Darl Bower and Kenneth Quay,
the finest of men

Turn: The midway point in an eighteen-hole round of golf. Making the turn means you have finished the front nine holes and are facing the back nine. Commonly a short break golfers take to use the restroom, grab a hot dog or refreshments from the clubhouse, or clear their minds after a poor showing on the front.

To turn for home.

The only thing a golfer needs is more daylight.

—Ben Hogan

Welcome to Twin Peaks Golf Course

Northern Colorado's Best Golf Value!

Remember to respect the course and play with a positive mindset at all times.

Muni—A municipal golf course, owned by the city and its taxpayers. You're standing on one. Do not mistake this for your own personal playground. You hit into somebody, damage a house, start a fight, pee on the course, or otherwise act a fool, we will *throw your ass out* and send you the bill. Yes, we're talking to YOU.

Tees—If you have to ask which ones to play from, you're not ready to play from the tips.

Golf swing—Yours needs work. Schedule a lesson with our club pro, Coach Lowry.

Attire—Collars are preferred, but who are we kidding. Just try not to dress like trash and keep it zipped up.

Breakfast ball—A free retee on the first hole because you drank too much last night or got stage fright. See also . . .

Mulligan—Free strokes are for chumps, but do what you gotta do to make it through another day.

Par—The expected score, in strokes, assigned to each hole.

Birdie—A score of one stroke under par on any given hole. It never hurts to dream.

Bogey—A score of one stroke over par on any given hole. You're going to see a lot of these.

Double bogey—Two strokes over. Relax. You suck at golf, just like 99.99% of the population.

Triple—For God's sake, stop counting, pick up, and move on to the next hole.

Eagle—Two under. A bird of prey you are not likely to see today or ever.

Ace—A hole in one. Congrats! You owe *everybody* in your group *and* the clubhouse a drink.

Divot—Repair the damage you are responsible for. That bottle of sand in your cart is not free cat litter.

Pace of play—Stop taking five practice swings and move your ass. Most people have lives, and you're ruining mine.

Ready golf—Never mind etiquette. If you're ready to hit, go. See "pace of play" above.

Ranger—The grumpy old bastard scowling at you for not following the rules. Has no real authority—he just needs something to do in retirement. Accepts bribes.

Gimme—A short putt your playing partners allow you to pick up without finishing. Common practice among golfers in deep denial about their abilities. Gimme? Gimme a break!

Golfy (a.k.a. GED or golf erection disorder)—An ailment that afflicts men who no longer have a sex life and turn to golf to fulfill their physical and emotional needs. Extremely common ages forty plus.

Handicap—The numerical measure of a golfer's ability, used to enable players of different abilities to compete against one another. Lower handicap = better player. A thing golfers lie about all the time.

Scratch—A player with a handicap of zero, even par.

Slice—A shot that curves violently to the right (for a right-handed golfer). Unfortunately, this is the most common ball flight in golf. The only cure is to quit the game or take lessons. See Coach Lowry.

Hook / snap hook—Opposite of a slice, ball moving right to left, usually short, not good.

Draw—A beautiful shot that curves right to left. Every amateur thinks they need one. Let it go already.

Fade—A lesser, much more desirable slice.

Flop shot—If your name is not Phil Mickelson, do not attempt this.

Shank—Laughably poor shot that fires off wildly in front of others. Strong indication you need to see Coach Lowry.

Pork missile—A hot dog, bratwurst, meat stick, or other elongated animal protein masquerading as food. Try the Dottie Special—a pork missile with chili, cheese, and jalapeños.

Piss missile—A stunningly well-executed shot that flies straight and goes forever.

Swing juice—One drink per nine holes = keeps you loose. Two drinks per nine = you're pushing it. Three-plus drinks per nine = how's your marriage these days?

White Claw—While there may be "no laws while on the Claws" at your fraternity house, rest assured there are laws out here. Don't be a shithead, or we will throw you out on your ass and send you the bill.

Fireball—If you like the taste of antifreeze and seek to compound all your life problems in one shot, by all means "fire" away. And NO, the cart girl will NOT do one with you. Stop asking!

Yips—Like leprosy, a contagious disorder we shall not speak of. Take a month off. Or just quit.

Thank you for playing Twin Peaks.
We hope to see you again soon!

player handicap -36

My tee time is six forty. I set alarms for five, five thirty, five forty-five, and just to be safe, six fifteen. I know what's coming. The pain. The game. My next chance at glory.

The Masters unfolded a month ago but continues to echo, with its eye-watering botanical glory, the players with their transcendent shots and unholy heartbreaks, the billiard-smooth greens, this great ode to tradition reminding me of my father even as the game summons me toward some indefinable greener pasture of my own. It's early May, and each day is a little longer and brighter, filling with the promise of a better start, a swing secret unlocked, my new personal best. I'm ready to take the next step in my game. In my life.

I was so excited last night that even though I told myself I would go to sleep by eleven, I was practically twitching until two. Drinks and more drinks and headphones pumping N.W.A., Eric B. & Rakim, and a little Miley to make my head swim while I rehearsed my takeaway in the home office. I managed to drift for a couple of hours until the *beep beep beep* woke me, and now I pound water as fast as I can. Half a whiskey and Coke left warm by the sink. Shudder, finish it.

Hot shower, full-body rinse in three minutes. Getting clean isn't the point. I stretch my back, letting the water pelt me in the ass as the steam loosens my sinuses. Hot, then warm. Then slowly dial back to lukewarm, cool, and finally ball-shocking frigid, Scottish-style. Brace myself against the tile, shiver out toxins.

SPF 50—check. Cool-dry underwear, ankle socks, joggers, the thermal-responsive Nike polo I scored at Marshalls for 80 percent off, my best quarter zip—check. Crack a beer in the kitchen, golf bag to the trunk, yardage watch charged and strapped on—check. Cooler filled with White Claws and a frozen Snickers—check. Balls, tees, phone, nicotine, cash for the cart girls and gambling—check, check, check.

Ready? Ready.

Peep my phone on the way. Ah, shit. The boys had to bail last minute. One forgot to tell his wife. Another is too hungover from playing poker all night. The third saw the forecast and said nope. A rare May chill in Colorado, a dusting of snow last night.

Screw it, I'm going anyway, can't waste a day. This might be the one.

In the clubhouse there are men. Men who would rather be here than anywhere else in the world. This is a place they understand and are understood. The TVs are always tuned to the Golf Channel. In the bathroom, someone's releasing their pre-round jitters explosively while a couple of the old dogs try to piss. "My dad taught me you're supposed to wash your hands after you piss," one says. "My dad taught me not to piss on your hands," his buddy answers. They laugh at a joke they have made a thousand times.

This is where you meet a man whose wife was up at four thirty to make her husband coffee, eggs, bacon, toast, and one big Bloody Mary with the right number of olives and a pinch of celery salt because she loves him and wants him to be happy, and she wants him out of the house for the next six hours because she has a life too.

What about the women? They're growing in number. Some are just along for the ride, reading books in the carts with blankets over their laps. But many more do play, in various forms: as one half of a young couple that's taken up golf as this season's hipster activity, the widow who golfed with her old man for decades before the coronary took him on one of the fairways, the ones who come for the social benefits of the women's league, and even the solo addicts, out here purely for the love of the game. Like the one we see here, dressed like a climber, small and geared for battle. Took up golf at her husband's request, was surprised at how the swing came naturally to her, and in no time she was beating hubby. He was all butt hurt and quit the game, they divorced, and she soldiers on with her GPS trolley, one hundred lessons, keeps the ball moving right down Main Street on her way to a seventy-eight.

But those are rare, like spotting a kit fox. This is still mostly a boys' club, a place where we get to dress up in bright athletic fabrics and strut around with high-tech weaponry, pretending our days of physical relevancy did not end after the varsity squad.

I check in, eyes barely open, hands a little shaky. I'm overweight and out of shape, on two different blood pressure meds. I drink too much. I always rent a cart. I don't take work or women or my finances or anything else seriously, except the chance to break ninety today.

I set up on the first tee in a pair of beater running shoes because I can't commit to real golf shoes yet, haven't earned them. Temperature is forty-one degrees, might reach sixty-five. The frosty fairway crackles under my steps. I force the tee into near-frozen ground. Place the white ball atop. Set my feet.

Empty thy mind. Clean white sphere: All I have to do is sweep through it, open my chest to the target. I hover, waiting for the confidence to manifest, and Jim Nantz narrates in his soothing bedtime voice:

The newcomer Sweet likes driver here, and why wouldn't he? It's only the straightest, flattest, widest par four within fifty miles. He's got nothing to fear but his own inner demons, the noble fight all golfers must join. Tiger, Phil, Koepka, Rory, even the singular Bobby Jones—all the great ones had their dark days on and off the course. What he wants here is a nice easy swing, nothing too cute, just harnessing all two hundred and thirty pounds of his battered, beaten, and self-abused form to strike one clean. The entire golf world knows just how hard it's been, shanking his career, multiple girlfriends, and that one hopeful marriage into the algae-covered pond that has become his sad-ass, self-defeating, shit-for-nothing, fucked-up life. It all comes down to this, friends. Will today be the beginning of A NEW ERA?

I bring the big dog barking—*whuPING!* Center face flex, arms finishing high. The ball soars, holding a nice cut. Maybe 250 in the fairway, just past the white stick. *Mmm, baby.*

Don't get too excited. One shot at a time. Let's try the eight here—always liked the eight. Nice mix of loft, control, distance. The ball takes off high, drifting left, missing the green, but manages to catch the shoulder, and I get the member's bounce as it kicks back across the dance floor until it rests maybe fifteen feet below right of the cup. Lucky, but we'll take luck. There's enough bad luck out here—gotta take the good when it comes.

So we're on in two. It's a par four. We have a real shot at birdie. Could start the day one under par. Skin prickling at the possibility. A gulp of that grapefruit White Claw as I unsheathe the flatstick and circle the glittering green, noting the slope from all sides. I probably won't make it because the first two swings were a fluke. I trace a line from the cup back to my ball and don't look up again, like Grandpa taught me thirty years ago.

Sweep. Listen for it, the sound like no other sound, that sweet *plottle.*

But no. It rolls over the left edge and keeps going; it won't stop. Jesus! Fuck! The comeback is six goddamn feet. Un-fucking-believable.

Okay, we can still make par here. Par is nice. Par is great. Stay above the hole. Let it crest and topple over. Read it. Settle. Go.

Maybe . . . !

Not even close. Short-sided it by three feet. Nerves. What the fuck is wrong with me?

No one is watching. I could cheat. Call that last one a gimme on the warm-up hole. People do it all the time. But who am I really doing this for? What is the point? No one will know, but *I* will know. And if we're not keeping the real score, why keep score at all?

Stop overthinking everything. Just putt the ball. Three feet straight uphill. A blind man could make this. Whatever. Tap.

It slides by the cup.

Tap in for a six.

I'm considering slitting my wrists as I press the plus sign on my watch twice. I am now plus two through one hole. Probably finish forty over. Sloppy mind, sloppy game, sloppy-ass life. I want to cry. Scream. Smash my putter into the cart and wreck everything. I should go home and go back to bed. I should sell my house and move to Guam.

I press on.

Over the next twelve holes, my life becomes a horror show. I can't hit anything anywhere I intend to. I lose balls, duff drives, chunk approaches, and continue to putt like Mr. Magoo. By the time I reach number fifteen, all seven of my White Claws are gone. I haven't eaten a thing. The morning is still cold, the frost giving way to wet muck. My lower back feels like a shattered beer bottle. The world has taken on a blurry sheen of simmering rage. I feel sick, cursed. The end is nigh. I don't know what this is, but it isn't fun.

Number fifteen is a short par four, 340 yards. Pretty little hole. A westward wind pushes at my back, makes my nose run. I decide to give this one hell, nothing left to lose. Everything drains out of me, including the ability to care what happens next.

I unleash and, beyond all reason, catch the sweet spot. The ball goes like a cruise missile, not moving an inch left or right, and the wind carries it way, way down there. I drive up and park beside the ball and look at my yardage watch.

Three hundred seven.

My laughter erupts. My dick gets an inch longer. A half-swing gap wedge lands me on the green, seven feet right of the cup. I read the bend and don't hesitate on the birdie putt. Smooth tap. Ball goes over the top, and gravity sucks it back down.

Plottle.

Inside me, something brighter than a rainbow shines. Something more mysterious than a woman lowers her hood to let me see her face. Something more than grace enters my blood.

For a moment I am immortal, and a fleeting thought stirs:

The rest no longer matters.

Work and women and illness and terrorism and mass shootings and viruses and greed and sadness and addiction and confusion and every other tragedy perpetuating itself across this absurd and fragile world—they can take the day off. I don't care about any of that. I only care about making this little white ball do more good things.

At last, I am home.

part one
finding fairways

the POS

I played some golf with my dad and a few friends here and there during my teens and twenties, but real golf—capital-*G* golf, that deliciously evil affliction that grabs you by the lungs and infects your dreams and empties your wallet, *that golf*—came to me later in life, right around the time basically everything else went to shit.

It was the time of the D-words. Dogs died (two). Divorce. Dad died. Diet (poor). Drinking way too much. Dick problems. I'd been drinking most of a bottle of whiskey nightly, a genuinely awesome (in the original sense: awe inspiring and scary) amount of booze for one man to consume. And the past ninety days had turned truly diabolical as I'd proceeded to suffer at least five panic attacks. Then there was that other number.

Forty-five.

Not a bad score for a recreational golfer on the front nine. But that was my age and not a golf score. You could say I was not playing well at the game of life, sliding into a moral and physiological decline from which I might never return.

I had a pretty good hunch my employment status would be

the next domino to fall. Over the past fifteen years, I had been a copywriter, product-marketing writer, UX writer, content producer, whatever title was in fashion that year. Now I was senior content manager at Flagstaff Solutions, a software company just outside Boulder, Colorado. I wrote enterprise-network and personal-security applications, and I didn't care about any of it. The job was boring but easy and paid well. I had been coasting in my career, but so what? Sometimes life is hard enough. Not everybody needs to become a filmmaker or entrepreneur or VP of something in order to sleep at night. I hadn't been sleeping very well, either, but that was likely the sauce. And the women. And just the state of all things Casey Sweet in general.

My boss, Dave Strickland, knew we had nicknamed him Diamond Dave behind his back, and instead of being angry or hurt, he wore the moniker with pride, pretending to be a big Van Halen fan. The day of reckoning, I arrived a little after eleven, and he was hovering around the creative team. He spotted me at once and snap-pointed toward his office.

"Lemme grab a coffee."

Dave looked displeased as I dropped my backpack and headed to the break room. I poured myself a large coffee and added three sugars and three creams. I sipped, burning my tongue. My hands were shaking, but only a little. I was still drunk, but the world felt normal, comfortably fuzzy, inconsequential. I was dreading the next six hours in my cubicle more than whatever Dave had in store for me.

"Hey, Casey!" Lauren said, entering the little kitchen. "How are ya?"

"What's the story, morning glory? How's the Arapahoe cart optimization coming along?"

Today Lauren wore a long sweater that looked like a duster

or a cape, her tall brown boots, and a hat with an actual feather in the brim. Country chic. We'd been working together for almost three years, and there was a time when I carried a painful torch for her. But I'd never made a move, because even though she did not report to me, a relationship gaffe could nuke an entire creative team's chemistry, not to mention my career. Or hers.

She swept by to refill her water bottle. "It's almost there. We can chat later. I want to show you my new flow and some options for the CTAs."

Call-to-action buttons. Cart flow. More complex than one would imagine, especially considering we were trying to convince IT pros that purchasing a ten-grand-per-month security solution really was as easy as buying a new pair of shoes on Zappos.

"Perfect. I'll catch up with you in a bit."

"Thank God it's Wednesday," she said, and I wondered when we had all started thanking God the week was barely half over. As an office, we were running out of banter.

"I like your hat," I said on the way out. "It's so you."

"Thanks."

"Have a seat, Casey."

Dave wore a blue oxford shirt, khaki "work" joggers, and silver Adidas trainers, just to let the team know he wasn't a total corporate dick. The only things on his glass desk were a small laptop and a wireless mouse. No monitors or files or paper of any kind. He was fussily neat that way, but it made you wonder how much work he really did. He was our senior vice president of marketing and had come from international banking. He was not great at product development, design, or marketing. He was a whip, a game show host, the enforcer. I knew he liked me on some personal level, but I also sensed he wouldn't trust me to park his car.

"Casey, how are you?" he said as I sat down.

"Thank God it's Wednesday." I sipped more coffee. "How are you?"

"You went home sick yesterday?"

It was a little more dramatic than that. I'd had a full-blown panic attack in the men's bathroom, on the toilet to be precise. But as funny as that may seem, it wasn't. At that point, I had no idea these experiences were panic attacks. I had no idea what a panic attack was. I lost my breath, my entire body went into a tremor, and my vision darkened as if occluded by raging black drops of poison. Each time, I was convinced I was dying, having a stroke or a heart attack. Each was the most terrifying two hours of my life. Each was a new horror and always felt like the end.

"I had a headache, so I worked from home the rest of the afternoon."

"Oh, so you *were* working. You should have told someone. We were worried."

"I should have emailed."

Now he went to his office door and closed it softly. "Is there anything you want to tell me, Casey?"

"About . . . ?"

"Anything. You can talk to me."

"Thanks, Dave. I appreciate that."

We had a standoff. I didn't know what he wanted me to say, but I sure as hell wasn't going to say it.

"I need to be clear here," he began. "And I am saying this with concern: You don't smell right, Casey."

I frowned. "I smell?"

"You smell like alcohol."

"Now? I smell like"—nope, not gonna say it—"that now?"

He nodded. "Did you have a big night?"

My anger was rising. My personal life was none of his business. "What do you want?"

"I want to help."

"Fuck off." I think we were both surprised by this.

"Hey now." Dave put his hands up. "Easy. We're just talking."

"Fire me," I said. "Please. You'll be doing me a favor."

Dave scowled. "That's what you want? To be fired?"

"I don't need this," I said. "So do what you gotta do."

Dave sighed. "Casey, if I wanted to fire you, I could have done that months ago." He stood and began to pace before his whiteboard, blue marker in hand. "Hear me out. I think this will make sense to you."

On the board, he made a list:

ROCK STAR
GRINDER
AVERAGE EMPLOYEE
CRUISER
PROBLEM
PIECE OF SHIT
COMPLETE BAG OF SHIT

"Do you know what this is?"

"A little early for my quarterly review, isn't it?"

"Let's call it a sliding scale." He began to walk me through it. "You got your rock stars, the one-in-a-hundred killers. The people who are both super talented and hard workers. We're lucky if we can find one of these every few years—they're mostly extinct. Next you have generally excellent employees, the grinders. No geniuses here, but they're our real workhorses. They put in hard hours, and they care about the mission. Below your grinders we have the average employees, self-explanatory. Next comes what I like to call a cruiser. Not an outright bad employee—the cruiser is a decent worker, not overly talented but dependable, kind of just always there. Hell, most companies run on these types of folks because they can be slotted into roles no one else wants.

"For my first two years here, you were a grinder, you had your teeth on the bone, and maybe, just maybe, you could have become a rock star. You made me wonder, I'll give you that. Then gradually you backslid through average and became a cruiser. Okay, everyone has ups and downs. But you didn't really pull out of the slump. You did your work. You skated the rules a bit, but essentially no one noticed or worried too much, at least until about nine months ago, when you became a problem. Coming in late, leaving early, setting a poor example for the rest of the team, several of whom look up to you. Your work turned sloppy. You looked increasingly annoyed, resentful of meetings—"

"Everyone hates meetings," I said.

"You've taken twelve personal days this year—make that thirteen counting yesterday and this morning—and now here you are, reeking like a distillery, eyes like deviled eggs, and it's time we acknowledge where you are on the scale. You've become a piece of shit, and most days you're doing your damnedest to earn your next merit badge. The real problem I'm facing now is a simple question: Is Casey Sweet merely a piece of shit, or has he become a complete bag of shit? Because when you're just a piece of shit, people see it, but they will still like you, they will forgive you. There's still hope for you.

"But once you become a complete bag of shit, there's no turning back. Family turns on you. Friends write you off forever. You get shitcanned. You stop paying the mortgage, the

child support. Soon there is a default on the car lease. You develop gout, maybe have a stroke. You've somehow become all the things you never wanted to become, and you don't care about anything or anyone anymore because you're such a—"
He snapped his fingers and pointed at me.

"Complete bag of shit?"

"You got it. Now you tell me, Casey. Are you merely a piece of shit, or have you become a complete bag of shit? Because one of these has a future and the other does not. I just want to be clear on what we're dealing with. So I can help."

He capped his marker and sat back in his chair, fingers laced across his chest.

I sipped some coffee. "That's heartwarming."

"We're here for you. If you can convince me it's not too late."

Oh, this was good. Perfect. I had been unchained.

"I'm not in the mood to convince you of anything, Dave. I don't like being here. The fluorescent lights make me feel sick. My cubicle is a litter box lined with felt. I'm under surveillance from the moment I walk in, yet you don't have any idea what I accomplish in an hour, let alone eight. You're a quota guy. You think what we do is the same as building trucks on an assembly line. How many rivets did he rivet today? You don't have the first fucking clue how truly collaborative creative work leads to brilliant products. And here you are, trying to recruit me for a job I already have. You remember how the Folsom app began? Our first consumer product. No one asked me to do it. There was no creative brief. It was my idea. I pitched it. I wrote it in sixty days, and it was flawless. Folsom now has three hundred twenty-seven thousand four hundred fifty-eight users at five bucks a month, and it's made you and this company a pile of money. So here's the news about my status: You make ten times what I do, and I think *you're* a phone-it-in cruiser piece of shit. I think you're in above your head and you need people to blame. I think your silver sneakers are silly, and so does the rest of the team. And regardless, I'm too old for rah-rah shit like this"—I stood and pointed at the whiteboard—"to work on me. I quit, effective now."

Dave barked a faux laugh and got to his feet. "There he is. The funnyman writer, using his words. Full of it now, aren't you? You quit on us months ago, pal. So don't tell me about quitting. You don't get to quit! But here's what you can do. Are you listening?"

"Probably not." I dropped my coffee in his trash can, and it sloshed up the wall.

"You put some years in around here, so let's call it a sabbatical. It's April. I want you to take the summer. You will be paid for medical leave, seventy percent of your current salary. HR will handle all that bullshit. But you take a vacation, get some help, go clean yourself up, and don't become a complete bag of shit. Come back and see me around Labor Day. If you still want to quit then, I'll shake your hand and pay you out thirty days. But if you do come back, I want the Casey Sweet I knew two years ago. I want you to come back stronger than ever and become my next director. I believe you can, and I believe that if you don't, things in your life are going to go very badly. You have a real opportunity here. Up to you."

On the wall to the right of Dave's desk was one of those generic corporate motivational posters that aspire to the profound. This one featured a mountain climber on some ridiculous snowy peak, his parka a red speck among the terrible elements. It said:

NEVER GIVE UP
Your next step might change the world.

"I may not punch in at eight and stay till six," I said, "because I am not a robot, and the work I shepherd and deliver is not something one of your AIs can do. Ask every person in this company if they've ever had a problem with me, if I've ever caused them to miss a deadline. You won't find one. So I'm thinking, basically, the fuck else do you want from me?"

Dave put a hand on my shoulder and sounded like he might shed a tear. "Casey, I know you lost your dad a few years ago. That's never an easy thing. But the bottom line is, you aren't here. Even when you show up, you don't *show up*."

We had one last standoff. I realized I would not be free until I gave him some sign that any of this meant something.

I raised my hand to high-five Dave. "Today is the first day of the rest of my life!"

Dave stood there blinking at me, then turned back to his office and shut the door.

I fetched my backpack and considered making the rounds to bid the team farewell. I felt I owed them an explanation, Lauren most of all. But that was Dave's responsibility now. I thought it unlikely I would ever set foot in this building again. My work was done here, and I was free to do whatever I pleased.

On the way home I stopped at the liquor store and bought a handle of Seagram's Seven and a six-pack of Diet Coke.

cord-cutting

I didn't tell anyone about my sabbatical at first, not my mom, my friends, or my ex-wife, Blair. We'd been divorced for seven years but still spoke every couple of weeks, and it was always Blair who called me to check in. I harbored no delusions of getting back with her. She was remarried and had a family now. In our current reality, we were more like siblings—she the assertive and successful big sister, I the delinquent and disappointing younger brother.

But in the little amber sphere where I preserved her, she was still Ideal Blair, the Blair of our courtship through, say, the first two years of the marriage. Ideal Blair was the one who had brought out my A game, my first great lunge at a proper middle-class life and lasting commitment. She was the woman who could—all in the span of a Saturday—build a spreadsheet for our future, paint and refinish the cabinets in our first apartment kitchen, run six miles, paint her toes while idly reading forty pages of literature and watching me cook dinner, finish a bottle of wine without slurring, and then fuck me like she was trying to brand me for life. That was the Blair I tried not to dwell on, because she was as beautiful and painful as a Pearl Jam song.

After she left, I didn't feel destroyed or act crazy. Instead, I buried my emotions and embarked upon a slow, years-long descent into numb depravity. I was stoic through the dissolution of the marriage. Rather than seethe, I mellowed. Instead of fighting over furniture, I helped her load the moving truck. I didn't cry. I was too busy consoling my crying mother. Blair insisted on leaving me the house for a year. She wouldn't be needing it, seeing as how she was moving in with Carl.

Every marriage has its star, and Blair's light retreated slowly, leaving me cast in the role of recently divorced, not-quite-forty, shambling but still-marketable guy. Women, including some of our friends and colleagues, seemed to sense Blair's cattle brand on me, a USDA stamp of alpha-woman approval lurking somewhere beneath the unkempt hair and hoodie rotation. I lost some weight and took on the nervous, tail-wagging gait of a shelter pup. Probably why I adopted Jojo then, my three-legged bulldog.

The consolation calls and offers to meet for coffee spurted forth through my phone, flirt-bumped through the aisles of the grocery store, sprayed over the mulch at the dog park. I had the Sport Clips lady do something different with my hair. I bought new clothes. One night on a vodka-tonic roll, I charged into the dating apps with fearless confidence. I'd just lost an amazing woman but still had game—she was proof. As a writer, I had the small advantage of being able to string together a no-nonsense profile with a few clever lines, and the messages I sent were constructed to let the women know I had actually read their profiles. For my profile pics, I chose six photos, the ones Blair always said were good, and those seemed to work fine. The one or two photos that Blair happened to be standing in with me worked even better.

That's your ex-wife? Wow, what
happened, dude? You must be
de-VUH-stAY-ted!

It's all good, we ended things
amicably. I support her growth
100%.

Something about my data points pleased the algorithms. I matched with an array of women ages thirty-three to forty-nine, messaged many, and was soon guffawing at how quickly we reached the decision to plunge our tongues into each other's mouths, take off our clothes, suckle and pet and probe, and hey, we're already rounding third base, why not slide into home and tag fifth before we pass out? This happened at their place, my place, in cars, outside bars, and once in the women's bathroom of a fancy brunch place in Denver where the champagne was flowing a bit too freely and the bartender shouldn't have turned up Maroon 5 that loud.

There was little time for introspection and few expectations. Some were long-term single; others were similarly paroled from happily-ever-afters gone wrong. Some were still married, and some claimed Big Daddy was cool with sharing. They told me they were embracing life, working on themselves, up for adventure. They were unafraid to tell me over drinks what was going to happen next, probably tonight. They were unafraid to ask the hard-hitting questions. *What did you do to make your wife leave? You're not a psycho, are you? I already had one of those—he's still stalking me, in fact. You seem like a nice guy, so are you? Am I going to regret this?*

I don't know. No. Yes. Probably.

Blair had always been generous in bed, willing to try most

anything, and our sex life had followed a satisfying cadence right up until the last year. Still, after a certain amount of time with your spouse, you've seen and felt it all. You don't imagine you will ever be close to another woman, ever have another first kiss, ever know a new scent. Then you get divorced, and every woman becomes not just a new experience but a whole new milieu, another planet. There was a lot to take in. It was hard to tell how long I should stay. Sometimes after only two dates I could imagine moving to this welcoming foreign country permanently, but for all I knew it was ruled by a dictatorship. But if I fled too soon, I might miss the next great scene, like Seattle or Austin before the corporate money put all the weird on lockdown.

These dalliances played out in terms of weeks, sometimes months, but never long enough to fall back into the L-word, the one we were not ready to utter again. I was having an absolute ball not thinking about the specific things that had really led to my divorce. I was content to dwell in this middle ground of almost-relationships, this space where sex wasn't totally random and cheap but still felt weightless.

"We deserve this," one of them told me after our second date. Heidi the real estate phenom, top-five agent in her hotly trending market and climbing. Oh, how she wanted to reach number one. "And I will, Casey. Don't ever doubt me!" I didn't. She was almost militant with her black pageboy hair, her biceps swollen like lemons, her thick little CrossFit feet. When the making out turned breathy, she seemed on the verge of angry laughter. "I'm done pretending to be the good wife. *Ha-grrr.* I just want to feel alive again, right? Get in here, dude! *Uuungh-huh!*"

It all felt amazing, until it didn't. Somewhere around the two-year mark of my "swinging Larry from *Three's Company*" days, everything that had seemed effortless became a slog. Frictionless communication turned into delayed texts, drawn-out phone calls, odd silences, poorly timed happy hours, morning headaches. All this driving back and forth to Denver—going out late, staying up later, actually having sex, and then sexting more the next day—took its toll. I was drinking more, at random times, because if you're going to Monday-night bowling with fifty singles and the costume theme is pimps and hos, you're not doing that sober.

So maybe I was getting tired, cranky, a little lost. I stopped trying to meet new people and settled into a few (I call them the Final Four) that could be lumped into the general category of relationships, if not serious ones. The Final Four lasted three months, six months, a year, tops. Sex got scheduled. Small gifts were exchanged. We began to fight as our commitments to one another waxed and waned. Intimacy issues, more than one said. Translation: I had become simultaneously emotionally unavailable, sex obsessed, and barely able to get it up except when they threw a particularly naughty curveball my way. And none of them liked me seeing other women, though some of them saw other men.

Okay, look. I sincerely believed we were just casually dating, that this was understood by all involved, and while there is probably something unseemly about a man in his forties chap-sticking the platypus with four different women *on a yearlong basis*, I didn't believe I was violating any specific policy agreement. But feelings were hurt, including mine, so I must have been doing something wrong. In my defense:

Elise was separated but not divorced and was still in pity-love with her not-quite-ex-husband. I was good for happy hours, hookups, and long conversations on the phone. But in the rest of her life, to her family and friends, I was a ghost, a secret. A dildo hidden in a drawer.

But maybe that's just how not ready for prime time I was.

Katie had been ostensibly single but "just not really in a good place right now." Ever. Her life was filled with tragedies, one after another. Like her cat being sick, her sister not supporting her arguments with their mother, and her tummy aching because the waiter lied about the gluten-free pasta.

But maybe that's just how not sensitive I was.

Paige was always hiking, attending spiritual yoga retreats, and continuing her personal journey. She was one of those women who have a lot of male friends. I guess I was one of the lucky ones who made it through the gates occasionally. We never said goodbye. In a war of attrition, the calendar won.

Or maybe that's just how not on the journey I was.

Genna was a woman I knew from a job I had ten years ago. After my divorce, I curiosity-pinged her on LinkedIn. We had sex like five times and realized we weren't meant for each other but could still talk occasionally and sometimes have phone sex. She was moving to Japan.

And that's definitely how not Japan I was.

In this age of apps and texting, it seemed to me that your exes were rarely ever truly your exes. We were all hedging, and no one was ready to invest their whole heart into anything but themselves (and even that was a hard maybe). We all wanted the semblance of a relationship, especially the attention, but with maximum freedom and minimal expectations. Also, everyone was "crazy busy." Work was "so insane lately," and the world was "ending any day now." Who could deal with an actual relationship?

Eventually I realized they saw me as an easy hang. But once they started looking beyond the hang—to the commit, to the cohabit, to the rest of our goddamn lives—they didn't like what they saw any more than Blair did. I couldn't blame them. I was a piece of shit, after all. I was nice, even when I drank, but I drank all the time, and I had no idea where I was going or what I wanted. I was tired of romance, so I stopped trying. I stopped returning calls and texts, checking the apps. I stopped taking care of myself. This is a dangerous era one enters: male, single, wounded, hungry, with no woman or other governing forces in the vicinity.

Still wildly aroused, my spank bank chock full of recent material, I decided as long as I didn't complicate other people's lives, it was a free-for-all, "all" being me and my dick. The freedom in this was like going keto. Eat as much meat as you want, just avoid carbs, and get high on your body devouring itself. I opened the porn spigot wide.

First the dusty DVDs Blair and I had watched together, the tame Adam & Eve "romantic couple" stuff. Then the stuff I had only ever looked at when Blair was out of town, the direct stuff without storylines, churn and burn. Then new kinds of porn I had never considered, things that even scared me a little. But as the novelty of gonzo stepfamilies and glory tables wore off, I realized I had reached a Rubicon. Like Pinocchio after he smoked that nasty cigar and turned green, I scurried back to a Geppetto's workshop of "mainstream" staples.

The kind of porn that didn't seem so bad because the performers were authentic, consenting, progressive. Solo women sharing quietly. Hipster couples who seemed to be almost as in love with each other as they were in love with showing the world how depraved they could safely be in their own loving marriages. Porn made by women, for women. OnlyFans, where workers retained creative control of their content, and where I met regular girl-next-door types and eastern European types and yoga MILFs and had the pleasure of not only their porn but also their conversation. Lana Del Emotional became my primary virtual paramour. She not only sexted and video chatted me at what seemed value prices for this market (real-life dating had been costing me a helluva lot more than fifty dollars a week) but checked in during the day to ask how work was going, what shows I liked, how my cute doggy was doing. Pretend-girlfriend stuff. Sure, why not, at least everyone's expectations were clear. And wasn't a confused, recently divorced guy who feared the next major commitment even as he romanced multiple women also kinda, ya know, destructive? Wasn't it better that I limit the damage to myself and my laptop?

As porn's efficacy trended downward, I was forced to conjure new strategies. I would start with some of my top ten clips until my attention wandered, then close my eyes and replay a highlight reel of the most inspiring sessions I had shared with the real women. And when those stopped working, I returned to Blair. In the end, Blair was the only foolproof measure for defeating a sad boner. Sad Boner still loved Ideal Blair so much. Sad Boner was not about to let Ideal Blair (and by extension Ideal Vagina) go quietly into the night.

And that's how it went for another year and a half (or two, three?). I could barely remember what a real woman felt like. I felt burned, and I did not expect someone else to lick my wounds. I had alcohol for that, but it took its toll on my libido. What had always been a healthy sex drive before and during my marriage, then had become a sort of inferno EDM rave postdivorce, was now a swaying balloon not unlike those flapping air dummies you see out in front of the discount-furniture outlets and used-car lots. Each time I inflated it for another clearance sale, it was a little less tumescent, until finally it melted across the hot deserted parking lot.

Which is why, on the first full day of my sabbatical, I deleted WhatsApp and all my porn: the bookmarks, the downloads, and the photos my hookups had sent me. I even canceled my Only-Fans subscriptions. Lana Del Emotional would hound me for weeks—*Lana miss you, Sweet Boy, where are you? I'm so bored at home today, why you not entertain me no more?* Admittedly, this was not a good time to abandon her. Her father needed a foot. Not foot surgery, a whole new foot. But if I wanted to cut clean, I had to be merciless. We all needed to sacrifice during this difficult time. Lana's three children, the little Del Emotionals, were going to have to find another way to fund their gaming and vaping habits.

I had been done with real women for a while. Now I was done with the virtual. And my dick was done with me. The whole mess reminded me too much of what it was like to be in a real relationship, dedicated to someone else and something bigger than ourselves. You know, the good old days. Back when love was still a thing and I still had fucks to give.

copperheads

Phase three of my demolition commenced. Somehow being a bum was easier to stomach when I was supposed to be at work. But after a solid week of sabbatical boozing and sleeping late, I was repulsed by my own lethargy. My house needed tending. I decided it was finally time to clean out the garage.

My dad had been an "avid collector" of many things. A hoarder, really. Not the kind who saved old newspapers and TV dinner cartons. He hadn't been living in filth. But the house had been full, all the way full, of a whole lot of *stuff*. Dad had been thrifty, always on the hunt for a deal. As a snapshot:

Seventy-plus wristwatches, none worth more than twenty dollars. A couple of hundred pairs of off-brand blue jeans. Four hundred–plus shirts, the sort you got at dying mall stores like JC Penny. Fifty-plus cheap pairs of sunglasses. An entire hardware store's worth of tools acquired from discount outlets in Denver. He loved pocketknives, had a tackle box containing nearly three hundred of those. His furniture was too old to sell, so that all went to the dump. The clothes went to the VA. We held yard sales. Everything that was left was stuffed in the garage. I'd already rented a roll-off dumpster three times, but the garage was still overflowing.

My dad died a little more than five years ago. I have no siblings. He and my mom divorced when I was still in Little League, so I inherited his house while his second wife, Janey, received the rest of his assets. It was a fair breakdown. He and Janey had divorced when I was in college but remained committed until his death. They loved each other, just couldn't live together. I hadn't owned a home since Blair and I divorced seven years ago, and buying a home in Boulder County required a chunk of change and a credit score I had not managed to build on my own. Dad had worked as a distribution-center manager most of his life. His estate was worth approximately $700,000, half of that being the house.

If someone had handed me $350K and told me to go buy a house, I would not have chosen this one. A modest trilevel built in 1984. About 1,300 square feet, fenced yard, two-car garage. It was not my childhood home, so I had no sentimental feelings attached to it. But once I was in here, I realized Dad must have seen something in it that suited him in his late bachelor years. It was very livable, with open floors and vaulted ceilings, perfect for a single guy. I could mow the yard in eleven minutes.

Initially, I planned to bring everything up to modern standards, flip it for a nice payday, and then find a house more my style. Janey was very pragmatic and fine with this. "It's your house now. He would want you to do whatever makes the most sense for you."

I took out an equity line and spent most of a year acting like a general contractor, hiring out the work except for a few things I knew how to do myself, like the subway-tile kitchen backsplash and some accent paint. I started with a gut job, then had new paint and flooring done, new kitchen everything, including appliances. New tile showers in both bathrooms, new concrete sinks. It was thrilling to choose everything according to my taste, not Blair's. Vintage rock posters (tastefully framed, of course), books in almost every room, cobalt leather sofas. The formal "family room" became my writing lounge with a tall beverage fridge, dartboard, and elite sound system. If I had a decor style, you could call it Dude Eclectic. Or maybe just Wifeless.

When I finished, the house was appraised at $530K, but I was too comfortably rooted to start all over again. Now I doubted I would ever sell it, unless I met a woman who had a better house and a better life.

"Does it feel like your home now?" Janey had asked when I gave her the tour.

"Mostly," I said. "I know he's gone, but he's always here. You know?"

"I know. And that's a good thing."

"Yeah." But I wasn't so sure.

The best thing about renting a dumpster is that they come with a deadline. The fourth had been delivered yesterday, and I had a week to fill it up. I clipped Jojo to her rope in the front yard. She had lost a hind leg when she was a puppy, after her first owner had let her run into traffic. She was six now and still loved to pogo her way around in the grass. I turned on Dad's old AM radio in the garage and dove in. I made three piles in the driveway. One for stuff I thought I could sell, another for stuff worth donating, and the third was the dumpster.

My neighbor directly across the street was a seventy-something German man named Klaus. He was short with flowing gray hair and used to be a software architect but now drove buses for the city. He had known my dad and welcomed me when I moved in. We would make polite conversation whenever we ran into each other at the communal mailboxes located at the end of my driveway. He usually dropped by when he saw me clearing out more stuff.

"Ah, at it again, I zee," he called out as he crossed the street. His German accent was thick, but his voice was soft and a little high. "You should not throw so much dis valuable away. Better zell and make zum money."

"I've tried, Klaus. Feel free to take whatever you want."

He stood with his hands on his hips, surveying things. So far, I had given him three folding bicycles, five ice chests, a few buckets of garden tools, and many pairs of white leather gloves. For some unfathomable reason, my dad had left a bag full of white leather gloves, maybe fifty pairs, brand new. Klaus loved them. He wore them for gardening, driving the buses, riding his BMW Adventure cycle, and God knows what else.

"Does ya fazzah leave kind of posaw?" Klaus asked.

"Sorry, what?"

Klaus moved beside one of the big trees in my yard and made a sawing motion. "You know, da branches?"

"Oh, polesaw. I haven't seen one yet, but I'm sure it's in here."

Klaus peered into the garage with admiration. "Ya fazzah love dis tools, *ja, ja*."

"He sure did. Help yourself, please. I want it all gone."

Klaus frowned. I knew he thought I was a spoiled-rotten American man-child with no respect for the real value of a dollar, and he wasn't totally wrong. Eventually he shuffled off.

I worked all morning, until the dumpster was about half full. It all made me sad, but I was getting the first real exercise I had had in a long time. I worked up a sweat, got my hands dirty. I went to the store and bought a can of snuff and a case of shitty beer. I was on task and making good progress.

Then I stumbled onto it. The thing that changed everything.

At the back of the garage was a small lane that he had preserved to access his beer fridge in the corner. I started that way, and my left foot snagged on something heavy, causing a strangely familiar rattle. I stopped, breath catching in my throat. I suspect every boy is tantalized by something his father cherishes and keeps strictly verboten—the heirloom pistol, the Pioneer hi-fi system, the keys to the Mustang—and here was mine.

The copperheads gleamed in a shaft of dusty sunlight coming through the south door. Black full-grain leather Ping bag with a complete set of Ping Eye 2 beryllium-copper irons. Old-school two iron through lob wedge. Titleist driver. Ping Anser blade putter. I pulled the seven iron, sniffed the copper grooves, massaged the dried grip. I gave it a practice swing and shattered a fluorescent light overhead. Bits of glass and powder rained down on me.

"Hey, Pop, can I try one of your sticks?"

"Absolutely never," I could hear the old man reply. I was fourteen or fifteen, and we were playing a rare round together. He didn't like to take me along on his golf outings. For one, as much as he loved the game, he always viewed golf as a financial indulgence, and he probably felt that taking me out for a round was like burning fifty dollars in a trash can. I had not comported myself well on the occasions he had let me join him. I didn't have the emotional fortitude for golf, he announced six holes into our first round.

"Golf isn't football or basketball or even tennis, where your anger and physical power might help you overcome your opponent. Golf is man against himself. Most humbling game ever invented. It requires respect and grace, and you have neither. No, my son. These are the finest golf clubs ever made, and you will never swing one as long as I am alive. No one touches my copperheads."

My father wasn't a cruel man or even really a hard one. I had come to understand this was a side effect of his hoarding disorder—almost everything he owned was protected, precious, *his*. At least until he died.

I glanced west toward the mountains. The sun was still high. *Sorry, Pop. My clubs now.*

mulligans

Longmont had three courses. I chose Twin Peaks because it was Dad's home course and only about ten minutes away. I left the garage open and the stuff piled on the driveway, hoping someone would steal it all.

Before I checked in, I gave the bag a thorough shakedown. Dad had left it stocked with about a dozen Pro V1s, old but unblemished. Tees. Golf pencils. A divot-repair tool. A brown glove dried and shriveled like a turkey neck. A windbreaker. A couple of whiskey shooters and a desiccated cigar. I even found a roll of ones and fives wrapped in a rubber band, probably around a hundred dollars in all. The old man's stash for wagering with his dick buddies. I drank the shooters in the parking lot but decided to leave the money in the bag, for karma or whatever.

There was one thing missing. I remembered how he'd always carried a little green book with his initials embossed on the cover. Made of water-resistant paper, it had been filled with sketches of all the holes here at Twin. Lots of numbers and calculations and his loose but artistic renderings of each fairway, its various hazards, shaded textures for the quality or depth of grass, and

the greens with arrows indicating slope. He would consult it
on every hole, as if he had not already played the same course
several hundred times. During his rounds, he'd note the club
selection, leaving little *X*'s in the spots optimal for ball place-
ment. Sometimes he would continue fussing over it in front
of the TV after his round, a Scotch breathing beside him. I
once rifled through it to see what brilliant insights the old
man had come up with. I hadn't understood most of it but
was surprised by the quietly poignant bits of guidance he'd
left for himself.

> be mindful of fatigue holes 14–16
> long par 3s still the dickens—try 7w
> deloft gap at 70–80 yd.
> hybrids—call me a nonbeliever
> Sept. grass like a fleeting lover

Many of the sketches had been erased and redrawn, his notes
often cribbed into tight corners. He spent years on the same
green book, and I sensed it was a thing that would never be
finished. No chance he'd thrown it out. It was probably buried
somewhere else in the garage or the basement, and I made a
mental note to look for it later.

"You have a tee time?" the gentleman working the pro shop
asked. He was short with gray hair and a deep tan. He stood
rigidly in his white Mizuno polo like he was in the navy. Name
tag: *STEVENS*.

"No, sorry. Spur of the moment."

He looked displeased as he checked the time sheet. "Single?"

"Hmm?"

"Just you, or do you have partners?"

"All my girlfriends broke up with me."

Stevens didn't miss a beat. "They must have finally gotten new glasses."

"Good one, Captain. Just me today. Haven't golfed in like twenty years."

He raised an eyebrow. "What brings you back?"

"Found my old man's clubs in the garage. He used to play here. I had a day off, figured what the fuck. Excuse me, what the hell."

"Yeah, watch your fucking language around here, spunky." He surveyed the course through the large south-facing windows. "Nine or eighteen?"

"Oh, just nine for now."

"Walking or riding?"

"Cart, please." I grabbed a new golf glove off the sale rack. "And this too."

He nodded. "Take number eleven. I'm sending you off the back. If you decide you want to play more than nine, come see me again."

"Will do."

"Forty-six and change with the glove. That's a good deal on those."

I handed him my card. He looked at it briefly, then gave it a harder inspection.

"Casey Sweet?"

"Yeah."

"You're not Roger Sweet's son, by chance?"

"I am."

Stevens smiled warmly. "Hell, I knew your dad. Roger was a terrific member. Very consistent golfer. Called himself a twelve, was probably an eight. Impeccable scorecards. Didn't know the meaning of the word 'gimme.' Boy, I was sure sorry to see him go. He was too young."

I was a bit shocked by this man's impromptu eulogy. "He was. Yeah."

"And he left you his clubs?" Steven said. "Those BeCu Pings?"

"Yep." Guilt crawling up my leg.

"Well, that's how it should be." Stevens raised his chin, and for a moment I thought he might salute me. "Yes, sir, Roger Sweet was one of the real ones. Always a good steward of the course. Always on time. Always a perfect gentleman."

Stevens was probably being sincere, but I couldn't help feeling like he was setting a high bar for me to live up to.

"Thank you. I know he liked it here," I said, wishing for this to be over. "Anyway, uh, what did you mean about the back?"

"Back nine. You start on number ten. Right over there. Our beverage-cart girl is running late today, probably hungover again. But she'll be out in an hour or so."

"Gotcha."

"Tell you what . . ." Stevens ran my bank card through his machine once more, then handed it to me with a new gleam in his eye. "Welcome to Twin Peaks, Casey Sweet. Your first round is on us. Go have some fun. Play as many holes as you like this afternoon."

I swallowed. "Thank you, sir."

I rolled up to number ten, relieved no one would be joining me. I slipped on the new glove, put a handful of tees and two balls in the right pocket of my joggers, and pulled the driver. I stepped onto the tee box and stretched while trying to remember what little Dad had tried to teach me.

Stack the hands. Interlock forefinger and pinkie.

Shoulder-width stance. Bend the knees. Stick your butt out.

Pick a small target away from the trouble.

Just swing like you're throwing a bucket of water. Let the arms pull you through.

Keep your goddamn eyes on the ball.

I planted a tee. Couple of practice swings. My entire body felt coiled, tense. I was squeezing the grip as if trying to choke it to death. Five minutes ago this was a lark, just a way to kill a couple of hours in the spring sun. Now I could feel him breathing behind me.

Enough with the horseshit practice swings. Fire away.

I brought the big boy back slowly, gaining momentum near the top, then came down around like Sammy Sosa. The force of it threw me back on my heels, and I almost fell over. The ball just sat there on the little tee, laughing at me.

"Fuck's sake, moron." I looked around. No one was watching. I waggled.

Settle down, for Christ's sake, the old man said. *Quit squeezing it like it's your dick. Swing easy and trust the club.*

This time my tempo was a bit smoother, but I topped it just short of the women's tees.

"Oh, for the love of . . ."

I teed up another. Rolled my shoulders. My eyes locked on the ball so hard I could feel them straining from their sockets. The sound of the shaft whipping through air, the solid clang of an aluminum baseball bat. Echoes of summer youth. I looked up to see the ball arcing high and wide right. It climbed and climbed, drifting toward a pond as it lost steam over a big tree.

Damn. That felt good.

I was happy to find the ball resting in some nice grass just short of the pond. The path back to the fairway was treacherous, full of large pine and cottonwood trees. I had never learned which clubs to use for which shot, yardages, different types of swings, any of it. Going on instinct, I tried the six iron and just chunked it about forty feet. I thought the eight iron might give me loft, so I gave that one a bash. Better. Up and over a tree, to the left side of the fairway. Chip. Chip. Chunk. Skulled one over the green.

"Fuck! You suck! Worthless piece of shit!"

"Take it easy," someone called out behind me.

I turned to see a stout middle-aged woman in gardening boots and a tank top watching me from her backyard. This fairway was lined with large 1970s ranch homes with huge walk-out basements, elevated terraces, immaculate lawns.

"Sorry, ma'am," I said.

"That's all right." She waved her watering can around. "But voices carry out here."

"Yes, ma'am."

"Ma'am? Gimme a break." She turned away.

I four-putted. I had no intention of keeping score, but that had to be twelve or thirteen.

Things went a little better on number eleven. My drive was short but surprisingly straight. I kept the next three close to the fairway, had a decent little chip, chipped again, three-putted.

Probably a nine.

Number twelve was a 160-yard par three that started downhill before rising again to the green. A residential street full of apartments on the left. I teed it lower and hauled off with the five iron. The ball hooked downward as if magnetically pulled to the street. The bounce was incredible. It shot up to strike a second-story balcony, where it rattled around. I cringed, waiting for someone to come yell at me, but they never did.

Eventually I loosened up and fell into a sloppy rhythm. The voices in my head quieted, and I played faster, finding a semblance of flow. I noticed another single guy banging his way around a few holes back. I lost him for a while. Then he appeared on the shimmering horizon, like a figure out of a spaghetti Western, still far away but doggedly approaching, his jostling cart a galloping steed, his inevitable arrival portending some fate that I could not precisely decipher but that heralded trouble, immense change.

I was reloading with balls as he caught me on the box at number fourteen. He was tall, with tattoos filling out most of his long arms. Hoops in each ear. Thick and pointed goatee with a fair amount of gray in it. The kind of guy you see and think he might be the former lead singer of some Seattle band, or maybe an arms dealer. Probably not on the short list of candidates to join Augusta National. He was vaping and staring at me with an unnerving intensity.

"You can play through if you want," I said. "I suck."

He stepped from his cart and released a blue dragon from his lungs. "Well, you can't possibly be worse than me, so I'll tag along if you don't mind."

"Cool. I'm Casey."

"Good to meet you, Casey. I'm Vince." We shook hands. He spoke with a slight Southern drawl laced with urban cynicism. He removed his ball cap and wiped his forehead. "Par five? What's she playing today?"

"About five thirty."

"Giddyup, son!"

My state of calm wrecked by the presence of another, I just let it rip. I connected, but the ball flew forty-five degrees left, a line drive that landed on the wrong fairway.

"Shit," I said. "That's not it."

"You're fine," Vince said. "At least you got some yardage out of it." He set his tee. "You ever see a monkey tryna fuck a football?"

"Can't say I have."

"Then I apologize for what you are about to witness. And I'm a lefty, so stand back if you want to live."

Brand-new FootJoys, blue-and-white saddle-style, big as gunboats. Expensive-looking Nike polo and pants. The Callaway bag looked mint, the clubs high tech. His swing was wide open in a way that didn't seem right, even to me.

Bang—hard left. He looked over his shoulder. "See? We both suck."

"I haven't golfed in twenty years," I said.

"I played in my teens, but my stepfather was a real cocksucker, so I don't count that. Wife's been wanting me to get out of the house, so now I'm making a jackass of myself in front of total strangers." Vince opened a black cooler and offered me a tallboy of IPA. "Who knows when the cart honey will be back."

"Thanks. I'll get next round."

"Whoa, check out these sticks," he said, pulling one of Dad's irons. "Vintage copper. When did you get these? Late nineties?"

"My dad's. He died about five years ago. I just found them today, actually."

"Sorry to hear it. You like 'em?"

"He always said they were the best."

Vince slipped the club back into the bag. "They stopped making those because the manufacturing process was too dangerous. Milling that copper released all kinds of toxins. Complete sets are going for about two grand on eBay. If they don't hit well, you could sell them, set yourself up with a whole new bag with five hundred to spare."

"Huh."

"To slapping it around," he said. We toasted.

"It'll get better," I said as we settled into our carts. "It has to, right?"

"Oh, you're an optimist? That's adorable." Vince stared off

at the mountains. "I hope you're right, Casey, because if it gets any worse, I'm throwing this brand-new six-hundred-dollar driver into that fucking pond on sixteen."

But it did get better. We had nearly the same terrible golf game. Occasionally one of us would get a clean strike along the way and make a bogey. As we took the box on number eighteen, his Bluetooth speaker kicked into Soundgarden's "Searching with My Good Eye Closed," and those grinding, glorious guitar chords put us in some kind of state.

"Last chance to be a hero," he said. "Finish strong."

"I want par, Vince. Not double bogey. Not bogey. Par."

"Go get it."

Number eighteen was a long par four with a dogleg right. I went at it. The ball had a nice rising trajectory on its way to the driving range, but as it neared its peak, it began to fade and landed nearly dead center, up by the white 150 marker.

"Sweet chicken," Vince said. "If that doesn't stiffen your shaft, what will?"

"Best one I've had all day. Or in my entire life for that matter."

"Okay, big shooter, enough bragging. My turn." He went into his backswing and came through like a sledgehammer. The ball went forever. "I kill anyone on the practice green?"

"Close, but no one's fallen down yet."

I used the five iron on my second and left it right under the green, on the apron. Vince had left himself about 130 yards and managed to land high above the pin but still on the table. I didn't want to blow the opportunity by using a wedge, so I putted. A good thirty-foot uphill roll, and damned if it didn't almost go in. I finished with a tap-in.

"And that's a par," Vince said. "You trying to hustle me, Casey?"

He two-putted, also for par. We grinned at each other like we had won a prize.

"Did we just become golfers?" I said, walking over to give him a bump.

"Fuck yeah, we did. Time for a drink!"

nineteenth hole

The man behind the clubhouse bar was one of those burly, chapped-faced, sixty-year-old guys made of granite. He wore nylon track pants and a Twin Peaks quarter zip and had a towel around his neck, his gray-black hair damp like he'd just finished a shower. He bumbled around, slamming a metal cooler door.

"Coach Lowry," Vince said. "How's it hanging, big dog?"

"She forgot the goddamn ice again."

"Kids these days."

"You're telling me. What can I get you?"

"Double Jack and Coke plus whatever my boy here's having."

"Make it two," I said.

I offered Vince a twenty and he put a hand up. "I got it."

Coach Lowry filled each cup about three-quarters of the way with whiskey and then waved a Coke can in the vicinity. He had the surprisingly delicate hands of a string musician. Vince tipped him ten dollars. Coach's eyes were quick and penetrating. He met my own gaze for a moment, taking some measure, then nodded as if he had filed me appropriately.

"Thank ya, fellas."

We carried our drinks to the patio overlooking the range and the eighteenth green.

"He's the club pro," Vince said. "Only goes by Coach Lowry. Don't ever call him anything else. He lets the locals mess around a bit because this is a muni and they gotta have some place to play Happy Gilmore. But you start a fight, wreck a cart, harass one of the girls, any of that shit, he'll bust your ass right out of here."

"You said pro. Like from the PGA Tour?"

"Club pro is usually the big dick in charge, regardless of any real professional experience. But in this case, yeah, there are rumors he was on his way to the show. All-American in college. Won a few pro-ams. Folks were writing articles calling him the next Ray Floyd. Got a few exemptions to play a couple stops on the Tour but never did get the card. Something went wrong, and it all went up in smoke. He grew up on this course. Came home, became the club pro, and that was that. So they say."

"I bet my dad knew him," I said. "What do you think it was? Injury?"

Vince tossed his cap on the table. "Might have fucked some-body's wife. Might have been drugs. Or just fear. People like to blow up their potential for some reason. Self-sabotaging out of fear of success."

I thought about my own career for a moment.

"So what's your story, Casey? You married?"

"Divorced."

"How long ago?"

"About seven years."

"And how old are you?"

"Forty-five."

"And that was your first? You haven't remarried?"

"Nope."

Vince scoffed. "Fuckin' rookie. What's a matter with you? Get back on the horse. I'm on my fourth and I don't regret a damn thing."

I liked this guy immediately. He seemed confident, unafraid to speak his mind. I'd never had so much fun playing golf, hadn't even realized it could be fun. "Today was good," I said. "I needed this. Just getting away from the screens, playing in the sun."

"You on spring break or just take a day off?"

"I'm on sabbatical."

"Funny, I didn't take you for a professor."

I told him I was a product-marketing writer for a tech company.

Vince looked at me skeptically. "So what triggered this 'sabbatical'? You have a lot of extra vacation time or . . . ?"

For some reason I found it easy to open up to him. He didn't know me. I might never see him again. "I've been half-assing it at work," I said. "Underperforming. Missing days. Drinking too much. Boss called me on it."

Vince was intrigued. "But he didn't fire you? Just suggested you take some time off?"

"Yep."

"You must be worth something."

"I'm not a complete bag of shit, yet." I laughed. "According to my boss, Dave."

"At least you admit it. So what's the problem? Is it the job? This Dave character an asshole?"

I took another drink. A deep one. "I don't know."

"Some gal eat you up and shit you out?"

"Eh, I was more or less crushing it in my thirties. Married, good career, house, wife. Then in a span of like three years we got divorced, my dad died, both of our dogs died. Losses piling up, you know?"

Vince nodded. "I do."

"I should be over it all by now, but anyway."

"Sometimes things just go to shit one on top of another. For me it was in my twenties. I did all the drugs. Bar fights. Thrown in jail in Mexico for a week. Then I focused on work and became a VP at the age of twenty-seven. I was King Kong. I raged at my employees. Pushed my first two wives away. The third was a cheating bitch. I ran around the country wrecking agencies and relationships. I had to get it out of my system."

"What changed?"

"I met the right woman. I found a way to turn my insecurity into professional discipline. I was a workaholic. Still only sleep about four hours a night. But I learned to work on myself. I paint. I trade stocks, and I'm studying all this crypto bullshit. Play the guitar. Working on the ukulele next. And the golf thing. Think I'm getting the bug bad this time."

"That's awesome, man. What was your career, anyway?"

"I started in creative, and that turned into high-level branding and sales. Mostly agency work, then started my own digital shop. We worked on BMW, Coke, Toyota, some of the big fast-food chains. But I was bored, so I sold my share of the agency to my partner two years ago. I'm fifty-four. Figure I'll give it another year or two, and if I can't find a way to enjoy retirement, I'll just buy a bar or go back to fishing in the Northwest."

I sat there digesting how different we were. Vince was a world-beater. I was more of a beater-offer.

Vince stared at me again, processing. "So never mind the paycheck. What do you love to do just for the sake of doing it? Besides parring out."

I finished my drink. "I have no idea. How sad is that?"

"You've never had something that was just a pure joy? Not even as a kid?"

"Well, sure. But nothing that makes a career."

"We can figure that out later." Vince looked at his watch. "Shit, I got to get home to the lady. But do me a favor."

"Okay."

"You're on sabbatical. I'm retired. Meet me back here at nine tomorrow. We're playing another eighteen, my treat. In the meantime, tonight while you're sitting there on the couch with Grindr and Netflix, write down three things you love to do. Or used to. Three things that made you happy in the moment, no matter how silly they seem now. Collecting baseball cards, bartending, building a deck in your backyard. Whatever. Write them down, and we'll go over them tomorrow while you're schooling me on the fairways. Sound good?"

We stood. "Sure. I don't have anything else planned."

"My man." Vince shouldered his bag and headed toward the parking lot. He raised his fingers. "Three things!"

"Got it!"

I stood on the patio. The sun was setting over Longs Peak and the rest of the Front Range. The sky was pink and blue and purple, ribbed with gray flannel clouds. The geese were settled in their clusters. The fairways were dark and calm. A lone blue heron stood vigil in his pond. It was like one of those motivational posters in an executive's office, but this one was alive. I could smell the grass. The land seemed to breathe. I'd lived in Colorado my entire life, and I hadn't seen it for so long.

If I had been tasked with writing the caption for the poster, it would say:

RELAX
There are places left just for you.

the little things

So that's how my new golf addiction started. Vince and I played the next day, and the next, and then five or six times per week through April and May. We'd usually play in the morning, sometimes in the afternoon, but rarely on weekends (too slow, too much riffraff). Saturdays I'd hit the range for an hour, then spend another thirty minutes putting. After practice, I'd ease my way onto a stool in the clubhouse and knock back a Bloody while listening to the gamers brag about the shots that made their days or bitch about the malevolent forces that had cost them par.

I was in love. I fed off Vince's enthusiasm, but I think even if I hadn't met him, I still would have fallen for the game. For one, it gave my days some structure and gave my mind something to latch onto. It had its own language, a curriculum, an excuse to gear up and forge your own style. And the golf swing itself, the elusive technique, endless facets to dissect and fiddle with.

My drinking regimen changed, spreading out over the day. After that first round, I felt so good I went home and, like an asshole, drank too much, giving myself a nasty hangover I regretted the next day as I shot my way to a glorious 124. Vince limited himself to four drinks per round, but the other guys and I liked our Fireballs. Birdies became Firebirdies, a mandatory shot every time. First six holes a disaster? Better have a Fireball to loosen up. White Claws were our staple. Shameful to drink at home but somehow perfect for golf.

Most days, the hours in the sun wore me down, and I drank less at night, went to bed earlier, slept better, and woke each morning with that pleasing soreness in new places.

Vince had the "elite membership" at Twin Peaks. Two thousand dollars a year for unlimited golf, carts, and range balls. Once I did the math—sixty dollars per round with no membership—I ponied up for the same. It was cool to feel like I belonged somewhere. No need to hand Stevens my debit card anymore. We'd just check in, sign for a cart, and go.

Golf kept me from sulking around the house, dwelling on my exes or my career or my mom, who was seventy-five and struggling with arthritis and various other minor ailments. She was doing good overall, but I couldn't help worrying that something big was waiting for her around the corner, just like it had come for my dad.

He had been just sixty-six when he was diagnosed with a small tumor in his bile duct. Turned out to be cholangiocarcinoma, a cancer that afflicts about one in three hundred thousand people. Nine percent of cases survive five or more years. Dad fought hard, made it four and a half.

During his last week he would sleep a lot, the morphine sending him away for ten, twelve, sometimes twenty hours or more. I tried to share something meaningful whenever he was awake. The last conversation we ever had, we were sitting in his bedroom and had just finished watching *Smokey and the Bandit*. His stubble was all gray, and he was down to about 135 pounds.

I thanked him for teaching me things. How to ride a bike, use a pocketknife, make a pot of chili, fix things around the house. How to share a meal with a woman and be a gentleman.

"You taught me so many things, Dad. I'm gonna be okay without you because you taught me . . ." But then I was crying and couldn't talk anymore.

Behind the morphine, he still had a gleam in his eye. "And I'm still teaching you."

I understood. "Yes, sir."

I'm teaching you how to fight and then go with grace.

I am teaching you how to die.

Living in his house was a mixed blessing. I felt closer to him than I would if I'd lived somewhere else, but I still felt guilty, like I had pulled one over on him. After how tough he had been on me in my teens, then how he'd cut me off financially when I turned twenty, I wound up owning his house. I hadn't done anything to deserve it. I was just his son.

I don't believe in ghosts, but sometimes I would see him turning a corner into one of the rooms or hear him clearing his throat as he climbed the stairs with a laundry basket. Small flashes out of the corner of my eye. These moments didn't happen often, and they didn't bother me when they did. Sometimes I told myself they were just echoes from a weekend I'd spent with him watching football. Other times I did believe in ghosts. Or at least his.

But when I was playing golf, even with his clubs, he retreated into the shadows. His impatient voice, browbeating me for my adolescent temper, went away. I came to understand part of why he loved the game. Because out there on the course, surrounded by nature, away from my desk, golf, with its many bits of etiquette and ritual, was pure engagement. It required such focus to bring the shot you imagined into being, you hardly thought about anything at all.

I won't say I got *good* at golf in that first month or two. But I *did* improve. The scorecards that started 117, 121, and 112 were now 102, 105, and sometimes a 98.

Part of my improvement was simply playing so much. There was no time to get rusty. And when I wasn't playing, I was usually reading golf books on the couch or surfing YouTube for tips and drills. I ordered some real golf shoes, a few polos, shorts, hats, ten dozen Vice balls. I soaked the copperheads in Coke overnight and then polished them with Brasso until they shone like new. I had the fitter at Twin put fresh grips on them. Someday I might get fitted for my own irons, but I knew I would never sell Dad's. Of all the things he had left behind, the clubs were the magic beans that made the rest grow.

A good deal of my improvement was owed to Vince. While he was only marginally better than me, he knew far more than I did. His advice on "the little things" was invaluable. Most of the little things were about creating consistency, eliminating variables, minimizing risk.

Tee it up at the same height every time.

Find a setup routine and stick with it.

Swing three-quarters of what your instinct tells you.

Think about where's going to be your worst miss, your best miss.

Play loose, like every shot matters but not enough to anger you. You're not good enough to get angry. When you land in trouble, take your medicine and get out. Don't be a hero. You're not good enough to be a hero. Always aim for the center of the green, regardless of the pin position. You're not good enough to attack the pin. Otherwise, take dead aim at your target.

Most of them he had taken from Penick's *Little Red Book*, and he knew how to dole them out right when I needed them.

I still hadn't found Dad's green book, but I started jotting down my own notes after each round.

> Too many tops today. Work on mobility, rotation, compression.
> Take more wrist out of the short chips.
> Practice lagging. Picture a Hula-Hoop around the hole.

Vince's nature was to lead, speak freely, help others. I had always been more passive, rarely assuming I knew what the hell I was doing. The two of us fit one another in our shared mission, and he became something of a mentor as well as a friend.

One day we were having our post-round cocktail on the terrace while he tallied our scores. He snorted and spun the card at me. "Chap my ass."

I picked up the card. "Damn, you bagged a ninety? That's great, Vince."

"I shot the ninety-nine, you dick. Next row. You just beat me by nine strokes. Congratulations."

I was floored. "That can't be right."

"I didn't want to say anything and get in your head. But your swing looked almost effortless today. You were so chill I thought you were bored. You only drank three Claws and didn't lose a single ball. That's most of it. A few lucky breaks, but you played clean golf."

"I wasn't bored," I said. "I just wasn't overthinking every shot."

"Don't worry, tomorrow you'll shoot one hundred four again."

He was right. I didn't sniff ninety again for a while. I met someone else on the golf course, and my newfound state of zen went completely sideways.

Eighties Boy

Vince and I were waiting to go off the first hole.

"Hey, what about my three things?" I asked. "I finished the homework assignment a month ago. When do I get the grade?"

That night after our first round, I had written down the three things I used to enjoy. Though I hadn't planned it, all three had come from my childhood:

Working on bikes (BMX) in dad's garage
Mowing lawns for summer pocket money
Writing short stories, usually sci-fi and horror

"I haven't forgotten," Vince said. "I'm working on your audit. Another week or so."

"Sure."

"Here." He pointed toward the ninth hole. "See that kid about a hundred yards out?"

"Yep."

"Watch him."

The kid was short, thin, looked about fifteen. He wore a

lime-green T-shirt and plaid Bermuda shorts. Faint music was issuing from somewhere. He had no cart, just a brown bag with a stand. He lined up and went into a swing unlike any I had ever seen. His body seemed to dip and sway just before he pulled the club back, then reasserted itself with precision as he came through. His swing speed was mild, but the ball took off high.

"It's like he has a tic," Vince said. "But that tempo is smooth jazz."

The ball came down with a thump. The kid walked briskly. He wore no hat or sunglasses. His face was blank. His eyes cold, never wavering from the target. His ball was sitting about twenty feet from the cup.

"Watch the finish," Vince said.

The kid set his bag on the collar and muted his speaker. He pulled his putter and walked around the hole once, then set up. He was playing barefoot. His dark-brown hair was long and sloppy, like he'd cut it himself. His putting stroke was almost mechanical, delicate, but the ball took off with a surprising burst. He was already walking after it as it slammed into the stick and sank. He retrieved it, shouldered his bag, and went striding off toward number ten. The music resumed. Billy Idol, "White Wedding."

"Damn. Looks like he's been at this awhile."

"Eighties Boy," Vince said. "That's what I call him. The Maui and Sons clothes. He's always bumpin' eighties music. Out here every day, early in the morning, just flows through the course like an assassin. Walks eighteen in under two hours. Scratch golfer."

"What's scratch?"

"Handicap zero. He averages par."

"Jesus." We assumed the tee box. "He play for his high school team?"

"He's actually twenty-one-ish, even though he looks like he's twelve. He's Coach Lowry's nephew or related somehow. He's another Mowgli, like Coach was."

"A what?"

"*The Jungle Book*. Mowgli. Grew up out here, a feral child turned prodigy. He never knew his father. His mom was always working two jobs, and she's Coach's sister or whatever, so after school and every summer the kid would just spend all his time out here. Most of his bag has been cobbled together from the lost and found. He never even checks in. Just comes and goes like a ghost."

The first seven holes were a grind. When the cart girl found us on number eight, we were ready for the swing juice. Most of them were in college. Now that it was mid-May, they came to work earlier.

"Morgan!" Vince called out. "We need shooters!"

Today she wore camo leggings and a Nike compression top. Her blond hair was in braided ponytails. Her shoulders gleamed like ripe fruit. When she leaned into the ice cooler, I noticed the outline of a thong. When she faced us again, a lace pattern impressed itself against the V. I forced myself to look away and shook my head.

Morgan said, "Is cinnamon Jim Beam okay? I'm out of Fireball."

"That'll do." Vince paid. "How was your semester?"

"Great! I'm taking accounting classes this summer, but I'll be around. Probably Tuesdays, Thursdays, Saturdays, and Sundays."

Vince tipped her twenty dollars. "You gonna do one with us?"

She giggled. "If I start now, I'll fall asleep in my cart. Are you guys playing eighteen?"

"You bet," Vince said.

We toasted and drained our shots.

She smiled at me. "What's your name again?"

"Casey."

"Right. Cool. Want me to grab anything from the club-house? I can bring sandwiches or whatever you want."

Vince handed her the empties. "We'll figure it out. You go make some more tips."

"'Kay. See ya soon!" She drove off.

Vince looked at me and raised his eyebrows. "Rocket fuel, huh?"

"Unreal, dude."

We walked to the ninth tee.

Vince said, "Don't get any ideas, Casey. 'Respect all em-ployees at all times.'"

"Don't worry. My dick is on sabbatical too."

Vince tallied our scores in the parking lot. I notched a hum-bling 106.

"Beat you by eleven, Casey," he said. "Lock it up."

I sighed. As always, we shook hands after the round. "Same time tomorrow?"

"Nine sharp, so don't forget to stretch." Vince walked to his black Land Rover, the electric hatch opening as he neared. "CBD bath, stretches, bourbon."

As I was loading my bag into the car, Eighties Boy came around the clubhouse, his bag over one shoulder. I lingered as he approached a sand-colored Toyota Land Cruiser with gra-dient accent stripes of brown, red, and orange. One of those FJ60s from the eighties, but this one looked nearly new, as if it had gone through a complete restoration. Something about the rig raised a memory flag. I knew I'd been in a Land Cruiser like this long ago, same color, same accent stripes.

He glanced at me as he loaded his clubs into the double hatch and nodded politely. I started my car and watched him try to do the same, but it didn't respond.

"Come on, Honeybear, you can do it." But the truck did not oblige. "Balls."

He popped the hood and got out, peering into the engine bay. He fiddled with something, then looked around with a defeated expression.

"Need a jump?" I asked.

"Thanks, but that won't help. It's a bad wire from my stereo. It's been shorting the battery. Now it's cooked something else. I should have redone it all a month ago."

"Need a lift?"

"I'll call my mom. We live nearby."

"Well, good luck. Saw you on nine this morning. Impressive." He squinted. "You new here?"

"Just started playing a few weeks ago."

"It's a good value. Better grass and fewer snobs than pretty much every other track within fifty miles."

"Seems like it," I said. "My friend Vince says you're like a scratch golfer, huh?"

"Better than that most days." Humble pride. "How about you?"

I chuckled. "Mid-nineties is a special day for me."

"But you can't stop, right? Having fun?"

"Absolutely."

"That's all that matters." He pulled his phone and turned away. "Hey, it's me. Honeybear out of commission again." He hung up and looked surprised to see me still there.

I was staring at the Cruiser. "That truck is in really nice shape for its age. What is that, an eighty-nine?"

"Eighty-seven."

"Looks like new."

"It was my mom's," he said. "She gave it to me when I turned sixteen. Said it was the last time she would ever buy me a car, so now I take care of it."

"You do the work yourself?"

"All of it. Rebuilt the engine two years ago."

"How'd you learn?"

"YouTube." As if this were obvious.

"That's cool, man. Good on you." I drove off.

The rest of the evening, I couldn't get it out of my head. How many forty-year-old beige Land Cruisers with those stripes could there be in Longmont, a town of about a hundred thousand people? Someone I had known way back in the day had that truck.

Red, brown, orange stripes. Not high school. College? A girl I knew, even though it was an unusual vehicle for a girl to own. Drinking wine coolers in that truck outside a party. Her breath like cherry cough syrup. Thick brown hair. Hands on me.

"She's my Honeybear," she said. "I love her. She gets me through everything."

Then I remembered all of her, and shit got real.

preshot routine

She came back to me with her physical presence, her energy: the way her short, curvy form fit inside my arms, her rounded shoulders and small waist, her wide feet. The whole of her deceptive at first glance, her softness hiding ferocious strength. Thick brown hair. Pale skin. A small nose with broad cheeks. All-natural, no perfume or makeup, a girl of the earth. Her boobs were the biggest I'd gotten close to at that age and probably since. Rounded and magnificent in their own marbled mass. A girl harboring a sexuality independent of men, of anyone but itself. She used to come very easily, even with the minimal skill set I had at the time. Two fingers inside and about two minutes of firm tongue, the little pulses clenching.

We met at Front Range Community College, where I was taking one final semester to fill out a few missed undergrad requirements. It was a small campus, so we had several classes together. She was a couple of years younger. She was the one who had talked first. Confident, assertive without needing to lean on her looks.

"What's your story? You don't look like you have to be here."

"Can't get my bachelor's until I finish these prereqs. How about you?"

"Can't afford real college."

"What about financial aid?"

"Maybe after I decide what I want to study."

"That's practical."

She sniffed. "Poverty is never practical."

We started sitting together. One class was a survey of major religions, which I didn't think I would enjoy, but we both did. The prof was a tall, thin man in his early sixties with a goody-goody way of speaking, always bright eyed, finding the positive in every faith. He would say things like, "Isn't Judaism just lovely in that way? You can join the club anytime!"

"You should join," she said, side-eyeing me.

"You should become a Mormon," I replied.

"Why, so we can marinate?"

"Huh?"

"You never heard about that?"

"No. What, like a food thing?"

She was trying not to laugh. "We can explore that later. Hey, wanna go to a party tomorrow night? It will probably suck, but we don't have to stay long."

"Sure."

She insisted on picking me up and driving us there. Maybe she wanted to see where I lived or just keep me from bailing early? I was very full of myself back then. I wasn't athletic or well put together. I was the kind of guy girls called cute, never handsome or hot. But I was low key, I knew how to make people laugh, and when it came to girls, I tried to be nice without pushing. This routine had been working well for me since about tenth grade. I'd had several girlfriends in high school, but in college I was never able to sustain interest in one girl for more than a few weeks. I didn't lie. I didn't cheat. I just slid from one to the next.

For the past year, I had been living at my dad's house while working part-time retail jobs. The girls I met through work all seemed to be in love with the boyfriends they'd met in college. I had fallen into some kind of depressed phase, and I resented having to go to junior college. Until her. *Damaris. Damaris Parker.*

She wrote it down in my notebook one day. "Spelled like that," she said, then added her phone number.

"Interesting," I said. "I've never met a Damaris before."

"No, you definitely haven't." Her eyes challenging me.

"I like it."

"Good, now give me your address."

We didn't stay at the party for very long. Most of the people there were her friends from high school, more of a punk crew than I was used to. Lots of leather jackets, heavy mascara, creative piercings. I was still in my basic-Levi's-and-clever-T-shirt days, so most of them looked at me like I was lost. We had a drink, and then Damaris wanted to go outside for a smoke. We sat in her Land Cruiser listening to KTCL, the alt station out of Fort Collins. We drank wine coolers she had brought.

"This is a really cool car," I said.

"She's my Honeybear. I love her. She gets me through everything."

"You could take this baby anywhere. How long have you had her?"

"My dad gave her to me a year ago, right after my mom died. I think it was partly out of guilt for him moving away and partly to protect me. He said he would never let me drive a small car."

"Oh shit. I'm so sorry. What happened to your mom?"

"She had this rare form of meningitis. It kind of came and went a few times, then went into her brain. You can't live with a brain that's swollen up like a melon."

"Damn. I can't imagine."

She took my hand. "Sorry, I don't mean to be a bummer."

"You're not. I'm glad you told me. Where'd your dad go?"

"Back to Ohio. We have family there, and they found a really good job for him. I'll probably go see him this summer."

We kissed for a while, and she put my hand on her chest. I was suddenly very aroused by the assertiveness. She gave my dick a little squeeze through my jeans as if testing it.

"Let's go," she said.

"Sure."

"I've wanted you since the first class we had together."

"Really? Why?"

"I used to be fat."

"Don't say that. I'm sure you—"

"Okay, I was *bigger*," she amended. "Everybody looked right through me."

I laughed at her bluntness. "You look great now."

"Thanks."

Leftover high school insecurity. We all had it. It was following us into our twenties and might never end. The missed opportunities. The haunting what-ifs. I'd never been with a girl like Damaris, so this was turning into a new thrill for me too. Most of the girls I had dated were preppies, white suburban girls from upper-middle-class homes. They drove new Jettas and shopped at J.Crew. They liked to go out for frozen yogurt and make it a Blockbuster night. They were beautiful and clean and would soon tire of me.

Damaris was the girl sneaking into dive bars at age sixteen. She smoked like she couldn't wait for someone to tell her smoking is bad for you. She wore turquoise jewelry, army-surplus tanks, short little motorcycle boots with silver chains on them. The sex was good right away, and once we got going, it reorganized my entire repertoire. At once heated, tender, giving, and messy. She was confident in ways that were new to me.

"Do you have a condom?" she asked the first time we went to bed, the night of the party. I was licking her nipples and unbuttoning her jeans.

"I wasn't planning on this. I'm sorry." Classic excuse. "But we can save it for next time."

I don't know if this was a conscious strategy on my part, but I hated condoms. My last two girlfriends had been on the pill, so I had grown used to the real thing, and going back was like having to retake seventh-grade algebra.

"Fucking guys." Damaris growled in frustration and rolled away.

"We can go to the store," I said. "There's a 7-Eleven somewhere."

"We can't drive drunk." She stared at me. "Can you control yourself?"

"Sure. Yeah."

She took my face in her hand and squeezed. "I'm serious. I can't take the pill because it messes with my skin and makes me fat. You have to pull out."

I nodded vigorously. "I promise."

So that's how it went. I never did buy the condoms. We started hooking up almost every night and sometimes in the parking lot on campus. She got off on public sex. Damaris was the first girl to ever masturbate in front of me. Sometimes she'd burn one off real quick before I even got inside her. Sometimes she'd go again after I finished. I worried I was never enough, but that wasn't it, she explained. She was just built for multiples. She liked being watched. We would have sex until she had her first orgasm, and then she would pull me into her mouth and finger herself until we came together. She had zero shyness about bodily fluids. Mine, hers, ours, anywhere, everywhere. She was completely scentless, with no discernible taste except for a delicate, almost imperceptible sweetness. I remember think-ing, *Crystal Pepsi.*

She never pressed me about other girls or asked for a com-mitment. I began to wonder if she saw other guys, but I didn't ask, because things were nice and simple just the way they were. We went on dates too. It wasn't just a fuck-buddy thing. I took her to dinner, movies, brunch on the weekends. She would drag me to see bands I had never heard of, which I'd usually end up liking. She bought me a few articles of clothing, things I would never have chosen for myself. A heavy black shirt with pearl buttons. Boxer briefs instead of my baggy-ass boxers. My first pair of Doc Martens (blue, eight-eye). She encouraged me to grow my hair longer. I sensed she was trying to morph me into a grunge bro of some kind, but I embraced it. It was like she could see some future, cooler version of me but also under-stood these evolutionary steps away from rugbies and oxfords had to be taken incrementally.

This all happened in only eight or ten weeks, maybe three months at most.

One evening she took me to Twin Peaks. I thought that was a strange choice. We sat on the patio and had beers and te-quila shots. I told her my dad played here and asked her why she would choose a golf course just for happy hour.

"My family is full of golfers. My uncle works here. My dad used to play almost every day before he moved away. I don't play, but somehow, I've always been connected to it. I like it here. The view. It's peaceful, right?"

I took her to my mom's place for dinner once. Mom seemed surprised we'd found each other, but she liked her. Damaris was talkative and confident, which my mom respected.

"Be careful with that one," Mom told me a few days later. "She acts tough now, but she could get hurt very easily."

"What the hell does that mean, Mom?"

"Casey, you know what it means. She's very attached to you already."

"What if I like her more? What if she breaks my heart?"

"Good, you could use a kick in the balls." My mom liked to make herself laugh with comments like that. Keeping me in check.

Our breakup happened as quickly as our relationship had started. Damaris missed a few classes near the end of the semester. When I called, she said she had a bug. She sounded tired, her voice a little hoarse. I offered to bring her food, pick up medicine.

"That's sweet, but I just need some time to myself, if that's okay."

"Sure. Did I do something?"

"Let's just not dig in right now."

A few days turned into a week. I left a message every other day and even stopped by once, but she didn't answer the door. What had I done? Who was the other guy? I felt like I should be doing something more but had no idea what.

I knew I liked her a lot, but did I love her? Did I even know what real love was? Part of me wanted to do something to fix it all, while another part of me was starting to think I'd be fine either way. She had a few shades of darkness that I didn't, or so I reasoned. But I missed her, and not just the sex. I missed her energy, her push, her curation of me.

She finally called me back about two weeks later. "Sorry for being so far away. I've been working through some things. Now that the semester is almost over, I think I need to get away from Boulder. I'm going to Ohio. My dad finally settled. He has a place on a lake. I think that's where I should be. At least for the summer. Maybe longer. I don't know."

"Wow," I said. "I didn't see that coming."

"I know. I'm sorry."

"Did I fuck this up?"

"It's really not about you. I just haven't ever been happy here."

I chewed on that, searching for an argument.

"You're a good guy," she said. "You deserve better."

"That doesn't make sense," I said. "I'm not better than you."

"Anyway, I need to do this."

She was dumping me. I wasn't hurt, but it was weird. Yeah, maybe I was hurt.

"Okay. Then thanks for telling me." The line was disturbingly quiet. "Hey, let me know how you're doing, okay? It just seems weird this might be the last time I talk to you, you know?"

She sighed. "Thanks, Casey. I should go."

"Okay."

We never spoke again.

I guess everyone has that special someone from the past, the one who got away. But here's the thing, at least in my case—you don't realize she is the one who got away until it's too late. Slowly she becomes preserved in time while your memories build a shrine.

For a week or two, I pretended I was relieved, free. But soon the pain crept in. The more time passed, the more certain I was that the pain was not a reflex after being dumped. She was a really cool girl, a good person, unique, funny, bold, sexual, smart. Her absence became a serious hurt that lasted longer than we had been together. She left a gaping wound, and I trudged through life for months.

But I was young. I started going out with my friends again. We always found a group of girls to hang with. And through a friend of a friend, I met Amy, and she was like a return to my previous type. Blond, chatty, a little naive. The chemistry was nothing like it had been with Damaris, but it was nice, uncomplicated, good enough to keep me moving forward. I learned to forget about Damaris for the next twenty years. At least until I ran into Honeybear. And the kid.

You have to pull out.

He never knew his father.

Single mother, always working two jobs.

She's Coach Lowry's sister or whatever.

My family is full of golfers.

And then I did the math. Eighties Boy was twenty-one or twenty-two? Twenty-two or -three years ago, she was all into me, then vanished. Why did she suddenly need to escape to Ohio?

"No, no way," I said to Jojo, who was sleeping beside me. "No. Fucking. Way."

But there were too many coincidences for it to be a coincidence.

part two
swing thoughts

body work

"I'm sorry, we're not accepting new patients," the lovely-sounding woman on the phone told me. "I can put you on our wait list? We're about seven, no, ten months out."

"That's not gonna—I need to see someone now."

"Yeah, no, there's nothing until March."

"What if I am really a psycho?" I blurted. "Seriously, some guy completely out of his tits, you're just going to let him walk around out there?"

"You'd be surprised."

Seeing red, I crossed Dr. Alfred Spangler off the list. That made twenty-seven rejections over three hours. Twenty-seven psychiatrists and none would help me, for one of three reasons: not accepting new patients, not accepting health insurance at all, or booked out months, sometimes a year or more.

Here's the thing I was quickly learning about my little sabbatical—it was a pain in the ass. What started out seeming like an easy break was turning into a bureaucratic odyssey through paperwork hell. The Family and Medical Leave Act, a great thing in principle. When Dave said "HR will handle all that bullshit," he forgot to mention that for me to collect any paycheck at all, I would have to see a doctor (which in my case was turning into multiple doctors because no one knew what was wrong with me). I would need one or more of these elusive doctors to diagnose me and give me a file explaining why I could not perform my job. I would have to fill out a shitload of forms for HR and the partner company that paid the reduced salary. And even then, it would take forty-five to sixty days before the first check was processed.

My first appointment back in April had been with my new primary care physician, Dr. Nathaniel Bretner, a solid, relatable dude. He was only a few years older than me, broadly built like a former jock. He was bearded and soft spoken and never rushed. I liked him.

I hadn't had a real physical in years, so he ran me through the gauntlet: lifestyle, family history, blood pressure, breathing, fondling my balls. When I asked if he would need to do "the whole ass-check-and-piss-tube routine," he just frowned and said, "We don't need that yet."

I described my panic attacks in great detail. The sudden bouts of vertigo, how my computer screen would start to shimmy and quake, the ringing in my ears, the shaking hands, the inability to breathe. I gave him a synopsis of my failed relationships and my dick's lack of dependability for the past six months.

"I can help with whatever is going on physically, and we may yet get you an MRI just to make sure you don't have a brain tumor. But I want you to talk to a psychiatrist or a psychologist about everything else. A psychiatrist because they can prescribe actual medicine, but a psychologist is fine too. I'll get your panel over to the lab, and we'll see if anything is off with your blood sugar, liver activity, cholesterol, things like that."

"Yeah, okay."

Then, instead of continuing our conversation face-to-face, he picked up a little microphone attached to his computer and began dictating my take-home orders.

"Your weight, two thirty-two . . . Family history of cancer . . . These are a bit of a concern . . . Blood pressure is very high. I am prescribing you losartan, one pill a day, and metoprolol, also once a day. I want you to buy a blood pressure machine—they're only about thirty bucks on Amazon—and keep checking your BP at home at least every few days . . . If it stays around this one-sixty-to-one-eighty range, I need you to come back so we can make another adjustment to bring this down. Right now you're in a risk category of around twenty percent of having a stroke or cardiac event within the next ten years. My job is to get that back down to one or two percent. I'm also including a prescription for Cialis. If it is not effective, let me know, and we can try another medication or check for other causes, such as prostate trouble."

He paused, sneaking a glance at me, then returned to the screen.

"I'd like you to get some exercise. Walking your dog and playing golf is good, but let's find some moments of intense cardio, at least ten to twenty minutes three or four times per week . . . More greens, fruits, whole grains. Let's try to avoid the carbs and sugars as much as possible. Less red meat.

"Your drinking is a quite serious concern. Five to fifteen drinks per day, whether they are beers or cocktails, is really, really hard on your body. I want you to remember that alcohol may help alleviate stress for a few hours, but it's affecting your sleep, your digestion, and the next day you will feel more anxiety, often overwhelmed with racing thoughts. If you need help for alcohol treatment, there are many options available, and I am happy to help you find a program.

"I want to see you again within sixty days. We will print copies of today's visit and include a list of mental health professionals who may be able to help you gin up an erection more than once a year, cure that slice, stop topping easy approach shots from perfectly good lies, learn how to read a goddamn green once in a while, and by God, have you shooting in the low eighties by July. End notes."

Okay, that last part was wishful thinking. I shuffled out, disoriented and feeling like I was failing at that simple game, the one called DON'T LET YOUR ENTIRE BODY, MIND, AND LIFE GO TO COMPLETE SHIT BEFORE YOU TURN FIFTY.

Super fun game.

headjob #1

After the twenty-seven -iatrists rejected me, I decided to call a few -ologists. Everybody just wanted the drugs, I reasoned, so all the psychiatrists were overloaded. But the first four psychologists gave me the same excuses. Do not accept insurance, no new patients, Dr. Dieter von Hindenberg is traveling for the next seventeen months, we don't like the sound of your voice, you seem angry at us already, et cetera.

The fifth one answered her own phone, and somehow I knew right away she would take me. She explained that she was between practices but was very experienced in working with depression, anxiety, loss, divorce, abuse, and family matters. She sounded a little older, with a touch of the career smoker's vocal fry, but I preferred that to some robotic industry professional.

"I have an opening tomorrow at four," Dr. "Call Me Lisa" Greyson said. "I do take insurance, but not until after the first fifteen hundred. I charge one fifty per session, so that would give you ten sessions before you can start being reimbursed, and who knows, you might be cured by then." Light laugh on her end, followed by a cough.

I was in no place to negotiate. "Sold."

She gave me the address and explained that it was a house, not a medical office, and that I should park on the street, not in the driveway. I arrived fifteen minutes early. I supposed this must not be all that unusual, a psychologist using her house for her practice. But without the sterility and professionally clad staff of a clinic, it felt too intimate, too vulnerable, with no place for my twisted, alcohol-and-anxiety-fueled musings. The failed screenwriter in me couldn't help wondering: What if the patient was a psycho and the treatment didn't go so hot and the doctor was pushing his buttons a little too hard and now was his chance to star in his own Lifetime movie? The kind that came with trigger warnings?

Albert had already become familiar with every room in her house. First he was her patient . . . then her captor! He came for help, but when the lonely Dr. Lisa said there was no cure for his brand of evil, he took treatment into his own hands!

There was a sign on the door, black marker on yellow legal paper.

DON'T KNOCK
PLEASE COME IN AND
STAY QUIET UNTIL YOUR SESSION.

The foyer was narrow with a set of curtained French doors immediately to the left. A warm yellow light glowed inside, and I could hear a woman talking. She sounded miserable, her words coming low and severely strained. There was a padded bench with a couple of magazines. I sat down, my knees almost touching the office doors. The woman inside began to cry, and I squirmed and got up.

I waded deeper into the house, to a large family room and

open kitchen. It looked like a house that had been staged for Generic American Family, with all the furniture, bad artwork, and even worse family photos, as well as a bowl of perfectly arranged fruit on the island. I sat on the couch and flipped open a magazine aimed at today's more aspirational version of a homemaker, equal parts decor ideas, healthy recipes, parenting tips, stress relief, and relationship advice.

I got lured into a piece about how to shake your husband out of his workingman doldrums ("Five Ways to Turn Any Weekend into a Romantic Sex-Romp Staycation"). The first step was *getting your naturally beautiful "down-there hair" waxed*, the perky author asserted. *And yes, even your butthole—he'll see that you understand him and won't be able to contain himself!* Before I could get to the second step, the office door opened, and the doc and her patient murmured goodbye.

The patient was younger, late twenties, with mousy hair, a huge sweater, and pink mittens. Something about the mittens in May made my heart hurt. I hung back, not wanting the woman to feel self-conscious. She was still wiping her eyes, and I felt like I had intruded upon some family tragedy. Jesus, I didn't belong here. This was a place for battered women, suicidals, the helpless and ravaged. I was just another overprivileged white male who needed to drink less and find a better job. Who was I to clog up the system?

After a moment, a late-middle-aged woman with brightly dyed blond hair and a lot of colorful makeup peered into the living room, looking concerned. "Casey?"

I stood. "That's me."

"I'm Lisa. Please don't come in here. This is not my house. I'm just renting the office. Stay in the foyer next time."

"Oh, sorry."

"Come in."

The Romantic Sex-Romp Staycation would have to wait. She led me into her office, a simple study that had been primped into a Pottery Barn day spa for emotions. Had to be at least eighty-five degrees. Shelves filled with self-help books with Eastern-philosophy-meets-spiritual-warrior-sounding titles. Dim lamps, a scent diffuser misting orange-almond cyanide, a deep couch strewn with fluffy decorative pillows. A series of little metal chimes sat on one end table, next to a box of Puffs Plus. At the foot of the couch was a massive red velvet pillow with a tiny gray dog resting on it, a yellow bow in its head hair.

"That's Christina," Dr. Greyson said. "I hope you're okay with dogs. Have a seat."

"I love dogs." I reached a hand down.

Christina began to growl and tremble.

"She doesn't allow petting until at least the third session," Lisa said. "Don't take it personally."

I managed not to make the obvious joke on that one.

Dr. Lisa Greyson looked mostly like she sounded. I guessed she was in her late fifties or early sixties. She was well put together. Work had been done. Her cheeks and forehead were tight and shiny. She wore a sort of bohemian pantsuit with a thin shoulder wrap. One of those women who are always cold, even in summer. Red-framed glasses. Probably had been a real knockout fifteen, twenty years ago, but somewhere along the line husband number one or two had abandoned her for the younger version, leaving her with just enough of a settlement to finish the PhD that might help her understand just what the fuck happened.

If that sounds judgy, it is, but it's based on the few personal details she came to share with me and, it must be said, her apparent inability to respond to my confessions with anything less than a full-on opinionated assault of the sort you'd expect from your mom, your wife, or a daytime talk show host, not a calm and objective mental health professional.

Ultimately, I came to respect her for this. It saved us a lot of time.

She began with all the usual questions: *What brings you in today? Tell me about your work. Family, marital status, any recent traumas? Oh, I see, when did you lose your father, your wife, the dogs? What's your manager like? Are you experiencing any physical manifestations lately? Other than the panic attacks, vertigo, blind spots, toe tingles, nightmares, cold sweats, hot face, early tremors, insomnia, dry mouth, back pain, sudden onsets of rage?*

I answered freely, never skimping on the real dirt. A few of Lisa's highlights:

On my dad dying: *So that was some time ago. Maybe it's time to let go?*

On my divorce: *Do you resent her need to change? Why do you think you still talk to her so often?*

On my work situation: *I used to want to be a writer. Can't you do that from home? I work from home. All you need is a computer and Wi-Fi.*

On my drinking: *My God, Casey, that is a* terrible *amount of drinking. I'm amazed you're not already in a hospital. You're absolutely destroying your body, and your mind doesn't sound like it's doing too well either. Have you considered checking yourself into a facility?*

On the paperwork I needed her to fill out so I could get my leave pay: *Oh dear, hmm. I'm really not comfortable with that. It's not very . . . It takes a lot of time, a lot. I would have to bill you, unfortunately . . .*

This pissed me off. If you work in a giant warehouse lifting boxes all day and you blow your back out, the doctor tells you to stay off your feet, get surgery, whatever, it's there, in your file—you're taken care of. All I was asking was for her to sign the form and share it.

"Fine, how much?" I steamed at the end of our first session.

Lisa tapped a pencil on her chin, obviously making up a figure on the spot. "Well, it's about three hours of paperwork, at least, and I bill one fifty an hour, so . . ."

It all became very clear then. She was renting part of someone's house, probably living in the basement, watching Netflix on her iPad while kickball Christine ate bonbons from her lap. She wouldn't bill my insurance until I'd covered the $1,500 deposit. She dressed Beverly Hills circa 1988, but that wasn't the life our thwarted shrinkess wanted. No, no. She wanted back in the game. Aspiring writer? Shit, she wanted her photo on the back of a self-help book. Working title: *The Goddess Rising: Turning Our Traumas into Fierce Energy*. But first she needed to round up enough scratch to lease a real office and, more than likely, an abode of her own. I wrote her a check for $600 and let it float down to her desk.

"I need the forms emailed to me by the end of the week, please. Signed and emailed, because I don't have a scanner. We good?"

Lisa frowned, considered further negotiations, then carefully placed the check in her little black calendar and patted it shut. "See you Tuesday at eleven."

Exiting, I nearly tripped over the knees of a heavy man in construction clothes and muddy boots seated on the padded bench. He did not look up from his issue of *Motor Trend* as I said excuse me and left.

His name is Mitch, I thought on the way home. *He's a site foreman who can't sleep. He drinks five bottles of Chablis every night watching* Yellowstone *reruns. He has walking night terrors and micturates in the closets, the hamper, the plants. He claws holes in the walls. His wife and children have come to fear him. He seethes at his boss, his workers, even people in the grocery store. He thinks he has low testosterone, but after just two more sessions with the Diabolical Dr. Lisa, he will recall how when he was ten, he and his best friend, Glen, used to get a little goofy watching* Facts of Life *reruns and play tummy sticks, and maybe, just maybe, the real reason he doesn't want to pork his old lady anymore is . . .*

When I got home, I poured myself a huge Seagram's Seven and Diet Coke and then called Stevens to make a tee time.

Stevens clicked a few keys. "Sorry, rest of the day is fully booked."

"Come on, Doc," I pleaded. "I need help. You gotta get me on today, even just for nine holes. This is your boy Casey Sweet now, not some swinging dick up from Denver. Please, *please* help a brother out?"

"Jesus, you got it bad already," Stevens said. "Come by around three thirty, and I'll see what I can do."

I laced up my golf shoes and felt better immediately.

pullout boy

It wasn't always just Vince and me. When we were paired with guys who shared our sense of humor and knew how to keep the pace without taking themselves too seriously, we would exchange phone numbers after the round. It was a form of man dating. Some lasted only a few rounds before getting scared off. But there were guys (and one woman) we played with semiregularly, and they all had their signatures.

There was Sam, who we called Sam That Was the Line, because he never made his first putt, and no matter how far off he was, he would always say, "But that was the line!" Then there was Sunset Ronnie, who always arrived late and always had to leave early because his wife was a ballbuster and hated that he golfed. The woman was Jenny P. She played seriously, had a very disciplined routine, and shot well. Once, we asked her if she wanted to play a buck a hole, and she acted like we were trying to take her 401(k), so from then on we called her Jenny for a Penny.

We even brought the cart girls into it. The girls who had fun and used their personalities often made over $1,000 on a Friday, Saturday, or Sunday. Morgan became Morganic, for her all-natural goodness, but she said she had a man who'd kick our asses if we tried anything funny. The newer one was a Black girl named Shyla, and she was in fact shy, so we named her Turtle. Taylor was a short brunette who was leaving us at the end of this summer for a career in pharmaceutical sales. She had a fiery personality and knew just how far she could push the guys to make huge tips without encouraging outright lechery. We called her TaylorMade. Taylor made for summer, Taylor made to hustle guys like they were in a strip club. We told her this and she loved it. She'd roll up on us every three holes and holler, "You sorry-ass bitches ready for another shot yet?"

But mainly it was about the boys.

Soon we had a regular text thread with six or seven guys to schedule tee times and share swing videos, funny golf memes, and just bullshit in general. We forged a loose kind of golf gang. Most of our crew were in their late thirties to mid-fifties. We all had too much time on our hands and were obsessed with the game. We all had problems we were trying to get away from. We all talked trash and told stories from our past, most of them involving nights gone wrong and embarrassing sex, the dirtier the better.

A couple of days after my Eighties Boy shock, Vince and I met up with two of our other regulars for a Friday-morning round. I hadn't told any of them about my possible paternity situation yet. Today we had Mike, who we called Mellow Mike. He always played in flip-flops, a ratty tee, and basketball shorts but was hard on himself. He'd shoot eighty and still call himself a "fucking nut sack" for leaving six putts out there. He had a thin beard and spoke softly but never shut up. He would mumble through every stroke, ours and his own. He had quit alcohol but made a lot of comments about pills and better living through chemistry.

Our fourth was Jamie, a handsome dude of ethnicities so well mixed even he wasn't sure what to call himself. His own take went something like, "My grandma was Korean, my grandpa was a Caribbean brother, my mom is white, my dad was Hispanic, and I have an uncle who's *Black* Black, but I'm just Jamie motherfuckin' Delacorte, one-man United Nations and all the best of the PGA rolled into one!"

"You told me you were Puerto Rican," Mellow Mike said after one of these roll calls.

"That's my cousin Alejandro, dumbass. And he will knife you."

"You just claim everything so you can be racist to everybody," Mike said. "It's kind of brilliant."

"Don't call me a racist, honky gringo bitch."

Whatever he was, Jamie had served in the army about ten years ago, three tours in Iraq and Afghanistan. He was aggro fit and always wore a lot of red. After his tours ended, he fought on the All-Army mixed martial arts team, pounding his way across Southeast Asia to win the mid-weight title belt. He worked out at Gold's Gym five days a week. He was on a partial military disability and didn't have a full-time job. He had a side hustle of some sort, but he never revealed exactly what, and we decided it was better we didn't know.

Jamie could drive the ball 350. He'd use a sixty-degree wedge from 140 out. He'd only taken up golf two years ago and was already a minus-eight handicap. Jamie was hilarious and incredibly social, but he could get a little intense when his game deserted him. Some days he wouldn't drink at all. Others he might hammer down eight White Claws and ten shots of Fireball in a single round.

We reached the fourth hole, a 180-yard par three that was backed up with at least two groups. The temperature was already in the high eighties. We parked our carts in a patch of shade and waited. I felt cranky, and not just because I was playing like shit.

"All right, Casey, what is it?" Vince spoke loud enough to get everyone's attention. "Our boy here is humping his way around the course like he hasn't gotten laid in a year."

"Maybe he hasn't gotten laid in a year," Mike said.

"Yeah, what up, man?" Jamie said. "You need a drink?"

"Oh, it's been way more than a year." I accepted another White Claw. Took a deep hit. "And I have a lot on my mind."

"Well, spit it out," Vince said. "That's what time with the boys is for."

"Leave the man alone," Mellow Mike muttered. "You guys are always pushing."

"Might as well." I told them everything I had pieced together about Eighties Boy and Damaris. How the Land Cruiser seemed to be the key, how Damaris called it Honeybear, just like Josh did, and how Damaris and I had lots of sex without protection. They didn't interrupt as I went through it. "So now I don't know what the hell to do."

"That little bastard is your son?" Vince said. "Oh my God, this is fantastic!"

They started laughing. I did another shot of Fireball, my fourth of the morning. I was sweating, my guts tied in knots.

Jamie slapped my back. "Johnny motherfucking Appleseed over here!"

I was not amused. "I promised to pull out," I said. "And I always did."

This sent them all into more howls of laughter.

Mike: "Did they not have sex ed in your school? Oh, Casey, I'm so disappointed in you."

"Man says he pulled out, he pulled out," Jamie chimed in. "Shit, you should be relieved. You just dodged twenty years of fatherhood."

Mike: "You have nothing to feel guilty about, Casey. You

precummed that boy into existence. And that kid's a scratch, so you're definitely entitled to some of his winnings when he hits the Tour."

I could only shake my head as they ran with it.

"I can hear the college recruiter now," Vince said, getting into character. "Sir, your son is a prodigy. We'd like to offer him a full ride to Oklahoma State. But how in the world did you not notice his talent until now? He's a natural!"

"We haven't been close for a while," I said, playing along. "We've only recently reconnected. Over golf, in fact. He shoots just like his old man did back in the day."

"Thought he lipped out," Jamie said. "But homey sank a hole in one."

"Wait, how many times did you screw this chick?" Vince asked.

"Plenty."

"And what about diseases? That ever cross your mind?"

"It was Boulder in the nineties. We didn't worry about that."

"You should give seminars on pulling out," Mike said. "Go to high schools like one of those reformed coke dealers and tell the kids how you ran amok and now you're stuck paying your debt to society."

"My man," Jamie said. "Going in bareback. That's old school."

"God dammit, I pulled out!"

"You pulled out," Vince said. "Maybe you just forgot to pray."

"Yo, you gotta enter the father-and-son tournament out here," Mike said. "Take that trophy home."

Vince added, "The names on the trophy plaque are Eighties Boy and Pullout Boy."

"You gotta find the mom," Jamie said. "Start hittin' that ass again. Get that good ol'-fashioned negligent-father makeup sex."

Vince, deadpan: "Yeah, but only if she still lets you pull out."

Then we were all laughing so hard my stomach hurt. A residue of Fireball kicked up into my throat. I started to cough, and then it all came up. I puked all over the tee box.

"My man," Vince said. "Livin' his best life out here at Twin Peaks!"

They joked about it the rest of the round. But in between holes, Vince and I went over the scenarios, possible next steps.

"Maybe I should try to get in a few rounds with him, pretend it's a coincidence, casually ask about his family?"

"You can't start with the kid," Vince said. "That wouldn't be right. Find the mom first. See if it's really her."

"So I stalk them? Follow the kid home one day?"

"Here's the thing. Do you really want to know? Because if he is your son, there's a reason she never reached out to you. Maybe she had no way of knowing for sure—"

"She wasn't like that."

"I'm just checking all the angles. Okay, maybe she just didn't want a man involved."

"I would have helped," I said defensively. "It's not like I was such an asshole I would have left her hanging."

"Okay, good for you. But now the kid's all grown up. You want to have a relationship? Help him financially? Maybe he ends up hating you for it and you throw a wrench in his life for no reason. I think you need to know why you're doing this before you mess with someone's life. Including your own."

"Maybe I just need to know."

"So she tells you what's up, and you just say, 'Thanks, I just needed to know'? I promise you, it won't be that simple."

"But I don't have any legal obligations at this point, right?"

"Shit like this can get complicated real fast."

"But if I'm *not* his father," I said, "then at least I *will* know. I can't sleep with this."

Vince took my hat off and studied me closely.

"What?"

"I wish you had longer hair," he said. "I'm trying to decide if you look like him."

I hadn't even considered this yet. "Do I?"

Vince snugged the hat back over my brow. "I think you might."

drugstore creep

I began playing early mornings, a few groups behind Eighties Boy, usually just nine holes because he played so fast and would roll off by eight. I would park on the street and wait for his car to leave the parking lot.

The first day, he went from the course to the grocery store and then to a house close to the course, in a subdivision of plain ranch homes from the sixties. No name on the mailbox. If there was another car, it was in the garage. I lingered for about an hour but didn't see anyone else.

The second day, he stopped at a CVS on Main Street. He was in there for about ten minutes and came out with a small plastic bag and a bottle of Gatorade. From there he went to McDonald's, used the drive-through, and wound his way out of town toward the interstate. I already knew where the house was, so there was no point in following him.

The third and fourth days, he went right back to the same CVS. That seemed strange. Either he had some medical thing going or they had good prices on Gatorade. Then he would usually go home, park in the garage, and leave the door open as he worked on Honeybear with his shirt off, listening to eighties tunes. I took off before he could notice the same silver Audi lingering on his street.

As I was driving home, it hit me. The CVS. Maybe his girlfriend worked there?

Or his mom.

I went home, changed out of my golf clothes, and walked Jojo around the block. Was I really up for this? I wasn't sure. But I needed toilet paper and some Advil anyway. I headed back to the CVS.

I parked, went inside, and made a casual loop of the entire store. Two teen girls working the front registers. An Asian woman and a brown-bearded white man behind the pharmacy counter. One Hispanic man stocking the snacks aisle. No women around my age.

I picked up my Advil and a twelve-pack of Charmin. When I arrived at the checkout, the two girls up front were gossiping. The one on the left was saying, "He was screaming at Reyna right there in the grocery store, threatening to steal her car, high on that shit again."

"He's a problem."

"She needs to get her ass—"

"I can help you here," the one on the right said. She was a thin redhead with pointy glasses, celestial tattoos under her wrists. "Did you find everything okay?"

"I think so." She started to scan the items. "Oh, hey, is Damaris working today?"

"No, she's not on—" She seemed about to say more, then gave me the up and down. "You a friend or something?"

"Something." I figured I'd better not lie. "Long time ago. We had some classes together in college."

Red bagged my Advil. "Keisha, is Damaris closing tonight?"

"Yep," Keisha said. "Thank God I'm off at six."

They exchanged a knowing smile. Damaris must be their manager. A toughie.

"I'll catch her another time," I said.

On the way out I clocked the store hours on the front window. Eleven p.m. Perfect. I'd come back around ten thirty and try to strike up a conversation. I went home and took a nap on the couch with Jojo. I had bad dreams.

I had been better about the drinking. But since this Eighties Boy thing started to reveal itself, I had been wobbling. I started drinking vodka and tonics with a splash of juice. Four or five stiff ones at night.

Don't become a piece of shit again.

So the night of my return to CVS, I limited myself to two drinks over a period of four hours. I forced myself to eat a decent dinner and put on some real clothes. A fashionably wrinkled linen shirt, khaki shorts, black sneakers. I wet my hair down and brushed my teeth as if I were going on a date. I was first-date nervous too.

I got to the store at around ten forty. The parking lot was mostly empty but for a small Ford truck and a light-blue Toyota RAV4. Damaris's brand loyalty now that she'd passed Honeybear along? Inside, the store was bright, and the music was playing a little louder than normal. The cashier was a young Hispanic man reading his phone.

I made another loop. As I turned the corner into the pet supplies, I caught a glimpse of a woman crossing the middle aisle, a good-sized booty and a trail of sandy-blond hair in a ponytail. My heart sped up. Damaris had brown hair back in the day, but women change their hair color all the time. I picked out a rawhide bone and a fuzzy toy shaped like a rabbit for Jojo, then headed after the blond. She was reorganizing the cold-medicine section, stacking the boxes, aligning the little price cards in their tracks. Just like a manager would before closing.

I pretended to study the allergy medicine, hoping she would approach me first. She finished there and headed to the back of the store. I switched aisles until I found myself among the condoms and other "personal health" products. I was mildly surprised to learn that your average drug chain now carried a variety of lubes, vibrators, and a few other treats in tasteful, energetic packaging.

The 3-in-1 Ecstasy Ring. For him and her.

Strawberry-Flavored Massage Oil. Safe for external and internal use.

This progress was comforting. We were no longer perverts in trench coats. Our desire to throw some lube and battery-powered accessories into our regimen was to be treated as unremarkably as home hair coloring or bunion pads. Condoms had a new shape too. The front two inches or so were like a loose sack, according to the diagram, I guess to emulate the sense of freedom. Maybe it wasn't too late for me to learn. I was considering buying a three-pack for a jerk-off trial run when a woman's voice startled me.

"Finding everything okay?" She was standing at the end of the aisle. "Sorry, we're closing in five, so just wanted to make sure you got what you needed."

I turned. "Oh, no problem. I think I'm all set."

She nodded. I met her eyes. It was Damaris. She had some new lines around them. Her brown roots were showing at the top. She was a little heavier, a little tired looking. My reptile brain made that nearly subconscious and instant calculation that men so often make—would I have sex with her? Answer: absolutely.

I held up a finger. "I, uh . . . Are you . . . ?"

She waited, raising her eyebrows politely. I was stuck, and something changed behind her eyes. Like she knew something was off here but wasn't sure what.

I cleared my throat. "Sorry. You look familiar."

She crossed her arms protectively. "I don't think—"

"Damaris." I was unable to frame it as a question.

Now she took half a step back and really looked at me.

"I think we had some classes together," I said. "Front Range Community?"

She looked away and shook her head. *No, no, we're not going there.*

"Casey. Casey Sweet, remember?"

"I couldn't say. But we're closing, so you should check out now." She walked away.

I followed her around the corner to the food aisle. I picked up a package of Golden Oreos and some milk, as if this would make me seem harmless, just a guy who had some late-night shopping to do.

"We dated. For a while actually."

She kept walking to the front of the store.

"I think I met your son on the golf course," I said. "It was crazy because I remembered the car. Your Land Cruiser."

Now she stopped and whirled on me. "What did you say about *my son?*"

"I just met him a few days ago. He golfs all the time, right? I see him out there sometimes. He was having car trouble, and I offered to give him a jump. That's when he told me about Honeybear and—"

She looked horrified. "Did you follow me here? Are you following him?"

"No, it's not like that, I just—"

"You just *what?* Who the fuck are you?" She was walking

toward me now, fists bunched at her sides. "How did you know I work here? Did he tell you that?"

"No, he doesn't—okay, look. I did follow him once or twice because I wanted to see you. To see if it was you."

"Dude, I don't fucking *know* you," she said, "and this is *really not* okay. I have pepper spray in my pocket, and I have security cameras all over this store, so I think you better pay for your shit and get the hell out of here."

I put my free hand up in surrender. "Okay, I'm sorry. I should not have—I just wanted to say hi after all these years, and I didn't know how else to do it."

She let out a breath. "Fine, Charlie. You said hi. Now goodbye."

"It's Casey."

"Goodbye, Casey."

"But maybe we can catch up sometime? Like normally? Maybe a cup of coffee?"

"A cup of coffee?"

"Sure. Why not?"

"Why do you want to have a cup of coffee with me? Why not go have a cup of coffee with anyone besides me?"

"Hey, look," I said, trying to cool her off with a little laugh. "I liked you back then. I figured, what the hell, might be nice to catch up. People do that, right?"

"I don't." She took my handbasket and marched to the checkout. "Javi, ring this up and lock the doors once he leaves."

"Yes, ma'am."

"Damaris, there's more," I said. "Please? It's important."

She turned back, pressing her wrist to her forehead. *Why is my life like this?*

"You know what I mean," I said. "I never knew why you left. Back to Ohio. I was worried, and now—"

"You're worried? That was twenty years ago, dude. What do you want? An apology? Okay, I'm sorry."

"Yeah, but—"

"But what? You're going to have to find some other old flame to rekindle with, all right?" She took the bag from Javi, shoved it into my gut, grabbed me by the elbow, and started to drag me to the front doors. Javi seemed amused.

"Okay, I'm leaving. One last question, then I'll go, I promise."

She released me. The automatic doors whooshed open.

I'd had no intention of being this direct right away, but now that the whole encounter was sinking, I couldn't seem to stop myself. "Is he . . . Is his father . . . Is that why you left? Were you, you know, preg . . . with child?"

Damaris shook her head tiredly. "Jesus Christ, Casey. I barely remember you. You were like the third-best lay of my junior college career. Get over yourself. My son and my life are none of your business."

"Third?!"

She shoved me in the chest. I stumbled backward, and she stepped to the right and flipped some kind of switch. The doors whooshed shut between us.

She just stood there with a faint smile of satisfaction.

"IS HE MINE?" I said to the glass. "JUST TELL ME THE TRUTH. I CAN HANDLE IT."

She cupped her hands around her mouth. "GO FUCK YOURSELF."

She stomped away. I waited. Javi walked over and stared at me. He held up his cell phone and waved it back and forth. I decided to leave before Javi called the cops.

I eased my way out of the parking lot deliriously, hands shaking. *That wasn't too bad, right? Oh Christ, it was a disaster! You're a goddamn stalker now. What the fuck were you thinking?*

That you could charm her like old times? That she missed you? You scared *her.*

I checked my rearview mirror as if expecting to be pulled over soon. I was flooded with guilt. I wanted to go back and apologize but quickly realized that would only make things worse. So this was it. I'd taken a shot. It hadn't gone well. Whoever Eighties Boy's father really was, I needed to let it go, move on. Leave these poor people alone.

And so I did.

Black Mamba

I stayed away from the course for a few days. I thought it was better to let Eighties Boy and his mom digest the encounter. I doubted she would tell him everything, maybe just that some ex of hers had been creepin' around and to let her know if he did anything else funny. Maybe she wouldn't tell him at all.

I cleaned the house, caught up on some phone calls. My new driver arrived. A Titleist TSR2 with an upgraded graphite shaft. I'd gotten fitted for it at Golf Galaxy a few weeks ago. The launch monitor had shown a distance gain of about forty to fifty yards and a tighter dispersion compared to Dad's old thumper. It was a beautiful thing, all black, so of course I named her Black Mamba in anticipation of our forthcoming dominance off the box.

I hadn't seen my mom for a few weeks, so I took some lunch over to her house. She lived on the north side of Longmont, only about ten minutes away. I mowed her lawn while Jojo and Carol, my mom's basenji, wrestled around in the back-yard. I moved some planters around for her, mounted a small bookshelf. She acted like I was the best son in the world, even though we both knew I wasn't.

Linda Sweet—she kept the name—had been a wild one, something of a Boulder legend. After she and my dad divorced, she spent the next twenty years acting like she had just turned twenty-one. Eventually she found a stable career as an executive assistant–office manager at one of Boulder's most prestigious real estate brokerages. Everyone knew her and loved her. She didn't take any shit and she had no filter.

She was getting around well in her retirement. She still cooked and cleaned for herself, got her exercise walking her dog and gardening in the backyard. The house looked good, cleaner than mine. She knew about my sabbatical but not how much the drinking had been a factor. I didn't want to worry her more than I already did.

"Are you still golfing all the time?" she asked as we sat in her kitchen and dug into our take-out boxes of carne asada. "You look tan. You've lost weight. Are you happy?"

"Yep, lots of golf. I'm good."

"Did that Vince offer you a job yet?"

"He's retired," I said.

"But he's got money. You never know. What about Dave? Have you heard from him?"

"He emailed me a week or so ago. Said they miss me, but I should take the time I need."

"I think you should find something else. That place wasn't healthy for you."

I shrugged. "It's not their fault I hate working in cubicles."

"You're a writer. Can't you find some company that will let you work from home?"

"Probably. If I update my portfolio and send out a bunch of résumés."

"My friend Gloria says her son works from home now. But he and his wife fight every day. I read that domestic abuse is on the rise because these people can't stand being at home all the time together. Isn't that awful?"

"Yep. That's why I just have Jojo. I can't imagine living with a woman again."

"You lived with Blair for a long time. How is she? Have you talked to her? How are the kids?"

Blair and Carl had two kids whose names I could never remember. One was hers, the other from his previous marriage. I had resisted having children with Blair, but that wasn't the only reason she had asked for a divorce. She had said over and over it wasn't about wanting me to make more money. It was about wanting me to do more, be more. But I knew it was also about money. Blair had always envisioned herself with a family, a big house, expensive vacations. For the past few years, she'd been killing it as a VP of human resources. Her husband was killing it even harder as a corporate lawyer for a fracking firm. I called him Carl the Kangaroo, after a baby kangaroo that had been born at the Denver Zoo and become the subject of fascination on the local news the same week Blair left me for him.

"Not for a while. She's still married to the kangaroo, living off the fat pouch." I stuffed a tortilla filled with beans, meat, and jalapeño salsa in my mouth.

"Tell her I said hello. I always liked her."

I laughed. "You said she was a selfish bitch on wheels."

"Only at the end, when she hurt you."

"I deserved it."

"You'll find the right girl soon," she said, patting my hand. "My son is too special to be all alone."

"For Christ's sake," I said. "I'm not all alone. I'm fine."

"I know, honey."

"I actually ran into an old girlfriend the other day. Remember Damaris Parker? When I was about twenty-three?"

"Was she the one who fled to New York?"

"That was Amy. Damaris fled to Ohio. Brown hair. You said she was edgy."

My mom's eyes brightened. "The one with the big boobs!"

"Yes, that one."

"How did you find her?"

"Just ran into her at the CVS over on Ken Pratt. She's a manager there."

"How was it? Where's she been all this time?"

"I don't know. We didn't get to talk much. The store was closing."

"Are you going to see her again?"

"I don't know."

We ate in silence for a minute or two. I decided to tell the whole story. My mom was a realist, she wouldn't judge, and I valued her input. When I finished taking her through it all, she stared at me with blank confusion. Slowly, her eyes widened all the way around.

"Are you shitting me? You have a son?"

"Funny, right?" I tried to downplay it. "Maybe. Probably not. It'll be okay either way. I think I just need to know. He's really quite the golfer—"

"Does he look like you? Oh my God, I have a grandson!"

"Whoa, whoa, slow down."

"But why didn't she tell you? Why just run away? It's not like you kids were sixteen."

"That's what I don't understand. Maybe it wasn't mine. I just have this weird feeling it was. He is."

My mom sat back and drank her iced tea, shaking her head. "Well, I just never imagined. This is like one of those TV shows. Aren't you scared?"

"What's the worst that could happen? Maybe we become friends. Maybe more."

"What if she wants all your money?"

"We were never married. The kid is like twenty-two now."

"She could sue you."

"For what? It wasn't my choice to leave. And what would she get out of it? I'm not an NBA player over here."

"You better be careful, Casey. She could get her hooks into you."

"Mom, she's not going to *get her hooks* into me. She might not want the kid to know. Which I have to respect."

"How did she get pregnant?"

"How does anyone get pregnant?"

"Didn't you use birth control? Did the condom break?"

"Mom, please."

"Well? *Something* happened."

"We might have been a little irresponsible in that department."

Mom gave me her best frown of disapproval. "Casey Sweet. Your father had those talks with you, I know he did."

"He did."

"But there you went, running around town with your dick."

"Jesus, Mom."

"Sport fucking. That's what it was called back in my day." She gazed off at some distant memory, a trace of a smile creasing her lips.

"Jesus, Mom. Hello?"

She snapped out of it. "Do you think she tricked you?"

"Why would she trick me and run away?"

"Your father gave you good genes."

I rubbed my eyes. "Yeah, well, it's too late now. How it happened is irrelevant."

She turned hopeful. "Do you want to bring them over for dinner? I can make my meat loaf."

"No. God, no. Something like that is a long, long way down the road. One thing at a time."

"You better tell me what happens. I'm gonna be a nervous wreck!"

"I will. Relax."

She carried her tray to the kitchen. "Life is funny. Maybe you were meant to be a father later down the road. Not with Blair. More like this."

Sadly, I knew what she meant.

father-and-son time

I couldn't avoid the golf course forever. Vince and I had a tee time that Thursday at ten twenty. I parked and looked around for the Land Cruiser but didn't see it. The kid had probably already finished for the morning.

I checked in with Stevens. "Haven't seen you for a few days," he said. "Take a vacation?"

"This is my vacation, good sir. Just had to take care of some stuff at home."

"You and Vince today?"

"Yep."

"Go ahead and sign in. You guys are playing with Josh," Stevens said. "Try not to let him take all your money."

"Josh?"

"You know, the younger fella with the bare feet. Josh Parker."

So that was his name. Would I have named him that? Would I have had a say?

"He's a good kid," Stevens said, trying to reassure me. "Scratch golfer. You might learn something."

"I thought he preferred to play alone."

"Every now and then he'll mix it up. Have fun!"

Was I imagining it, or was there a mysterious little twinkle in Stevens's eyes? I was probably being paranoid, but this felt like a setup.

The blue RAV4 pulled in while I was loading my bag onto the cart and tying my shoes. It parked a few spots over from me. Eighties Boy removed his bag from the hatch. "Thanks for the ride, Ma." He shot me a quick glance as he headed toward the clubhouse.

I heard another door slam. Oh shit.

"Well, look who it is," Damaris said. "The Longmont Stalker." She wore dark jeans, pink running shoes, and a sheer blue blouse with frills at the cuffs, a black tank underneath. Big celebrity sunglasses. Her hair had returned to its natural brown. She looked good. Better than good.

"I didn't follow anyone today," I said. "I promise."

"I know." She raised her glasses to her forehead. "I called the pro shop and asked for your tee time."

"I see."

"All Josh knows is that we dated a long time ago. Because that's true and that's all there is to know. Don't fill his head with any ideas, because they're not true. Understand?"

"Yes, of course."

"He's an adult. Treat him like one."

"I will."

She looked at me for a moment. "You married?"

"Divorced."

"How long ago?"

"About seven years."

"You cheat on her?"

"Excuse me?"

Damaris nodded as if I just confirmed her suspicions. "Are you seeing someone now?"

"No. And what's with the interrogation?"

"I ran a background check on you," she said. "At least you're not a sex offender."

"Well, that's a relief."

She handed me a business card. "Next time use a phone like a normal person. Don't come to my workplace."

The card had her name, a variety of skills, and a telephone number etched into an eggshell background.

DAMARIS PARKER

Massage. Reiki. Desensitization Therapy.

"Desensitization therapy. What's that?"

"Google it."

I put the card in my golf bag. "I'm sorry about the other night."

"Are you really that desperate? Or you just get off on harassing old flames?"

"I told you, I just wanted to understand why you disappeared and if—"

She put her hands up. "Cool it with that shit. I mean it. We can have coffee sometime, but not if you keep on with these absurd conspiracy theories."

I smiled. "Fair enough."

"And only if Josh likes you. He can tell a lot by golfing with someone, so don't blow it."

I laughed. This was too much.

"What's funny?"

"So this is a screening thing? Josh helps decide who you date?"

"It's not a date. And I had to tell him something so he'd

watch out for you. You're the one who used him to find me. So now you have to own it. Prove you're not a shithead."

"Okay. Thanks. I think."

"I'm late for work." She left.

I exhaled. Jesus Christ. This was going to be some round.

I filled Vince in on the situation as we waited at the first tee.

"Be cool," I said. "No jokes. Don't even hint about it."

"I got you, homey. 'S all good." But he was grinning, loving every minute of it.

Eighties Boy walked up in his usual golf attire: ratty old Quiksilver tee, red Bermuda shorts, camo neck gaiter, no shoes, and a pair of blue Oakley Frogskin sunglasses. He crossed the gravel cart path as if he were walking on felt.

"You guys ten twenty?"

"Yep. I'm Casey. We met before." I offered my hand and he shook it.

"Josh."

"Hey, Josh, I'm Vince."

"Cool." They shook.

"We usually play from the whites," I said.

"Is that so?" Josh lowered his glasses and gave me the Clint Eastwood. "We're playing from the tips today."

"About time we pushed ourselves," Vince said. "We're ready to get schooled. Go ahead, Josh. Show us the way."

He cleared his throat and spat. "You guys go first. People in front of the green."

The green was 380 yards away. Carts right up next to it. No way he could drive the green. Not this little guy. Vince and I looked at each other dumbly.

"Well, I know I can't reach it." Vince stepped up. His drive went about 240, up the right side.

"Good stuff," I said. Under the spotlight again. I took an extra practice swing. Reminded myself to breathe and take it nice and easy. One . . . two . . . three . . . GO.

I looked up to see my ball hooking left. Maybe 160 yards. "And that's why we play the whites," I said.

"You have a clean line from there," Josh said. "You were standing too close to the ball."

Vince grinned, eating it up.

Josh set up. Took a very slow half swing, then went into his weird little hitch move before unleashing. His body was a rubber band, twisting into pure rotation, full extension. The physics made no sense. He was maybe five feet seven, 145 pounds. He swung as easily as I might use a gap wedge from 100 yards. But the ball went on a perfect draw and seemed to have endless steam. It landed center fairway about 20 yards short of the front edge.

"Un-fucking-believable," I mumbled.

"See you up there." Josh shouldered his bag and began peeling a banana as he set off.

Vince and I sat in the cart. He said, "This is going to be an education."

"He just drove three fifty like he was sleepwalking," I said. "There's no way he's my son."

We didn't speak much for the first six holes. What was there to say? Eighties Boy—Josh—shot the best golf I had ever seen outside of the PGA on TV.

Holy-Jesus-on-every-shot golf.

He birdied the first, eagled the par-five second, then birdie, birdie, and parred the fifth, but only because he missed his birdie putt by an inch. He got distracted by his phone and parred number six.

His drives were monstrous, towering. His approach shots were low flying and sticky. Hitting the green was as easy for him as pouring a vodka tonic was for me. He sank putts from eight feet, thirteen feet, twenty-four feet, and what must have been thirty-six. And all through it, he acted like this was just another day at the office. Golf wasn't even a challenge for him, I realized. It was subconscious equations, like driving a car half awake.

He rarely spoke, except when one of us exceeded ourselves. He might say "Nice roll" if we made a long putt. Or "You got that one" when we had a solid drive. But mostly he played like we weren't even there. He didn't respond to our compliments either. He'd hole one from thirty feet, and we'd holler in approval. On number nine, he had to work a punch shot from one hundred twenty out. He proceeded to thread it through five trees, in and out of the greenside bunker, and onto the green. We whistled and clapped, and he just nodded. "Sometimes I like to practice hitting out of the trees."

"You hear that?" Vince said. "He went into the trees on purpose."

"Little fucker," I said.

On the tenth box, we had a short wait. I asked him if he'd fixed his truck yet.

He never met my eyes when he spoke. "I got the wiring sorted out. Now I need to replace the driveshaft."

"Sounds expensive."

"It's a double Cardan, about five hundred bucks. I have the part, but I can't find the right U-joint puller. The old joint is seized up, so I need a commercial-grade puller. The one I want is back-ordered."

"Sure, makes sense." I didn't understand mechanical stuff, but the tool rang a bell. My old man the tool fanatic would have known.

We pressed on. As far as I understood, it was generally poor etiquette to give another golfer unsolicited advice. But that didn't stop Josh. After I missed several putts ranging from four to sixteen feet, he said, "You're aligned right. Open your stance and square your shoulders. Get your beak over the ball." When I was pulling long irons, he said, "Your takeaway is dooming you. You need to get wide and not so high; it's about load efficiency, not power."

We drank our White Claws. Offered him one. He declined. He had his Gatorade and was always eating something. Protein bars. Bananas. Nuts.

Vince tried to strike up some conversation on number eleven. "You in school, Josh?"

"No."

"Do you work?"

"Yes."

"What do you do?"

"I'm a trader."

"Stocks?"

"Some, but mostly crypto."

Vince became animated. "Nice. I've been playing around with some of that. I'm holding about twenty grand in Bitcoin, Solana, Cardano, and a few others. Anything working out well for you lately?"

Josh shrugged. "I mostly study alt coins. They're harder to spot, but I like playing the long game."

"Alt coins?" I asked.

"They're like penny stocks," Vince said. "Also known as shitcoins."

Josh responded as if mildly insulted. "That's like saying BTC was a shitcoin when it started out. They're not shitcoins when the tech is real and the team is proven."

Vince nodded. "So you're making a little cash from your setup at home?"

"Here and there." Josh dropped his ball on the tee box. "I got in on Binance when it was eighteen cents."

Vince's eyes widened. "Whoa. How many were you holding?"

"Twelve hundred."

"Uh-huh. And are you still holding?"

"I sold at four hundred dollars."

Vince turned pale. "You're joking."

"Nope."

Vince mumbled the math, then whispered to me, "If he's telling the truth, he turned two hundred bucks into almost half a million."

Josh teed off. Another fairway, dead center.

"That's a helluva profit," Vince said. "What'd you do with the cash?"

"Paid Mom's house off. Put a chunk in Nvidia low. Diversified the rest."

"Should have at least treated yourself to a new set of clubs," Vince said, gesturing to Josh's old bag of lost and found sticks.

"Why?" Josh seemed genuinely perplexed.

"My man," Vince said with a laugh. "We need to play together more often."

Josh smiled. "Check out Verasity. Trades under 'VRA.' You can pick that up at about point zero zero four cents a coin right now. My model has it going to ninety cents in eighteen months or so."

"VRA," Vince repeated. "Thanks, bro. I'll look into it."

I chunked my tee shot.

"Try that again with your eyes open," Josh said.

But Josh was not immortal, it turned out.

We were on number sixteen, where a big pond spanned

most of the fairway's right edge. Josh's driver scuffed the ground, and he blocked the shot right. The ball sailed about 240 yards around the bend and bounced into the water. He just stared at the pond for a while. We weren't about to say anything.

For the first time, he turned and looked at me directly. "So now I know why you were so interested in my car. I guess you dated my mom way back when, huh?"

I swallowed. "I did, yeah. We were about your age."

"Why did it end?"

I looked at Vince. He looked away.

"I'm not really sure. I liked her a lot. We didn't fight. But then she moved away."

Josh dropped his driver into his bag. "You trying to date her again?"

I knew I needed to be honest. "Maybe. Might be a little too early to tell. We've hardly had a chance to catch up."

He stared at me, hands on his hips. "I don't believe you. You're trying to fuck my mom."

"Oof," Vince said.

"What?" I felt gut punched.

"Don't lie. You want to fuck my mom! You're trying to take her away from me."

I was horrified. "Jesus, no, I'm not—"

Josh pointed at me and started laughing hysterically. "Did you see his face?"

Vince started laughing.

Josh was beaming. "Dude, I'm just messing with you! Chill out."

"He has a sense of humor," I said, shaking my head. "Good one, Josh."

We went up to find our balls. Vince and I hit our seconds, then waited while Josh took his drop.

He glanced back. "And just so you know, it doesn't matter to me one way or another. Mom can date whoever she wants, and you seem all right. I won't be here much longer, so I hope it works out however it's meant to. She definitely needs to get out of the house more."

"I'll keep that in mind," I said. "Appreciate the thought."

His next shot ended up on the shoulder at the back of the green. He chipped short, leaving himself about twenty feet above the cup. He missed the putt. It was the only lost-ball double bogey I ever saw him make at Twin Peaks.

tools

The next day I was back to digging around in the garage, separating the tools from the rest of Dad's stuff. I was looking for a U-joint puller. Google showed me what they looked like. Kind of a horseshoe-shaped thing with a heavy-duty threaded bolt running through the middle and a coupling at the end. I started opening the plastic cases. Drills, sanders, Dremel kits. Buried under the tool bench, I found a black case that said *Tiger Tool*. I popped it open. I couldn't be sure, but I thought maybe this was close to what he wanted.

I texted Damaris and asked her for Josh's number. I told her I had a tool he might be able to use on his truck. **We had a good time on the course**, I added. **Hope all is well.**

She responded about an hour later with just the phone number, nothing else.

I texted Josh and asked him if I could swing by. I might have something for him.

Sure I'll be home all afternoon.

I didn't ask for the address, and he never asked how I knew where to go. He was in the garage with the door open when I pulled up. He was shirtless, and his hands were dark with grime. Honeybear was on jacks, one wheel removed. A little digital streaming amp in the corner was playing a New Order deep cut.

"How's it coming along?" I asked.

"Same shit," he said. "Now that I'm in there, might as well do the brake lines and new pads. I can never just do one thing."

"I don't even know how to change my oil," I said.

"That's easy. Take it to Jiffy Lube."

I smiled and handed him the Tiger Tool case. "I don't know if that's the one but thought you might give it a look."

He set the case on Honeybear's hood and popped it open. He looked at me. "Where'd you find this?"

"In my garage."

"It's brand new."

"My dad left a lot of tools behind that he never used."

"You just had this in your garage? Seriously?"

"Yep."

"Your dad a mechanic?"

"No. But he was obsessed with tools. He'd see a good deal at Harbor Freight and buy two whether he needed them or not."

"Harbor has a lot of cheap stuff, but this is nice. Can I borrow it?"

"You can have it," I said. "I'll never use it."

"This is like a three-hundred-dollar tool. I'll buy it from you."

I scoffed. "Tools are meant to be used. I've got an entire garage full of shit and can't find the energy to sell it off piecemeal."

Josh looked at me like I was trying to trick him into something.

"Really, it's yours, man," I said. "In fact, you do all this work yourself—someday you should come over and ransack the garage. It's full of stuff I can't even identify."

"Thanks. I appreciate it."

"Sure thing. So when are we gonna play another round?"

He set the tool back in its case and wiped his hands with a rag. "Wednesday morning if you don't mind going early. I like to jump the first tee time, so probably five thirty?"

"Cool. All right. See you early Wednesday."

"Thanks again," he said, and I could see he appreciated the visit. He had his own money; he could find his own tools. But sometimes when a thing just works out between people, it carries more weight.

I thought my dad would have been okay with it.

That was a nice thing to do, Damaris texted me that night. It was around nine, and I was watching the Golf Channel with Jojo, sipping on a vodka soda.

> No problem. Hope it works
> for him.

> He's still working in the garage
> right now.

> That's great. How are you?

A few minutes passed, and I wondered if she was debating whether to have an actual conversation with me.

> My feet hurt. I've worked the
> past nine days in a row. Off
> tomorrow thnk god.

Retail is hard, I replied. I used to work in a bookstore. I loved the conversations but not the hours.

I keep trying to quit but they
keep giving me a raise.

You must be good at it.

It's a drugstore. Not much to it.
What do you do anyway? How
come so much time for golf?

I'm a writer. Corporate hack. On
sabbatical for the summer.

What does that mean?

What the hell, might as well give it a shot. Can I tell you about it over coffee tomorrow?

At least twenty minutes passed, and I figured I blew it. But then:

Coffee isn't really my thing.
Might as well eat. Late lunch,
early happy hour. Like 3:30?

Sure. Any place you prefer?

Mike O'Shays. Huge menu.

OK. Cool. I look forward to it.

I looked at her business card again. Desensitization therapy. The Google search gave me a lot of possibilities. I added in the other two skills on her card, the massage and Reiki, searched again. About half a page down, the results showed desensitization therapy designed to treat premature ejaculation. I imagined some poor guy on her table. Damaris giving him a regular massage. The guy already aroused. What then? She gets him riled up, maybe slaps it around a little, telling him not yet, not yet? I wondered what she charged for an hour of that.

Well, she always had been good with her hands. Who was I to judge?

headjob #2

My second session with Dr. Lisa was focused on my work and drinking habits. She really dug into both and the relationship between them.

One of the first things we landed on was how I used to love the writing, but I had come to despise being at my job. The work itself wasn't the real problem. It was the environment. I was surrounded by executives who liked to chat at full volume in the middle of our department. I had more than forty tickets on my hotlist, and there were daily stand-ups with the project managers, weekly show-and-tells for our creative director, plus weekly meetings with each department—product, e-comm, enterprise sales, consumer sales, dev, security, and senior leadership. In this magnificent swirl of corporate buffoonery, it had become impossible for me to get into the groove where I normally flourished.

Lisa was convinced that my anxiety stemmed from this trap I had fallen into. I was so uncomfortable at work, so stressed from not being able to do my job properly, I had taken to drinking from the moment I got home to the moment I passed out in bed, every night for the past two years. I was trying to seal myself in a cocoon, one that would protect me through the night and into the next day. For a while it had worked.

More work, more money, more pressure, more booze . . .

Lisa's confidence that this cycle was the culprit eased my guilt. I wasn't just some joker who one day woke up and decided to not care about my job. Yes, I was responsible for my choices, but I wasn't a flat-out failure. I wasn't just a drunk; I was self-medicating. For the first time in a long time, my plummeting trajectory made sense.

As I was writing the check for our session, Lisa had some parting thoughts. "You have an interesting opportunity here," she said. "Your sabbatical. What I'd like you to consider is what you want out of this time. Not just our work but your time before you go back to work. It could be one big goal or several smaller goals. Work choices, lifestyle choices, anything you want for yourself. Besides lowering your golf scores."

"Hey, golf is probably my only healthy outlet at this point."

"I'm suggesting that not everyone gets this kind of opportunity. Write something down. 'By the end of summer, I'd like to X, Y, Z.' Whatever it looks like, let's find a way to get there."

For once I did not have a snappy response.

the MILF

I didn't know what the hell I was doing, but I was doing it anyway. What did I want out of this situation? A girlfriend? A son? Someone to notice me? Did I really just want to put my mind at ease, like I had told Vince?

If Josh wasn't my son, we could all proceed as friends and things would be clearer, easier. If he was my son and I had missed his first twenty-two years, I would feel pretty shitty. But there was something weirdly romantic in the possibility that this tenacious, genuine, difficult, beautiful woman from my past and I had spawned this odd but brilliant young man. Maybe we could all develop some kind of healthy triad that wasn't really a family but was close enough to make the next thirty years more meaningful than my current one-man puppet show.

"Maybe it's just happy hour," Vince said when I called him to go over it. "How about we just start there?"

I went for a haircut that morning and then ran the entire male bathroom decathlon: shit, shower, shave, trim the pubes (because you just never know, and besides, it was summer—my boys were getting hot out there on the course), exfoliate the face, moisturize the body, pluck the nostrils, trim the nails, floss, brush, mouthwash. I settled on my saffron terry polo, gray jeans, white Stan Smiths.

O'Shays was at Fourth and Main, only about a mile from my house, so I decided to walk. It was a classic Longmont pub that had been there for over forty years. High ceiling, long bar, brass railings. The place drew an older crowd, folks who didn't feel safe ordering sushi, Indian, or farm-to-whatever gluten-free stuff. I arrived early and took a seat at the bar. I wanted a Guinness but decided it would be more polite to wait. She arrived some twenty minutes later.

"Sorry. Parking in back was full. Longmont never used to get this busy."

"No problem. Good to see you. You look great." Her hair was clipped up in a cute-but-not-trying-too-hard way. She wore light-green capris, a short-sleeved blouse, and gladiator sandals.

She looked down at herself. "Oh, please. I look tired."

"Not to me."

Eye roll. "Do you want to stay at the bar or get a table?"

"Maybe a booth?"

She scrunched up her face. "How about the patio? It's not too hot out." She did not wait for my response. The patio it was. We ordered beers, and Damaris added the artichoke dip. "I'm starving. Do you mind?"

"I like artichoke dip."

I had decided I would be completely honest about my past. Not just with Damaris but with all women, everyone. I wasn't some habitual liar, but I realized that even before my meltdown at work I had been padding the truth, downplaying the bad things in my life. I told her about the breakups, my drinking, the panic attacks. She seemed to take it all in stride. She laughed. Tilted her head in sympathy once or twice.

"Wow, that's a lot to go through," she said. "Sounds like you did need some time off."

I told her how much golf was helping, how being outside so much had changed my entire mood spectrum, how it had led me to new friendships with Vince and the guys.

"And that's how you found me," she added with a crooked smile. "I can't believe you remembered my car."

"Not at first," I said. "But then a lot of it came back. More than just Honeybear."

"Like what?" She seemed to be dreading my answer.

"Everything. The time we spent. Even our last conversation."

She looked away. "That's crazy. I hardly remember anything. No offense. I guess I wanted to forget how unhappy I was back then."

"I don't remember you as unhappy. I mean, I knew you had been through some heavy stuff, losing your mom. But you seemed pretty strong and positive most of the time."

"I was hiding the pain." She sipped her beer. "Everything from sixteen to twenty-five was bad."

"I'm sorry if I didn't pick up on more of that at the time."

"We were kids."

We were at that junction point again. The abrupt breakup. Ohio. But I decided to let her choose whether to bring up the big topic. The waitress came back. Damaris ordered the Reuben burger. I went with the fish and chips. More beer.

"I never married," she said. "What did I miss?"

"Don't ask me," I said with a dismissive laugh. "No. It was good for a while. The first five years, which were also the last five years. She wanted more than I could give. It ended peacefully. We still talk now and then. She's in Denver, remarried with two kids."

"What couldn't you give her?"

"A bigger life. A Range Rover. Kids. A mansion in Cherry Creek. Vacations to Greece. Did I mention money?"

Damaris smiled. "I bet you could have. You just didn't want to."

I shrugged. "Sometimes I wish I had just jumped in, worked harder, done whatever she asked me to do. But I also remember feeling overwhelmed. Like I had no voice in it all. There was her plan A, all hers, and plan B was divorce. Like, what's wrong with a modest life? Why does everyone need to live in a TV show?"

"My friend McKenzie was in the same boat," Damaris said. "Her husband wanted the country club life and four kids and a cute little wife who stayed home and blew him every night. She wanted to live in a loft downtown, go to art galleries, travel, open a little pottery shop. He never supported her in anything. She finally just said buh-bye."

"Good for her."

"She's an artist now. We decided we don't need men."

"You probably don't. So has there been anyone serious? Or recently?"

Damaris sipped her beer. "No, but I get why you ask. I haven't been all that nice to you."

"I could have done better with my approach."

"God, I miss smoking." She took a piece of nicotine gum from her purse and popped it into her mouth. She offered me the rest of the foil packet. "Want a little hit?"

"I'm good. Actually, yes." I popped two.

"Anyway, Kenz and I take a trip every year. We go to the same area in Costa Rica every January for two weeks. We do yoga, diving, camping in the jungle, everything. It's amazing. We drink, get high, dance, and run naked on the beach. It's like our big cleanse for the New Year. I would die without it."

"That's cool," I said. "I've always wanted to go there."

Damaris stifled a laugh and blushed. "You're going to think I'm awful."

"I won't. Promise." I could tell she wanted to tell me. "Come on. I spilled my secrets."

"Okay, okay." She leaned in. "We each have a boyfriend down there. Not like a real long-distance thing. There is no relationship when we're at home. But for the two weeks we're down there, it *is* a relationship. A real one."

"I think I'm confused."

"It's the same guys every year. They plan for us. They dote on us. They do literally whatever we want. It's perfect."

"Whatever you want," I repeated. "You mean sex?"

Damaris barked laughter. "Yes! Of course. Tons of it. The best sex ever. Uninhibited. Tantric. All the time. Six times a day. Massages. Threesomes. They wait on us. I know how it sounds, but it's not some cheap thing. They love us. We love them. We look forward to it every year, and then we come home happy for another eleven months."

So this is what we've come to. The modern single mom's ideal relationship. Or at least Damaris's. And: *January, which means she hasn't been laid in at least four months.*

"So it's an arrangement. You pay for the services and—"

"No! We don't pay for anything! We're all friends. It's not prostitution, though there is plenty of that down there too. But this is different. I'm telling you."

"I guess that makes sense. Guys don't need to be paid."

"It's spiritual," she said. "We found a harmony and it just works."

Spiritual. *Does Josh know the real point of your winter escape is a bacchanalian drug-and-dick fest?* I wanted to ask but resisted.

"And what do these guys do for the rest of the year? Go back to their wives? Take care of more American women?"

Damaris looked insulted. "Hell no. They build houses on the beach and run tours. They don't have wives or children."

"So they say." I winked.

She did not find this amusing. "Think what you want, Casey. I'm not a fucking idiot."

"I'm sorry. I didn't mean to suggest you were. It just seems too, uh, convenient?"

"We all bring documentation for STI checks every year. We're safe. It's respectful *and* romantic."

"Mm. Sounds like it."

She threw her water straw at me. "Don't be a wiener."

I laughed and leaned back. "So what's his name? Your fella?"

"You just want to make fun of me."

"I won't. Come on. Tell me his name."

The waitress returned with the new beers.

"His name is Ferdinand, but I call him Black Mamba," Damaris said, glancing at the waitress. "He's from Nicaragua. Darker skinned."

I froze. Black Mamba? No. Not the name of my new driver.

"Kenz says he looks like Kobe Bryant," Damaris added.

"Uh-huh."

"He has the most beautiful skin. It glistens in the moonlight like a baby seal, like a—"

"I got it," I said. "Sorry I asked."

The waitress hurried away. The $600 club I'd just bought. I doubted I would ever be able to hold it again.

"You wanted to know my situation," Damaris said. "Now you do."

Humbled, I said, "Look, I'm happy for you and anyone else who finds the thing that works for them. God knows it's hard enough."

"Thank you," she said.

The food arrived. We ate, not speaking much. Near the end of her plate, she looked at me somewhat warmly.

"I remember your green eyes," she said. "You have kind eyes. I remember feeling safe with you."

"I hope so."

"You were always so casual. Most guys made me feel uneasy, self-conscious about my body. You were comfortable. I needed that back then."

"I thought you didn't remember anything about me?"

She slipped a lock of hair behind her ear. "Not much, but what I do remember is good."

"You might be the last woman who could say that about me."

"I doubt that."

I folded my napkin over my plate. "So Josh is a smart kid. He told us about his crypto thing. That's wild."

"He's a genius. No one teaches him anything. He just locks onto something and then becomes an expert at it. Sometimes I don't believe I gave birth to him. I'm just in awe of him."

"Proud of him."

"*So proud*," she said, and hitched a little, fighting back tears. "Sorry, I just can't . . . He's a miracle. You know by now Josh is different. He's had challenges. For his first few years, we thought he was suffering from autism. Or 'suffering' isn't the right way to put it. Processing the world in a very different way. We could never get a clear diagnosis. 'He's on the spectrum,' they kept saying, and I was like, 'Spectrum of what, humanity?' We're all on the fucking spectrum. So we focused on finding things that work for him and let go of so-called normal expectations. All I've wanted is for him to make his own life. To grow up and get an education, see the world, meet new people, whatever he wants. I don't care what he does as long as it's *his* life."

"Of course."

"But what does he do?" She threw her hands up. "He saved up his own money from working at the golf course all through high school and bought himself these computers. He taught himself to trade stocks, crypto, futures. Things I don't even understand. And in three years he makes more money than I will ever have. What kind of kid pays off his mom's mortgage twenty years early?"

"The good kind."

"I provide for us just fine. My father left me a modest inheritance, and I work retail management so I can have the health benefits and write my own schedule. I would never ask for his money. But he has power of attorney in case something happens, and he just did it without telling me."

She was crying. I offered her my napkin, and she honked into it.

"I stopped fighting it because he's going to end up with the house anyway. But he saved me. I thought I was going to have to work until I was eighty. Not anymore. Because of that kid who won't even treat himself to a new set of golf clubs."

"That's really something," I said. "He loves you very much."

She wiped her eyes. "I try to treat him, but the truth is he doesn't want much. He likes making things last. He loves fixing Honeybear. He's proud of being so self-sufficient. I ask him what he's saving it all for, why not live a little now while he's young. He says, 'I'm already living the life I want to live. When I want something else, I'll figure it out.' And the thing is, he's not joking. He could retire now. He's twenty-two!"

"He's done that well?"

"When he paid the house off, I insisted on knowing how much he had left for himself. He showed me his books. He has ten times the house in assets."

Houses like hers in Longmont were probably worth around

four or five hundred thousand. Which implied he was worth around four million. You read about these kids, the new entrepreneurs and crypto wizards, but you don't meet them playing barefoot on a municipal golf course and maybe they're your offspring.

"Well, that settles it," I said. The beers and conversation had gone to my head. "With those brains and his financial acumen, he's definitely not my son."

To my surprise, we both laughed. It was a good, stress-relieving laugh. I raised my beer.

"To Josh," I said.

"To Josh."

We toasted and sat enjoying the summer breeze for a moment.

"The thing is," Damaris said, "I think he might be."

"Hmm?"

"I'm sorry, but it's possible, Casey. Like, it's almost certain. Josh is your son."

part three
grinding for par

headjobs #3-4

My third session was unremarkable. We spent most of the hour rehashing the same topics (work, drinking, grief) without breaking new ground. It felt like a waste of time and money.

"I sense there is more," Dr. Lisa said at the end. "Other things you may not be ready to talk about. And that's fine. It's your time. But I don't know how much progress we're going to make unless you're willing to open up."

I went into our fourth session guns blazing. I told her about Damaris and Josh, summarizing the entire situation in less than a minute. *Had a good week, shot ninety-four the other day, and oh, by the way, I might be the father of a millionaire golf prodigy.*

Always the impartial professional, Lisa reared back. "Oh dear Lord—you're just telling me this now?"

"I thought we had enough to sort through," I said. "And so far, it's not a problem. We're all getting along great."

Lisa shook her head in disbelief. "You are just a revelation every week, aren't you? Honestly, Casey."

"Honestly what?"

She crossed her arms and sniffed. "What exactly are your intentions with this woman and her son?"

"My intentions?"

"What are you hoping comes of this? What are you willing to invest?"

I laughed. "You don't have many male clients, do you?"

"What has that got to do with anything?"

"You react like some drunken frat guy stumbled into your office and peed on the floor," I said. "You're horrified by my life. Like I'm the only guy who has these problems, and what—I chose them? I got bored and decided to make a real mess?"

Lisa sighed. "Okay, look—"

"Forget it. I knew I shouldn't have told you. Christ, even my mom was happy for me."

Lisa put up a hand. "I'm sorry. I shouldn't have reacted that way. I'm just surprised. With everything else that's going on, I thought this would be much more distressing for you. But the way you mentioned it was more like you happened to make a nice score at your golfing."

"What if this is my chance to be a fazzah?"

"A what?"

"Father. Dad. Proud papa."

Lisa blinked a few times. "That's what you want? To be a father? Because when you talked about your marriage to Blair, you said she wanted kids and you didn't. Has something changed?"

"Maybe I didn't want kids with Blair. Maybe now I'm just trying to own my own shit."

"Own your own shit," Lisa repeated. "What does that mean to you?"

"I'm trying to be open to the right thing with her and the kid. I'm playing it cool, but I have rights too, don't I?"

"I'm not sure I follow—"

"I'm not, like, going all Mel Gibson." I pulled out my cell and pretended to be listening to someone, my face contorting with rage. "Give me back my son!"

Lisa just waited.

I set the phone down. "*Ransom*? No? Okay, how about *Heathers*?" I shifted gears and became the distraught, sobbing father. "I love my dead gay son!"

Lisa looked exasperated.

I broke character. "I'm just messin' with ya, Doc. Settle down."

Still not amused. "This is what I mean. This routine of yours."

"Want to hear my Sean Penn in *Mystic River*?"

"No."

I began to claw at my throat as an imaginary throng of policemen held me back. "IS THAT MY DAUGHTER IN THERE?!" I wailed. "IS THAT MY DAUGHTER . . . ?" But I couldn't contain my own laughter.

"You need medication," she said. "You're sick."

"No pills. The psychiatrists still won't accept me." I shot her a wink. "It's just you and me, kid. But we're making progress, aren't we?"

"Well. I hope you think so." Lisa straightened her skirt and fought a smile. "I think, yes, I can understand how this development might be exciting for you. It's a lot of *new* at a time when you've been somewhat stuck in the old, so to speak."

"I've been in the shitter, Doc," I said. "But I'm ready to become a family man."

Lisa put a hand on her forehead. "Can we just—I can't tell if you're being serious or still making jokes."

I leaned back and stared at the ceiling. "Women always say they want total honesty. But I'm not so sure. This could all be for naught. I'm not even sure if he sprang from my seed."

"Let's table all that for a moment. And please don't talk about your 'seed.' There's something I've been mulling over for you. Have you ever been diagnosed with ADHD or a similar disorder?"

I sat up. "No."

"That's not surprising, given your age," she said. "Hardly anyone was diagnosed with ADHD when you were a child. But that doesn't mean it wasn't there."

I was intrigued. She asked me about my childhood, specifically my experiences in grade school, middle school, high school. I explained that I had been a good student when I applied myself, and I thrived in certain subjects, but my report card often ran the gamut, from A's to D's with an F thrown in now and then. I was usually labeled the class clown. My parents, especially my dad, would say things like, "Where is your head today, kid?" I was easily distracted by girls, friends, a knife, a new rap CD some kid had brought to school that day, jokes, lunch, my dick, anything but a social studies lecture.

On the other hand, when certain assignments struck me, I would go all the way in. The consensus on Casey Sweet ages thirteen to eighteen: basically good kid, smart, doesn't apply himself, socially gifted but has no discipline, at risk of falling behind, we all hope he sorts himself out someday.

Lisa whipped out her battered copy of the *DSM*. It was marked with many Post-its. "Can I have you take a quick test?" She landed on a page. "It's not official, but I just want to get an idea if we're in the ballpark."

"Sure."

"Just answer yes or no, and don't overthink things too much." She began. "Do you often get impatient standing in line at the grocery store or post office?"

"Yes."

"Do you often find yourself finishing other people's senten—"

"Yes." I cut her off and she frowned.

"Do you find it hard to stay focused while someone is presenting information for more than fifteen minutes?"

"Jesus, yes, of course."

"Do you find yourself fidgeting? Wagging your feet, moving your hands, readjusting yourself in a chair?"

I wagged my foot, readjusted myself on her couch, scratched my ear.

"Do you find the majority of your tasks boring or repetitive, making them difficult to complete?"

"Isn't that what a job *is*?"

"Are you easily distracted by activity or noise around you?"

"My cubicle is like working in a marching band."

"Do you frequently misplace things or have difficulty finding them?"

"No, but only because I'm so fanatical about my keys, sunglasses, wallet—everything has a place because for years I couldn't find shit."

Most of these questions seemed too obvious. Like, who doesn't get frustrated waiting at a red light? In all, she asked me twenty-five questions.

"We could dive deeper into this," she said, closing the book. "And there are other, more reliable tests. But you answered in the affirmative to twenty-three of twenty-five, which strongly suggests someone coping with ADHD."

We added this new possibility to everything else I had been dealing with at work. We discussed the risks of leaving my job. What if I couldn't find something better? Freelance was an option, but I was still paying the equity loan on my remodel, and my 401(k) was years behind.

"There is always risk in change," Lisa said. "But where has staying the course gotten you?"

"You're good. I might actually keep doing this."

"I think you should keep searching for a psychiatrist," Lisa continued. "They can perform a more complete test, give you a second opinion, and if they arrive at the same diagnosis, prescribe you Adderall or another medication to treat it. I can email you some names."

"Okay. And thank you for doing the paperwork. My company was able to process everything, and I qualified for my medical-leave pay. You saved my ass."

"Happy to help." Then, as I was about to leave, "Have you considered attending an AA meeting?"

"I've considered it." This was true. "But I don't think I really need that."

She stared at me.

"I need to try it my way first."

"Do you?"

Yes, Mom. "Yeah. I do."

"Okay. Next Thursday then."

I paused at the door. "How about *Forrest Gump*?"

"Get out. Now."

"I'm not. A. Smart. Man. But I. Know what. Love is."

Lisa bit her lip.

"How about in Spanish?" I offered.

She looked like a woman trying to remain stoic during a bank robbery. I went all in, as if the Oscar were on the line.

"*No soy un hombre inteligente. Pero sé lo que es el amor.*"

No laughter. No smile. She looked down, embarrassed for me.

"You're not feeling it? Let's try it in German."

Head bowed, Lisa covered her eyes. Heartfelt Gump was gone.

I delivered in the tone of an inflamed SS officer. "*Ich bin kein kluger Mann. Aber ich weiß, was Liebe ist!*"

Lisa began to hitch, and I realized I'd cracked the fortress. "It's not even funny," she whispered. "Why would you know this in three languages?"

"More, actually." I launched into Mandarin. "*Wǒ bùshì yīgè cōngmíng rén. Dàn wǒ zhīdào ài shì shénme!*"

The dam broke. She howled, waving me away. "No, no more, please, go, get out . . ." *Gwah-ha-ha-ha!*

I took a formal bow and exited. The young woman with the pink mittens was sitting on the bench in the foyer, gazing up at me in bewildered repulsion.

"Apologies," I said. "I have movie-quoting disorder. It's common among men who don't know how to express their real feelings, but I'm working on it."

She wrinkled her nose. "Good for you, Forrest."

desensitization therapy

Every text, phone call, and hangout with Damaris was a delicate dance. During that first happy hour at O'Shays, when she told me Josh was almost certainly my son, everything that had been theoretical became terrifying.

I had tried to come up with a calm, mature response. "Really? Yeah, no, so he . . . as in he's *probably* . . . or I guess there's not, like, a percentage we can put to this situation? I mean . . ." I started to cough.

"There's a lot you don't know. Maybe things you don't want to know. And that's fine. You don't owe us anything."

"But you're not a hundred percent sure I'm the one?"

"There was one other guy around then," she said, looking guilty. "I'm sorry. I should have told you. It was mostly over. We weren't having sex when I was with you. But then we did one last time, at the very end of our thing, and it screwed everything up. But I've ninety percent ruled him out."

"Oh, I see. How?"

"He was Black. Or is Black, I should say. Unless he died somewhere along the way."

"Right, right. So probably not the father. Maybe ninety-eight percent . . ."

"We can just walk away, no hard feelings. But if you want to be sure, I guess we'd have to look into DNA tests and all that."

"Do *you* want to know?"

"I quit thinking about it years ago," she said. "Now I go back and forth. But we have three people whose lives are affected by this, and I think everyone should at least have a say."

"Does Josh have any idea? What does he want?"

"We haven't talked about it directly," she said. "I always told him I had to do things on my own, for my own reasons. He's always accepted that. But he's curious about you, about our past. I think he's catching some kind of vibe, piecing it together."

I was nodding along, trying to think.

"Breathe," she said. "You're doing fine."

I exhaled. "I think, yeah, I *do* want to know. That's why I've been trying to talk to you, right? Not the only reason. I'm attracted to you, but it's all mixed together, you know?"

"Yes."

"I still don't understand why you didn't tell me, even if you weren't sure. I would have tried to help. I think I would have been decent about it."

"It's hard to explain now, but the reasons were impossible to explain back then. My mother had just died. She almost died giving birth to me. She had a medical complication, and it made her pregnancy with me extremely risky. She caught meningitis. And they figured that out, but her immune system went haywire. For years and years. Later she developed multiple sclerosis and a few other things. I have some of the same risks. I have fibromyalgia and chronic fatigue so far, waiting for the real shoe to drop. Aren't I a catch?"

"I think you are," I said. "I'm just sorry it's been so hard."

"I'm fine, really. I have periods where it all catches up to me, but I'm okay. Some of this stuff is hereditary; some they don't know. So when I was pregnant, it wasn't just about having it or not, or who was the father. I had to think about my health, the baby's health, all this other shit." She took a drink of her beer. "I was overwhelmed. After I moved away, I kept thinking, *I'll tell him someday soon.* I kept thinking I would answer a few things for myself, or the doctors would tell me something that would make everything clear for me. But another week passed, then another, and then I was like three months along, and you and I—that seemed so far away. And eventually I just decided it was my problem, my choice. It was messy. I had no right to put all these big decisions on you."

"Of course you did. You had every right to involve me. At any time."

"And I had every right *not* to," she added. "But now I wish I had, but I couldn't see that then. I'm really sorry. You should hate me."

"I don't see the point in that," I said. "Twenty-two years have passed. Sure, maybe there was a whole other life we could have had. Would it have been better? Worse?"

"Or just different," she said.

Some golf advice came back to me. "We each took a swing. Good swing, bad swing. Either way, the only thing we have now is the next swing."

She looked relieved.

Over the next week, we saw each other three times. Once for a long lunch, once for another happy hour dinner, and then we spent a whole Saturday at one of those gatherings small cities heap together, a combination of music in the park, farmers' market, and food-and-art festival where all the restaurants put

tables on the street and the city closes down six blocks of traffic so everyone can walk around dropping money and feeling
part of the community.

We shared a pizza at Rosalee's, then trekked down Main
one more time. A young couple walked toward us, their little
kid swinging between them, laughing while they looked bored
and tired. Could have been us back then. I imagined Damaris
and me swinging twenty-two-year-old Josh between us now,
his face a mask of glee.

When we got to the corner of Third, she dragged me into
the Speakeasy, a dark, garden-level joint in an old historic building. Not much of a crowd, maybe fifteen or twenty people
scattered around. There was a terrible band trying to play some
kind of jazz-bluegrass fusion. We ordered martinis and found
one of the side rooms where we could hear ourselves talk. She sat
next to me with our backs against a wall and patted my leg like
we were in cahoots, waiting for the bad guys to come after us.

"I used to love this place," she said. "It's all dusty and full
of old people now."

"We're not exactly young," I said.

"But we can pretend."

We'd had beers earlier, and now she put away her first martini in three big gulps. She offered me the last olive, and I bit
it from her fingers. She flicked some gin in my eye, and I went
to the bar and got us another round. She asked how my mom
was doing, and I filled her in.

"She didn't like me," Damaris said.

"She actually did. She liked your confidence. You were just
different than most of the girls I dated."

"She thought I was a goth slut trying to corrupt her
only son."

"What? Stop it. No."

Damaris side-eyed me.

"Okay, maybe a little."

She slapped my arm. "Oh my God!"

"I'm kidding."

"No, you're not. What did you tell her? Does she know we're hanging out again?"

"Um . . ."

She grabbed my arm. "Casey! Did you say anything about Josh?"

"I thought we weren't going to talk about this for a while."

"Oh, for God's sake." Damaris released me and gulped her drink. "Now she thinks I'm a slut who's after your money."

I laughed again. "Absolutely not. She wants to meet you both. She asked if you wanted to come to dinner."

Damaris let her head fall to the table. She was adorable. Pulling at me with that combination of tough but vulnerable. Sensual and a little ragged.

"I remember you," I whispered in her ear. I put my hand on her thigh, near her hip. "I think I still like you."

"Of course you still like me," she said. "I'm amazing."

"Yeah," I said. "You are."

She turned and kissed me on the lips. Then we kissed again, longer, legs shifting, her breast pressing into my arm. It was new but familiar, and the echo between the past and this moment was heady.

Damaris pulled back. "Whoa-ah, you might have to drive me home. I'm a little drunk."

"Good."

"You hoping to take advantage of me?"

"I would never."

She looked into my eyes, searching. "We'll see. Ready?"

I dropped a ten on the table, and we weaved our way outside.

We held hands walking back, and it felt nice, normal. When we got to her car, she asked me where I had parked.

"I walked again. I can drive you home and Uber from there."

"I think I'm fine," she said.

"No, you shouldn't drive."

She thought about it. "Okay, you drive my car, show me your house, and then I'll go home."

"Deal."

I pulled into my driveway. Dusk had ended. Night was here. The two big trees in my front yard were hanging over the drive like a canopy. I'd mowed yesterday. The air smelled like cut grass, lilac, and meat grilling in someone's yard.

"This was your dad's house?"

"Yep. Want to come in for a minute? I have coffee and tea."

"Coffee and tea," Damaris said. "Does that line actually work on the other women?"

"The women I've dated over the past few years, it was always at their house, if ever a house at all. So no, none of my lines work."

"You've been here five years and never had a woman stay over?"

"Jesus, when you say it like that."

"Dude, what happened to your game?"

"It's Longmont. Most of the girls lived in Denver. Like an hour away."

Damaris wasn't buying this.

"I've had sex!" I blurted.

"With other people?"

"Yes!"

"How long's it been?"

"I think we're getting off track here," I said. "I also have seltzer, wine, beer, vodka . . ."

She touched my arm. "How long?"

"*Sex* sex? Like, not just online—because I was in this weird emotional relationship where we fooled around, just not actual, you know—"

"Casey," she said very softly. "How long has it been since you put your penis inside a real vagina? Not a doll or a website?"

I gripped the steering wheel.

"It's okay, baby," she said. "I'm just curious."

"I don't know."

"You're a man. You know. To the day."

"Eighteen months? Two years, tops?"

She decided she'd pushed me far enough for now. "See, that wasn't so hard. And it doesn't matter. Do you think I'd be impressed if you were out screwing a bunch of women?"

I felt relieved. "Come inside and meet Jojo. She'll love you." I reached for the door, but Damaris held my arm.

"Let's sit for a minute. This is nice. Being in the car."

"Yeah? Okay."

"I feel like we used to spend a lot of time in the car." She sighed happily, leaning on my shoulder. "We had fun, right? We were good together?"

"I always thought so."

We were facing my garage door like we were parked atop some romantic hill overlooking the town. I kissed her forehead. She looked up and kissed me back. She put her hand on my face, and I was running my hand along her thigh again. She had good legs. Her arms were strong too, green veins visible along her forearms, over the backs of her small hands. She shifted her hips, breathing harder.

Car memories flashed, those times we hooked up before class, before heading into a restaurant, sometimes just driving around town, bored, until we found a shopping center or a park. The risk of exposure, the thrill of stealing a moment.

Sometimes just hands. Or mouths. Sometimes she would shuck her jeans down to her knees and sit on my lap. It had all seemed so natural and easy.

Until she got pregnant.

I ran my fingers under the hem of her blouse, touching her warm belly. I was fully aroused in a way I hadn't been for a long time. She noticed.

"Oh, hi there." She moved her hand back and forth, coaxing the genie from the lamp.

I raised her shirt and pulled the cup down until her pale breast was exposed and put my mouth on her, tongue flicking. She moaned softly and leaned into me, fumbling for the button on my shorts.

"We have to let this poor guy out," she said.

"Okay."

Her pants had a drawstring and elastic waist, but the navigation was tricky. I tried the side door, fingers working under the hipline of her panties. Soft skin, stubble, then a sudden warmth, wetness.

Damaris tensed, locking my hand between her thighs. "This is crazy, right?"

"Is that a trick question?"

She kissed me again, then retreated. "I'm sorry, I just don't want things to get confusing."

"I agree." But how much more confusing could it get? I withdrew my hand and gave her some space.

"I want you. I just want us to know why we're getting into whatever this is. You know?"

"Yes."

She placed her hand on my erection again. "Are you okay?"

What was I supposed to say? *Yes, I'm fine, totally not painfully aroused? No, I'm not okay, let me pressure you like a sixteen-year-old idiot in hopes you will get me off so you can resent me later?* The failed marriage had taught me at least one thing.

"Look." I eased her hand away. "We'll know when we know. Let's do things the right way."

She nodded. "And what way is that?"

"No idea. But I'm crazy for you. I was then. I am now. I don't expect you to feel the same way, but for me, you're that one . . . the one who got away."

"You really think that?"

I nodded slowly. "I do. I'm not big on faith, but this all feels like it's happening for a reason. My dad died and left me his golf clubs. And I went golfing because I could finally play with his precious clubs. And then everything . . . Somehow the one who got away came back. And she has a son. And if he is my son, our son, shouldn't I try to be someone real to him? Someone real to both of you?"

"I think you're being real, and that's all I can ask."

"I'm tired of fucking things up."

"You're not fucking things up." She put her hand on the back of my head and rubbed. "I don't see you that way. I know you're trying to do good things."

"I'm not sure how to steer this," I said. "I'm not smart enough. Stay, go, be a friend, more than a friend, forget I ever saw you—I'll do whatever you want. Whatever Josh wants. I promise."

Her eyes were glassy. "Thank you, Casey. That means so much. You don't know." She kissed me again, then just held me. "I do want to see your house, but I'm fading fast. This was a lot for me. Not just the physical part."

"I know. For me too."

She raised her hips and fixed her pants. "I'm sorry I got you all worked up."

"It's fine. I'll probably still call you tomorrow."

"Probably?" She smacked my shoulder again.

I stood in the driveway and watched her drive off, waiting for my erection to go away. It was around ten, and my neighbor Klaus had just gotten off work. Doing his slow walk to the mailboxes.

"*Hallo*, Casey, how ah you?"

"Good evening, Klaus. How was the bus driving today?"

He stopped with his key in his mailbox. "All day I drife, all night. You cannot belief dese people. They falls asleep, leave da trash, shit and piss and prick selfie on my bus."

"That sounds awful."

"*Gott* damn animals." He retrieved his mail and closed the box. "Has you find da posaw?"

I took a moment to translate the question. "Oh, for the trees. No. Not yet. Why don't you come by tomorrow and just take whatever you want?"

Klaus stared at me. Then he wagged his finger. "You should not give way ya fazzah's things so easy. My fazzah has one pot to piss in! We all kids use dis pot to piss. And don't start me vit da shitting!" He laughed and laughed.

"Good night, Klaus."

He was still talking to me from across the street as I shut the door and locked it.

I had just finished brushing my teeth and was about to text her to make sure she'd gotten home all right when my phone beeped. She had beaten me to it.

> Thank you for a really nice
> night. You make me feel things I
> haven't felt in a long time.

Attached was an image. I tapped it open, expanded it.

Her point of view. She was lying on her bed. The frame cut off above her belly button and just above her knees. The pants she had been wearing were pushed most of the way down her thighs. Her panties were violet blue with yellow floral lace, her left hand resting just above the waistband.

So much for a good night's sleep.

slippage

Like an animal sensing an approaching storm, Damaris went to ground. No calls, no texts, no replies. Dead silence. I tried to play it cool. Obviously, she didn't owe me anything. Just because we'd had some kind of breakthrough didn't mean I deserved daily check-ins now.

But her sudden absence triggered feelings from the last time she disappeared, and I couldn't help wondering if this was a pattern for her: playing tough for a while, then a sudden "hey, let's just have fun!" escapade, followed by regret or fear, and then poof, gone.

I dropped a few texts here and there, to no avail. After nearly a week, I called and left a message asking if she would be interested in going to a street festival in Boulder where some of the local bands that had been big back in our day (the Samples, Big Head Todd) were playing a reunion gig. She didn't return my call but texted back some twenty-four hours later.

Thanks I can't. Work is bad. Maybe lunch in a week or so, she countered, without an iota of the playful energy or warmth we'd just found. Sorry just been really tired.

Sure, let me know when you're
free.

I restrained myself from asking if everything was okay, the words in my head sounding even more needy and immature now than when I was twenty-three. She might be regretting how close we had come to agreeing on a DNA test. Or letting my hand inside her pants. Or maybe she really was just busy and tired.

I threw myself back into my golf routine with Vince and the guys and occasionally Josh. I wasn't playing very well. Instead of shooting ninety, ninety-four, ninety-seven, I started double- and triple-bogeying everything. Instead of losing one or two balls per round, I was losing seven. I drank more to try and loosen up, but that just made things worse. By the fourteenth hole, my scorecard would be so ugly I'd stop playing for score and just do shots, Jamie and me drinking our faces off while Vince looked on. First with mild disapproval, then with outright scorn as we got sloppier and sloppier.

After one particularly shitty round, I followed Vince to the parking lot. He was quiet, cold, all business.

"That was a shit show, huh?" I said as he loaded his clubs into his truck.

"Not my brand of golf, Casey," he said.

"Not mine either," I said. "This thing with the kid . . ."

"I get you're going through some stuff, okay? And maybe I own some of this because you and I usually have a few pops out here." Vince chucked his golf shoes in the hatch and stepped into his flip-flops. "This is supposed to be relaxing. I'm happy to have a few beers, but I don't come here to play clown rounds. Waiting for you to take your fourth piss on the back nine. Jamie arguing with everybody. You guys doing a shot on every hole. If that's what you want to do, knock yourselves out, but leave me out of it."

"Nah, man, don't say that. I'll clean it up."

"And you definitely shouldn't drive," Vince said. "I'd give you a ride, but I'm late already. Fucking around out there for almost six hours. Don't be a dipshit. Call an Uber."

"Okay, yeah, no problem." I felt like a real asshole. I'd let Vince down. And myself. "I'm sorry I got carried away."

Vince retrieved something from the back of the Rover and handed it to me. It was a thin manila file with some printed paper inside, about thirty pages clipped together.

"Your three things," he said. "Sorry it's late, but you gave me three ideas. There're three business plans. Do what you want with them."

"What? Holy shit. Thank you." Disgusted with myself. "I'll look at these carefully."

"Catch you later." Vince left.

I stood there feeling like a terrible friend. It's a funny-not-funny thing how much you can drink on a golf course. You don't realize it while you're out there laughing in the sun, driving toy cars around, whacking away at a stupid ball. Then you get off the course and contemplate getting behind the wheel of a real car, and it hits you—you're loaded. You didn't mean to take it this far. Now you're just another drunk idiot with a scorecard showing 109 in your back pocket. Time to go home and yell at your wife, if you have one, which I didn't, so instead I had the Uber driver stop at the liquor store. I bought a fifth of Seagram's and a single can of Diet Coke because at this point mixers were for show.

At home, I sat on the couch, checking my phone for a text from Damaris, watching shit TV, and talking to my dog while I transported myself from daytime-golf-course drunk to privately-at-home-flat-out-shit-hammer wasted.

At some point, maybe around midnight, I texted Damaris. I was so drunk I had to close one eye to focus on the screen as I typed.

Did I do something wrong? I miss you. We should just talk. We always have good conversations. I like talking with you. It doesn't have to be this difficult. We can just be normal and sweet. Let me be sweet to you. Damaris, spelled like that (I remember you perfectly). Followed by a smiley face emoji, hot face emoji, dog face emoji, and XOX.

Took me fifteen minutes to peck that message out.

A little while after that, when she had not responded, I sent an angry one:

> I don't get this. If you're not into
> me, just say so. We're not 22 and
> preggo this time. You can reply
> to a text. News flash: Men have
> feelings too.

Then I was leaning sideways on the couch, sipping my drink, and half of it spilled down my chest and all over the couch, and Jojo got scared and ran away from me. I passed out with a chew stuck in my lip, drooling on myself, the TV on, my phone soaking in a puddle of whiskey and Diet Coke.

The next morning, when I was able to sit up, I looked at my phone, my stomach already turning with sick paranoia. The feeling you get when you know you did something dumb, but you don't know what or how bad the fallout will be. I saw her response first:

> What is this supposed to say?
> What is wrong with you?

I cringed, then read what I had sent her:

> Dij I sometay wong? I piss yo. We
> shud just talcum. Wee alays good
> converess. I like talling w0 you. It
> dollar have tobe diffirentcult. We
> can just be nooml and sheet. Let
> me be shine you. Damris, spell lik
> it, I member u pufedry.

But at least I'd gotten the emojis right! Oh, wait—no. Somehow the guy in the wheelchair emoji made his way in there at the end, which made a sick sort of sense.

And: I dog gt this. If your not in me, just say no. We're not 222 and preggo gid rim. You repeat a text. News flesh: men have finger so

Coughing, I threw my phone aside and staggered to the downstairs bathroom. I had grains of tobacco stuck in my throat. I tried to toss water into my mouth but couldn't stop coughing, then gagging, and then I pivoted to throw up. But the toilet lid was closed, so I spewed yellow and brown fluid across the floor and up the vanity and into the sink. I gagged on my own vomit and my stomach turned itself inside out until I was panting, eyes watering, blood running from one nostril. My heart felt like a kettlebell slamming on the floor.

Dave was right. You are a piece of shit.

give yourself a chance

I asked myself, as Dr. Lisa had encouraged, what I really wanted out of this time off. I made a short list one morning before heading to the course.

> Shoot 85.
> Make career decision—return to Flagstaff
> or resign and find a new job.
> Damaris—DNA test or not.

And last, the most pressing issue:

> Stop drinking.

Once it was on paper, it was like someone else wrote it. Stop drinking? Really stop? Stop forever? Or stop for a little while?

The night before last was exhibit A. I definitely needed to stop doing that. I had spent the entire next day sick in bed, gyrating and twitching in a land beyond hangovers. A headache, upset stomach, dehydration—these were nothing compared to the hell

I was raining down on myself by now. Imagine curling into a ball in your bed, eyes closed, begging for the internal earthquake of vertigo to stop even for a minute, like some colossus was shaking the house, stirring your brain with a steel spatula. Sweating, freezing, leg muscles seizing. And the million racing thoughts, rushing on currents of guilt, fear, self-loathing, outright terror.

Please stop, please stop for a minute, please let me go, I'm so sorry, I didn't mean to go this far, I was doing better, I can be better, I promise, just please don't make me have a stroke, a heart attack, I will figure it out, oh God, my head, my fucking brains, I'm full of poison, this is a prison, I'm going to die soon, nothing helps, I need a shot of anesthesia, just put me under for twenty-four hours, I can't stand being in my own skin, my wrecked body, my life, oh, my poor mom, I'm so sorry, Dad, can you see me now, I'm rotting, it's not your fault, my friends at work, Lauren, look away now, my fucking libido, women, all the sex in the world isn't worth this, leave Damaris alone, your son deserves better, not the failure you are, go away, sell the house, quit the job, move to Costa Rica, cough cough cough, my poor dog, she can see it, she knows, I have to stop everything, maybe I should call 911, go to the hospital now, today, rehab, really tell everyone everything, the truth, I am so fucked, I am so sick, but first I just need to ride this out, is that blood on the pillow, more blood, oh no, I have to shit but I can't walk, I might die on the toilet, just stand in the shower, shit down your leg, no one will know, you sick fuck, why are you crying, why did you do this again, why can't you just stop?

All that, and worse, for hours and hours. Wasteland days after drinking an entire bottle of the brown fire. The worst thing about this day, each endless minute and hour, was that it was one of a hundred days just like it, more, days when death sat in the corner, waiting, watching, ready for me, and there would be more, many more, worse, endless hell . . .

Unless I stopped.

By seven last night, I was through enough of it to shower and dress myself. Those next few beers were the only thing that could make me feel better, level everything out until it was time to go back to bed, so okay, maybe a few beers, six, nine, and somewhere around the eleventh IPA, I was just tired, not even drunk, really, just dead on my feet. Last night a good sleep, and today it was like a storm had passed. I was basically fine.

This was the real problem. The cycle. Carry on, steady for a week, two, until the next bad day made me buy another bottle, until the next big stress made me feel I had the right to cut loose, no limits, just keep pouring the drinks.

I'd always scoffed at the academic-medical definitions of an alcoholic, a word that obviously implied a problem. I always reasoned that anyone who had three beers a night and otherwise lived a normal, functioning life and had no health problems did not, by any sane definition, have a DRINKING PROBLEM. The way I saw it, you either had life problems that could be attributed to alcohol, which meant you had a DRINKING PROBLEM, or you did not.

Now it was much more complicated, and I saw that I had a drinking problem. I had known this for a while but had always kept it tucked into the corner of my mind. Something to deal with later. But now I was tired of avoiding it, and the problem had become a PROBLEM. Whether alcohol was the beginning of that problem or the symptom of another problem was debatable. But I had reached a point where alcohol was messing up my health, my sleep, my professional drive, my judgment, my friendships, my relationships, my basically everything.

As I looked back, I realized that since Blair and I divorced, I had not kept up any of the friendships that had flourished in our married-life social circle. I had stopped being social at all, at least outside of work. Once in a while, an old friend would blow into town, and we'd do a happy hour or I'd cook and we'd get hammered at my house. Or there'd be a company happy hour or holiday outing where I'd stand around resenting all the younger creatives who were just now getting engaged, getting pregnant, buying homes, all shiny and optimistic as they began their glorious ascent into their thirties. But mostly for the past seven years, all I had done was go to work, go home, waste six hours drinking too much in front of the TV, and go to bed.

My drinking had screwed up my ability to feel naturally happy, or at least more or less content, because HAPPY—as in smiling and rolling through life in a state of upbeat fun on a daily basis—well, no adult was HAPPY, not day in and day out. Maybe you were mostly content and fighting the good fight and winning more days than not, and you had moments of genuine HAPPINESS, but those were brief, not a baseline. Or maybe you were off the rails in some way, life was kicking your ass, and your problems outweighed the good times, and not only were you not HAPPY, but you weren't even CONTENT. You might even be SERIOUSLY FUCKED UP.

But was I ready to say I was an honest-to-God ALCOHOLIC? The kind who had to swear off drinking altogether, forever, because anything less was just fast-tracking a downward spiral? Or was there still some in-between? Could I go back to being the guy who came home from work and had a few beers in front of the TV without getting drunk? A guy who could drink a few Claws on the course and *not* go home and finish the rest of the liquor bottle and every last goddamn beer in the house?

No, not lately. Not for years. But then, I hadn't really tried, had I? Somewhere along the line—sometime between my divorce and my dad dying, living alone with no one to tell me to knock it off and come to bed—I had given myself permission to drink basically as MUCH FUCKING BOOZE as I wanted. But if I set limits and really tried to stick to them? I honestly didn't know. And that worried me.

You're not giving yourself a chance.

Years ago, when I was maybe twenty-six, about a year into my first real corporate job doing phone sales, I had been sharing an apartment with a good friend from high school who was also doing well for himself. Kyle's dad had shown him how to set up his own real estate appraisal business, and almost overnight he was on track to make $75,000 that year.

We were no longer faking our way through Thursday-night happy hour on the Pearl Street Mall with $25 in our pockets. We were flush. Ready to take the world by the balls with our newly leased sports sedans and new button-up shirts and *GQ*-approved shoes and hair, hitting bars three nights a week and throwing a little money around at dumb things like $500 leather jackets and Nuggets tickets and buying rounds for tables of expensive-looking girls. Sometimes Kyle would get ahold of a little coke, and he'd really get charged up, drinking all night and into Saturday, starting fights in the bars where I thought we were just trying to get laid. I was afraid of cocaine, afraid I might like it too much, afraid of Kyle when he was on cocaine, so I never tried it. But even sticking to booze, I was wearing myself down.

During this time, my dad noticed my haggard state one day and called me on it. We were out on the lake in his ski boat. Janey was with us (they were still married), and my dad looked put out in some way. Janey was reading her book up in the bow. We were at the stern, kicking our feet in the water while our fishing lines sat lifeless, bobbing in the greenish surface of Boulder Reservoir.

"You look tired, kid," Dad said. "Pale. Everything all right?"

"Work is busy. I don't get outdoors much." But I had seen the dark circles under my eyes in the mirror just that morning.

"You've lost weight," he said mildly. "I remember what it's

like. You're making money now. Nice little car. Snazzy clothes. Women notice. It's a fun time. Young man about town."

I was smiling, nodding.

"Just be careful you don't try to fuck everything at once."

I laughed. It wasn't like my dad to talk that way.

"Don't think I don't know," he went on, nudging me. "I used to work eighty hours a week, hit the bars, run around every weekend with the guys, riding motorcycles, camping, raising hell, and pissing your mom off. It's good to go after it while you can. Just be careful. You can easily dig yourself a hole."

"Yeah, I know," I said, a little defensive. "I'm up for a promotion. I'm making my quota, and they're letting me write press releases, some copy for the site."

"That's great," he said. "I'm proud of you. Just, with the booze and cigs . . ."

"I know."

"Hey, I'm not busting your nuts here, okay? Have your fun. But you have to be careful what's a celebration and what's now the everyday shit, you know? Because you can get away with this for a while. I did, believe me. But eventually when you're thirty-five, forty, you can't juggle it all. Know what I mean?"

I did and didn't. "I hear you. I probably need to cool off now and then."

"Here's a thing," he said. "Every once in a while, every year or so, prove yourself again. The minute you think you've arrived, that's the exact time you probably ought to humble yourself. Look at your life, your habits, your bank account. Even if it seems real nifty all around, challenge yourself. Go a month without the booze. Get back in the gym. Paint your house. Do that extra side project at work no one asked you to. Whatever it is, prove to yourself you're the one still in command. You get me?"

"Yeah." And in truth, I liked the sound of what he was describing. It sounded reassuring, another kind of manly. Being in *command* of your life.

"It's not that hard to make a change," he continued. "That's one of the things about being young. It's not that hard to break the pattern. But someday it will be. Someday when you need to change careers, or get out of a shitty relationship, or lose fifteen pounds, or stop smoking and eat more kale, whatever it is, it's going to be a lot harder. Because the patterns become set in your fabric. So prove it to yourself from time to time. Surprise yourself. Because if you don't, you're not keeping your options open. You're not even giving yourself a chance."

He smiled at me, hands open: *How simple is that?*

"I like that," I said. "It's good."

He patted me on the shoulder. "I love you, bud. I just want to see you keep on thriving, that's all."

"I appreciate it, Dad."

I took all he said to heart for a week or so, then ignored it for most of the next twenty years. And now here I was, writing in my little notebook, trying to figure out what to do on my sabbatical, the one my boss had put me on because I was—*Can we say it now, Casey Sweet?*—an alcoholic. A fucking drunk. A man decidedly *not in command* of his life.

I decided right then I was going to stop drinking.

Definitely. For now. Probably for a while.

Forever?

Maybe.

I needed to prove to myself that I could. I wanted to know if I could play eighteen holes, spend a night at home, go on a date, or enjoy everything else in my life without alcohol. If I couldn't, then that would be something more to deal with. But maybe I would discover something else along the way. Maybe

I would feel better on the sober side. Time would tell. How much time? I figured I needed a goal to measure my response.

Thirty days seemed awfully cliché but still felt like a good number. Enough time to really clear out my system, but not so much as to feel like a life decision. What was a month? I could put up with anything for a month, right? Today was June 17. By August, I would need to make a decision about work, so I settled on August 1. About six weeks. No problem.

Resolved, I walked to my smaller fridge, the one I used just for beverages, 95 percent of which was beer and hard seltzers, and I grabbed a White Claw, as was my usual preround tipple. Then I stood there leaning on my island in the kitchen. Staring at the can. Was I starting the NOT DRINKING now? Or was I going to play one more round and start tomorrow? I knew when I got home I'd want to keep the buzz going into the evening, because what else would I do? Fall asleep in front of the TV? Drink water?

But isn't that the whole point? A voice spoke up inside me. Mine or my dad's, I couldn't say. *What's going to be different tomorrow? Why not today?*

I cracked the Claw, chugged half, and then poured the rest down the sink. Silly, I know, but it felt like a compromise. I did not load my golf bag with more Claws. In fact, I removed the extra shooters I always seemed to accumulate from the cart girls and poured them out. Feeling bold, I took the rest of the Claws out and drained them in the sink. I looked at the bottles on top of the fridge. Big ones. Handles. Jim Beam, Seagram's Seven, Bulleit, Casa Noble, Myers's Dark, Stoli. Like $400 worth.

I wavered. Jojo was watching me as if trying to understand why I looked so lost.

Do it.

I dumped it all. Every last drop.

I gave Jojo her rawhide, then texted Damaris:

> I fucked up. I'm sorry. It won't
> happen again.

green book

"How's Black Mamba hitting for you today?" Vince asked for the third time that morning.

"Shut up." We were on the tee box at number eight, and I was trying to concentrate. "Seriously. I should never have told you."

"It's just a golf club. It's not like you're holding . . . *it*."

"I think she was just trying to mess with my head." I sliced my drive into the pond. "Son of a bitch."

"Hit another," Vince said.

"Stop talking."

He kept quiet for a moment. Then, "Would you feel better if I just called it Kobe Bryant? The original Black Mamba?"

I stomped back to the cart and shoved the driver into my bag. I pulled the three iron.

Vince laughed. "The three isn't going to shoot nearly as far as Black Mamba. It doesn't have that big, shiny, bulbous head."

I tried to focus on the ball, but all I could think about was Damaris in a jungle hut, holding some guy's enormous penis.

"Next time ask her if Black Mamba had a draw bias," he

added. "Maybe a special grip. Some kind of edge you could in-corporate into your—"

"Will you shut the fuck up!" I roared. Some men on the ninth green looked up in shock. "My bad," I called out. "We're fine!"

And I was fine. After the first couple of holes, I didn't think about drinking much at all. When Morgan came around, honk-ing the cart's ugly little horn, Vince got a big Coors Light and I ordered a Gatorade. For a moment I felt like I needed to explain myself, but Morgan didn't bat an eye. Before we'd started this morning, I'd told Vince I was taking a break from the piss. He didn't make a big deal of it or remind me how badly I needed to, only said, "Cool. Is it going to bother you if I have a beer?"

"Nope. It's on me," I said. "No one else."

"Hey, have you guys seen Josh?" Morgan asked as Vince paid our tab. "I don't think he's been out for a few days."

"I've been meaning to text him," I said. "I'll check in."

"Tell him to call me," she said, a little pouty. "He prom-ised he would."

After she took off, Vince asked, "Morgan into your boy?"

"No idea. Never seen them together."

"Would make sense. He's out here all the time. He's a good-lookin' kid once you get past the hair and caveman feet."

I realized I'd never asked Josh about girls, other friends. Golf and his mom seemed to absorb his entire existence. I texted him on the next hole.

Hey dude, I'm at the course. Morgan says call her. Then I added, **Girlfriend?**

He didn't respond until hours later, when I was home, drinking nonalcoholic seltzers in front of the TV while super-not-thinking about booze at all. But I was doing okay. I would have *liked* a cocktail, but I wasn't *craving* alcohol. I was mostly tired.

OK, thanks, he replied. That was it.

What's new on your end? I sent. We should get another round in soon.

Not much. Been busy helping
Mom.

Everything good? She all right?

I still hadn't heard from her, and I wasn't going to use Josh to be my messenger boy, but something felt off. Had I freaked them both out?

She's fine, he answered. Her usual.

As if I knew what that meant. I decided not to press.

Want to hop on tomorrow
morning?

Can't. Dr. appt. Maybe Thursday
around 4pm?

It was weird he wanted to play at four. A twilight golfer Josh was not.

Thursday it is.

By the time I went to bed that night, I was irritable. Everything felt off. I was no longer tired, and I really wanted a giant glass of whiskey. I was no detox expert, but I knew that for people who'd been drinking daily for a long period of time, going cold turkey carried risks. You could have seizures. You could die.

One of my exes from a few years ago had given me some of her Xanax, after a night that left me with a nasty hangover. She'd given me just five pills and told me to only take one when I was in a really bad way, because they could be highly addictive. I'd taken one at the time, and it had worked beautifully.

I dug around in my medicine cabinet and found the pills. There were four left. I decided I would take one each night to help me get through the worst of the detox, and then I'd have to do the rest on my own. I popped one and sat in bed reading Mark Frost's *The Match*. Around two thirty, I finally felt groggy, turned off the lights, and slept marvelously.

I made it through the week. Other than the insane detox dreams and almost comical outpouring of sweat, the body aches, the phantom itching in weird places, and my inability to stomach anything besides soup, yogurt, and grapes for three days, I felt a lot better. By the time I met Josh for our twilight round, my hands no longer shook, and I was feeling physically shot but lucid and emotionally kind of giddy. Cautious but proud.

One day at a time. One swing at a time.

Josh and I didn't say a whole lot through the first five holes. There was a minor art to getting the kid to open up, I was learning. It wasn't that he was antisocial or had nothing to say. He just didn't do small talk. I focused on golf and waited for a natural opening.

I was surprised how easy it was to spend time with him. By which I mean that I wasn't constantly looking at him thinking, *Is he my son? Look at my son smashing that beautiful drive! That's my boy!* Despite the whole 98-percent-sure thing, the reality was still sort of abstract. Maybe it would have been different if he were five years old, or thirteen, but Josh was just a young man I'd come to know a little through golf. He'd made it twenty-two years without me or anyone else as a father. I imagined he must see me in a similar way. The question of whether we were related was out there in the air somewhere. Maybe neither of us was in a hurry to touch it.

He played brilliantly as usual, going birdie, birdie, birdie, par, birdie through five. After carding a snowman on number one, I fell into a decent rhythm of bogeys. Morgan found us on number six, and I hung back while Josh went to chat with her.

She practically smothered him, rubbing his hair, shoving her hips into him as she laughed at whatever he mumbled. He gave her a half-assed hug in return. She handed him two bottles of Gatorade (no charge), then hung around his neck, swaying between kisses. *If he's not throwing his A game at this girl yet*, I thought, *he's wasting precious time. And she won't wait long.*

He said, "Sounds good. I'll be home around eight." She slapped his ass before sliding back into her cart. He walked back to the tee box as if nothing had happened.

I whistled in admiration. "Well, well, well . . ."

He looked uncomfortable as he planted his tee.

"Dude," I said. "That's working, huh?"

"I guess."

"You guess? That girl has it bad."

He looked at me with what I had come to think of as his Viktor Hovland stoner squint. Eyes narrowed to slits, cheeks high and rosy, mouth sealed in an uncomfortable smile.

"What's the problem? You don't like her?"

"Morgan? Yeah, she's cool." He wagged his driver.

"But?"

"Eh. She's only got one more semester, and I'm probably . . . I dunno, future's up in the air, for both of us."

"Uh-huh. She moving away for a job or something?"

"She has job offers in Denver, but that's not—I just can't really get too involved."

He set up. The ball cut the pond's left corner and went 280 into the fairway as usual. The little prick.

"So what's the hang-up?" I teed up and tried to align myself away from the pond. "Not to pry. I'm just curious."

He Hovlanded me again. "I have a lot to deal with. Not much time for stuff like that."

"For a relationship?"

He was watching my feet. "Check your alignment. You miss right on this one."

I opened wider left and waited for approval.

"Better. Strengthen your grip. Right hand down lower."

The grip felt weird.

"Just try it," he said. "And let your arms assume control of the forward swing. Throw your hips at the target."

"Throw your hips at Morgan," I said.

He chewed the inside of his cheek and waited for me to hit.

I gave it a go. The ball took off left, did not fade, and held its line all the way into another fairway. "Dog shit."

"Well, you hit that one straight," he said. "That's an improvement. Now do the same thing on the next hole, but line up straight."

He began walking, and I paced him in my cart. "You're young," I said. "You should be out having fun, flying off to Mexico with Morgan." He wouldn't look at me. "What else do you have to do besides trade coins and come out here to humiliate people like me?"

"Same as usual. She's been good for a while, but the past week, things have gotten rough again."

I realized he was talking about his mom. "Right. The tired thing. I haven't heard from her much."

"Most of her episodes aren't too bad, but this one was." He gave me a look. "She told you, right?"

"Actually, she did. Chronic fatigue. Fibromyalgia. I didn't realize it really knocked her down quite this bad."

"Her immune system is super sensitive. I probably wasn't supposed to say anything." He looked torn now. "Most of the time it's fine. The meds keep it in check. But every few months, one of the meds stops working and she gets terrible headaches, nausea, joint pain. Sometimes she's stuck in bed for a while. It's an inflammation of the spinal nerves."

"Jesus. That must be awful. And scary for you."

He kept his eyes on the green ahead. "We have a routine, good doctors. It takes a few days for the new drug to kick in, and then she's her old self again."

"Is there a longer-term solution?"

"She's on a wait list for this new immunotherapy thing. We're hopeful that can even things out."

I had driven the cart out to my ball, and he'd followed me without realizing it. He looked around as if he had forgotten where we were. Between my ball and the green was a line of tall pine trees forming a border between fairways.

"What should I do here?"

"You don't really have a line," he said. "One forty-four to the front. A well-scooped eight might get you over the trees, but only if you're feeling confident. A punchy five to stay under the trees and hopefully roll up is the safe play."

I got out of the cart and pulled the eight. "You help her," I said. It wasn't a question. "You take care of her when she's down like this."

He nodded.

"You're a good son, Josh."

"You want max loft here, so play the ball a little more

forward in your stance, like this. More weight on your right side. Visualize your path on an upswing and follow through to a high finish. Confidence is everything. Act like you own this bitch, or else put that staggie back in the quiver right now."

"Staggie?"

He looked confused for a moment. "The club, I mean."

I exhaled and went after it. Felt pure. My ball sailed over the trees and stalled high, landing on the green with a beautiful little thump.

He smiled. "Whoa, that was rowdy, Casey."

My first golf compliment from the kid. I savored it. "You should caddie for me more often."

We had to wait on number seven as the group ahead acted like they were contending for a major, marking balls a foot from the cup instead of finishing out, taking forever to four-putt. Josh was cleaning his wedge with a towel as I stepped up beside him.

"Your mom and me, we're still trying to sort a few things out. Maybe we'll just be friends. Maybe something more. I'm just trying to be a positive presence here, not add more bullshit, okay?"

"I hear ya." Josh stepped onto the tee box.

"I want to help. You, her, whatever. I'm sure you guys have everything under control, but I'm here. She needs a ride to an appointment, you need someone to hang around while you take Morgan to a proper dinner or the zoo or whatever, I'm your guy, okay?"

Josh smiled a little. "The zoo?"

"And that's not a get-in-her-pants thing," I said. "It's just a friend offering to help."

Josh laughed. "Okay. Got it. Now shut the hell up."

The wind picked up a little, and Josh noticed, watching the trees bend and sway. He backed off his ball, returned to his bag. He removed a notebook. He flipped it open and found the page he wanted. I did a double take. It was about six inches wide, nine inches tall, with a green vinyl cover. The pages were well thumbed.

"That your green book?" I asked.

"I hardly use it anymore, but this little par three is a chameleon. Every time I'm sure it's my fifty-three, it plays longer. Soon as I go to the forty-seven, I fall short. It's like the wind does something weird off these pine trees."

I sidled closer. We studied the page with a sketch of this hole. The little *X*'s stood out, and for a moment the streaks indicating slope shimmered, making me dizzy. The handwriting.

Wind likes to carry left. Aim rt. short.

"Where did you get this?" My voice was weak.

Josh didn't look up. "Coach Lowry gave it to me years ago. One of the older members here retired. Or he was sick? I forget. Anyway, he left this with Coach. Coach told me to learn it inside out. It's insane. Super, super detailed. There's like ten sketches of every hole, plus more for the greens. This book took four strokes off my game in a single summer. The old guy was some kind of obsessed genius. By the time I thought to thank him, Coach told me he had already died." Josh made the pages flutter by, the whole course unfolding like a comic strip come to life. "Pretty cool, huh?"

"Come here," I said, walking to the cart. I reached around the old leather Ping bag and unbuckled the ID tag. I held it out for Josh to see.

"RKS," Josh said. He held up the green book. Bottom right corner of the cover: *RKS.*

I tapped the initials with one finger. "Roger Kennerly Sweet. He was my father."

get in the van

We finished a little before dusk, and I asked Josh if he wanted to grab a bite to eat.

"I should get home," he said. "But I'm hungry. Can we make it fast?"

I drove the two of us to Phở Hương Việt, the only good Vietnamese place in town, as the course would be on the way back. Josh had never tried Vietnamese food.

"Start with the barbecue," I said. "You like steak, chicken, shrimp, pork?"

"Yeah, all that."

A quiet server appeared. "He'll have the grilled combo with rice. I'll have the grilled beef. And let's start with the Saigon rolls."

"To drink?"

"Diet Coke for me," I said. Josh ordered the same. The server left. "You don't drink alcohol, do you?"

"Tried it a couple of times in high school," Josh said. "I didn't like the way it made me feel, and everyone around me seemed to get dumber."

"Smart man."

I was riding a buzz of serendipity. Everything seemed connected. First his clubs, then the course, then Josh, Honeybear, Damaris, and now the book. It was like my dad had some secret life here at Twin Peaks and had left clues for me to piece together.

We'd played the back nine using my dad's guidance, talking through each shot and consulting the green book. Between my dad's notes and Josh's own insights, I shot my best ever nine holes, a forty-two coming home. Josh abandoned his usual game to help me, and there were several eerie moments when he seemed to occupy not only my dad's strategy but some of his stern, studious character. When I realized there was a genuine possibility that three generations of the Sweet bloodline were working together on those nine holes, I was moved to something approaching tears.

"I still can't believe you wound up with that book," I said now. "I remember it from when I was a kid, and I've been looking for it since I found his clubs."

Josh tensed. "You can have it back. I feel bad."

I waved him off. "Don't even think about it. My dad knew I wasn't a golfer. I'm sure he figured Coach would put it to good use, and clearly he did."

"He must have been a real baller. You can tell he had that obsessive golf mind."

"The funny thing is, I don't think he was ever better than a ten handicap. But he loved to tinker. With his cars, the house. He'd buy a new boat, then spend more time modifying it in the driveway than he did on the lake. He loved gear. He was an outfitter. I imagine he liked working on that book as much or more than he liked working on his swing."

"Like me working on Honeybear," Josh said. "Half the time it's just to do it, not because something's broken."

When our food arrived, I was thinking about the "three

things" challenge Vince had set me, and I decided to push a little more.

"So Josh, I'm curious. What do you want to do with yourself?"

Josh glanced up, a couple of grains of rice stuck to his lip.

I continued. "College? Travel? Any ideas for a career? Obviously you've done very well already with your trading. That gives you a lot of options, right?"

"What do you mean?"

"I mean, what's the plan? I'm sure you don't just want to hang around Longmont and play Twin Peaks every day. Don't get me wrong. It's a nice town. Good courses. I'm settled here, but my life is half over. You have it all in front of you. Like, in an ideal world, with no limits, what would you like to do?"

Josh considered.

"And for the sake of argument, forget about your mom. Pretend she's fine. It's just you. What would you do?"

"Buy a Sprinter van," he said.

"A what?"

"Sprinter van. One of those really nice Mercedes vans with a bed, shower, bathroom, kitchen, cargo rack, everything loaded. They're like a hundred grand, at least for the one I want."

"Okay, I've seen those. And then?"

"Drive around the country, a full year on the road. Just playing everything I can get onto. Bandon, Pebble, Torrey, LACC, TPC Scottsdale, Riviera, Bay Hill, Sawgrass, all the big ones. I know a guy through Discord. Dude's worth like a hundred million. Says he can get me on at Augusta. His dad's a member or something. Probably full of shit, but we'll see."

"So a big vacation. See the States. Play like the pros."

"More than a vacation. I need to be sure my game can travel," he said. "Before I go to Q-School."

"What's that? James Bond stuff?"

"Qualifying school," he said. "To qualify for the PGA Tour."

"Ah, you want to make a run at it. Like, really turn pro."

"Yep."

I didn't know enough about this process to form an opinion. I knew that Josh was a phenomenal golfer, easily the best at Twin Peaks and probably in our entire area. But the PGA?

"Everyone thinks I just play at Twin," he said, reading my skepticism. "But I get around. I've played all the best courses in Colorado, some in Nebraska, Utah, Oklahoma. They're not that tough. If your game is solid, you can play just about anywhere. It's course strategy. I wrote an algorithm specifically for my game, factoring in every stroke I've made for the past three years. I have a machine learning program I can sync with any course, and it gives me an attack plan based purely on my game, no one else's."

I smiled. "That does not surprise me one bit. Does it work?"

"You know Castle Pines?"

"Sounds familiar, but no."

"It's down in Castle Rock. Nicklaus designed it. It's ranked top fifty in the US. They've hosted several PGA events."

"And?"

"Went down last fall and played four rounds in two days. I shot sixty-eight, seventy-two, sixty-six, and a sixty-four."

"And those are pro-level scores?"

"More or less, but that was just me flying solo, no competition. I don't have the college experience, so I need to find other ways to test myself in the real fire."

"Why not go to college? You're a couple years older, but with your game I'm sure you could get a scholarship. Probably find a great coach, get your name out there, work your way into the conversation."

"I don't want to go to college. I don't want to be on a team.

Go to classes. Waste another three or four years. All I care about is finance and golf. I'm set financially. Trust me. I've looked at every option, and this is the right way for me."

"I can't argue with that." I pushed my plate away. "What does your mom think? She supports you, yeah?"

Josh turned sheepish. "She says it sounds fun. I think to her it's another thing that's someday, someday, maybe someday."

"*Is* it real? You really gonna do this, or is it just another *someday*?"

He picked at his food.

I added, "Because I think it's the best thing I've heard in a long time."

He perked up. "Really?"

"You're young, financially independent, talented as hell. Now is exactly the right time to take a big swing, Josh. This makes all the sense in the world for you. Even if you don't make it, you'll learn so much."

"You don't think I can make it?"

"Of course you might make it. My point is anything could happen. And whatever happens, you'll grow, meet people, see the country, and have the absolute time of your life. In fact, now you *have* to do it because I won't be able to relax until you do."

Josh laughed. I could see that my enthusiasm was sparking him. "Yeah, I really think I have a shot. I've studied as much as I can on my own. Coach says he can hook me up with more coaches who can help me as I travel. Everything is swing anal-ysis now, metrics, data, psychology. I can do some of that on my own, and I can pay for experts, renting time at facilities. All that's doable. But really I need to prove it. When some kid who grew up at a country club and had everything handed to him is staring me down on the back nine on a Sunday, I need to find a way to handle myself, play my game, and beat that guy's ass."

I smacked the table. "Hell yeah, man. I'm getting pumped here. I got half a mind to go with you. *Color of Money*–style. I'll be your Fast Eddie. Drive the van and carry your bag while you dial it in and smoke those clowns." The reference was lost on the kid, but I wasn't done. "I'm serious. This is some *Free Solo* shit. You see that documentary? That crazy guy who lived in a van and climbed El Capitan with his bare hands?"

Josh spoke reverently. "Honnold. Dude's a psycho. Straight-up gangster with zombie strength."

"Right! Do you think that guy gave a shit what others thought? His girlfriend? A career? A family? Hell no! He got in a van with a bag of shitty clothes, and he went and did it. That's you, Josh. Don't even talk about it. Just get in the van and go. Soon." I looked at my watch. "We can pack up tonight and be on a course in Dallas tomorrow afternoon."

"I wish it was that easy."

Of course. His mom. Maybe something more. Maybe a kid who had never lived any other way and was afraid to go it alone.

"I'm not like Honnold," he said softly.

"No, but you don't have to be. Nobody is. You can do this your way."

He picked up a wad of rice with his fingers. "Easy for you to say."

"Fair." The check arrived, and I gave the woman my card. I tried to think of some kind of fatherly wisdom to share without pouring it on too thick. But my life was a mess. What credibility did I have?

Josh just sat there mashing his rice together.

"Do you have regrets?" I asked.

He glanced at me but said nothing.

"Something you did and wished you hadn't?" I continued. "Doesn't have to be anything big. Could be something small.

Something your mind goes back and chews on, and the taste is bad?"

"I don't know. Haven't thought about it."

I nodded. "Actually, that's normal. You're young. You have a routine that works. You're not a troublemaker. You probably haven't had to make a big decision or done anything to hurt anyone yet."

"What's yours?" he asked, still unable to make eye contact.

"See, I'm glad you asked. Because I'm not in any position to lecture you about the future or how to handle your business. But I do have experience, simply because I've lived longer. And I do have regrets, plenty."

Now he looked at me, his expression equal parts curiosity and mild dread. *Careful now*, I warned myself.

"I won't bore you with the details," I said, "unless you ask, which you're free to do. But yeah, man, I have regrets. Made bad decisions. Hurt people. I left jobs too quickly. I didn't put my best effort into relationships with women. I didn't take the most pivotal years of my life seriously because I didn't take myself seriously. I fucked up. I left money on the table. I hurt people's feelings. I sabotaged myself out of fear. It's kind of strange how you can be selfish and think you're doing something for yourself, like taking the next job for more money or leaving some girl who's just admitted she's so in love with you, because you think you found something or someone better. But a lot of the times, what seems like it's best for you winds up hurting you most of all. Does that make any sense?"

Josh shrugged. This wasn't going anywhere. I felt lost, useless. Then he surprised me.

"I got better and didn't tell anyone." He looked miserable.

"Better at . . . golf?"

"My mind. The way I saw things, how hard it was to be around other people. Schoolwork. Focus."

I sat back, trying to decipher his words. "Okay, tell me more about that."

He seemed torn, then caved in. "I don't know what my mom told you, but I had a lot of problems when I was little. Like, I didn't talk for a couple of years. I couldn't go to school. I was very emotional, so much it was like everything was raging inside me, so many thoughts I just turned into stone."

"Was this just a phase like kids go through, or was there some kind of diagnosis? I mean, did you see a doctor?"

"All kinds of doctors. Nothing helped. Nobody knows what's wrong with me."

"There's nothing wrong with you, Josh. Everyone is different, but you're an amazing—"

"You're wrong," he said with more force than I had ever heard from him. "I am different. Good in some ways, and pretty fucking bad in others. You have no idea."

"Okay." I kept my voice as easy as possible. "You're right. I don't know. But I would like to know."

Josh exhaled. "You asked me what I regret. Well, let's say from age five till about eleven, I put my mom through hell because I had, whatever, autism, or close enough."

"If so, that's not your fault."

"I know that. What I'm saying is, around the time I hit eleven or twelve, I was a lot better. Things started making sense. I felt this strange kind of pressure disappear. I could think the way I pictured normal people thinking. I could go to a movie and enjoy it without forgetting where I was and running out screaming halfway through. I started to make friends."

I realized we were only scratching the surface of something here.

"By the time I was like twelve, I was fine. Mostly. I could

function. Ride my bike to the course. Take care of myself. Shower every day. But with Mom, I faked like I was still messed up."

I was thinking about his mom's experience in this, and something clicked. "You didn't tell her you felt better."

He nodded fast and smiled, but it was not a good smile. It was a little scary.

"Do you know why? Why you kept it to yourself?"

His menacing smile fell away. "I guess I thought I had a special secret. Like, I finally got what all the normal kids had—happiness. But I didn't want her to stop paying attention to me. And I didn't really want to have to do the same stupid shit all the other kids had to do. Go to school, read this book, dress like whatever, fit in with the cool kids."

"Yeah, that's understandable. But again, not your fault. You were still a kid. You were reacting to change."

He looked at me like I was dense.

"She suffered," he said. "Constantly worrying about me. Her own health problems, but mostly me. I drained her like a vampire. And I knew I was doing it. I was in complete control, but I made my mom fucking miserable for another two years. Sleepless nights, afraid every time I left the house. Arguments with my teachers. And honestly, when I think about it, I kind of never stopped. Even after I told her the truth, she couldn't let go. Because I kind of messed her up. I'm not sure if she can ever stop worrying about me."

Then he laughed. Too loud. We were both uncomfortable. I tried to think of something to put him at ease, but I was struggling.

"That's a lot to carry on your shoulders," I said. "Too much. Because no matter what you could have done or should have said, you were a kid. You didn't do anything wrong."

"I know what you mean," he said. "But I can't accept that.

I know what I did. I knew it when I was doing it. It was wrong. Can we go now?"

I felt short of breath. I drank some water, disoriented, and I really wanted some booze. "Sure. We can go."

I drove us back to the course in awkward silence. I pulled into the parking lot beside his truck. A rain was starting to fall, steaming off the asphalt with that summer smell.

"How's Honeybear holding up?"

"I'm still messing with the brakes, but everything else is good."

"You want me to just drop you at home?"

"Nah. Thanks for dinner." He opened the door, then looked back at me. "Don't tell her what I said. The whole van thing. Any of it."

"Of course. That's between you two."

He turned away.

"Josh?"

He hesitated.

"Whatever you did then, it's over. You already took those swings. You're not a kid anymore. You need to think about the next swing. Because that's the only shot that matters now."

He smirked. "Golf wisdom."

"I was scared," I said. "Too scared to take a big swing. To commit to the shot. And the thing about fear is it's comforting. Once you play it safe, it gets easier to do it the next time, and the next. It's safer to live your life punching out of the trees back onto the cozy little fairway instead of taking the hero shot. But life isn't always a fairway. Life is trees and sand traps and shitty lies in the rough. You can't win unless you go for the green. You only get to be young and fearless once, Josh. I sure hope you follow your heart."

He seemed paralyzed. Then, slowly, he looked at me, really looked at me. Our eyes connected and locked on one another, and because of who we were to each other, it was in a way neither of us had ever looked at someone else before.

Then he gave me a nod and shut the door. I watched Honeybear weave her way out of the parking lot and up the street to the stop sign, and then she was gone.

Blair

By the time I finished walking Jojo around the neighborhood, it was almost ten, and I was irritable from the stress of everything with Josh and, of course, the fact that I had just stopped drinking and felt like a glass that might shatter at any moment. I should have known better than to answer a call from my ex-wife.

"Hi, Blair."

"Hey, hon! I'm glad I caught you. Is this a bad time?"

"Not really, but I am kinda—what's up?"

"I just realized we haven't talked in almost three months."

She waited for me to explain this anomaly, but I wasn't in the mood for another recap.

"Everything okay?" she ventured, and this irritated me too. She texted me this all the time, as if I were a walking time bomb and she feared bad news at any moment.

"Everything's great. You?"

"You sound different," she said. "What's going on?"

I sighed. "Don't you think it's weird you keep asking me that? What does it really matter now?"

"Keep asking you? I'm just—"

"I'm not some lost soul who needs his ex-wife's supervision."

Audible gasp on her end. "Sorry, I wasn't trying to supervise you. I care, that's all."

"Yeah, but why do you care?"

"Okay, clearly you're not in a good place, so—"

"I had a great day, Blair. Look, I don't mean to sound shitty. But doesn't it ever seem odd to you? Calling me like this?"

"Talking to someone I shared a deeply meaningful portion of my life with? People do it all the time."

"Do they? Like this?"

"We're friends. I will always consider you family."

"But we're not family anymore, and we're not even really friends because friends are part of your real life. Friends do things for each other. All we do is have these empty phone calls where you tell me about the kids and some girlfriend of yours who's getting divorced, and I tell you how I'm still the same idiot you divorced."

"All right, Casey, Jesus. Obviously you're angry. I don't know if something happened, but if you don't want to talk, we don't—"

"Did I call you?"

"What?"

"No, you called me. You call me because *you* want to talk. If I wanted to talk, I would call you."

Silence.

I barreled on, not raising my voice, simply stating the facts in a neutral tone. "And the reason you call me is so you can still have a say in my life. You always craved control, and it kills you to think I might start living my life without your opinions. So you call me once a month to make sure I haven't met anyone serious or gone off the rails, because while you don't want the Casey who loved you and tried to save our marriage, you also can't imagine me living anything other than the same static, semishitty life you expect. You can go to bed and sleep soundly next to Carl now that you've done your check-in, everyone's fine, the world makes sense, right?"

Was she crying? Was that sniffling I heard?

Blair spoke in a whisper. "Is that what you think of me?"

My phone was beeping, another call coming in. I ignored it. My instinct was to apologize, comfort her, and settle into our usual routine.

"Yes," I said. "It's not all I think of you, but it's how I think you see me."

Her voice hardened. "I see. How long have you felt this way?"

My phone beeped again. I ignored it.

"Longer than I've admitted it, even to myself," I said. "And that's on me."

"Did I do something wrong? Was it something specific?"

"I've been alone for the past seven years, Blair. I've learned to live on my own because that's what you asked me to do. I don't need your input on what to do with my house, my career, my mom, or anything else. And maybe you should ask yourself why you need that."

Now a series of blips came through, someone texting me repeatedly.

"I'm sorry. I thought we would always be part of each other's life in some way. I thought we'd made peace with that. But if that's not what you want . . ."

I was sober and exhausted and beyond tired of my ex-wife. I was severely pissed off at myself most of all, for letting this charade go on and on.

"Look, I have to go. Someone's calling," I said. "But since you asked, I quit drinking, I'm taking time off work to make some big decisions, I golf five times a week"—my phone beeped four times in a row, then twice more, a blast of texts—"and I'm dating a woman I used to date when I was twenty-three. She has a son who is a really great kid, and for the first time in about a decade, I am happy. Or maybe I'm starting to see how happiness starts. Everything feels new, and Jesus H. Christ on a flagstick, I've really been needing something new. You must relate to that, yeah? You found yours; now let me find mine, all right? Can you do that, Blair? Can you let me find happiness my own way, without needing all the details and casting your vote?"

"Wow."

"Yeah. Wow."

I hung up on Blair and went to my texts. They were all from Damaris.

> Where are you???

> What happened?

> Answer your phone goddammit

> Josh is in the hospital. What did
> you do?

> Did you make him drink?

> You fucking

> Fucking call me!!!

> Josh accident losing my mind

I played her voicemail. She was hysterical. "What did you do to my son? What happened? What did you do? He said he was with you, and now he's in the hospital. Oh God, oh God, I can't, I can't . . ."

I closed my eyes and squeezed my phone. My heart was stampeding. The room seemed to elongate as my skin rippled in a cold sweat, my legs turning to rubber. It was how every one of the panic attacks started. My brain seemed to be on a gyroscope. I couldn't breathe . . .

Nope. No time for that bullshit. I grabbed my keys and ran out the door.

7-Eleven

Longmont had two hospitals. The newer UCHealth facility on the east side of town and the old Longmont United in the central-west part of town. This older one also happened to sit almost directly between Twin Peaks and Damaris's house. Before I shot out of the garage, I called her back. When she didn't answer, I texted: Which hospital? On my way.

I couldn't sit and wait for her reply, so I took a guess and headed toward Longmont United. Every race to a hospital is scary, but this was especially eerie because I was tracing a path right back to Twin Peaks, where I had last seen Josh. The rain was falling, but not like it had been earlier. The storm was moving on, but the streets were still wet, glossy, the streetlights casting long candlesticks of blurry red and yellow across the intersections.

I drove north on Hover Street, and as I neared the turn for Twin, I tried to map out his path home in my head. If he hadn't taken any detours, he would have come down Mountain View Avenue and turned left at the light where Mountain View met Hover.

Which was exactly where I was now, slowing, even though the light was green and there were almost no other cars on the road. I glanced at my phone—no new texts from Damaris. I glanced left, thinking, *Okay, he comes off Mountain View, and then what?*

And then I saw it.

On the northeast corner of Mountain View and Hover was a 7-Eleven. I'd stopped there many times on the way to the golf course to grab a drink or a can of snuff or a granola bar. Being on the corner, it had only a small triangular lot with four gas pumps, plus a few extra spaces on each side for parking.

The digital sign displaying the gas prices was blasted to pieces, its brick base scattered like Legos. Yellow crime scene tape stretched all the way around the property. A tree near the sidewalk had been snapped from the ground and was lying on its side, leaves scattered into the street. I pulled to the side of the road and came to a stop. A police sedan was parked at the north entrance, its lights flashing, but I saw no police officers around. I opened the door of my car and stood, glancing around, noting the sparkling pebbles of glass and other debris.

And there was Honeybear. I almost didn't recognize her, and when I did, my heart sank into my bowels. She was upside down and turned away from the street, her roof smashed down at the back end almost to the seats. The front end was not quite as bad, but the windows were all shattered, and the A-pillar was badly bent, both doors on the driver's side hanging open. The lovingly restored pinstripes were scraped all to hell, and the front axle looked like a twisted baby's rattle, one tire blown and hanging sideways.

He hadn't just hit something or been hit. Honeybear had been smashed and rolled hard, tumbling from the intersection into the parking lot. I could see it. I could feel it. I was amazed that whatever violence had transpired here had not tossed Josh and the vehicle all the way into the 7-Eleven itself. I was vaguely aware that my breath was coming in ragged gulps. I wanted someone to explain it to me, but there was no one here. No police officers, no firefighters, no ambulance . . . no Josh.

Inside the 7-Eleven, a clerk was pacing by the door, smoking a cigarette. I thought of running to him, but what for? It was plain to see what had happened. Everything I needed to know, everything I needed to do, was not here.

I jumped back into my car and raced the last three blocks to the hospital.

waiting room

"Are you a member of the family?" the woman at admin asked.

"Not exac—yes, I'm with the family."

She stared at me.

"He might be my son," I said. "I was with him before the accident. His mother called me." I showed her the texts. "Can you just give me the room number and let her sort it out?"

"He's in three thirty-one, but you need to remain in the waiting area until—"

I bolted for the elevators. The door to 331 was closed, and there were no windows. I knocked gently. I could hear voices. A woman who did not sound like Damaris. When no one opened the door, I texted.

I'm here. Right outside the door.

Then I paced in the hall. A minute. Five minutes.

A doctor emerged, along with what I assumed to be a nurse, both in blue scrubs. The doctor was a Hispanic woman of forty or so, athletic, serious. The nurse was a short white kid with a ginger buzz cut. She handed him some forms and spoke with authority but no real urgency.

"Get those to the lab and tell Neurology we need an MRI as soon as a bay opens. Get the mother some water and keep checking on them until I return."

"Yes, Doctor." He left.

She started down the hall and gave me a quick, dismissive glance.

"Are you his doctor?" I asked. "Josh Parker?"

She paused mid-stride. "Are you a relative?"

"He was with me right before it happened."

"You'll need the mother's permission to go in. You can wait down at the end of the hall." She was already moving on.

I grabbed her arm. "But is he stable?"

Something in my eyes got through. "He needs some tests, but yes, he is stable."

I knocked again. Another minute passed, and I was about to walk away when Damaris opened the door. She did not step back to allow me in. I caught a glimpse of Josh in the bed. His eyes were closed. A bandage covered one side of his forehead and the top of his cheek. There was an IV hooked into his arm but no other tubes.

"Keep your voice down," Damaris hissed. Her eyes were red and puffy. "He's resting."

"Sorry, I got here as soon as I saw your messages."

"Have you been drinking?" She stepped closer to smell me.

"Not a drop. I swear. We had dinner, Diet Cokes. I saw the car on the way. I'm so sorry. What did the doctor say?"

"He's lucky to be alive," she said. "He has a concussion at the very least." Her eyes darted all around as if she were shielding him from monsters in the hall. "He was talking when they found him. He was able to stand."

"That's positive," I said. "What can I do?"

Her face hardened. "There's nothing for you to do."

"Hey, I know this is scary. I can stay. I thought—"

"What were you two talking about?" Her anger was increasing. "You golfed. You went to dinner. What else? Did you upset him? What did you tell him, Casey?"

I ran it back in my head. Even though I was pretty sure I hadn't done anything wrong, I felt somehow responsible. She must have sensed this.

"You know what, it doesn't matter," she said. "Go home. I'll handle it."

"He seemed fine, okay? He said something about the brakes, and I offered to drive him home, but—"

"The brakes? The brakes on his car? What are you talking about?"

"When I gave him that tool, he said he was redoing the brakes, but that was like two weeks ago, and then tonight he mentioned it when I dropped him off. I don't know, maybe—"

She pulled the door shut and kept herself from shouting, barely. "All I know is you come around giving him tools, giving him ideas, you send me some drunken text, and all of a sudden you're golfing and taking him to dinner? Why would you do that?"

"We had a good day. I thought he might be hungry."

"You weren't drinking, fine, but what did you say?"

"I didn't—why do you think I said something?"

"Because that's what you do! You can't wait to open your mouth, and you have no idea how destabilizing this has been for us because you don't think about anyone but yourself."

"Hold on, hold on. I know you're upset—"

"Upset? My son is in the hospital. With a brain injury!"

"Damaris, I know."

"Everything was fine until you showed up and decided to,

what? I don't even know what you're doing. And I don't think you do either, Casey. We don't need the drama, so please just leave."

Some other medical professionals were walking toward us, and this was about to become a bad scene.

"Leave?" I asked. "Right now? Or for good?"

She took a deep breath and glared at me. "Pretend you never met me. Clear enough?"

"All right, Damaris. I'm sorry. I didn't mean to cause a problem."

"But you did cause a problem, didn't you?"

"He's going to be all right," I said as softly as I could.

"You don't know that! You don't have any idea what he needs. Stay away from my son, and stay the hell away from me." The fire in her eyes was jet blue.

"Okay. I'm leaving."

I kept backing away, hands up in surrender. She shook her head in disgust and slipped back into his room.

I walked away. He wasn't in the ICU; he wasn't being rushed into surgery. So this wasn't that bad, was it? Maybe I *had* upset him more than he'd shown. My speech at dinner, combined with whatever else he suspected about me being his dad. Maybe he drove off distracted, in a stew of emotions, and then what? He ran the red light? Someone blindsided him? I had to admit it was possible—maybe it was on me.

I walked to the end of the hall, to the waiting room. She wasn't in her right mind, and that was understandable. The boy was everything to her. Everything. Who was I? A romantic mistake twenty-two years ago, a romantic possibility a couple of weeks ago, no more. I was trouble, confusion. And now in her mind I was the one responsible for his accident. A concussion. What if it was worse? Really bad, like brain damage?

Please, God, don't . . .

I should go home. I wasn't helping anything here.

"Even when you show up," Dave had said as he sent me on my sabbatical, "you don't show up."

"You're not here," I said to the waiting room. "You're not family."

"Oh, I'm just waiting for my sister-in-law," someone said. There was a balding, late-middle-aged man in a light-blue sweater seated below the TV. He had a magazine in one hand, a foam coffee cup beside him. His face was round, his bald spot glossy. Reading glasses hanging around his neck. He looked like a professor, a financial planner. "I'm not immediate family, but she's working and her husband is useless, so I'm waiting until one of them can be here. My nephew cut himself on a broken beer bottle or some damn thing. What are you in for?"

Like we were in jail together.

"Hmm? Oh, my friend. Our . . . her son. Car accident."

"The young guy I saw come in about half an hour ago," he said. "About eighteen?"

"Probably. His name is Josh."

"That's it. Josh. He was complaining about the wheelchair. Said he didn't need it."

I brightened. "So he was talking?"

"Talking. Walking. Cracking jokes."

"No shit."

"Mother was a wreck, but the doctors kept telling her it wasn't as bad as it looked. I think he cut his forehead—stitches would be needed, someone said."

"But he was normal otherwise?"

"Well, I guess you never know, but it didn't seem too serious from what I saw."

I paced some more. Looked at my phone. No new texts. "She told me to go home."

The man studied me, setting his magazine aside. "When in doubt, stick around. That's my general policy for hospitals, marital disagreements, sketchy situations."

"She was really pissed," I said. "She wants me gone."

He stood and stretched one leg. "Maybe. Whatever you think is best. Want a coffee? There's a kiosk, not one of those machines. Almond milk. The works."

"I'm good, thanks."

He wandered off. I paced. Checked my phone.

"You don't show up," Dave had said. "You're not in this marriage," Blair had said. "You not tip enough for Lana text you more ass photo," Lana Del Emotional had said.

I needed to respect Damaris's wishes, and I needed to be here for Josh.

I took a seat.

part four
match play

congratulations, it's a boy

I tried to stay awake but nodded off sometime around two thirty in the morning. It was that particularly hellish dozing reserved for airport lounges, long bus rides, and hospitals. You're folded up in a chair that was designed to make you want to move on, head lolling like a doll's, stray bleats over the intercom slapping you awake right at the precipice of real sleep.

Dawn was making itself known through the windows when I finally fell into a dream involving an Indian doctor giving me happy news and patting my arm, with Blair smirking at me with a look of *I told you so*. My bladder woke me. I stretched and found the men's. When I came out, I started toward Josh's room, and Damaris and Josh were walking toward me as if we had timed it.

Josh was in the same clothes as yesterday. There was some blood on his T-shirt, a new, smaller bandage on his left cheek, and a purple line of stitches over his left brow, but otherwise he looked fine, just sleepy. He seemed surprised to see me, glancing at his mom, who looked thoroughly wrung out and had no reaction to me at all. We all came to a stop.

"Hey, buddy." I had no idea what else to say.

"Casey? What are you doing here?" Josh asked.

"My wife's in labor. She's about to pop, bless her heart. We're going with Tiger if it's a boy. Annika if it's a girl."

Josh smiled. Damaris just blinked at me.

"I'm sorry about the accident," I said. "How are you feeling?"

He pointed to his head. "Mild concussion. Eight stitches. Probably from the window shattering. Truck's trashed, but I'm fine."

"I'm sorry about Honeybear. I saw her on the way." I shuddered. "I know how much she meant to you. Both of you. But I'm really relieved you're all right."

He shot a glance at his mom. "It was so stupid. I was just driving home and got to the light at Hover. The left arrow turned yellow, and I hit the brakes, but the pedal just went to the floor. Gone. I sailed into the intersection, and this guy in a big truck T-boned me, flipped Honeybear into that 7-Eleven parking lot. It was super rowdy."

"Jesus. Sounds like it. And scary."

"Looked way worse than it was." Another glance at his mom, and it occurred to me he was trying to convince her I was not to blame. "I screwed up. Shouldn't have driven her. I knew something was off. I'm guessing lines were leaking, and when I stomped on it, everything gave out."

"You're never working on your own car again," Damaris said.

He elbowed her. "Hey, cheer up. Honeybear saved my life."

"We need to go home," she said. "You need to rest."

Josh turned to me. "Thanks for yesterday. I really appreciated what you said. I think this was a sign."

"A sign of what?" Damaris snorted.

"Big swings." He winked at me.

"I'm just glad you're all right," I said. "You guys need a ride? Anything from the drugstore? Breakfast?"

"Mmm, yeah, I could use some Egg McMuffins?"

"We're not going to McDonald's," Damaris said. "For the love of God. We have food at home." We all waited for her. She finally looked at me. "Well. It was nice of you to stay. For Josh. He—we appreciate it."

"Don't even think about it," I said. "Let's get out of here, huh?"

"What about your wife?" Josh asked, and I couldn't tell if he was in on the joke or still loopy. "You're about to be a father. I should get you a cigar."

"Josh, cool it," Damaris said. "Jesus."

I walked them to the car. Damaris tried to help him into his seat. "I got it, Mom."

She came around and looked at me. "I haven't slept in two weeks. I know he told you about my condition. I'm sorry I didn't explain it better before, but I'm fine. We're fine. I'm not mad at you. I'm just processing."

"I understand. Let me know if I can do anything, please? You're completely capable of running the show, but you know, maybe don't put everything on yourself?"

She hesitated, then stepped forward and gave me a hug. "He really likes you. God knows why." She let me go.

"Thank you," I said.

Josh gave a tired salute as they drove off. The sun was rising on another day.

headjob #5

I returned to my PCP, Dr. Bretner, at the end of June for my follow-up. I had lost nineteen pounds. I had a serious golfer's tan. My feet, lap, and torso were fish-belly white. Everything else was bronzed, and the contrast made me look like a dead man whose limbs had been dipped in wood stain.

"You look good," Bretner told me as he wrapped the Velcro sleeve around my bicep. "How are you feeling?"

I told him about the booze ceasefire.

"Really? That's excellent. The very best thing you can do for yourself. Stick with that." The BP machine hissed as it deflated. "Your numbers are down too. One thirty-one over eighty is better, but let's stay on the meds a little while longer. Keep up the progress, and we can probably drop one in the next few months."

The rest of the exam was cursory, and he asked me if I had found a therapist. I gave him my sob story about being rejected by the psychiatrists (now thirty-six and counting) and about the work Lisa and I had been doing. He had my file from her, with all her notes.

"I'm more than a little peeved," I told him. "I realize I'm not the worst case out there. I'm not suicidal or severely depressed. Thank God, or else I guess I'd be in real trouble. She says I have ADD, but what the hell am I supposed to do with that? Concentrate harder?"

Dr. Bretner rolled his stool back from the table and put his hands together as if in prayer. "On behalf of the entire medical community, I am sorry. I know it's bad out there. A lot of people are struggling right now, and there just aren't enough doctors. So here's the deal. I can help you. I can prescribe you whatever you need, but you need to talk to me. You need to tell me what your life is like, the ups and downs, everything."

A flicker of hope appeared in my little health-care-hardened heart. I summarized everything I had discussed with Dr. Lisa. He asked a lot of questions about my job, the feelings of cubicle entrapment, my relationships past and present.

"You know, I think everyone has a phase in their life where the really hard things come in clusters," he said. "Like a cyclone. Kind of a lifenado. My lifenado hit me in my late twenties. I lost my mom and my first wife, and I blew out two discs in my back. For you, it seems like the past few years have been your lifenado. What's important is realizing a few things. One, it won't last forever. Things will get better. It takes some time, but you've got to keep your head up and keep working at it. Second, you have resources, and you need to lean on those. Your family, friends, doctors. It's good to talk about it and get the care you need. You're already doing that, which is really a huge start. I'm guessing you do have some form of ADHD. A lot of people are struggling to stay focused these days. Try to put your phone away for a few hours, especially before bed. Minimize the social media."

"I hate that shit anyway."

"Me too. Read a book instead. Stay away from the screens. Your work desk, TV, phones—cut it all way back."

"That's the best thing about golf, I think. It's four or five hours away from a desk."

"Good. Keep at it. With the rest of what you're describing, I do see a general anxiety piece here, but one that should continue to lessen as you get used to going without alcohol. I'm going to write you a prescription for Adderall, a fairly low dose for now . . ."

Suddenly the skies opened. It had never occurred to me that a regular doctor could do much of what a psychiatrist would have done for me. My man was full-on seizing the initiative. I felt like we were conspiring, sticking it to the corrupt system, and I was so grateful I almost cried.

"But you need to come back in another sixty days so I can keep an eye on you, all right?"

"Absolutely. Thank you for taking the time to listen to me."

"Good luck with your return to work, Casey."

I stood and pulled on my quarter zip. "Am I allowed to hug you?"

Bretner chuckled. "Sure."

I hugged him. Hard.

"Okay, okay." He patted my back. "You're all right, amigo."

I finally let go. "Yeah. I think so."

People throw the term *life changing* around with far too little consideration. *Oh my God, this new yoga routine changed my life. These new stretch jeans, this new coffee diet, that new Titleist golf ball*—these things might improve a given experience and make us feel a little better for now. They do not change lives.

So while I will not say that Adderall *changed my life*, it was an absolute game changer in terms of my ability to think clearly and stay focused and productive. Far from amping me up (I had imagined it being like speed), Adderall was not so much a high or a boost as a *clear*.

Just ten milligrams in the morning, and for the next six to eight hours, I felt more awake, I could think through problems ten times faster, and I flat-out got shit done. I was no longer stifled by the weight of my to-do list. Everything now seemed manageable. Following up on emails, writing in my journal, cleaning the house, shopping for groceries, or tackling some yardwork—I sailed through these activities in record time.

Before Adderall (BAD), this big swirling mess of career, relationships, health concerns, finances, and daily stresses had been like trying to decipher a big splat on the wall. After (ADD), everything snapped into place like someone had turned the dial on the microscope, allowing me to see every collapsing molecule and wiggling flagella. Adderall did not solve my problems. It just allowed me to take it all in without feeling overwhelmed, and then act.

Golf? Oh yes, golf too.

The difference was evident on the first tee box. I felt more awake, more attuned to my body's ability to swing the club on the desired path. The ball itself, perched on its bamboo tee, stood out like the world's only target. While I shot only marginally better on Adderall, shaving maybe two or three strokes, the real difference was in my ability to stay focused for the entire eighteen holes. I didn't let a few bad holes turn me into a slappy. The absence of booze was also a big factor. The mid-nineties became my new standard, with several tantalizing forays into the high eighties, culminating in an honest-to-God eighty-five that all but made my dick hard.

"Someone's feeling golfy today," Vince said as we circled the flag on number thirteen.

"Full-on golfy, bro. I wake up with a morning golfy every day now."

This was true about a lot of things. Adderall provided a heightened sense of psychological arousal to things nonsexual, but what passed for my sex life was also impacted. Laser attention to detail, the effortless absorption of visual data, rapid awakening of the senses, culminating in bodily responses . . .

I realized I had to choose my maze wisely. Adderall's nearly magical effects, the way it sharpened fascination into a spearhead, could send you deep down a tunnel of research, study, writing, golf, or bird-watching with equal intensity. If you weren't careful where you pointed this spear of energy, you could very easily waste three hours exploring some esoteric subject like, say, vintage golf clubs on eBay or bunker-shot tutorials on YouTube. Or porn. But after one shameless detour, I decided to save myself for Damaris. I needed to be able to perform, if the stage was granted.

If quitting alcohol returned me to the land of quality sleep, healthy bowels, proper hydration, grounded self-esteem, and naturally brighter spirits, Adderall topped off the tank and put a high-gloss sheen on the whole production. Within two weeks, I felt ten years younger. I was driven to make up for lost time. I was hungry again.

I was ready to take my own big swing.

But first I had to deal with Dave. Over the past week, he'd sent me three emails and left two voicemails. His tone was friendly, but I knew he needed an answer to the fundamental question: *Are you coming back or not?*

I decided not to call him, because he was a salesman and I didn't want to be put on the spot. This was my sabbatical, my health, my future, and I needed it to be about me. I hit reply:

Hi Dave,

Thanks for checking in. I'm doing a lot better these days. I have seen several doctors and I have a much better handle on the issues that caused my performance to decline. I am not ready to declare anything with respect to my future, but I anticipate being able to do so within 30–60 days.

I appreciate that you have a team to run, and that you may need to make any decisions that will impact my role at Flagstaff before I reach a decision. I am grateful for the opportunity the company has given me over these past six years, and for the time you have granted me to work on myself. This generosity will be one of the important factors in my consideration of all possible next steps. I'll be in touch when I have something more concrete to offer. I hope you and the team are well.

—Casey

the Swede

All I know about surfing came from *Point Break*, the original masterpiece with Swayze and Keanu, which introduced me to the concept of territorial surfers. It makes sense: With a finite amount of good waves at a given beach, fights break out. I thought of Bodhi and Johnny Utah when things turned territorial at Twin Peaks.

For guys like Josh, Vince, Jamie, and me, Twin was our home course. It was just a muni, but it was ours. Most of us were scrappy, and we never took ourselves too seriously. But we couldn't help noticing when a group of guys from one of Denver's lesser suburbs like Northglenn or Westminster crashed our scene.

They were usually young, decked out in loud, heavily branded apparel or "hilariously" ironic white-trash denim and trucker caps. They acted like they'd just pulled off a *Heat* score for smuggling in twenty Coors Lights and a pint of grapefruit vodka. They blasted 2 Chainz and Post Malone and nauseating *uhn-tiss-uhn-tiss-uhn-tiss* club remixes from the shitty speakers mounted to their carts while they peacocked around like the cameras from *Full Swing* were following their every stroke, joke, and brofus move.

Why'd they come all the way here rather than playing somewhere else around Denver? Easier to get tee times here. The quality of grass was better than a lot of courses charging $90 or $120 per round to Twin's $60. And yes, the fairways were forgiving. On paper, Twin screamed *easy to dominate.*

But it was deceiving. At least half the holes were lined with relentless trouble up one side and challenged you to do one of the hardest things in golf—play dead straight from tee to green. And the greens were where the course struck back. Nearly all featured tall shoulders, steep slopes, and ridiculous pin placements from the snickering groundskeepers. Many a self-proclaimed four handicap had come to Twin cockily counting on an easy snatch and grab against one of our twelve handicaps only to be sent home five hundo lighter in the wallet.

The morning of July 1, Jamie, Josh, and I found ourselves grouped with a swaggering single by the name of Dolan Johanssen. Six four, maybe 220, wavy blond hair, shoulders like an ox. He wore Miami-bright Puma everything, his lemon-yellow bag loaded with polished blades. He wore a black glove on each hand, suggesting a strong desire to strangle someone. He introduced himself with a knuckle-crunching handshake and the overly polite presence of a TV evangelist, his blocky head looming so close you could smell the grains of protein powder from his performance shake stuck between his picket fence teeth.

Jamie was a natural chatterbox, and immediately he and Dolan had their dick rulers out. Dolan was a club pro at TPC Fort Collins some thirty miles north, a former top-ten Division I prospect out of Indiana. Had some success on the European and Korn Ferry tours before folding up shop to take a stake in his family's car dealerships opening across Northern Colorado. He made it clear that today was a slumming lark. Of course, he'd be happy to play for twenty dollars a hole, even ten dollars, or no money at all, *whatever, my dudes, I'm just here to knock it around a bit.*

I didn't like him, and the chemistry of this setup felt bad from the jump. "I'm not good enough to play for money," I said. "But you guys do your thing."

"I'm down for twenty a hole," said Jamie, who, we shall recall, was a true degenerate. "I'm an eight, but this is my home course, so spot me three per side and I'm in. I can show you my GHIN."

"I trust you, bro," Dolan said. "I'm a plus three. Pushes double on next hole? And double for birdies?"

"Yep, yep, all that." Jamie was six inches shorter but strutted like the ex-MMA fighter he was. "No mullies, count every drop, USGA rules across the board?"

"Yes, sir."

There was more I didn't understand, but I knew enough to grasp that they were exchanging handicap indexes and laying ground rules. A GHIN was the US Golf Association's handicap-rating system, and every player was responsible for keeping an honest handicap, usually by turning in their scorecards signed by a witness. Jamie was a minus eight, Dolan a plus three, which meant Dolan was even better than scratch, some eleven strokes better than Jamie. Jamie was giving Dolan two strokes for the home field advantage, so Dolan had to beat Jamie by nine strokes to tie, ten to win. On holes that ended in a tie, the stakes would push and double to the next hole. If a player won the hole with a birdie, he won double the stakes on that hole. There would be no mulligans; all penalties would apply, just like at a real pro golf tournament.

Jamie came back to the cart. "This chump's a piker, and I'm going to take him for a wad."

"Keep it cool," I said. "Easy on the sauce, no smack talk, no fighting."

"Bro, don't worry about it." He promised not to get fucked up, but I knew he'd drink a lot if he was winning and even more if he started losing.

Josh walked onto the box in his usual throwback threads and bare feet. A week had passed, and his bandage had come off, but he still had the little caterpillar of purple stitches on his cheek. We'd been texting, but this was the first time we'd golfed together since the accident.

"How you feeling, champ?" I asked.

Josh inhaled the morning. "I missed this."

"What about you?" Dolan asked, pointing at Josh's feet. "You're Josh Parker, right? I've heard about the barefoot wonder down here at Twin."

Next to the big Swede, Josh looked like a Gelfling. "Yeah, what'd you hear?"

"Just that there's an absolute killer smashing his way around Longmont. Some no-name kid who plays long as Rory and stalks pins like Scottie. I had to come see for myself."

"I don't know about all that," Josh said. "But I'm good for whatever you guys want."

This surprised me but shouldn't have. Hadn't Josh just told me he needed to test himself more? Play in real competition? Well, here it was.

"What's your cap?" Dolan asked.

Josh pulled his phone, as if he didn't know it. "Plus two point four. I'll throw you two strokes for home field advantage."

"Appreciate that, but let's call it even, cool?"

"Cool. You're our guest," Josh said. "The honor is yours."

"Why, thank you." Dolan set up between the blues.

"You sure you feel up for this?" I whispered to Josh.

"This is not a coincidence," Josh said. "He came to play me. I've been expecting him."

"All righty then. Smoke him."

Dolan had a prototypical big-guy PGA swing. Like watching Finau, the clubs reduced to toys. His pale Nordic ape arms hung down nearly to his knees, and his first drive went 325.

"Holy shit," Jamie said. "I should have asked for more strokes."

"You can have two more," Dolan offered as he stepped off.

"Hell no. I honor my bets."

Jamie set up and cocked into his usual baseball player's stance. From the back he looked like some kind of crab, the carapace of his deltoids, lats, and triceps stretching his red polo to its limits. His combat injuries prevented him from making a full swing, but he brought so much brute force between three and nine o'clock, it was a wonder his ball didn't howl in agony.

The drive launched like a home run, eating up the left side of the fairway before turning. His pride guaranteed he would outdrive Dolan but also bought him some trouble, leaving his bright-red ball in a sloping patch of clover and hard-packed dirt some fifty feet from the green.

"Fuck me," Jamie said. "I didn't slice one fucking time on the range this morning."

Dolan was not concerned with Jamie. He was studying Josh.

My dude stepped between the gates and watched the trees for a moment, then stuck his tee. He carefully set his lines to parallel before lowering the head of his battered old driver to the grass. I couldn't help but worry the accident might have taken something from his game. Rolled his car eight days ago, and now here he was, up against a legit beast.

Josh went into his unique hitch move before unfurling like a ballet dancer whipping a magic wand, flicking lightning. The flight was a low-rising draw I thought was sure to fall short, but it had wings upon wings. The ball touched down just inside the right rough and rolled out maybe ten yards behind Dolan's ball.

Shaking his head in admiration, Dolan said, "I simply do not understand how a body that small makes a ball go that far. Really beautiful, Josh."

"Thanks."

Dolan and Josh were walking today. Jamie and I shared a cart.

"We got ourselves a fucking match!" Jamie slapped me on the back. "Time for a drink!"

"I'm sober now," I reminded him. "But that might change today."

"Side action—a hundo says Josh takes this clown to Chinatown."

"Thank you, but no."

I didn't think Josh would be humiliated, but if he was bested here today, the blow to his confidence could shatter his trajectory for a long time.

Regardless, it was on.

sticks

Twenty dollars per hole doesn't sound like much, and for guys like Josh and Dolan who have a lot of lettuce to throw around, it's not. But when egos are involved—and in golf, egos are always involved—the action escalates quickly.

What began that morning as twenty dollars per hole soon skyrocketed. Dolan took the first hole with a birdie to Josh's surprise par. Something looked off with the putter. He missed an easy ten-footer, and not by a little.

On number two, Dolan proposed twenty dollars for the longest drive that stayed in the fairway. Jamie countered to fifty, Josh agreed, and Jamie won. Then it was closest to the pin for another fifty, which went to Josh. Number four, a par three, was one hundred dollars closest to the pin—Dolan. On number five, they all tied, and somehow, through a series of equations I could not follow, by the time we got to number six, the three of them were playing for five hundred dollars on one hole. Jamie had gotten an accounting degree before he began his service in the army, and Dolan agreed to let him keep track of all this using his "Vegas Baby Vegas" spreadsheet. He'd created it for golf gambling and carried it on his phone.

"Nifty," Dolan said.

I knew Dolan saw Jamie as too much of a roughneck for the game. Jamie was loud and bashed everything in his way. But Dolan was like a Glade scent diffuser of smirking condescension. It was in his manner and especially in his habit of turning obvious yet mundane observations about other people's golf shots into insults.

The barely missed putt: *Oh, one more inch would have been so nice.*

The fat pitch: *Grass is giving itself up cheap today.*

The plain old bad decision: *I was wondering how that was going to work out for you.*

As if we needed a commentator to explain what went wrong. Jamie was getting pissed, but if any of this bothered Josh, he wasn't showing it.

My own game was rendered meaningless within a few holes. I slapped a ball around here and there while Jamie and Dolan chirped at each other and ran up a big tab. Josh stayed quiet, which was his usual style, but which Dolan mistook for added concentration under duress. There was no real getting in the zone for Josh. He lived in the zone.

The three of them tied with birds on the ninth, so they lingered on the green and had a putt-off to decide a winner. Jamie lost a chunk. Josh escaped with a minimal loss. Dolan was grin-fucking all of us. When we gathered at the turn, Jamie announced the standings. Par at Twin was seventy, thirty-five each side. Through nine they stood:

Jamie: 42
Dolan: 34
Josh: 39

Josh either was tuned out or did not hear the scores. Either way, he betrayed no concern. I asked him how he felt. How was the swing? Any headaches?

He peeled his third banana. "Feels good to be back at it. How's Jamie doing?"

"You're not keeping track?" I asked.

"Nope. Don't care."

"But Dolan is—"

"Don't tell me my score. I never count strokes until I finish."

A few other regulars were starting to catch wind of the action and began to hover around the patio facing number ten. "That's Dolan Johanssen? He's huge," one said. "Josh is gambling? He never plays anybody," another added. "Better not let Coach find out."

Coach Lowry was down at the corner of the driving range, giving a lesson at his station. He had developed a keen ability to give attentive lessons while also maintaining a sixth sense of what was happening on his course. He glanced our way but didn't wave.

I got in the cart, and Jamie showed me his spreadsheet. The money standings:

Jamie to Dolan: −$1,850
Jamie to Josh: −$425
Josh to Dolan: −$800

"You're down that much already?" I asked.

Jamie laughed. "He can eat a dick. You know the back is nine where I shine."

"If you say so."

"Wait," Jamie said. "I forgot to show you yours."

He scrolled down the spreadsheet. "Oh, there you are."

Casey to everyone: $5 because I'm a pussy ass bitch.

Jamie brayed and I shook my head. "Josh isn't himself. I don't think he cares about the money, but this could get ugly. Don't push it, okay?"

"Swing juice!" Jamie did a double shot of Fireball and offered me one. I declined. Jamie coughed. "God, that tastes like shit. Why do I drink it?"

"All that sugar. It's literally the worst thing you could drink besides antifreeze."

"Bro, I have fifteen more in my bag. Wait, you can drink antifreeze?"

"Okay, see, please don't do that."

Jamie's eyes shrank. "I know guys like this from playing pool. He's going to stumble soon, and when he does, he will completely unravel. Just watch."

Morgan came bumbling out in the beverage wagon. "Are you guys trying to take my man's money?"

Dolan just smiled.

Jamie got up. "Morgan, can I put my Fireballs in the cooler? They're hot as fuck."

"Sure! As long as I can follow along."

Josh shook his head: *Please don't.*

"Too bad! It's slow inside and I'm bored."

Jamie finished dumping his shooters in the wagon's cooler and grabbed his driver. "Yo, Dolan. I'm down two G's. How about two hundred per hole on the back?"

"Sure."

"Make it three," Josh said.

"Sure," Dolan repeated.

"Ooooh," Jamie teased. "Josh's got a golfy! Fuck yeah. Three bills per hole. Pushes double, and let's do five-hundred-dollar birdies and . . ." On and on.

Josh and Dolan agreed to it all.

Whatever hopes I had that the short break and Morgan's cheer-leading might turn things around for Josh quickly went out the window.

Number ten was a 435-yard par four doglegging left. Severe tree trouble immediately after the tee box, plus houses and a drainage canal all the way down the left side. A pond deep right. The fairway was one of our narrower ones, rising to a slim elevated green that was steep front to back. Today the pin was tucked way up in the top left corner.

Driver was risky here. Didn't stop Dolan. He bombed one three hundred something to the right edge. Josh went with driver as well and put a nasty little sting on it, hewing to the left side of the fairway before its spin caught hold and parked him in the VIP section. Not as far, but it was pure artistry.

Jamie blocked his drive hard right into the water. "Noooooo!"

"That one's wet," Dolan said.

"Yeah, I know, motherfucker, I just hit it." Jamie slammed his driver into his bag. "Morgan! Shooter!"

"You better tip her," I said, "the way you got her running around."

Jamie gave her a twenty. "Stay close, huh? You look nice today."

She was all smiles and teal spandex. "Thanks, Jamie. How's your round going?"

"Like shit." Jamie did another double, and we headed off so he could take his drop.

Josh's second was an aggressive pin seeker that overshot the green, bouncing on top of the back shoulder before disappearing. Dolan tucked his second just under the cup, leaving him an uphill ten-footer for birdie.

What happened next was ghastly. Jamie was hitting three off the drop, and the Fireball was coursing through his veins.

He launched his ball way, way over the green, into someone's yard. His laughter was like something coming from an asylum.

Josh's ball came flying high from the back, landed past the pin, and rolled down the sloping green, gaining speed, still going, oh dear God, still going, before finally slowing all the way down at the front apron. He was lying three with sixty feet of uphill putting to go.

Dolan holed his birdie to get out of the way. Josh three-putted for a jaw-dropping six. The hole cost him at least a grand and gave Dolan a three-stroke bump to what was now an eight-stroke lead. Jamie and I drove around to meet him on the way to number eleven.

"Bro, what happened?" Jamie asked Josh.

"Golf."

Number eleven was one of the easiest holes on the course. You could miss the fairway by 30 yards on either side and not be in serious trouble. It played another 425. They all drove well, leaving themselves somewhere between 130 and 150 yards on approach. Only Jamie faced some trees in his path. He did another shooter before grabbing his club.

"Don't make it too easy," Dolan said. "That's a lot of juice."

"Pipe down, Swedish meatball," Jamie replied. "Have a drink and lighten up."

"Sure, I'll take a beer," Dolan said to Morgan. "IPA if you have one." She served him a can of Insane Rush.

Jamie grabbed his 56-degree wedge and scooped a beauty over the trees, got a nice kick off the left shoulder, and skittered to the right edge of the green. "I'm dancin'! Dancin' and romancin'!"

Josh's approach was pin high but wide left.

Dolan had an easy wedge to get there, but his hands went

wonky right before impact, and he flipped the club away as if it had burned him. "Jesus Christ!" he said, stumbling back. "Get it off! Snake! A big fucking rattlesnake!"

We all cruised over to have a look while Dolan hopped around like a maniac. Indeed there was a snake lying in the grass, but it was neither big nor a rattler. It was a bull snake, probably a yearling, maybe two feet long.

Jamie started laughing. Morgan cowered in her cart. Josh calmly walked over and lifted the creature with his club head. The snake slipped off, and this time Josh just reached down and picked it up with his bare right hand. The snake didn't bite or even hiss.

"Just a little bull snake," he said with a grin. "Completely harmless."

"Get that thing away from me!" Dolan shouted.

Jamie said, "Guess they don't have snakes in Norway."

Dolan flipped him off. "I'm from San Diego."

"That explains a lot," Jamie said. "Philip Rivers smack-talking jagoff."

Josh carried the snake to the deep grass lining the canal. He let it down easily, watched for a moment, then came back. "Was that a stroke?"

"No," Dolan said. "I jumped before I hit."

"Bullshit," Jamie said. "Your ball went like twenty feet, bro. That was a stroke."

Dolan looked incredulous. "I'm supposed to play with a goddamn snake hanging off my leg? Are you serious?"

"Bro, I am so serious," Jamie said calmly. "It's part of nature."

"What the shit does that even mean?"

"It means it's part of the environment." Jamie rose from the cart. "Like the grass. You could have backed off and let it pass, but you made contact. End of story."

Dolan was fuming. "I didn't see it until the last second."

"Yeah, and I didn't see that ant crawling on my ball four holes ago. You gonna give me back a stroke for that? What's next? A speck of sand?"

"Whatever." Dolan turned away. "Goddamn muni. Gravel in the bunkers. Probably snakes and prairie dogs all over this shithole."

I admit that was when I really started enjoying the round. Dolan went to his ball, still shaken and angry, and took a swipe at it without even getting set in his stance. He topped it badly, plonking the ball forward only another ten feet or so.

"Asshole!"

"That's me," Jamie said.

I tugged on his sleeve. "Easy, man. Don't make it worse."

"He was chirping at me all morning."

Dolan's fourth swing cracked the ball hard, sending it on a beeline that smashed into the front shoulder and kicked right, back down into the deep rough.

Josh sank his long putt for birdie. Jamie bogeyed. Dolan took a seven. He was no longer smiling or talking as we set up on number twelve, the downhill 170-yard par three with the gaping mouth of a bunker up front.

"Extra three hundo closest to the pin?" Jamie asked, knowing Dolan could not refuse. He was still up big, and they'd been pumping up the stakes on every par three so far.

"If you insist."

"Five grand for an ace," Jamie added.

Dolan shook his head. "Right. Sure. Go get your ace, big fella."

"I'm in," Josh said.

Jamie took a swig of Fireball. "Now go home and get your fucking shine box, meatball."

"What was that?" Dolan said, jutting his chin.

"Pickled herring," Jamie said, and cackled.

"You know what," Dolan said. "You're a real fucking asshole."

Jamie looked at Morgan. "He's not wrong."

I couldn't pinpoint the reason, but Josh looked calmer now. Settled. His swing looked like someone underhanding a basketball, almost sleepy as he sent his ball on an absolute knockdown rope that landed mid-green and crawled uphill . . . kept going . . . right toward the flag . . . Oh God, this was going to be close.

"You're joking," Dolan said.

Jamie was jumping up and down. "Get it! Get it! Bust that nut!"

. . . The ball slowed, crept, and stopped maybe three inches under the cup.

"Josh, you almost aced that!" Jamie yelled. "With money on the line! That was so fucking ice! Dolan, did you see that shit?"

Dolan sighed. "I saw it. And I can hear you just fine. You don't need to shout."

"What? What?" Jamie repeated theatrically. "Can you hear me now?"

"Just hit."

Jamie made the green, high above the hole.

Dolan took a long time setting up.

"He's using a pitching wedge," Jamie said to me, "from one seventy. He's showing off. No chance."

Dolan gave it a hard chop of a swing and thinned it, and the delofted wedge sent the rock over the green and into the street behind it.

"Whoa, traffic ball," Jamie said. "Fasten your seat belt, folks."

"Yeah, I know, motherfucker," Dolan said with a sneer. "I just hit it."

The beating continued on the next hole, a 470-yard par-4 beast. They all drove into the fairway, and then Josh used his heat-seeking eight iron to eagle out from 180. It came down maybe ten feet past the cup, spun back, and vanished. Jamie went nuts. Morgan ran from her cart and hugged her boy. I clapped slowly. Josh followed Morgan back to the cart to get some crackers.

Dolan just stood there with his hands on his hips. "What the shit is this? You went plus five on the front, and now it's two birdies and an eagle. Why do I smell sand?"

Jamie got out of the cart. "Yo, what did you say?"

"I smell sand," Dolan repeated, then spat.

"You sayin' Josh is sandbagging?"

"Not a chance," I said. Even I understood that in competitive golf there were few things worse than a sandbagger. As if Josh had tanked on the front nine to hustle Dolan.

"Awfully convenient," Dolan said. "He's draining everything now, you're hollering in my ear, and he's juggling snakes. I'm being clowned."

Jamie stood a foot from Dolan and became very still. I could see his nostrils flaring.

Oh shit.

out of bounds

Dolan and Jamie were about to come to blows. Josh was watching as if this all had nothing to do with him.

"Are you calling the most honest kid I've ever met a hustler?" Jamie asked. His voice was quiet but full of menace. "Choose your answer carefully. Are you calling my friend a piece of shit?"

"We both offered to show you our index," Josh added.

Dolan held out his hands. "Hey, I don't know you guys. You have cash, he's got Venmo, you're yelling at me. Let's just see the money, okay?"

"Oh, now he needs to see the money," Jamie said.

"Jamie, chill out, all right?" I said. "You're all whining like a bunch of little shits."

Josh held out his phone for Dolan. "That's my account," he said. "My Venmo is attached."

Dolan blinked a few times.

"He's got four hundred and sixty-eight grand in his account," Jamie said. "I think he can afford to throw you a couple if he loses, which he currently is not doing. Satisfied?"

"Sure," Dolan said.

Jamie went to his bag and pulled out a Ziploc bag full of cash. "And here's ten grand. Tell you what. You don't like me. I'm losing anyway. I'll pay you out now, everything I owe plus five hundred dollars for my forfeit. But only if you agree to play Josh straight up over the last six holes for a grand per hole."

Josh spoke up. "You don't need to do that, Jamie. I don't play for money when there're bad vibes. We can call it now for all I care."

Dolan perked up. Maybe he took Josh's reluctance for fear; maybe he just liked the idea of cutting Jamie out of the equation. "How much are you into me now?"

Jamie checked his spreadsheet. "Fifty-three fifty. Call it six K to cash out. You can play Josh a grand a hole on house money, big fella. You down?"

"Absolutely."

Jamie looked to Josh. "Take his money, Josh. Please. Let him bury himself."

Josh glanced at me, squinting.

"No one cares what I think," I said. "Play if you want to play." Then I stood and addressed them all. "But if we keep going, each and every one of you needs to cut the shit. No more arguing. No smack talk before, during, or after shots. No more accusations. Trust each other completely, or go home right now. Understood?"

They all nodded in agreement.

As we headed to the fourteenth, the gallery had grown to almost twenty people. A foursome of older men walked off the seventeenth green to see what all the fuss was about. Then a few more people from number five. They kept coming, and Morgan kept setting everybody up with cocktails and bags of chips. Jamie had Morgan give him a big cup with ice, and he filled it two-thirds of the way with Fireball, the rest with Coke. I took a Frappuccino on the rocks and put a wad of Skoal mint in my lip. Nothing like a speedball of caffeine and nicotine to calm the nerves. Morgan did a shot with Jamie and asked Josh if he needed anything. He accepted a bottle of water, and she kissed him on the cheek.

"You got it, baby," she said. "Do how you do."

Number fourteen was one of the easiest holes on the course, a long par five. Both Josh and Dolan birdied it, doubling the bet to $2,000 for number fifteen.

"But double for birdies," Jamie said. "Not just a push. So four grand."

Josh nodded. Dolan agreed but looked a little queasy.

Number fifteen was my favorite hole at Twin Peaks, a simple yet beautifully designed little par four that only went 355. Someone had nicknamed it Layla, after a woman who had grown up here and gone on to play on the LPGA Tour for a few years before starting her own accounting firm. Number fifteen had been her favorite hole, probably for the view. Layla played west, driving into the Front Range of the Rockies, a living postcard that framed the two peaks—Mount Meeker and Longs Peak—the course had been named for.

There was something about Layla's simplicity, her diminutive size, her flat approach, and that killer view—all of it came out from the center of the course and, like your cute high school girlfriend who was smarter than you, stood there naked, baring herself with a coy smile, daring you to not screw this up. Daring you to sneak inside her contours, those little cutouts where the pin stood blowing you kisses and laughing at your macho hubris, your useless power, your inability to understand her great simple mystery.

Josh took a sensible approach and birdied Layla.

Dolan tried to drive the green, blocked it wildly right, and came back for par, leaving him –$4,000.

Josh birdied number sixteen. Dolan parred, putting Josh up $5,000.

Number seventeen, a merciless 230-yard par three with a nasty cattail swamp short left of the green, was the hole everyone dreaded. Josh pulled his six iron.

"You don't like woods or hybrids?" Dolan asked, trying to make Josh second-guess himself here.

"Don't trust hybrids," Josh replied. "I have a five wood but only like it for stingers."

"Whatever works," Dolan said.

Josh didn't just make the green—he stuck the bull's-eye, less than six feet from the cup.

Dolan went with a hybrid and pulled his tee shot into the cattails. Reteed, made the green, one-putted for a bogey. Josh canned his birdie putt.

Jamie did the math as we shuffled over to number eighteen. "Told you he would implode."

Dolan to Josh: –$7,000

"You got me on the run," Dolan said. "How about we play the last one for double or nothing? You win, it's fourteen to you. I win, we're clear."

Josh looked uncomfortable.

Dolan shifted on his feet. "Come on, gimme a chance to walk out of here with my dignity."

Josh nodded. "Fine."

Coach Lowry was giving another lesson. Number eighteen ran parallel to the driving range and played right back into his station, and I knew he must be aware of what was happening by now. Maybe not the stakes but the gist. We had almost forty people in tow.

The hole was not an easy par four. It ran 455 yards, narrow fairway with a right dogleg. The entire left side was lined with out-of-bounds markers to keep you off the driving range. Up the right side, a few mature pines and three or four hulking cottonwoods got into the mix. The green featured one short-side bunker but no real shoulders or crazy slopes to contend with.

Josh played the left-to-right power fade, his ball flirting with the driving range for a long time before coming to its senses. By the time it turned over, it had a lot of catching up to do. The fairway was out of the question. He'd be lucky to keep it in bounds.

"Oh my," Dolan said, licking his lips.

The ball came back over the last two pine trees and a metal electrical box, plunging into some nasty wet rough not fifty feet from Coach Lowry's teaching station.

"Out of bounds," Dolan said.

"No," Jamie said. "He's in."

"Like hell," Dolan said.

"We'll see," Josh said.

Dolan's drive went like a torpedo, fearlessly passing the edge of the big trees to cut the corner, leaving himself about 125 yards. He couldn't have asked for better.

The out-of-bounds markers were white iron poles spaced out about every 50 to 75 yards, forming a loosely curving line. When we got up there, Josh's ball looked out of bounds, until you walked around it and traced the line up the other way, in which case it seemed in play, just barely. The two of them tried to negotiate. Dolan would not concede.

"I'm telling you," Dolan said, raising his voice. "This is ludicrous. The line must be defined by the poles. It's pretty goddamn obvious."

Jamie got out of the cart and sidled up. Soon everyone was arguing again.

"You don't know what you're talking about!" Dolan said to Jamie. "And you're not his babysitter, bitch."

"Dude, fuck *you*." Jamie stepped into Dolan's personal space again.

Dolan pushed Jamie in the chest. "How about you back the fuck away from me!"

"WHAT THE HELL IS GOING ON?"

We all turned to see Coach Lowry stomping toward us in his usual attire: track pants, a Twin Peaks polo, full-length white SPF sleeves, and his straw bush hat. No matter how much sunblock he used, his face was always red, which made it hard to tell if he was just sunburned, overexerted, or pissed off. The other thing about Coach Lowry—he was one of those guys who didn't swear much, but he had chosen one good swear word and wielded it like an all-purpose survival knife. For Coach, that word was . . .

"Why are you making such a GODDAMN racket on my golf course?" He glared at each of us. "I could hear your goddamn nonsense three holes ago, and now you're itching for a little donnybrook in front of my clubhouse? Explain yourselves before I throw you all out for the rest of the goddamn season." His eyes settled on Josh.

"Sorry, Coach," Josh said. "We just need a ruling on this OB line."

"Why do you need a goddamn ruling? Are you GAMBLING?"

"Yes, sir," Josh answered.

"How much money is worth making goddamn idiots of yourselves at this fine gentleman's game?"

"Just a few bucks," Dolan began, as if he could smooth it all over. "No hard feelings here, really. Josh has been—"

"HOW MUCH?" Coach yelled at Josh.

"We're up to seven." Josh failed to conceal his smile. "Thousand. Actually, fourteen."

Coach slowly removed his mirrored sunglasses and tucked them into the neck of his polo. He rubbed his eyes and pinched the top of his nose. "Four . . ." He lost his breath. "You're playing golf at Twin Peaks for fourteen goddamn thousand dollars?"

"Yes, sir," Josh said. "But actually just on this hole. We settled the rest."

"Fourteen thousand on one lousy hole. Are you tugging my titmouse?"

"No, sir," Dolan said. "He is not."

"What's a titmouse?" Jamie asked.

Coach took a deep breath, and I thought he was going to blow his stack again. But very calmly he asked, "Who's winning?"

"Josh is," Jamie said.

"We're tied," Dolan said.

"Well, which is it?"

"Depends where we go from here," Josh said. "Dolan believes my ball is out of bounds. I believe it is in play."

"And now you," Coach said, pointing to Dolan, "think I'm going to rule in favor of this little pecker here because he's my nephew. Is that about the size of it?"

Jamie chuckled. "Pecker."

"You shut up," Coach said, stabbing a finger at Jamie. "You drink too much."

"Yes, sir," Jamie said.

Coach sighed and looked around. "What the hell do I know? I've only been the club pro here for seventeen years. Only spent the first twenty years of my goddamn life playing here. I only helped dig the bunkers and drove the goddamn Bobcat back in thirteen when we renovated two, four, six, ten, thirteen, sixteen, and this hole right goddamn here. I'm just the guy who supervised the entire goddamn architectural plan and site construction and rewrote the goddamn yardage files and submitted them myself to the USGA, City of Longmont, Boulder County, and State of Colorado—what in the sweet cheese would I know?"

Dolan did not like where this was going.

Coach smoothed his mustache. "If you don't have faith in my integrity, you won't have faith in my ruling, so why should I bother?"

Dolan squirmed. "Sir, I know your reputation as a man of unparalleled respect for the game. If you say the ball is in bounds, it's in bounds."

"Electrical box." Coach pointed to the green electrical box standing just a few yards away. "That's the goddamn problem."

We all turned to look at the box, as if it were going to reveal a great mystery.

"Tree roots prevented us from putting the goddamn box anywhere except there or on my practice green, so that's where it went. It was my decision, after many hours of consultation with three different course architects and my own goddamn common sense, that the box should not be considered in bounds lest it become a goddamn unnecessary obstacle and stick out like even more of a goddamn sore thumb than it already do. The debate came down to a matter of six feet, four inches of bend spread between these two white stakes fifty yards apart. Hardly discernible to the goddamn naked eye."

Coach began pacing off the line, stepping toe to heel like a drunk driver taking a road test. He paused with one foot up beside the electrical box.

"That box is out of bounds. But it does not itself serve as a marker. It cannot, according to the rules. But was I allowed to plant a steel rod next to the electrical box, which happens to be filled with enough juice to power my clubhouse and the entire goddamn neighborhood? No, I was not. Because this is a goddamn municipal course, and as such it is city property, no different than a public park, and when it comes to matters of goddamn public safety, the city—the same city that lets all the public lunatics blast off enough fireworks to reenact the bombing of Hanoi every goddamn Fourth of July—would not look the other way, or they could wind up tripling their hazard insurance if the goddamn inspector or the goddamn power company ever found out. And this is why my foot dangling here is the goddamn line. This is the marker, not the electrical box, and as you can plainly see, that goddamn golf ball right there"—he pointed to Josh's ball using his extended middle finger—"whoever the hell it belongs to, is one hundred percent IN BOUNDS, by a yard and probably more like a goddamn yard and a half. The ball is in fair play, there is no penalty, and you guys are all a bunch of dickheads who have nothing better to do than waste my goddamn time. Now, I am in the middle of a goddamn lesson that a respectable member of Twin Peaks, who is going to be twice the golfer any of you four turkey necks imagine yourselves to be, has paid good goddamn money for—"

We all looked over to Coach's station. A little blond girl who couldn't have been more than eight was watching us intently. She was dressed in a matching pink golf outfit, her hybrid slotted into the crook of her arm like a shotgun. She smiled at us and waved.

"—so if you goddamn idiots have no more questions, I'm going to return to my real job and ask that you let little Amanda over here work on her baby cut in a modicum of goddamn peace. Think we can do that?"

"Yes, Coach, yes, sir," we all said in something close to unison.

For the first time, Coach smiled. And the weird part was just how genuine it seemed. He even added a slight bow.

"Please enjoy the remainder of your round, and thank you for choosing Twin Peaks as your recreational outlet. We know you and your families have many options in the Boulder County area, and your patronage means the world to us."

He walked away, shaking his head. "Mandy!" he hollered. "Put that goddamn hybrid away, honey. It's time for the mighty two iron."

"Two iron?" Dolan said. "Is he serious?"

"Afraid so," Josh said.

"Why on earth is he making that poor little girl use a two iron? I can't even hit a two."

"Oh, he's not making her," Josh said. "It's an old tactic he uses on his best students. Uses it as a warning at first, a threat. 'If you keep screwing around, I'm going to make you spend the *rest of your lesson* on the two. The two iron will *ruin your life*.' You're terrified of it. And then he'll slip in a few stories to get you thinking it's a precious relic, a secret from the game's golden years. '*Only the best of the best* knew how to work the two. *Nicklaus loved* his two iron. Bobby Jones loved his two and used it to *win all his biggest tournaments*.' He keeps on with this romantic bullshit until you're begging to use the two iron, you dream about it, you'll do *anything* to convince Coach to let you hit the two. Because you're not a real golfer until you can stop a ball on the green from a mile away with the two. I guarantee you little Mandy over there dreams about the two the way most girls dream about a new iPhone."

Dolan smiled. "Jesus, he really messed you up, huh?"

"You don't know the half of it," Josh answered. "But it wasn't the two iron for me."

"What was it?"

Josh held up his index finger.

"The one?" Dolan was incredulous. "Shut the front door. Nobody hits a one. Not for decades. It's a relic. An abomination."

"Come here," Josh said, removing a shitty old club from his bag. It had a leather grip gone nearly black with sweat. The head was tiny, flat, dull. A garden spade.

"Holy shit." Dolan took the club and inspected it. "Hogan. What year?"

"Sixty-eight," Josh said. "It's a rare reproduction of the same one iron Hogan used to win the 1950 US Open. Coach found it at an estate sale in the last century, from an old couple who had lived next door to Hogan. He was never able to verify it, but Coach swears it spent its first few years in Hogan's personal bag."

Dolan whistled. "Can you hit it?"

"Used to. Haven't bothered in a few years."

"I gotta see you hit that thing," Dolan said. "Sling one for us, baby."

Josh put the club away. "Not today." He returned to his ball. "So we good here?"

Dolan nodded. "Swing away."

next man up

Josh won the hole and the match. Beat the Swede by seven strokes overall. More importantly, he'd shown that he could rally from behind an opponent with far more physical advantages and pro-level experience.

Dolan was quiet as they shook hands on eighteen. Josh seemed to take no pleasure in winning, probably because of the arguments that had come with it. In the parking lot, it was strange watching him stuff $14,000 into his bag and then toss the bag into a beater Mazda truck.

"It's just temporary until I figure out what makes sense," Josh said, stepping into a pair of shower flips.

"I'm having a little barbecue on the Fourth," I said. "Just my mom, stepmom, and a few friends. Love to have you if you don't already have plans. I'll call your mom later to invite her. Bring Morgan or anyone else you feel like."

"I'll let you know." He seemed mentally shot.

"Yo, Josh, hold up!" We turned to see Dolan hurrying toward us.

I tensed. Jamie was gone and I wasn't a fighter, so if Dolan had beef and wanted his money back, this wasn't going to go well for us.

"How about you settle down?" I tried to put up some kind of defense for the kid. "Slow it down, please."

Dolan put his hands up. "I come in peace. I just wanted to say how impressed I am by your game. I underestimated you, and you cleaned my clock for it, fair and square."

"You owned me on the front," Josh offered.

"You're gonna make a run, right?" Dolan gave a knowing smile. "At the Tour."

"Why do you care?" I asked.

"Because if you're not already planning to," Dolan said, ignoring me, "I really think you should. You got game, but a lot of dudes have game. You have that extra thing. That million-mile stare, like no one else even exists."

"I guess I don't think about it," Josh lied.

"That's what I mean," Dolan continued. "I did everything I could to throw you off, but you're unshakable. That can take you far. I know because I've been up against a lot of guys who had the natural physical skills, the experience, but not the temperament. At the elite level, that's what separates the contenders from the pretenders."

"Maybe," Josh said. "Thanks for saying so."

Dolan glanced at me before continuing. "I hate to be the one to say it, but you already know this inside—you're screwed. You have no choice but to go for it. If you don't, you'll hate yourself for the rest of your life. I know because I touched the sun. And the only thing that keeps me from hanging myself with the laces from my FootJoys is the knowledge that I gave it all I had. And that's all you have to do. Give it hell."

Josh coughed up a small laugh. "Yeah. Maybe."

Dolan continued. "So anyway, I got a guy. Dad and I

sponsor him through our church, but he's surpassed anything we had to give him. Name's Francisco Dominguez. Everyone calls him El Guapo, Frankie the Handsome. He's twenty-one, from Mexico City. Everyone says he's the next Mito Pereira, but that's just lazy because he's Latino. His closest analog is probably Cam Smith. Putts like a god. But that mullet can't drive like Frankie. He was in gangs from age seven. Grew up just as hard as can be. Parents gunned down, sister abducted. Rest of his adopted family got slaughtered, and they found him playing some course in the desert three hundred miles away, dying of dehydration. A cartel boss took him in. Hired all the best coaches. But deep down he's another feral, like you. If he doesn't win amateur of the year next season, I'll eat my sand wedge."

Josh was intrigued. How could he not be—there was another out there like him.

"Dad and I are sponsoring an exhibition. It was going to be another guy and Frankie, but the dude flamed out a week ago, nervous breakdown. Now we need a sub. We'll do a little fundraiser thing, donate the proceeds to underprivileged kids, gun control, shit like that. This is part of a national effort to draw more of the Hispanic community into the game. Local TV, probably get you a write-up in some of the national golf trades. What do you say?"

"Where would we play?" Josh asked.

"My home course, TPC Fort Collins. We host NCAA and Korn Ferry stops. We've committed fifty from the car biz, but we have other sponsors rolling in. Minimum purse a hundred, more depending on how our sales guys do."

Josh seemed distracted. "Can I think about it?"

Dolan shot me a look like, *What is wrong with this kid? Can you wake him up?*

"Josh, Josh, listen," I said, resting a hand on his shoulder.

"I'm not exactly up to speed on the Tour stuff, but this isn't the kind of thing that just falls in your lap all the time, right? I mean, forget the money, you have money, but isn't this kind of competition what you were just telling me you needed?"

Josh reared back and glared at me. "What did I tell *you*? I didn't tell you shit."

Now I was caught off guard. I smiled, trying to keep it light. "Just about wanting to push yourself, test your game at the next level. This is the perfect chance. The exposure. A real match." But somehow every word I said made things worse. Josh was fuming inside now. I had never seen him this angry.

"You should listen to your dad here," Dolan said. "This is super rare, and honestly it's perfect for you."

"He's not my dad!" Josh snapped. Then he really ramped up. "I barely know him any better than you. Jesus, I come out here to get a round in, and all of a sudden I am in not one but two matches? I got a coach up my ass, failed Korn Ferry guy here begging me to help him sell cars, and some rando drunk who took advantage of my mom twenty years ago—but suddenly all of you know what's best for me? All of you want a say in *my future*?!"

He shot daggers, daring us to respond. Dolan looked at me like he just now realized he had walked into a psychotic family-therapy session. He was backing away. I had to think fast, try to keep the door open and then untangle the real ball of yarn later.

"All right, all right," I said loudly, maintaining a big smile. "I was out of line, Josh. You asked for time to think about it, and I pushed you. I should not have done that. However, Dolan here has given us a generous invitation, so let's not be rude just because I stepped in shit, okay?"

Josh exhaled and looked away.

I appealed to Dolan. He was standing with his arms crossed, and I knew I had to stick the landing here. "Dolan, as I am sure you can understand, everyone is a little fried from the match you two gentlemen just completed. You probably did not know this, but Josh was in a car accident recently, and he's still recovering."

"I'm fine!" Josh barked.

"Yes, you are," I said quickly without looking at him. "Regardless, if there is an asshole here, it is surely me. I seem to have inserted myself into things without respecting a few boundaries. I am sorry. But if I may, one request to each of you before we blow out of here. This is a tremendous opportunity for Josh. Whether it is the right time for it, that's up to him. And Dolan, from what you have explained, you need another golfer or else your fundraiser is going to fall apart. And time is of the essence. May I suggest to each of you that we take the night, go home, hash it out, and reconvene by phone tomorrow?"

Josh opened his mouth to protest. I put up a hand.

"If either of you have already made up your minds, fine—I am not here to do any more persuading. Dolan, can you give Josh twenty-four hours? Josh, can you give it the night?"

Dolan had softened, but I knew he was waiting to see how Josh responded first. Josh was still agitated. Gently, I turned him around to create a semblance of privacy.

"Josh," I said, "I'm not trying to be your dad. Just a friend. If I overstepped, I apologize. Tell me to fuck off, I'll fuck off. But maybe take the night and ask yourself what you would have done in this situation a month ago, three months ago, before you ever met me. Maybe that's the move. And that's all I got. This is all you now."

Josh blew out more air and wiped a hand over his face. He turned to Dolan. "Sorry I insulted you. When is the match?"

"Saturday, eight days from now," Dolan said. "I can't move

it because we already booked the course and Frankie's got an exemption to play the Barbasol. He's leaving Sunday."

Josh shifted from foot to foot. "All right. I guess . . ."

"Let me know tomorrow," Dolan said, handing us each a business card. "I want you to be sure one way or the other. But if you decide to play, you gotta wear shoes. A collar. Look and act like a pro. And this is an exhibition, so don't be afraid to get a little wild with it."

"Like what?" Josh asked.

"Dress bold. Bring a walk-up song for the DJ. We're asking people to bring their families; we've got to put on a show. Have some fun, give them something to remember."

Josh nodded. "Okay, sure."

"Thank you, Dolan," I said. "Josh will call you in the morning one way or another."

Dolan hurried off. Josh was still trying to get his head around it all. I didn't know where to go from here. He glanced at me uncomfortably.

"Hey," I said. "I don't have any right to act like your dad. I don't deserve any influence on your life. I should have communicated better with you from the beginning. Spelled everything out. Man to man. Maybe I shouldn't have come around at all."

"No big deal," Josh said.

"But it is a big deal. You're a big deal. Your mom is a big deal. And you're right: I am a drunk. I have problems. I've done a lot of stupid shit over the years. But for what it's worth, I haven't had a drink since before your accident, and I am trying like hell to not drink ever again. I can't promise you I won't fuck up again, but in my heart, man, I really don't want to. I really want to be better. Not just for you, not just for your mom, for myself. And nothing about me is on you or her, okay? It's my shit to clean up."

Now Josh was staring at me. Not warmly, but maybe with new curiosity.

"I want to do better for myself," I said. "And I want you to do what's best for you, no one else. So go home, forget about me, talk to your mom, and you decide what you want to do about the match. And anything else that comes next."

Josh smiled. Then frowned.

"What is it?" I said.

"Dolan said it was an exhibition."

"Right. Make it fun. No big deal. It's not, like, on your permanent record or whatever the PGA considers for your future. At least I don't think—"

"*Rocky IV*," Josh said.

"Huh?"

"When Apollo fought Drago. That was an exhibition."

I pulled out my best Drago. "I must break you."

Josh didn't laugh. "Apollo died."

free solo

On the way home, I stopped at my neighborhood liquor store to buy a pint of Seagram's Seven.

I did so without thought, moving on autopilot. That's not an excuse. It's something that can happen to people who have deeply ingrained habits. I was mentally blown out. I was anxious about Josh. Partly for the match he had, for now, agreed to, but mostly about what I had done to this kid. How I had disrupted his life. Blundering in like a goddamn bull in a china shop, breaking something new every time I opened my mouth. My mind was everywhere except on alcohol, and before I realized what was happening, I was parking outside the dirty little storefront with the steel bars on the door and the giant Modelo signs on the glass windows. That's when it hit me. I was at a liquor store. My liquor store.

From that moment on, I was fully conscious of my actions. I exited my car, walked inside, and waved to Rajesh, the proprietor, who had come to seem like one of my friends. Over the years, we had developed a level of familiarity you would expect from your barber, your neighbor, an uncle. We had exchanged recipes, my mom's meat loaf for his wife's dal. I had educated him on the reliability and quirks of my Audi, a model he was considering for his daughter, who had just moved from Mumbai to Colorado to begin university. But he was not my friend. He wasn't evil either. He was a businessman. And for the past five years, I had been one of his best customers. Quite possibly his number one customer.

He knew better than to ask why I had not been here for weeks. He only smiled and said how good it was to see me, how was work, still on sabbatical? I responded vaguely as I made a quick left to the cooler reserved for the half-assed mixers places like this sell. *I'll show him who's boss*, I was thinking, as I carried my Diet Coke to the front counter.

"Pint?" Rajesh asked, already turning for the Seagram's. He could do this for me blindfolded. If I were a pro golfer, my polo would have had a big Seagram's Seven pint logo sewn into the tit. Pints, Jesus. The bottle you buy when you're afraid to bring home a handle because you know you'll drink much more than a pint in one night. For me it rarely worked; I'd usually be back in three hours for another pint.

"You know it," I said.

More small talk was exchanged. I swiped my card. I left the store with a small brown paper bag, the kind that isn't fooling anyone into thinking you don't have a bottle of hooch. I drove home and marched into the house like I was about to scold my children for leaving toys all over the floor. I set the bum bag on the kitchen island. My hands were trembling.

In the three minutes it had taken me to drive from the liquor store to my garage, my tired anxiety had jumped up into righteous anger like the blue flame from a crack pipe. My sweet Jojo came pogoing over to greet me, and I petted her and murmured something about what a shitty day, and then she ran out back as I opened the door for her. I was left standing in my kitchen wanting to smash every plate and bowl in the cupboards. I saw myself smashing my foot through the glass front of the beverage cooler. I could feel the glass shards embedding themselves in my calf, hear the pebbles raining across the floor. I was lit with a fury I had not known since Blair moved in with Carl two months after she moved out of the house we once shared. I was panting like a greyhound, and I hadn't moved a muscle.

Nothing was broken, yet. Including the seal on this bottle.

I stared at the brown bag, then removed the flask. I could smell the bitter cheapness of the whiskey before I unscrewed the cap. I could taste it, could feel the welcome burn sliding down my throat. Fuck Diet Coke—I needed to feel raw grain blooming in my intestines like a syringe full of gasoline.

I unscrewed the cap, tearing it from the safety ring, and put the bottle to my lips, just under my nose, then closed my eyes and inhaled as hard as I could. I shuddered in recognition. A couple of drops hit my lips, and my tongue flicked out like a snake's. This bolt of poison never changed, would never change, would always be here, waiting for me, anytime, all the time, in any quantity I wanted. And I wanted it all.

He's not my dad! I barely know him any better than you . . . some rando drunk who took advantage of my mom twenty years ago—but suddenly all of you know what's best for me?

Some kind of dreadful noise rattled out of me. I was still shaking, still furious. Without understanding what I was trying to accomplish, I set the bottle down, popped open the Diet Coke, and poured it down my throat vertically. It was ice cold, stinging sweet, and I swallowed hard until my sinuses burned with carbonation. When the can was empty, I threw it aside and went upstairs to shower. I took it cold from beginning to end.

Naked, I sprawled across my bed, and soon Jojo came to

curl against me. I held her and clamped my eyes shut, waiting for dark to fall. An eternity passed itself off as night. I did not sleep a wink.

The open pint sat down there on my island, waiting for me.

I left the house at three forty-five that morning at the beginning of July with Jojo in the passenger seat. I drove to Twin Peaks and sat in the parking lot, engine off, windows down, listening to the birds awaken. Mine was the only car. Everywhere was dark, but soon the sky would be slowly bluing toward proper dawn. The temperature was fifty-seven degrees.

I took off my shoes and socks. I set my phone in the console. I hadn't brought my yardage watch. Wearing only a pair of shorts and a plain black T-shirt, I removed my bag from the trunk and let Jojo hop out, and we walked to the clubhouse. It was dark inside, the door locked. Even the grounds crew had not arrived yet.

Jojo ran around the first fairway while I walked to the tee box on number one and leaned my bag against the flagstone marker. I waited for a while, watching the geese and listening for the music. I wanted to hear the music Josh heard, feel the course the way he experienced it with his bare feet. Soon my eyes adjusted to the darkness, and before the sun had crept up to point its first silver rays across the land, I set a new white ball on a tee and unsheathed my driver.

I stood over it and let all the swing thoughts flood in.

I hadn't had a drop of alcohol in seventeen days. My body still felt different, better but odd, a little weak, refamiliarizing itself with something other than numbness. I closed my eyes and breathed. I could still smell the Seagram's Seven as I'd poured it down the sink twenty minutes ago.

I thought of Josh. I thought of Damaris. I thought of my

father. My mother. My exes. My friends. My coworkers. I thought of the pointless hell I had put my body, my mind, and other people through over the past few years. I started to cry, quietly but freely, letting the shame and sadness and anger fall to the grass. I hiccuped and cried for a while. But after another minute, the tears turned to a sigh of soft laughter.

Let it go. Just let it go.

You already took those swings. You're not a time traveler. You're a human being. You are alive. You didn't kill anyone. You didn't land in a jail cell. You hurt people, but not irrevocably. You hurt yourself most of all. Now you're healing.

Forgive yourself. Swing for a new day.

I wiped my nose on my shirt. I spat. I didn't want a drink. I had so many things to do. Writing, golfing, reading new books, spending time with my friends, developing my relationships, maybe adopting another dog, maybe adopting Josh, maybe giving half my salary to him and Damaris . . .

Something primitive was happening. I had come to love them already. I didn't want to lose them. Not so soon, and not for a reason so stupid as alcohol. There was the love for them that had somehow sprouted within me, and they were a mystery, an unanswered question—what would my life be like with them in it? How would it look in another three months, in a year, in ten? I had no idea. Maybe they wouldn't be in my life at all. Maybe we were not destined to be close, like real family. But something more than where we stood today was possible. I could live with whatever we became to each other, I realized, but not if we fell apart because I couldn't control myself and turned back to drinking. I needed to stay sober so I could be here for them, so I could play whatever role I was meant to play in their lives. So I could play a different role in my own life. Then I heard a clear voice in my head.

Everything will be better without alcohol.
Every. Single. Thing.

What fell over me then was the greatest calm of my life. More sublime than love, rarer than ecstasy. It was a silver ray, cold and pure, running this calm through me and spreading within and radiating all around me. My blood was rejuvenating, my thoughts pure.

I felt like I had escaped some terrible spell. And here, beyond the prison walls, a glimpse of pride. I had a small thing to be proud of—a day when I did not drink, when I had fought back and won. There would be many more to come. I could see a future where the healthier me was someone to be proud of, where no matter what the day had thrown at me, I had accepted it like a man. A man? What was a man?

I had never felt like a man, not in forty-five years. It wasn't a masculinity thing; it was a maturity thing. To me, men were fathers, bosses, great athletes and artists, men of accomplishment, boys who had gone to war and come home changed. My dad had been a fucking man. Vince was a man. Coach Lowry was a man. You became a man after you had survived marriage or loss, brought life into the world, done something that required strength during terrible events. I had lost my father, lost my wife, blown my career, but I had not survived anything. I had crumpled like a child, whining and crying into my drink. I was stunted. Afraid. Weak. Lost.

Except—it came to me there in the blue dawn—all of that could change now. In this moment, right fucking now, standing on the grass of this shaggy, humble, yet fateful municipal golf course, I could do so much more than cry and drown. I could win my war. I could stand up. I could survive, carry on, join the next great cause, fight for my people, for myself; I could become my own version of a real man, the only man I could be.

And all I had to do was not drink.

It was in my power, no one else's.

I had chosen my path to this moment, and now I chose the path forward.

I knew then I would have to make this choice every day, and I knew that I would never drink again. No matter what happened, no matter who died, no matter whether Damaris and Josh let me in, no matter where my work took me next, I was going to live this way, not the other way.

I watched my sweet dog run around yapping after birds. She was in a new heaven, and I could be too. The morning was my peace, and across the fairways and greens was where I expressed my peace, my unshakable optimism, my love for my people and the strange life we shared. And today, for the first time I could recall, love for myself. Gratitude for my own life.

I golfed all eighteen holes before anyone else made the first tee, and I did not keep score. Jojo ran wild with me, and I remembered the feeling, not the shots.

I was free, and I played.

meet the Sweets

I had not hosted a real get-together of any kind since moving into Dad's house, and when most of the people I'd invited RSVP'd yes to my Fourth of July barbecue, I turned anxious and got to work.

Dad had owned seven grills, so I started by cleaning the largest two and refilling the propane tanks. I mowed and trimmed the yard, pulled weeds for two hours. Inside, I ran all the laundry while I swept and mopped every room, scrubbed the toilets, the whole house.

At the store I loaded up on hamburgers, bratwurst, ribs, buns, sides of potato and macaroni salad, cookies, chips, dip, ice cream, marshmallows, chocolate bars, and nonalcoholic beverage options. I even got some little red, white, and blue paper plates and napkins. I found some old tiki torches in the garage, along with the fuel, and planted them around the back patio. The secret to setting up for a party was to do the basic cleaning, then think like my ex-wife, Blair, for the extra touches. Feeling magnanimous (okay, I also wanted her to see Damaris and know I was doing great in my new life), I invited Blair and told her she could even bring Carl the Kangaroo.

"Why are you having a barbecue?" she asked.

"Uh, it's the Fourth of July."

"But you never host anything."

"I guess I have some new friends. Maybe I'm curious to see what it's like to have them all in the same place."

"Well, that's nice," Blair said. "But I thought you didn't want to be friends with me anymore."

"I'm sorry. You caught me at a very stressful time. I've been a little on edge since I quit drinking."

"You said that, but I wasn't sure if . . ."

"I'm taking it seriously, yes. But that's no excuse. I'm sorry for being an asshole. What I said came from a lot of pent-up anger about my own decisions. You've been supportive of me longer than I deserved it. I just wanted you to respect that I'm capable of living my own life. I'm Casey, not Head Casey."

The line was silent.

"That was a joke, Blair."

"Right. I never did have a sense of humor."

"No, not really," I agreed.

"I'll see what Carl has planned. What can we bring?"

"Just any alcoholic beverages you want. I'm off the piss, but it's not, like, a dry house or whatever."

"You're really doing it," she said.

"I am."

"How's it feel?" Hope and apprehension in her voice.

"It feels really good."

"Great. I'll let you know if we can make it."

The morning of my solo round, after I had committed to sobriety and danced through eighteen holes, I had texted Josh from the parking lot at Twin.

You're no Apollo Creed. He
was the heavyweight world
champion.

You haven't even stepped into
the ring.

Which makes you Rocky. In the
original. He didn't win.

But he went toe to toe with the
champ for 15 rounds.

And brought the world to its
knees.

He had not responded, and I had no idea if he would come to my party.

My mom came early so Jojo and her dog, Carol, could burn off some energy in the backyard. I was finishing the setup and prepping food while my mom hammered me with questions and blew cigarette smoke out the side door to the patio.

"What time is Damaris coming? Is she bringing Josh?"

"I don't know."

"What should I call him?"

I gave her a look. "Josh."

"Not 'my favorite new grandbaby'?"

"Please do not start with that again."

"Does Damaris remember me?"

"She does. Fondly, of course."

"She hated my pork chops."

"You remember what you cooked for her? Twenty years ago?"

"She said they tasted like boots."

"I am sure she did not say that. Would you settle down? Just act natural. Not *your* natural, natural like normal people. Try not to blurt out the first thing that comes to your mind."

"You're the one who's nervous," Mom said. "Look at you. I've never seen you Windex your stove before. You must be trying to get laid."

"I'm gonna go to the store and buy the world's largest bottle of whiskey if you keep pushing me. Put the goddamn cigarette out, sit down, and have your iced tea. It's a nice day."

Mom ignored me and fed the dogs some chips and dip.

Janey came next. I was always proud of how both of Dad's wives got along so well. Something about him dying had brought them closer. Maybe it was that they'd survived him, in more ways than one. I knew they exchanged emails and had lunch together now and then. They gave each other a hug. Then Janey hugged me and shook me by the shoulders.

"You look really good, Casey! You lost weight. You're so tan!"

"Thank you, Janey. I'm glad you came."

"He finally got sober," Linda said. "And he's got a girlfriend now. And a son."

"Jesus Christ," I mumbled.

"A son?" Janey looked like she thought we were pranking her. "That was fast."

"We're still trying to figure it out. But what I need today is for both of you ladies to chill out. Do not start asking questions about the past, about Josh—"

"Josh!" Janey said. "I always liked the name Josh. How old is he? About six months?"

"He's seventeen," Linda said. "He has Casey's eyes."

"He's twenty-two!" I barked. "And he does not have my eyes. You haven't even met him, for Christ's sake."

The widows Sweet repaired to the patio while more people filed in. Vince and his wife, Rita, were next. Vince wore a loud Hawaiian shirt and golf shorts. Rita was at least ten years younger and would not have looked out of place on the cover of *Rolling Stone.* She was indie-rock-artsy chic, with almost as many tattoos as Vince had, raven haired, gorgeous. She gave me a big hug.

"I'm so glad I finally get to meet the person my husband has been having an affair with! Vince says you're already a better golfer than he is."

"Negative," Vince said. "I said he might be someday if he ever gets his head screwed on right." He gestured to the can of beer in my hand. "What's with this?"

"For the bratwurst," I said. "You boil them in beer and onions before the grill."

"My man."

Josh and Morgan arrived with a cardboard crate full of cookies, chips, Gatorade, and a glass baking dish covered in foil. Two of the other cart girls arrived at the same time, TaylorMade and Shyla. They had dressed just like they did on the course, leggings and spandex tanks, but with added touches: new manicures, long nails, hair primped and wavy like 1984 *Penthouse* Pets', eyes dusted with glitter. Morgan and Shyla had little American flags across their cheeks. I grinned. Blair was going to choke on her pinot grigio when she saw this.

"I told you not to bring anything," I said, taking the dish from Josh.

"Mom insisted. It's her famous nine-layer Ohio dip."

"Because sometimes seven layers just won't cut it. Is she going to join us?"

"Probably." Josh was already stuffing Doritos in his mouth. "She was taking a while getting dressed."

"Not feeling a hundred percent?"

"She's fine. Just being a mom. I think she's bringing her friend McKenzie. You'll like her. She's kind of unhinged like you."

Everyone filed in around the kitchen and chatted as I dumped the beer over the brats and sliced an onion. Before I could stop myself, I asked, "Is she the one your mom goes to Costa Rica with every winter?"

Josh sidled up to me with a grin. "She told you about Costa Rica?"

I kept it vague. "Yeah, she mentioned some annual trip thing."

"Her guy down there, Ferdinand? She mention him?"

I tensed. "Was that his name?"

"Black Mamba."

"She told you about that stuff?"

"Of course," he said. "All about it. Drugs. Wild sex in the jungle. The volcano."

"Okay, that's messed up. Why would she tell—and what volcano?"

Josh shook his head. "Because it's all bullshit."

"Huh?"

"Yeah. A fairy tale she tells guys to scare them away." Josh started laughing. "She's never been out of the United States. She doesn't have a third-world side piece, bro. You believed her? Amazing!"

I was embarrassed but relieved.

Josh grabbed Morgan and Shyla. "You hear that? Casey believed the story, my mom's Costa Rica thing!"

The girls all burst out laughing.

"I'm not sure it's *that* funny," I said.

"Dude, you believed her and you *still* want to date her. Pro move!" Josh threw an arm around me. "This freakin' guy!"

He watched me for a moment, waiting for something.

"What?" I asked.

"Aren't you curious?"

"About?"

"The match."

"That's your business."

Josh scoffed. "I accepted, and I apologized to Viking Man. It's on. I'm not an idiot, you know. Of course I'm playing. Gonna get my ass kicked but whatever."

"I'm happy for you," I said, chopping more vegetables.

"That's it? Dude, come on. Quit being so melodramatic. Have some fun!" Josh slapped my arm again and wandered off.

"Goddamn kids," I muttered, grinning.

Damaris let herself in. She was with McKenzie. Damaris wore sandals, olive shorts, and a sheer yellow top with a not-subtle lace bra beneath. Her hair was blown out, and she looked like summer waiting to be kissed.

"Thanks for coming!" We hugged. "I love your hair."

"You're not looking at my hair."

"I also love your sandals," I said, turning to her friend. "And you're McKenzie."

"Hi, Casey." McKenzie gave me a hug. She was about Damaris's age, a reed-thin woman with very long, steel-colored hair. "Oh my God, your dog only has three legs. That's so adorable. Awww."

Jojo was barked at everyone, hopping around and nipping for a treat. I led the ladies out to meet the moms on the patio. "Are you okay with this?" I asked Damaris. "My mom is excited to see you again. Sorry in advance."

"Let's do it!" Damaris clapped her hands.

I signaled Josh, and he followed us out.

I had my outdoor speaker set up, streaming mellow indie rock. Suddenly I felt very weak, almost stoned, every detail of the scene taking on a glowing, terrifying significance. Every leaf on the aspens my dad had planted so long ago flickered like soft coins, and for a moment I could see him here, standing beside the grills, watching us. He wore his powder-blue corduroy OP shorts and a tee he had loved in the eighties, the one with an iron-on graphic of a sailboat. *Sailing Takes Me Away.* His skin was tan, his late-middle-aged legs bandy. When I looked into his eyes, he threw his head back in silent laughter.

Then he wasn't there.

Linda and Janey were sitting in the shade of the table umbrella. My mom had a chip in her mouth and looked up as if an alien species had arrived, which in many ways it had.

"Mom Linda, Mom Janey, this is Damaris, her son, Josh, and their friend McKenzie. Everyone, these are the moms, Linda and Janey."

"Well, hello, it's so nice to meet you all," Janey said, standing. Then to me, "Casey, I didn't know you had so many friends."

"He doesn't," Damaris said. "He paid us to show up and make him look good."

Linda got out of her chair and walked around the table. She peered intensely at Damaris, then McKenzie, then settled her gaze on Damaris's boobs.

"The one with the boobs," she said. "You're Damaris!"

"Jesus Christ, Mom."

Damaris stood hip to hip with Linda and threw an arm around her. "Hello, Mrs. Sweet. I remember your pork chops. They were divine. And your boobs are just as lovely as ever. What kind of bra are you packing these days? We gifted girls have to keep these puppies locked up."

Nothing could have pleased my mother more. "You're still

sassy," she said. "Just older. Why did you leave my baby for so long? He needed you. He's been an absolute wreck."

"We're working on that," Damaris said. "And I think he's done just fine without me. Now our job is to keep him on the righteous path."

I stood there and let them beat up on me. Josh seemed fascinated.

My mom was feeling herself now. "Oh, honey, he's just like his father. Just make sure he gets his weekly roll in the sack, and he'll do whatever you want."

Josh laughed. Damaris shot me a look.

"Would you like to meet my son?" Damaris asked. "Josh, introduce yourself."

Josh came forward and looked each mom in the eyes. "Hello, Mrs. Sweet and . . ."

"We're both Mrs. Sweet, but you can call me Janey. How old are you, Josh?"

"I'm twenty-two."

"He looks fourteen!" Linda exclaimed. "Why's he so small?" I knew we were one tiny step away from blowing the whole paternity thing out in the open.

"Don't be rude," I said, shooting daggers.

"It's my fault," Damaris cut in. "I'm only five three, and I never fed him right. He grew up on vegetables and saltines while his friends were eating cheeseburgers and soda."

My mom reacted as if this were true. "You poor baby. She's starving you to death."

"Josh can drive a golf ball three hundred fifty yards and walk seventy-two holes a day," I said. "He's fine."

Suddenly my mom stepped up and took Josh by the shoulders. She peered deep into his eyes. Josh just stood there, smiling uncomfortably. Damaris was wincing. Linda held his face. Then she leaned closer and sniffed. Sniffed his chest, his hair, his face. Her hand crept forward and began to gently caress his cheek.

"Mom? What are you doing?" I was about to drag her away.

Her eyes widened and she spoke softly. "I knew it. I just knew it. What a good boy."

Josh giggled nervously. My mom was gazing at him the way Bambi's mother looked upon her fawn. Her eyes turned glassy, and I was sure she was going to start bawling any second.

"You're a beautiful boy," she whispered. "A perfect *Sweet* boy." She threw her arms around Josh and held him tight. After a beat, Josh hugged her back. "We're here for you always. Don't be afraid. Casey is a good man, and he loves you so much."

The entire patio had gone silent. I was moved from embarrassment to shock to something like tender gratitude. Josh didn't seem fazed at all. In fact, he seemed to appreciate the moment. My mom could do that. She was so naked in her opinions and emotions, she could disarm anyone. Damaris was stunned.

"Thank you, ma'am," Josh said. "He's been really cool. He's been good to have by my side on the course and stuff. He helped me with my truck."

Linda released Josh and dabbed her eyes. She looked around at all of us and broke into a huge smile. "I love my family!" she cried. "I love you all so much!"

I maneuvered her back to her chair. "Okay, okay, easy. Let's just relax a bit, huh?"

"You didn't tell me he was so handsome!" she said. "He looks just like—"

"All right, who's hungry?" I called out. "Let's turn up the music and get that grill going."

People split into their own conversations. I went back inside to find Jamie bombing in with his cart cooler slung over his shoulder and Mellow Mike in tow.

"Doctor J in the house! Who needs some medicine!" He brandished—shocker—a huge bottle of Fireball. He pointed to me. "You stay away from this shit."

"I'll try."

"Nice pad, Pullout Boy," Mellow Mike said, wiggling a small prescription bottle. "Care for a lude? They're knockoffs but still make you want to put things in your butt."

"I'm cool, bro. Thanks for coming."

Jamie unloaded a platoon of frosted red shot glasses and lined them up on the island, spilling as he poured. Damaris and McKenzie came back in.

"Oh, for Pete's sake," Damaris said. "Gimme one of those."

The widows Sweet came in to see what all the fuss was about. "All right, you kids," Janey said. "You're not supposed to drink in Casey's house!"

Everyone looked guilty.

I waved her off. "It's fine. Everybody drink up, go on, I'm fine."

"Then I guess I could use a tipple," Janey said, and both moms joined in. Jamie topped everyone off. We ran out of shot glasses, and I passed around some little jelly glasses.

"Wait for me!" I turned to see my ex-wife, Blair. She was dressed in a tennis skort and an expensive lace top, her hair washed a new shade of blond, skin glowing.

"Carl couldn't make it," she said. "He's having a problem with his feet."

"What problem?" Josh asked.

Blair winced. "Ugh, he's got gout. It's really painful."

"Yo, that shit is no joke," Jamie added. "I had that when I was ten because my mom raised us on Twinkies and venison."

"Aw." Blair tilted her head in sympathy. "Carl might lose a toe, actually. The big one."

"I know a guy, we were in Iraq together, six toes blown off," Jamie said. Somehow, he already had his arm around Shyla. Like Morgan and Taylor, she was twenty-one or so. Jamie was thirty-eight. "We can save the toe. Or get him a new one. But you can totally get by without the big toe."

"What on earth is going on here?" I wiggled my finger at Jamie and Shyla.

"We just met yesterday," Shyla said. "On the course."

"We're in love," Jamie said.

I rolled my eyes. "Good for you."

My German neighbor, Klaus, sneaked in through the patio door, which meant he had somehow gotten through the fenced backyard like a rabbit. His long gray hair and beard were flowing, and he wore a pair of yellow nylon running shorts, knee-high tube socks, white New Balance sneakers from the seventies, and a Yoda T-shirt that said *May the 4th Be With You*.

May, July. Close enough.

"Everybody, this is my neighbor Klaus. He's got an awesome motorcycle, and he can drive anything with wheels."

Everyone said hi to Klaus. My mom watched him closely, and I knew she was hoping he would try to steal something. She didn't trust anyone with a foreign accent.

"Hello," Klaus said. My best translation of what he said next: "Nice to has you. Vhat are vee drinking, eh? A little of da herbal vines? In Germany vee know dis as da winter clover en *Alpenhütte*."

"Klaus!" Jamie poured Klaus a double shot. "Your family was in the Big One, right? Was your old man Third Reich?"

"*Mein Vater* join da resistance, not da SS."

"Fuck yeah, bro." Jamie slapped Klaus on the back.

So there they were. Aside from my coworkers and doctors, everyone I knew was standing in my kitchen. Most were people

I had met only in the past three months. It struck me then just how much had changed, how fast. I guess I got lost in thought for a minute.

"Casey?" my mom said. "You look tense. Do you need to poop?"

Everyone was waiting for the signal to do their shots. The whole kitchen smelled like a cinnamon toothpick dipped in gasoline. Blair watched me with concern. Damaris likewise. Josh was smiling until he realized something was off. Was this it again? Another panic attack? I felt chilled all over but hot in the face. My hair was heavy. The floor seemed to flex.

"Casey?" Damaris came to me. "What's up, babe?"

"I . . ." I couldn't finish a thought. "Everyone . . ."

"At ease, soldier," Jamie said.

"He's thinking about the drive he shanked on six yesterday," Vince said. A few people laughed uncomfortably.

Damaris leaned in until I felt her breath in my ear. "Be grateful," she whispered. "It's all happening for a reason."

I wondered if I was dying. I looked to Josh. He and his mom had the same eyes. Did I have the same eyes? What if I did? Did I want to? Did he get the mental stuff from me? Was he on the spectrum because of me? I had struggles. My dad had struggles, the OCD and anxiety turned hoarding. Was this all connected? I heard Damaris's voice again, *Be grateful*, and it was just an echo, but the echo snapped me out of it.

I looked around and smiled. "Sorry. I'm fine. Drink up!"

Relieved, everyone raised their shots.

"Wait!"

They paused, Fireball hovering under their noses.

"I just want to say, uh, thank you for coming. To my dad's house. My house." Janey nodded, glad I had corrected myself. "I know we don't all know each other that well. Yet. But we're friends.

I think we're friends. I hope we all get to be better friends. I . . . Sorry, I haven't had company in a while. Ever. I've lived here five years, and . . . it's been a different year. A very hard year back in winter. Then a very good year. And now one of my favorite summers. I wake up every day and I'm either golfing or thinking about golfing, and I'm usually doing something that involves at least one person in this room. And I guess it's kind of rowdy, as Josh would say. That something as silly as golf—"

"Golf ain't silly, bro," Jamie said. "Golf is life."

"Amen," Vince said.

"Hells yeah!" Josh said.

"But without the people, it's just a man in a field, walking around, beating a ball with a stick. I think, for the first time, I'm starting to understand why my dad loved it so much. It wasn't about his score. Some great shot. It was the people. Twin Peaks, the people who work there, the other guys, the people he walked the course with . . . I get it now. And I just wanted to say . . . you know, thank you for walking with me."

"Oh, Casey," the moms said. "Aw," the cart girls said.

Blair looked like she was seeing some guy she vaguely recognized but had never been married to. Like, *Who are these people who mean so much?*

I raised my can of grapefruit seltzer. "And summer ain't over yet! Let's GO!"

Everyone hooted and yowled and did their shots.

I chugged the rest of my seltzer.

Elmo

We ate. We drank. The dogs wore themselves out. We sat on the patio with the music and the torches and listened to the neighbors setting off fireworks. Klaus explained to Josh and the girls how to make a bomb out of a truck muffler. I worked the grill. At some point, Josh took over the music and fed us one of his golf playlists. The late afternoon filled with the eighties sounds Damaris had raised him on, which were also the sounds of our youth: Oingo Boingo, the English Beat, the Police, Duran Duran, Van Halen, Tears for Fears, INXS, A-ha.

By dusk, the older folks began to trickle out. The moms told me *this was so nice.* I walked them to their cars. Halfway there Linda gasped and yanked my arm. "I knew it! What's that old bastard stealing now?"

I turned to see Klaus digging in the garage. He was wrestling with something buried in the towering main pile, cursing in German.

"I told him he could take whatever he wanted," I said. "Settle down."

Klaus really put his back into it. Gritted his teeth. I grew afraid for him as the tendons of his neck started to flex like a cobra hood. He was committed, giving it hell, and the huge pile of goods swayed with a single tremor, a mountain losing its grip. And then we saw the handle move, the first glimmers. Like young Arthur pulling Excalibur from the stone, Klaus freed the mighty polesaw and held it up in triumphant awe.

"Mein Gott! Sie ist wunderschön anzusehen!"

He turned and looked at us with a proud smile. I think there were tears in his eyes.

"Look at that," Janey said with a twinkle of admiration. "He's strong as a badger."

I applauded. "She's all yours, Klaus. You earned it."

I was busing dishes when Damaris's friend McKenzie cornered me at the kitchen sink. We hadn't spoken much, and I asked her if she was having a good time. She sounded a little oiled up. Not drunk but enjoying her wine.

"It's lovely. Can I help with the dishes?"

"I'm just fussing around. How did you and Damaris meet again?"

"Josh and my son had soccer together when they were little," she said. "My Nevin worships him. I tried to get him into golf, but I think Josh's game intimidates him."

"Josh's game intimidates everybody."

"But not you," McKenzie countered. "You play with him all the time."

"More lately."

"Does he talk about leaving? Damaris is convinced he's going to leave town soon."

I wiped the counters. "It's come up. If he wants to give it a serious go, now's the time."

"You think he's that good?"

"Absolutely."

"But do you think he can handle it?" McKenzie moved closer. "Emotionally?"

I leaned against the island and nibbled on a leftover brat. "I guess that's the big question for all these guys. Josh is hard to read. He's unlike any young man I've ever met. She thinks I'm trying to push him away, right?"

"She doesn't blame you. But she is scared." McKenzie seized me by the forearm. "Not of being alone. She wants Josh to live his own life. She's been preparing for that."

"That's good," I said. "For both of them."

"She's worried what will happen to him if he loses his way."

"He's a good kid. He makes smart decisions."

"Of course. What I mean is, she's worried he won't be able to handle failure."

"Maybe he won't fail," I said.

McKenzie cocked her head like I was being dense. "But what will it do to him if he finds out he's not one in a million?"

"I think he's in it for the right reasons," I said, feeling defensive. "And honestly, who plans to fail? The only way you learn to cope with failure is by failing, then picking yourself back up again. Trust me, I know."

She must have sensed I was getting annoyed and changed the subject. "She's crazy about you, you know that, right?"

"I don't know that."

McKenzie set her wineglass down and crossed her arms. "She won't admit this, but the reason she's afraid of this whole thing is because she really likes you. Josh really likes you. She really respects what you're trying to do."

"What am I trying to do?"

"Um, the right thing? Be a better person?"

"Whoa, whoa, let's not get carried away."

"Cutting off the alcohol. Trying to make amends. Confessing all your worst shit. You're on the quest, my friend."

"Like a vision quest?"

"Was that a movie?"

"One of the best."

"The one with the women in the desert?"

"No. From the eighties. Matthew Modine, Linda Fiorentino," I said. "He's a high school wrestler. Based on the novel. An absolute classic."

"Oh, that was good. Madonna, right?"

"Right." Then it dawned on me. "Holy shit, that's it. He's not Rocky. Josh is Louden Swain. He's the one on a vision quest, not me. We're all just the bit players around him, and he's showing us the way. Damn, I forgot how great that movie is. Josh needs to see that one."

McKenzie wasn't getting my point. "So what does that make you, his coach?"

"Elmo," I said. "Remember the hotel cook? The down-and-out sage. Missed his shot at glory. But he comes through in the final moments. Louden is thinking about quitting, abandoning his big match, but Elmo won't let him."

Behind McKenzie, standing in the door to the backyard, was Josh. He was staring at us with a curious look. How long had he been there? I opened my mouth to say something, but he ducked back outside.

McKenzie resumed. "Okay, Elmo. Damaris doesn't date. And she doesn't screw around. She's got life-and-death shit on her mind, like, daily. You see what I'm getting at?"

"Maybe."

"She's afraid of letting you down, hurting Josh, letting herself down."

"Hey," I said. "People don't let *me* down. *I* let people down."

McKenzie laughed. "They both need you, in my opinion. Not like a lonely woman needs a man or a lost boy needs a father. More like you can't keep going along two against the world. Two's not enough anymore. They need a good third."

"I want to be the best late-addition third ever," I said. "Or best whatever they want me to be."

McKenzie smiled and hugged me. "I like your odds. Let me know if I can help."

"Thank you."

McKenzie pulled on her sweatshirt and let herself out. Just then Vince and Rita walked in and set their glasses down. Vince gave me the mob-guy hug / back clap. "Great party, mano. We need to get home to the dogs. But thanks for having us."

"Are you okay?" Rita hugged me. "That looked a little intense."

"I'm good. Thank you for coming, Rita, and for letting Vince get out with me."

"Stay focused," Vince said, punching my shoulder. "One swing at a time."

Blair came in next. Having her in my house felt odd. She hadn't been here since I first bought it. She'd tried to give me a million ideas on the decor, how she would have done it, unable to see that this one was going to be me all the way.

"Hey!" I backed into the kitchen again. "Sorry to leave you stranded out there."

"The host is in high demand," Blair said. She looked good. She took care of herself and maybe had put in a little extra effort for the occasion.

"Did you find someone to talk to? Meet everybody?"

"I still remember how to socialize." She eyed me with amusement. "I'm heading back to Denver while traffic is light. But thanks for inviting me. It was a nice gathering."

"Yeah? I'm glad you think so."

"Feels like a good crew for you." Blair washed her wineglass in the sink and set it on the drying rack. "Damaris is lovely."

"Did you two get to talk?" I was unsure how I felt about that.

"She told me about growing up here, moving back to Ohio, all her phases. She's had an interesting life. Mine seems boring now."

"Nah, just more sensible. You've always called your shots and made them come true."

"She's not who I would have imagined for you. But I can see it."

"Why do you say that?"

"Hard to put a finger on. She's a little edgy. She could be comfortable in places I wouldn't. She's got that tough-chick piece still in her, and she seems very in touch with herself."

"I can't tell if you're being cool or judgy," I said.

Blair looked wounded. "God, you really think I'm kind of shitty, don't you? The shallow suburban wifey. I'm sorry I managed to leave that as your primary impression."

"No, I'm sorry, I don't know what to expect when your ex-wife meets your new . . . whatever."

"My opinion doesn't matter anymore," Blair said. "You said so. And you were right. It really doesn't. But for what it's worth, I think she's great."

"Thank you."

"And Josh is brilliant," Blair said. "He's sweet and incredibly intelligent. He's got something special in him." Blair eyed me up and down, almost like she was flirting. "I recognized you in him."

"You did?"

"He's like you when we first met. You were on fire back then. But it was all inside, like it is with Josh. He's going to do something big, I think. Did he get that from you?"

I scoffed. "I haven't done anything big. Ever."

"You still have time."

"Maybe."

Blair's eyes filled up, and she stepped into my arms. Squeezing me like she would never see me again. She stepped back and held my hands.

"I love you, Casey. I want you to be so happy. I promise you, I want that. And I don't care what it looks like, who it's with. I just want you to be you and have everything you deserve. I wish I had done better."

"You were more than I deserved," I said.

Blair took a deep breath, holding back her emotions. "I wish I could have been the one who helped you get where you wanted to go. I was too focused on my own things."

"Hey, stop that. You lifted me up. You tried. The rest was on me. And we did okay. We figured it out. Maybe we're right where we're supposed to be."

Blair dabbed one eye. "Carl is a very good man. He's stable. But there's only one Casey Sweet. Stay sweet, okay, baby? Promise?"

Goddamn, woman. She was going to make me cry too. "I love you, Blair. I was lucky to have you while I did."

"I love you." She dabbed her eyes and kissed me on the cheek. "Still friends?"

"Always."

I watched her walk to her car, and there seemed to be something lonely in her gait. Carl. That marsupial bastard had better not let her down. That was the whole point of the Carls of the world. To do the shit the first husband couldn't. Be the rock. Be solid. Let the moss grow.

Now I needed to do that for a different woman. I was ready. Was she?

fireworks

As dark fell, the last of us settled out back around the Solo stove, waiting for the city fireworks to begin. It was down to Damaris, Josh, Morgan, and me. Josh and Morgan were public-display snuggling. I set my hands on Damaris's shoulders and leaned over her.

"Can I get you anything? Blanket? Another drink?"

"Thank you. I'm good." She pulled a camp chair beside her. "Here. Sit."

She was watching the sky like a child. She was layers, depths, the girl I used to have so much fun with going to concerts, staying up late watching movies, young and free. I could see that girl, now distilled and intensified in ways that made the idea of aging into herself a compliment. Blair was packaged with care, delicate, ornate. Damaris was a black Camaro with smoking tires, a few dents on the grille, and an engine that burned hot and loud. Smart, fun, serious, raw, emotional, passionate, high-octane sexual, and real. I wanted her to be mine, and if somehow this all fell apart, I was going to hang it up for the rest of my life. This was it for me. Tiger in 2019. My last run at a major.

Josh was telling a story about some crypto or gaming friends he knew online, guys who lived in Korea and Vancouver, how they all came together for these scheduled raids, and while I didn't understand any of it, I saw that he was talking about it the way my friends and I used to recall our most epic Saturday nights. Morgan was staring at him with that combination of adoration and complete engagement only girls and young women give so naturally, and which older women learn to protect because too many shitheads take advantage of it. I hoped Josh appreciated her for it, understood somehow it would not always be like this, and in turn treated her like the utter gift she was, that all women—

"I think I'll stay here tonight," Damaris said. "I don't feel like driving home."

I laughed.

"That's funny?"

I kissed her forehead. "I've missed you."

"Well, I'm getting tired, and you have a better view to the fireworks than we do."

"Yeah, okay, babe."

"Behave." Damaris stared into the fire. "I'm sorry I haven't been very available."

"It's okay. You haven't been feeling a hundred percent."

"I never feel a hundred percent. But I'm fine. I've just been thinking about things."

"I get that. And what do you think about things?"

"I think thinking about things is more tiring than doing the things you're thinking about."

"Makes total sense," I said.

"It's too bad we don't have some marshmallows. This fire."

I went inside and got the bag of marshmallows, graham crackers, chocolate bars, and skewers. I came back out. "Who wants s'mores?"

"What are s'mores?" Morgan asked.

"Is she joking?" I asked Josh.

"She wasn't allowed to have sugar growing up."

I passed out the sticks and handed the marshmallows to Damaris. "Show the kids how it's done."

I burned three marshmallows before Damaris would eat one. We got chocolate all over our fingers and clothes. Josh just started stuffing his face with uncooked marshmallows. Morgan and Damaris had a contest to see how many layers they could fit together and still take a bite.

"Hey, Josh," I said. "You tell your mom about your next move?"

"This tournament?" Damaris said.

"It's a match," Josh said. "An exhibition."

"It sounds like a setup," Damaris said. "One week's notice? Please."

"It'll be fun," Josh said. "Even when I lose."

I didn't like this. "Hey—who says you're gonna lose?"

"I read up on this dude, El Guapo. He's a bad, bad man. He could beat half the Tour guys tomorrow."

"Can someone please explain this to me," Morgan said. "What is it with you guys and golf? It's like nothing else exists. Why do you, like, obsess over something so hard? I tried it like twice, and I hated it. It's so . . ."

"Dumb?" Josh asked.

"It's not dumb, it's torture!"

"Smart girl," I said.

"Tell them, Joshie," Damaris said. "Tell them why. From the beginning."

Josh turned sheepish. "Eh, it's complicated."

"Come on," I said. "I want to hear this."

"It's really beautiful," Damaris said. "Go on, honey. Tell it. We need a campfire story."

Josh knew when he was cornered. He sat up and summoned something in himself.

"Golf is not a sport. It's not a hobby. It's not a pastime or a tradition. It may be those things for most people. Not for me. When my mom first started leaving me out there at Twin, I was seven years old, and I couldn't talk. Maybe a few words to her, but around everyone else I was mute. Not only could I not find the words, I had no idea what I was even trying to express. My mom thought I was autistic, and maybe I was. Maybe I am. So we went to all the doctors, speech therapists and regular therapists. Teachers, play dates with other kids with similar problems. Nothing helped. So my mom and my uncle, Coach Lowry, decided to leave me out there every day. Mom was always working. I couldn't handle school. We couldn't afford a babysitter. So Twin was like my day care. Coach didn't try to teach me anything at first. He just handed me some clubs and pointed to the other golfers and said, 'Watch, learn, play.' So that's what I did.

"Putting at first. Then chipping. Then the driving range. I was too afraid to go on the fairways. They seemed so long. But I wanted to play so bad I could taste the grass. I started sneaking around when no one else was there. Half a hole here, another hole there. At first it was just a big playground, a place to wander around. The second year, I started to play with the clubs. I was awful, but I didn't care. I was lost in the best way. Soon I was playing five or six holes every day, then nine, then eighteen. Thirty-six. When I started running into people, I'd just wave and play around them, or sometimes I'd hang with them for a few holes. When I was old enough to ride my bike there by myself, sometimes I'd play the course backward starting at four a.m., then front to back, whatever. I made up my own games, different challenges, and I was always trying new things.

"When I looked at the golf course back then, I didn't see

eighteen holes. Fairways, greens, flags. I saw geometry, tunnels of reality, different planes of earth. I saw golf in six dimensions and emotions like paintings of the sea, like galaxies inside me and all around me. Elementary particles. Consciousness. More I can't explain, even now. Probably I made it all up in my head, but after about a year, I was playing in parallel realities, I saw forests inside a corner of rough, one bunker became like the planet Dune, and the ponds were oceans, the geese my Viking longships. I chased down monster dragons. I fought marauding gangs to save the princess. I stormed castles and captured the flag. I played at night, at dawn, in the blue twilight, until I could nearly play this course blind. Coach saw the shots I could make as I rode into battle. He gave me more clubs. He told me the history of the staggies, which is what I called the clubs. He showed me the old books with the old Scottish names. Mashies. Niblicks. Spoons. Brassies. They sounded like a magician's tools. And somewhere along the way, I started talking. I would tell my mom about what I saw, the places I traveled, the things I learned to make the ball do. Then I started telling Coach, and he never made a joke of it; he just listened, and when he had something to add to it, he would give me a tip or two. Small things. Like, 'Use your palms to throw the ball when pitching. Think of the club as a sword; raise it high above your head to salute the gods on every shot. The ball is like gold, the rarest pearl on earth. Protect it. Respect this land, the grass; it is your birthright. Protect your flank. Always charge from the low side. Trickery is nothing without a keen strategy.'

"By the time I was ten, that was my handicap. By the time I was thirteen, I was a four. When I was seventeen, I shot a fifty-eight out there, but I was alone, so it didn't really count. Except I knew what I did. I explained it to Coach. He made me draw it up, every shot of my round, and then he believed me. He began to spy on me, because I was still fragile and he didn't want to break the spell. Anyway, golf made me a functional kid when nothing else would. It was the land, the sun, the sky, the motion of objects, the mental gymnastics, learning to listen to my body, feeling frequencies in my swing, the weather, the Lords and Barons . . ."

Josh paused like he had lost his train of thought, but I sensed he could keep talking this way until sunrise.

"None of that makes sense, I know. It sounds like mystical bullshit, and maybe it is. But I came to believe that my way of approaching the game was utterly unique, mine alone, and that if I followed it, I could use golf to go places no one else has been. I'd take a lesson with Coach now and then, and still do, but usually we just talk about what I'm seeing. The color of the sky, the winds. We'll play a few holes together, and he might offer one or two small comments. Like, 'Try moving your thumb over here.' Or 'Your back looks stiff today; move closer to the ball.' Or 'Look at the green—see how the grass is leaning this way? Roll 'em careful today.' But most of it is the way I taught myself, and Coach says if we mess with that too much now, the whole house of cards might fall down. So for me it's about what's humanly possible. I don't mean making money, winning events on the Tour, celebrity crap, any of that. I mean that golf can take me out of this world. I don't play to have fun. I play to feel something I cannot feel any other way, and see the world, other worlds, in ways that make sense. I play because I believe hidden inside this game there's something only deep practitioners of unnamed religions have glimpsed, and it is every bit what people mean or hope for when they talk about heaven, paradise in the ancient sense. A place only a few souls can find, and only after a long journey of penance. I've glimpsed it. It's more terrible than any drug, and more beautiful than money or anything we can touch. It's real. It's my great passion. And I want more of it. That's all. That's it. *That's* golf."

I realized I had goose bumps. Not because I felt the same thing or even truly understood what he meant, but because I could see that Josh *believed* it, believed it in his soul. He had lived in this ethereal place and built a kingdom of it. It explained so much about him, why he often played alone, why he protected it, and why his mother was afraid of what would happen if he were to try and carry it elsewhere, to the Tour, and it all fell apart.

"That's the most perfect thing I've ever heard," Morgan said, and kissed him. "You're my Beastmaster."

Damaris covered her mouth and looked away as if everything about her son, the beautiful and terrifying, was dawning on her all over again.

"That's really something, Josh," I said. "I don't think I will ever look at a golf course the same way again."

He sighed. "Better than being in a mental hospital."

"Golf has been healing me too," I said. "I feel focused. Awake. When I don't play for a couple of days now, I feel crabby, lost."

Josh nodded. "You're finding it. I can tell."

We smiled at each other, sharing our own Bodhi–Johnny Utah moment.

"Now we need to get this whole thing outfitted appropriately," I said. "I'm taking you shopping tomorrow. No argument. I'll pick you up at ten."

"Cool."

The fireworks started. We repositioned our chairs to watch as they went off over Fox Hills Country Club, less than a mile away from my backyard. Not a bad display overall, but definitely not as impressive as anything in Denver or at the university in

Boulder. After a few minutes, Damaris stood and tapped me on the shoulder.

"Time to go up."

"What about the grand finale?"

"I'll give you a grand finale. But you better hurry."

I popped out of my chair. "Good night, kids!"

"Good night?" Josh looked confused. Morgan got it and elbowed him in the ribs.

"Stay as late as you want," I said. "Or feel free to crash in the spare room downstairs."

"I guess we'll bounce," he said.

His mother was already inside, climbing the stairs. I realized I had forgotten to take one of my new Cialis. Shit. Maybe I could pop one as I brushed my teeth. Chew it up and hope it kicked in fast. I walked Josh and Morgan to the door, then went in search of my grand finale.

links frolic

Summer
Youth
Fireworks
The girl
The one who got away
And came back on wings of fate
Power fading back to the fairway
Scents of bug spray and honeysuckle in her skin
My hands peeling her clothes down slow
Down on my knees
Her little feet, tiny pearl toes
I hold her shaking hands, kiss her thighs
She starts to shudder, pressing my nose to her hips
Second cut around a manicured green
She turns to the bed and falls back
Be careful, she says, voice soft, voice heavy
Warning me because what's coming next is a force
The full Damaris
Lets me kiss everything

Glimmers of morning dew
Where I kissed before
Rolls me onto my back and sits atop
Upgrading my graphite shaft to ultrastiff flex
Areolas dimpled like Titleists
She slides down, notch by notch, until the flagstick
    is planted
The window glows pink, orange, blue, purple with fire
She is small in form, dense with energy
Soft cover demanding hard compression
Years and years have led to this
I'm going to fuck you so bad, she says
Fuck you until you forget your ex-wife's name
I believe you, I say, I want you to
You can't handle me
Yes, I can
Give me your worst
Uuuuggghhh, she groans, slides off, takes me into
    her mouth
Fitting me with new grips
Until I start to quake
She stops, backspin checking up
I'm stranded below, climax delayed, spilling weakly
Oh, good boy, she says
Fuck, I say, come on
She laughs, crawls up, and straddles my face
I lap at the collar, trace the green, finding the sweet spot
Wet from her navel to her thighs
She coaches my technique
Guides me to the back nine
Together we roll and I escape, reversing like Louden
Her hands on my headboard, grabbing rails

I climb, take her hips
Practice swings, club head testing the rough
I need it, she says
Stop teasing, fuck me
I visualize the shot shape
She stifles a moan as I move inside,
        time-lapse motion
Each millimeter a tight band of friction
I stop, wait
FUCK, she yells
I fall into her, fall in and out, fall deeper, harder,
        softer, longer
She comes
Slow but don't stop, breathe, keep swinging
It becomes an angry range session
Pounding balls, a whole bucket
She comes again
I am in the burn, sweating pure fuel, tireless
My back strong as Tiger's when he donned his first
        green jacket
Sweet, climbing the leaderboard
I hold her thick brown hair in a knot, she arches back
Takes my fingers in her mouth
We are upright in balance
She laughs, driving against me, trying to knock
        me down
We roll, I taste her skin, the bedroom sweltering
I am dying, I am reborn, dying, reborn
Inside her again, slow, careful approach
The crowd hushed
Her face streaked with tears
I love you, I say

She shakes her head no
I love you, I'm sorry but it's true
You can't
I do, I am loving you
She clutches, scratches me, bites my arm, kisses
    my hand
You can't, she says, I'm sick
I love you, I say
You don't know how bad it gets, she says
I can take it, I say, I want it all
She shakes her head
Never get rid of me, I say
Never again
I'm sorry, she says, I'm so sorry I left
She pulls me down, kissing my face, my neck
I was so in love with you, she says, did you know
Stupid scared young fucking idiot my mom dead I
    wanted to die
I know, I say, you had to
You left me, I say, but it never went away
He could only come from love, she says
I always knew it was love or else he wouldn't have
    come to me, she says
You gave me the most beautiful thing in my life
We are in something beyond sex now
I'm fucking terrified, soaring
I wish I could have been there, I say
For all of it
But you're here now, she says
Yes
Promise?
Yes

Promise?

Yes

It's good, right, she asks, we're good

So good, so good

I'll fucking kill you if you try to leave, she says

Fucking kill you, Casey

I'll never leave

You won't let me

Oh God, oh God, yes

I move faster and she comes

One drive after another, bombing over the hazards

I slow, draw it out, until we're still

Stroking me into herself, rubbing herself

Starts to quiver, animal noises

Focus on the cords, tendons flexing from her center
      to her thighs

I can't stop this time

I go and go and go

Damaris, I say, Damaris, Damaris

The gallery roars

Yes, yes, yes

Her energy compresses around me

Every sensation funnels to our center

We levitate

One more pure swing

She bites my shoulder and I release

Waves upon waves, pulsing in a tide

Like a man who hasn't played in twenty years

An escaped convict loosed upon Cypress Point

I howl as the ball rolls up, around the world, and
      spills into the cup

My heart is going to explode

Oh, baby, she says, and pulls me down to the bottom
    of the sea
Oh, baby, she says, so good, so good, all mine
I go blind, hover on the edge of blackness, orange
    stars, blood pumping
She holds me, smothers me
Her hair is soaked as a woman just out of the shower
We wallow in it
Jesus fucking Christ, she says
What's the matter with you, she says
What's the matter with you, I say
We laugh
We hold it as long as we can
The night is silence summer hot skin
Cool fairways freshly mown
Windless flags at rest
In the blue dawn
Staring into each other over a pillow
Everything that once was
Is no more
We have made the turn
We're heading for home

part five
the rowdy

fitting

When I picked Josh up at ten, I was running on three hours of sleep, and he looked almost as tired as I felt. He walked Morgan to her car, and they kissed goodbye. I briefly wondered if Damaris allowed her to sleep over, but of course she did. The boy was not really a boy anymore.

"Morning," he said, hopping into the Audi.

"Morning. You guys have a fun night?"

Josh gave me a weird look.

"Right," I said. "Let's focus on golf."

"Yeah."

"You hungry?"

"Not yet."

"We'll do lunch down by the PGA store."

"Where's that?"

"South Denver. Buckle up."

It was strange and incredibly fun for me to take the kid shopping. Like back to school but for golf. Even though he had his own money, much more than I did, we reached an understanding that today was on me.

"This store," I said, gesturing like a game show host, "is yours. Whatever you want."

"I just need a shirt and some shoes."

"You're really gonna play with your bag of lost and found clubs?" I asked. "Because now's the time, if you want some new wedges, irons, a new driver, the whole bag. I'm serious. You have a few days to adjust to new equipment."

"You think I can't beat him with my old shitty bag," Josh said. "Right?"

"I think you know better than anyone else. And I think you could, maybe, benefit from any and every possible advantage."

He stared at me for a moment, then went off to the shoe section, where he chose a pair of black Nike Air somethings that looked like the same black Nike Air somethings I used to wear in tenth grade, only these were golf shoes. He tried them on, walked over to a bay, grabbed a club, took a big swing.

"Jesus," he said, looking at his feet. "They're glued to the turf."

"Yeah, your bare feet don't have spikes, unless you managed to grow some. They fit? Not too tight?"

"These'll work."

"Polos," I said.

We browsed the clothing racks. I picked up a couple of Adidas polos for myself, and the next time I saw him, Josh's arms were full. He had eight or nine polos, six shorts, two pants, and a couple of sharp quarter zips.

"What balls do you play?" I asked.

"Bridgestone," he said. "But I have hundreds."

"You can't play with found balls, my man."

"I have almost a thousand still new in the box."

I found a Bridgestone lid and snugged it over his brow. With his long hair, unshaven lip, and diminutive size, he looked like

Rickie Fowler's little brother. We left the clothes at the front counter and headed back to the clubs.

One of the fitters came over and watched Josh wiggle some irons. "I'm Tim," he said. "I can get you a bay if you want to hit anything. Are you familiar with the new Callaways?"

Josh turned to him and smiled. "Thanks, Tim. Can you get me a bay and put a bucket of balls in there—and not those dud brick range balls, a bucket of tour balls. I'm not worried about all the stats and metrics. I can tell what will work."

Tim seemed a little taken aback.

"He came out of the womb with a gap wedge between his teeth," I said. "Thanks, Tim."

Tim went off to set up a bay.

Josh chose three eight irons, one of each from a set of Callaway, Ping, and Mizuno blades.

"Why the eight?"

"It's my favorite club. And that's the bridge where the manufacturers really start to play silly games."

I had no clue what he meant. He hit four balls with the Callaway before handing it over to me. I handed it to Tim.

"Wow," Tim said. "That's some swing."

"Better believe it," I said, full of dad pride.

Josh hit two balls with the Ping, handed it to me.

He took the Mizuno and studied the forged head, smoothing the contoured back with his fingers. His eyes seemed to glow. He set up, hit a ball, and held his finish pose for a few seconds. Nodded at something. Hit another. Held the pose. He glanced at me with a smile.

"Good?"

Josh turned to Tim. "Could you bring us the four through pitching wedge, please?"

Tim hurried off. When he returned, he said, "We can try

any shaft you want with those. Or do a mixed set. Mizuno has one of the best customizing programs in the industry."

Josh hit one ball, and one ball only, with each club, working his way through the four, five, six, seven, eight, nine, and P.

"The shaft that's two steps stiffer than these," he said. "Could you put that shaft in the eight, please?"

Tim hurried around, mounted the clubhead, handed it to Josh. Josh hit a few more balls while Tim stood behind his little podium and played with his computer. Josh's shot tracers were so boring you could be forgiven for not knowing what you were seeing. Like a machine drawing one line on top of another. He stopped after about ten balls.

"Can you show me the dispersion all at once?" Josh asked.

Tim pressed a few buttons. The dartboard came up. Almost every shot was stuck in a circle the size of a Hula-Hoop around the flag. I noted the distance. One hundred seventy-four yards.

"You're quite the golfer," Tim said. "How long have you been playing?"

"Awhile." Josh smiled. "We're good. Sold. I'll take the Mizunos, four through P with these shafts."

"Outstanding," Tim said. "I can place the order right away. Mizuno is running about four to six weeks, but some of our customers have been getting theirs as soon as three."

"You don't build them here?" Josh said.

"We keep the common sets in stock, but with a custom shaft we order everything from the factory. The nice thing is you get our warranty as well as theirs."

Josh turned to me in distress. "In four to six weeks, I'll be dead. I mean, why are we even bothering—"

I put a hand up to calm him. I turned to Tim. "Say, Tim. I realize this is an unusual request, but Josh has a really big match this Saturday. Is there anything we can possibly do?"

Tim cleared his throat. "No, sorry, we don't build the clubs here, sir."

"I understand that, but you repair them, right?"

"Sometimes."

"So I'm guessing you have a guy, someone here who knows how to do this. Maybe it's a little off the corporate script, but hey, let's have some fun. This is a huge opportunity for Josh. I am willing to pay for the time. Whatever it takes."

Tim's mouth creased. "Yes, well, we do have a gentleman who can do things like that. Not for customers, but on his own time. Unfortunately, Buddy is off today. But he'll be back Thursday. Even then, I don't think—"

"This is the PGA store!" Josh blurted. "The sign out front says 'PGA.'"

Tim glanced at me nervously.

"The match he's playing is against a PGA Tour member," I said. "How about this. Could we maybe call this Buddy and see if there's any chance he could come in today for this very special situation? We're going to be making a sizable purchase here, not just the irons but at least two putters, a pile of clothes, and a bag. Can we try to work something out?"

Josh's eyes were boring a hole into Tim's forehead. Tim looked lost.

I put on my best smile. "How about this, Tim. You have Buddy's phone number?"

"Uh, his personal number?"

Josh interrupted. "The number where Buddy can be reached right now."

"We don't, uh, I'm sorry, but—"

Josh removed a roll of hundred-dollar bills from his shorts and peeled one off and shoved it at Tim. "We need Buddy's number. Come on, dude."

I eased Josh back. "Please help us here," I said to Tim. "Blame it on me. Tell him I'm forcing you to call."

Tim cackled nervously and dialed. "Buddy, it's Tim down at the store. Yes, I know. How are they biting today? Hmm. Shame. So I have a customer here who wants to speak with you. Yes, he's serious." He handed me the phone.

"Hi, Buddy, this is Casey Sweet. I'm sorry to bother you on your day off. No, I'm nobody important, but my boy here is playing in his first PGA match this week, and he just fell in love with these clubs your excellent fitter introduced us to. Problem is, we can't afford to wait a week, let alone six. I was wondering if you could come down here today, as soon as possible, and build this young man's set. If you could do that, I'd be happy to put five hundred—call it a thousand dollars cash into your wallet. What do you say, Buddy? Can you help me get this young man off to a great start?"

A rough older voice said, "You shittin' me? A thousand bucks?"

"Not shittin'. Yes, one thousand."

"You better have cash in hand. Let me talk to Tim."

I handed Tim his phone. "We'll be back after lunch."

I hit the ATM, and we ate Vietnamese at a strip mall a mile away.

"Think Buddy will come through?" Josh asked.

"How much does a retail golf guy make, you think? Twenty an hour?"

"Maybe more. Thirty?"

"But money isn't everything," I said. "I learned that in sales. Being nice carries weight."

Josh nodded. "Sorry, I'm just nervous."

"I get it. I am too. And Buddy will deliver." I shoved a Saigon roll into my mouth.

When we got back to the store, Tim spotted us and hurried to the back room, then returned with a stooped old man dressed in jeans and a tattered flannel shirt, even though it was ninety-four degrees outside. He must have been seventy, but he looked ninety, with hands like red crab claws. He was carrying the newly assembled irons, all banded together.

"Buddy!" I said. "You are the hero of the day."

Buddy glanced at me, then Josh. "That epoxy needs to set overnight at least. Three days would be better."

"Understood," I said.

Buddy wasn't finished. "Those shafts are designed for swing speeds above one hundred ten miles per hour. They are tour-grade, extra-stiff, high-density composite graphite and run four hundred sixty apiece."

"Awesome," Josh said, and began peeling bills from his roll.

"Josh, we agreed." I pushed him out of the way. "Take everything up front."

Buddy licked his lips as I counted off ten hundreds, then added two more, and handed it over.

"Thanks again for your help. Sorry to bother you on your day off."

Buddy folded the bills into the chest pocket of his flannel. "Best of luck to you and the squirt over there," he said, and walked back out of the store.

When it was all said and done, we needed two shopping carts. In addition to the clubs and clothes, Josh had chosen two Scotty Cameron putters, extra grips, two more pairs of shoes, and all the tees, tools, gloves, magnetic towels, and other accessories you could possibly use on a golf course. We topped it off with a new limited-edition Vessel Lux bag in solid black. It retailed for $1,199 and looked like an assassin's carryall. The total came to $7,922.

"Are you sure, man?" Josh asked. "I might have gotten a little carried away."

Tim was grinning, waiting for my response.

"Goddamn kids these days," I said. "Spoiled beyond belief."

As we loaded everything into the car, Josh removed the eight from the box and held it to his chest. He was beaming at me.

"You gonna sleep with those tonight?"

He stepped forward and threw his arms around me. "Thanks, Casey."

"You're welcome."

It was a fine ride home.

practice round

The next day Vince met us at TPC Fort Collins for the kid's nine a.m. tee time. Josh was dressed in some of the new clothes, the new shoes, with his whole new bag. He'd kept his beloved old driver and wedges. The driver was a twelve-year-old Tay-lorMade with a white head that looked like a stale egg, but I wasn't going to argue with him. He only carried two wedges, a fifty-three and a fifty-eight, both Ben Hogan from a time when the actual Ben Hogan still oversaw the design and manufactur-ing of the clubs with his name on them. They looked like rusted junk, but he regrooved them every season and told me he knew them better than his own hands.

Vince and I hung back in a cart as Josh walked, playing three balls on each hole, trying out various shots. He had a new green book, a blank slate, and was taking notes as he went along.

Vince and I talked about my upcoming return to work. I needed to give Dave an answer soon, and we discussed the pros and cons. I talked about the "three things" he had given me, my pastimes that he had turned into business plans. He was kind of a genius at proof-testing ideas. The pastimes I'd shared with him were mowing lawns for extra cash, working on my bike in the garage, and writing short stories. In return, he'd given me detailed plans for viable businesses, each with a unique twist.

An eco-friendly community mowing co-op with profit sharing for every worker.

A retail store that sold and repaired bikes, plus a coffee café, with a nonprofit arm that did cycle-safety programs with the local school districts.

And for the writing path, he noted that this wasn't a viable business but a dream career in the arts and as such required extreme commitment to match the extreme risk. He suggested I take a year off, commit to writing my long-gestated novel as well as a feature-length screenplay and a pilot for a TV adaptation of the story. He provided a list of agents and producers, along with a boot camp timeline for delivering the work. His final note on this was to give it hell for the year, then get a position teaching writing as an adjunct while shopping the story for two years, after which time, if I had not sold any of the rights or earned a staff writer position in film and TV, let the dream go and never look back again.

All excellent ideas, with realistic outlooks. But I didn't want to do any of those.

"I have an idea for a golf app," I told him.

"There's a ton of those already in the market."

"I know. But I can't find one that does what I would like a golf app to do. And the best part is, I think it would be super simple to build. I could write the prototype myself and build out the wires in a few weeks. That's what I used to do at Flagstaff, design and write apps."

Vince stroked his goatee. "I might like to hear more."

I told him about it between Josh's shots. The thing I had in mind did everything every other golf app did—yardages, distances, scoring, a social component, tee times, deals.

"But here's my differentiator," I said. "I'm going to build in an entire, holistic health component. Not just your daily steps but stretching routines, exercises, workouts, practice recommendations based on your game, age, skill level, body type. And a mental health piece. Motivationals. Hours of daylight. Alerts for encouragement. Alcohol reminders, calories, ride shares. And psychological coaching tips, like my doctors have been giving me, but all golf related. I want people to know how much golf can do for their well-being, the whole lifestyle. We partner with sports shrinks, nutritionists, real experts. Eventually we bring in the pros and their team recommendations. Wanna do the same warm-up regimen as Rory? We got that. Wanna know what Koepka has for breakfast before a big round? We got that. Learn how Jon Rahm tamed his temper in five easy—"

"I got it," Vince said. "Do you have a name yet?"

"Swing Life. Or Life Swing. I'm not set on it yet, but something—"

"Sounds like an app where you find someone to fuck your wife. And you need to focus on one main thing first, not everything from the jump. Go with the health angle but pare it down for the beta and one point oh. You want to go into the pitch with one simple hook, a few others in your back pocket."

"Right, totally, but you think there's something there?"

"I'll chew on it."

He wasn't excited, but he hadn't dismissed it. I was encouraged. But with every hole, I grew more unsettled. Josh had played seven holes and looked all out of sorts. Vince noticed. "Is this really a loose practice round, or is he not playing well today?"

"He's got to work through the new sticks, get the feel and

yardages down. And he's trying to absorb this new course in six dimensions."

"What's that?" Vince asked. "Some new term you picked up in *Golf Digest*?"

"Josh's way of seeing the game. He explained it to me, and I still don't get it. He's like Rain Man counting cards, but with golf. He sees patterns, alternate realities, wormholes, dragons."

"Okay then."

But it wasn't just practice. Josh was getting frustrated, which I had never seen him do on a golf course. Swearing, slamming clubs back into the bag.

"This course is boring," he declared on the ninth tee. "It's just fancy lawns. Nothing grows naturally out here. The elevations on the greens have no purpose other than a guy jerking himself off while he made each one up. The bunkers are obvious and so long it's like they think challenging players with strategic choices can be measured in tons of sand. It's like a poor man's idea of a poor man's idea of Bandon in the middle of Colorado prairie. Morons."

Vince and I sat quietly. We should have brought Coach Lowry. Surely he would have some advice to help keep the kid on track.

Josh set up, then turned to us again. "Why did I agree to do this? That dude from Mexico is going to eat me alive. There's a goddamn sewer grate right there on the line to the hole. Stupid shit-pipe fairway even smells like shit."

"It's all new," I said lamely. "But you will crack it. Just keep taking notes."

Josh laughed and returned to his ball. He took a few breaths and fired. The drive looked incredible to our eyes. Josh slammed his driver into the grass. "Piece of shit!"

We drove off in search of the ball. It was resting in some

native grass about ten feet off the fairway. Josh walked up and pointed to the fairway bunker it had skidded through.

"See that? Why is that bunker shaped like a kidney and the one across the way there is shaped like a T? Because no one thought about it. They just drew it up on a piece of paper and said, 'Isn't this cute? Doesn't this look like a real golf course?' They call this the native grass. It's a protected species. God-damn weeds."

Josh hacked his ball out and landed on the green. He chuffed with dark satisfaction. "'Bout fucking time."

It was a long morning.

After, as we returned our cart, Josh walked by and slapped a scorecard into my chest. "Let's get the hell out of here." He stomped off to the car.

Vince patted me on the back. "Good luck. See you Saturday, if he makes it."

"He'll make it," I said. But I wasn't sure.

Josh didn't speak until we were almost halfway home. "I'm sorry. My head hurts. I need to hydrate."

I handed him a bottle of water from the cooler bag. "Is it the new clubs? Something we can adjust? Maybe that was a bad idea on my part."

"It's not the clubs. I'm out of my element. My plan was all wrong. I rolled in arrogant, tried to dominate it, threw my swing out the window. The course is fine. I need to go home and meditate."

"Okay, so you know what to work on. We could come back tomorrow?"

"Maybe," Josh said. "I'll draw it up and see what I see."

He pulled out his phone. Typed something. Sighed.

"What?"

"Coach wants to see me," he said. "Urgent. We have to go to Twin right now."

"Not something with your mom, I hope?"

"Says he has something for me. Just arrived by FedEx."

"Might be good to talk to your real coach. I'm useless out there."

"It's okay," Josh said. "Your job Saturday is to keep my mom from fainting."

"That I can do," I said.

"If I even play this stupid match."

magic stick

Half an hour later, we parked at Twin Peaks. I followed Josh into the clubhouse, down some stairs behind the kitchen, into a dark hallway lined with clubs, grips, boxes, cases of soda and beer.

"So this is what it looks like," I said. "Never been down here."

"The magician's lair. That's what I called Coach's office when I was a kid. It scared the shit out of me."

We reached the end of the hall. There was a small sign on the door:

WHAT HAVE YOU DONE FOR COACH TODAY?

Beneath the sign was a framed photo of Coach Lowry, age twenty-four or so, with muttonchop sideburns and plaid pants. He was standing on a green, holding a yellow flag and a golf ball.

"Where was this?"

"One of his aces," Josh said. "Augusta. I forget which hole."

My testicles shriveled and retreated into my abdomen. "Coach played in the Masters?"

"Not quite. Qualified as an amateur. Played his practice round. Shot sixty-six. Got that ace. Then was disqualified. Sent home. Banned from the PGA for life."

I stared at Josh.

"I don't know what happened," he said. "And don't ever, ever ask him about it. Ever."

"Jesus."

Josh knocked. "Coach?"

"Come in, for Christ's sake." Coach did not seem surprised to see me. Only nodded before addressing the kid. "You just get back from Fort Collins?"

Josh sat down in one of the vinyl chairs. I stood in the corner. Coach's desk was hiding somewhere beneath a pile of paperwork, empty Diet Coke cans, and small trophies used as paperweights. The room was dark and dank and smelled like Old Spice and grip rubber.

"Yes, sir."

"And?" Coach came around his desk and sat on one edge, arms crossed.

"It's not my favorite track," Josh said.

"Unmitigated disaster, then. I knew it would be."

"My plan was terrible. My mind was wrong."

Coach looked at me. "Was it bad, real bad, or just the worst goddamn thing you ever saw?"

"It was, ah, aggravating," I said. "He wasn't himself. At all."

Coach returned to Josh. "What did you see? Take me through it, big picture."

Josh removed his cap and scratched his hair. "A furnace. No trees. Fake grass. Dollhouses. Industrial waste. Leviathans in the bunkers. Slopes laced with razor blades. The greens were fast on the west side, slow on the east. Whoever's watering that place is drunk on gasoline fumes and pixie dust."

I understood Josh was trying to put words to his visions, his other dimensions.

"What colors?" Coach asked. "Start from the tee boxes."

"Steel blue from the tips. Dull grays in the fairways. Approaches were brown, like hard crystals. The greens were just plain green but like I said, artificial, AstroTurf, and the cups were filled with ox blood. I saw my headless body falling into a bunker because my actual head was on a pike and the cavalry rejoiced."

Jesus Christ.

"You got the heebie-jeebies," Coach said. "Sure enough. And there's only one thing that can snap a golfer out of those nasty buggers."

"What's that?"

"New clubs." Coach grinned.

"My whole bag is new," Josh said. "It's not the clubs. It's me."

"Of course it's you," Coach said, rising, walking in a circle. "It's always you. It's always me." He stabbed his chest with a thumb. "It's always him." He slapped the poster on the wall behind his desk. It was an old poster of Ben Hogan; even I knew that. The old Irishman. The bulldog hips, the pleated trousers, the heater dangling from the lip. "Even the Wee Ice Man before his tragic accident, he knew it was him, and whenever he got himself in a bad patch of that Texas sand and couldn't swing his way out of tarnation, he picked himself up with a new club. Usually one he designed or modified himself."

Coach went to a pile in the corner and pulled out a long slender box.

"His mean old drunk of a father taught him metalwork when he was barely old enough to hold a club. Young Hogan would break clubs from other players, other manufacturers, and write them letters until they called him in and asked him to help them create the clubs he wanted."

Coach pulled a ribbon of Bubble Wrap from the box.

"So that's what I've been doing the past couple of months,"

Coach continued. "Been on my mind for a long time, but I wanted to be sure your swing was ready. I think it's time."

Coach removed a club from the box, all wrapped in one last layer of packing paper.

"Now, I am not really a club designer. I don't have the skills, the materials, the tech they use now. But I have ideas. Piles and piles of sketches at home. And sometimes, when I think I've hit upon something, I'll send one off to my old friend Dave Kreiger—you remember him?"

"Your college roommate at LSU. You two played the NCAA championship together. You placed tenth. Dave placed twelfth. He works at Ping now."

"Used to work at Ping," Coach said. "Did a lot of good work over there. He was instrumental in bringing their wedges back into the realm of respectability. But they never cut him loose, not really. And his interests were always more in the driver. The driver is the big machine in the industry now. It's what excites the kids. It's the start of a long relationship with the brand. Give a man a driver he can carry far and not miss every goddamn fairway, he's already half sold on the rest of your line. So Dave got to talkin' with one of his buddies over at Titleist, where they been hungry for something new. 'We'd love to see anything you've been working on,' they say, 'nothing proprietary for Ping, of course,' wink wink, bullshit, 'have another martini.'

"Dave isn't an idiot. He knew we were getting close to something special. And he's not about to hand it over or get sued by his former employer, so he'd done this all on his own time. So he says to this friend, he says, 'I'll tell you what. I'm going to quit my job at Ping. I'm tired of it anyway. You bring me in as a consultant for six months, long enough to prototype this new design and test it out, and you either hire me or don't hire me based on this one club. If it doesn't outshine every other major offering from the top five, I'll walk away, without pay. But if it does fly, if you build it, I get one percent of gross sales. Globally.' Can you believe the balls? Dave always did have balls like an elephant. Cost him a lot of strokes in the heat of battle, but hey, we can't change our character, can we?"

Josh and I were both salivating now, and Coach knew it. He was having his moment.

"So Dave goes off to Titleist, and they get to work. But it was not, shall we say, bowling anyone over. The materials were too inconsistent. Too fragile. Like what's happening with carbon faces these days. Amateurs are cracking them like eggs. They'll iron it out. Carbon will stay. So he talked to me about it, and I sent him some ideas for new materials, new layering techniques I found they're using for extreme ocean submersibles. Okay, so there's a new way to shape steel, a new way to thread titanium within titanium, and new polymers to fill it up . . ."

"Coach, you're killing me," Josh said.

"Bottom line, Dave loves what I'm sending him, but we kept hitting the wall. We could build a bomber but lost the spin control. We could build a goddamn guaranteed fairway finder, but it hit like a rock and flew like a penguin. So we went back to the photos of the submersibles, these sea vessels designed for extreme pressure. But we'd been so focused on the materials, we hadn't really paid attention to the shape. Dave traces it with his finger. 'The shape. That's it. That's our club.' But when something is three miles under the ocean, the pressure is so immense a single point of weakness will cause the entire vessel to cave in like a beer can. Same thing here. 'The manufacturing process is going to be a nightmare. Has to be flawless,' I said.

"And the light bulb goes off. In three weeks we went and designed a very weird club. Like, forget what a driver is supposed to look like; design purely for the physics. We come up with this thing, and while we were testing it, we used film and analytics from your swing." He pointed at Josh. "Your body. Your build. Your hitch move. Everything. Because the big guys don't need any help hitting long. But it's the smaller guys now, like Rory, Rickie, Harman, fifty others, five foot six, five eight, a hundred and fifty pounds soaking wet. They can bulk up and swing out of their shoes, but that's gonna cost them years off their career. So we built a prototype for smaller guys, and it hits long and straight. It's based on your game, Josh. And now it's yours."

Coach handed the parcel to Josh. Josh stood and began to unwrap it. The grip had no markings. The shaft was glossy black with a milky-gray fade to it. Josh unwrapped the head. And my first thought was, *That's not even a golf club.*

Josh turned it over, his fingers caressing the head, the face, the hosel—but there was no hosel. "It's fused," Josh said. "Head and shaft. All one piece."

"From top to bottom," Coach said. "It's a fusion of titanium, graphite, and carbon laced with more titanium, with different flex up high that tightens as you get lower. Off the shelf is out the window with this one. Every single club sold will have to be tailored to each player."

The face was not as tall as most drivers, though about as wide. The crown had a depression sloping down toward the back end, where things got really weird. The sides of the heel were thick but concave in the middle and tapering to the end, where it narrowed like a fin. I thought of those Cadillacs from the 1950s, if they had been designed in the year 2050.

"Severely aerodynamic from the back. Stout up front." Josh let the head fall to the floor and waggled it. "Oh, wow. The balance is totally different."

"The weight is distributed in a continual gradient," Coach said. "It's not a chunk of metal that weighs a bunch more than the stick it attaches to. This is balance from top to bottom, front to back, inside out. We're calling it harmonium. Filed the patent a month ago."

"Is this even legal?" Josh asked.

"USGA approved as of last week," Coach said. "But no one's playing it yet. Dave is working on the premarketing pitch to get Tour players to try it out. It's going to scare a lot of them away. But if they can get over the look of it, see how it feels and how it makes the ball go, oh boy. That there in your hand is one of fifty prototypes in existence. The rest are sitting in boxes in Dave's office. He wanted you to have it for your match."

"No one has this?" Josh asked. "Not even Xander?"

"Nope. Hold the head up again," Coach said. "Tilt the sole toward the light over here."

Josh did, angling the sole of the club at the fluorescent light above. All I saw was solid black, so I moved closer.

"Whoa," Josh said. "It's like the chameleon paint they use on cars. Was that a logo?"

"Working name. People love it so far. What do you think?"

Josh turned the clubhead like a crystal, refracting prisms of light and then very faint white lettering. It reminded me of one of those Magic 8 Balls, how the little triangle inside would turn over and reveal a phrase.

"There." Josh grabbed me. "See it?"

The black surface seemed to shimmer, and then it rose up from inside like a ghost, a pupil opening. It seemed like a thing coming alive in Josh's hands.

SORCERER

Then it disappeared again.

My scalp felt like it was moving. Fingertips tracing up my

spine. I stepped back, mildly disturbed. It was by far the most beautiful golf club I had ever seen, probably the most beautiful ever made. But something about it seemed unnatural. Spooky.

"Sorcerer," Josh whispered in reverence.

"You like that?" Coach asked.

"That's what I called my twin," Josh explained for my benefit. "The boy who played on the other side of the kingdom. When I was little, I made up an invisible boy. He looked like me in most ways, but he was a little smaller, and he had red hair. He was always smiling. He had solid-white eyes, and we could read each other's minds between realms, here and on the other side of the Great Hoogan Sea. He lived in a castle, and he would sneak into his father's chambers at night and read from the Book of Link Spells, where all the golf secrets were kept. He would bring them back to me, like a caddie, or more like a little prophet. He told me how to do things no one else could. He didn't have a name, but he knew how to do magic. I called him my Sorcerer." Josh looked at Coach. "You remembered?"

Coach was no longer smiling. "I built it for you. I named it for you. And I named it *after* you. You were the Sorcerer, Josh, you know that. You still are. Now take your magic stick and go set the Sad Queen of Trinity free. She's been waiting for you all her life."

Josh's knees buckled, and he caught himself on the chair. He laid the stick across his thighs, his head lowered. That club might have weighed next to nothing, but in Josh's hands, with the road ahead, it carried the weight of destiny.

It was not until Coach walked over and set his hand on Josh's shoulder that I saw his shoulder was hitching up and down. Josh was crying. Coach looked to me and winked.

"Will you be there?" Josh asked, his voice tired and raw.

"I haven't taken a day off in fourteen years, since Lucy died," Coach said. "Maybe I'm due for an afternoon of spectating."

"Will you be my caddie?"

Coach knelt. "Look at me. No, Joshie. I won't be your caddie. For one, you've never had a caddie; that's not the way you play. That's not the world you created. To insert myself into that world now would be to invite ruin. And you know that."

"Yes, sir."

"For another, I have nothing left to teach you. You have already surpassed me. I could never do what you do with a golf club. Not even close."

Josh shook his head. *No, no, no.*

"Do you really not know that yet?"

"No, sir."

"Nephew, you are, without question, the purest, most natural talent I have ever seen. You are like Tiger was, but he had Earl driving him, shaping him, building him. You have done most of this yourself. Christ knows how, but you have something in you. I'm not even sure it's human. Like a creature from one of your goddamn visions out there in the moonlight. You are going to play on a different course, against a different opponent, with more people watching, but everything you need is already in here." Coach touched Josh's forehead. "And in here." Coach touched Josh's heart. "Go home. Go sleep. And when you walk onto the box Saturday morning, I want you to tune this world out. It's not real. The real world is inside you. Will you do that for me? Will you play your game, no one else's?"

"Yes, sir."

Coach stood. Josh got to his feet. Coach walked over and offered his hand to me. "Your father was a damn good man," he said. "He'd be very proud of you and all that you're doing."

"Thank you, sir."

Coach slapped my shoulder. "Now you two get the hell out of here. I got things to do."

We reached the door. Josh turned back. Coach nodded. Nothing more to say.

Josh shut the door behind us.

I didn't bother making small talk on the way to Josh's house. He seemed absent. I pulled into the driveway. He slid from the car and walked inside, his magic stick tucked under one arm. I carried his golf and gear bags to the door and waited a moment. Damaris came out from the kitchen.

"Everything okay?"

"Big day," I said. "He's wiped out." I set his bags in the foyer. I'd never been inside. Something smelled delicious.

"Do you want to stay for dinner?" she asked. "I made lasagna. He needs carbs."

"Better not. He also needs space."

"Was it that bad?"

"It was unusual."

She studied my face, then kissed me. "I miss you. I need more."

I smiled. "I miss you too. Come over later?"

She considered. "I need some help tomorrow with a couple of errands. Can I pick you up around lunchtime?"

"What are we doing?"

"Costco is having a sale on a sectional I like. I want to test-sit it."

I started to laugh, then saw she was serious. "Yeah, of course. Happy to help."

She slapped me on the butt. "Rest up, sport. Big game tomorrow."

free samples

Damaris picked me up at noon.

"Can we stop for coffee first?" I hadn't slept well last night, worried about the kid.

"Costco has coffee."

"Are we driving to Denver or something?"

She looked at me. "Um, they just opened a new one four minutes from your house."

"Oh. I'm not exactly savvy to the whole Costco experience."

She became excited to introduce me to the cult. "It's the best! They have my favorite juice, my favorite gummy supplements. You're gonna love it. I wish I could afford to go every day." She turned up the radio and sang along. I studied her. She wasn't joking.

Four minutes later she pulled in beside the gas pumps and filled up on Costco gas, saving herself eight cents a gallon. Then we parked. Along with her denim skirt, a faded Psychedelic Furs tee, and a pair of baby-blue Converse low-tops, she had some kind of hybrid purse-papoose slung over one shoulder. From this she removed a list and thrust it upon me. It was not a short list.

I groaned. Middle of a Thursday, and Costco was already crawling with eager shoppers. We had to wait in line for admittance, like we were going on a ride. A tough older gal with an aggressive smile checked the membership cards, front and back.

"Welcome to Checkpoint Charlie," I said.

The gatekeeper did not find this amusing. Inside, Damaris pointed me to the cafeteria and waited impatiently while I got the quarter-pound hot dog and a large Coke.

"A dollar fifty," I said. "This is a steal!"

"Try not to drip relish on the floor."

She had a cart the size of a dump truck, and I followed her around as she picked out bags of granola and chips, nutrition bars for Josh, some kettle corn she liked. All kinds of toiletries, tampons, lotions. I spotted the rack of condoms and began to browse.

"Would you say I'm more of a Magnum or Super Magnum?"

Damaris walked over and scanned the options. "Hmm, I don't see any junior sizes. And it's a little late for these now, wouldn't you say?"

I picked up a "Family Size" twin pack of Astroglide and tossed it into the cart. Damaris removed it and shoved it back on the shelf. "I don't need that shit. Wish I did. It gets tiring having an irrigation system down there all the time."

I was at once aroused and mildly alarmed. "For real?"

"Have to change my panties twice a day. Used to be three or four, so maybe I'm finally turning into an old lady."

"That's hot."

"Focus, please. We have a long way to go."

On the next aisle, she picked up a new four-pack of toothbrushes. "You can choose your color," she said. "Green, black, blue, or yellow."

"I get a shelf in the medicine cabinet?" I asked. "Maybe a drawer in the bedroom?"

"Don't push it. And you need to floss." She threw in a twelve-pack of mint floss.

Then she launched a targeted strike on the foodstuffs. Cereal, cans of yellowfin tuna, jerky, oatmeal, a forty-pack of frozen chimichangas, cases of coconut water, frozen fruit mixes, Greek yogurt, almond milk, a giant canister of protein powder. "Josh and I are on a smoothie kick." In the meat department, long slabs of salmon, chicken breasts, some kind of Hawaiian brisket that could feed eight people and cost sixty bucks. Unusual brands, quality stuff.

"How is he today?" I asked. "Has he said anything about the match?"

"His door closed the minute you dropped him off," she said. "I heard a car late last night. I think Morgan picked him up." She parked the cart in the clothing section beside a table stacked with leggings and matching sports bras. "Do you think they're having sex?"

"Most def. Cart girl is gaga for the lad."

She shot me an angry look.

"Well, they're young," I added. "They seem close. What do I know?"

"Would you folks like to try an egg roll?"

We turned to see a gray-haired woman in her Costco apron doling out one-inch pieces of some new Filipino-style egg rolls. Lumpia. With chili sauce.

"Yes, please." I took three of the little paper cups and started stuffing my mouth. I offered one to Damaris, and she balked. "These are delicious!" I threw a thirty-six-count into the cart. "Is the sauce included?"

"Yes, there are four packets in the box," the woman said. "You can bake or microwave them, but they're really best fried. I like to use canola oil. Three minutes per side."

"Thank you"—I noted the name tag—"Marjorie."

She beamed, proud to have turned another customer on to the lumpia. I took two more. "Do you mind?"

Marjorie winked conspiratorially. "I won't tell."

"You're my girl, Marge. Imma be back to see you soon."

She laughed. Damaris rolled her eyes. We walked on.

Damaris crossed some items off her list. "No more impulse purchases. We're on a budget." Then, as if somehow related: "I'm still sore. From the other night."

She could have been talking about a good deal on potato chips. But I knew something was simmering underneath.

"Me too. I forgot to tell you, my doctor gave me some pills last time I saw him."

She was headed toward the laundry detergent. "For what? Your blood pressure?"

"You know." I made a little flipping motion near my crotch.

"Huh?" Still not understanding.

"Boner pills!"

"Quiet! Jesus." She leaned in. "Is that what it was? Because you lasted an unnaturally long time for a guy who hasn't been laid in five years."

"One year, Damaris. I said one year. Maybe eighteen months."

"I'm not judging." She smiled. "If you need a little boost, I'm all for it."

"That's the funny thing," I said. "I haven't taken any. I meant to the other night, just in case. But I forgot."

She gave me a curious look.

"All you, baby," I said. "You're my rocket fuel, and we're going to the moon."

"Hmm. We'll see." She kept walking. I watched her legs. She had great legs. Sculpted calves. Her hips making that denim skirt switch back and forth.

"How much longer?" I complained like a little kid. "This is sooo boring."

She played along. "No whining, or else you don't get to pick out a video game."

She slowed next to a pallet of water picks on sale. Pretended to consider one, reading the box. "I can still feel you in me," she said. "So sore. But sooo sensitive."

I stepped closer, pressing my hips into her from behind. The aisle was empty except for us. This corner of the store was low traffic. I ran my hands over her hips. "What's under this adorable skirt?" I whispered, kissing her ear.

She exhaled. "Don't be naughty."

"You started it."

I wanted to see if I could get her going again like the old days. Damaris glanced around. No one nearby. She raised her skirt and pressed her ass into me. She wasn't wearing any panties. Stark tan lines. Pale cheeks dimpled with goose bumps.

"Casey, look . . ." A little breathless. "These motorized toothbrushes are on sale for ninety-nine dollars."

I kissed her neck, cupped her breast. "Seems like a good deal. Five vibration settings. Healthy gums."

She turned and I kissed her deeply. I ran my hand up the inside of her thigh. Higher.

"Wow," I said. "You're aching for it."

She bit my lip. "Not here."

"Just a touch."

I kept my fingers moving.

"Casey, you're crazy," she said. Her neck was turning spotty, arousal blushing. "We could get arrested. There's cameras all over."

I whispered dirty things in her ear.

"Are you trying to make me come in Costco?" she asked. "Oh God."

I made sure no one else was in the aisle and kissed her harder. She reached back to feel me. She was letting go, letting me bring her to the edge.

"Just like that, just like . . ."

Her phone chirped. She froze.

"It can wait," I said.

More chirping. The spell was broken. She slipped away and checked her phone.

"Oh Jesus. Oh no." Her face went slack.

"What?"

"Josh isn't with Morgan." She dialed. "She hasn't seen him in over twenty-four hours. He never texted her last night. We have to leave. Now."

We abandoned the cart.

I checked my phone on the way to the parking lot. Nothing from Josh.

Damaris spoke into her phone. "Morgan, honey, what happened?" She listened for a minute. "He didn't say anything else? And what time was this exactly?" Another pause. "Well, where else would he go?" Pause. "I heard a car leave. I thought he was with you." Pause. "Right. Call me as soon as you hear anything. *Anything*."

Damaris lowered her phone. "Where would he go? Where else does he spend time?"

"I don't know. He's never mentioned any other friends, places . . . How long has he been seeing Morgan, anyway? Does she normally text you?"

We arrived at the car and got in.

"Couple months. I gave her my number as soon as I met her, just in case something like this came up."

"He's run off before? This is a pattern?"

Damaris slammed her door and looked at me. "Josh has episodes, all right? When he gets anxious, he hides in his room or shuts down for a day or two. But he doesn't usually disappear unless something is really wrong. How bad was he yesterday? Don't downplay it."

She started to reverse hard and then braked, rocking us back and forth. "Get the fuck out of my way!" she yelled, and honked at the two older women pushing a cart behind us.

"Hey, easy, let's just calm down a minute," I said. "I'm sure he's fine."

Damaris shook her head. "He's not fine. He's freaked out about this whole stupid match you got him involved in, and now he's missing." She was weaving out of the lot. "I knew I should have checked on him last night. God dammit!" She banged on the steering wheel. "Call Coach. Use my phone."

"Damaris, slow down. Getting us in a wreck isn't going to help."

"You don't know anything," she snapped. "He's fragile. He's so fragile."

I dialed Coach Lowry. He answered after four rings, his gruff voice coming through the car speaker. "Hey, D, what's up?"

"Josh is missing!" she barked. "Have you seen him?"

After a moment, Coach said, "I have not seen him. I'll have one of the guys make a loop, but I haven't seen his car all day."

"He's not with Morgan. She's worried too. Where would he go?!"

"Fort Collins," I said. "Maybe he went back for another practice round."

"There ya go," Coach said. "Did you call them?"

"Not yet," I said. "I will now."

"Ask for Larry Waters," Coach said. "Tell him who you are

and that I asked you to call. He knows what Josh looks like. Tell him to send one of the marshals around."

"Got it."

"He's not golfing," Damaris said. "He ran away again. I know it."

"Hey now, calm down," Coach said. "He's a big boy. He's probably just taking some time to himself before the match."

"Why didn't you tell him this was a terrible idea?" she yelled. "He's not ready!"

"Honey," Coach said. "Go home. Wait for him. I'll call you back soon."

Damaris stabbed the phone off. She drove hard.

I set a hand on her leg. "Hey, it's going to be—"

"Don't talk to me right now."

I shut my mouth.

"Ninety-nine percent of the time, he copes with everything just fine. He has had what most people would call nervous breakdowns before. But with Josh, they're *hard* resets. I'm not just being overprotective. Josh has mental health issues that even his doctors can't fully explain. The last time he disappeared, a couple of years ago, he drove to Nebraska and tried to make his own campsite at Lake McConaughy. A ranger found him wandering on the beach, naked, covered in his own filth. He hadn't eaten or slept in three days. He wasn't himself for six months. So this is really not okay *at all*. You get it now, Casey?"

"Yes. I get it."

I was scared shitless.

lost boy

Josh's truck was not in the garage. We waited at their house.
Josh had left no note. Damaris and Morgan kept texting and
calling each other. I spoke with the people at TPC Fort Collins.
No sign of him. We all texted him, called him. No reply. His
clubs were in the foyer, where I had left them. We were out of
ideas. I made tea and tried to console Damaris.

"Take me through yesterday," she said. "Every second, from
beginning to end."

I did, but nothing helpful emerged. "He said he was going
to make a plan for the course. Mostly he seemed wrung out.
But he wasn't visibly upset."

"He doesn't show it. Everything just goes internal. He can
be unreachable, even when he's home, right there on his bed."

We sat with that for a while.

"It's too much," she said. "He can't handle this kind of pressure. And you two are running around talking about how he's
going to buy a van and go on tour like some wannabe rock star.
Can you understand why that sounds insane to me?"

"I do now. I'm sorry, I didn't before. He just seems so

confident. Like he always knows what to do. With golf, money. It's hard to see him as fragile or unsure."

"It's not your fault," she admitted. "You haven't been around him enough."

We waited all evening. All night. We slept little. Damaris woke every half hour to look at her phone. She called the police. They weren't helpful. She finally fell into a deep sleep around four. I woke up at five and checked his room, the garage. Nothing.

It was Friday, twenty-four hours before the match. I no longer believed he would just show up, ready to go. I didn't care about him competing, of course. I just wanted him to be safe. I wondered if this had anything to do with the fantasy world he had constructed around golf. The way he'd explained it was well beyond the imaginary games of your average boy. His fantasy land had been some kind of coping mechanism, a reality within his reality. He'd leaned into it for years. Was there some mechanism in his mind that could detach, take him away not just in golf but in the rest of his life? Maybe the destination was not always his golf kingdom but alternate states of mind, somewhere he could safely be *not here*. What if someday Josh had some kind of breakdown, went to his *not here*, and didn't come back for a long, long time?

The afternoon and evening passed without any news. No one knew anything.

"He'll come home soon," I said. She was standing at the front window like a dog watching the street. "He loves you. He needs you."

"You should go home," she told me. "There's nothing to do here. I'm fine."

I protested; she insisted. I went home to feed and water Jojo again, take a shower, and change my clothes. My house felt empty. Maybe it had been this way all along and I was just now sober enough to notice.

I grabbed my keys and led Jojo to the car. We drove back. Damaris brightened a little when she saw us, then deflated when she realized we weren't with Josh and had no news.

"Why'd you come back?" she asked.

"You're not alone in this."

Friday night was long. Hard. Bad.

Saturday.

I woke up at four thirty and made breakfast. Eggs, bacon, toast, juice. I brought it to Damaris, who was in bed, sitting half upright, staring at nothing.

"Okay, Mama Bear. You didn't eat all day yesterday. Let's get some bacon in you."

She shook her head at first. I persisted. Reluctantly she began to nibble.

"Here's what we're going to do," I said. The epiphany had come to me the moment I had opened my eyes. "We're going to shower, get dressed, and drive to Fort Collins."

"What for?"

"Because Josh has a tee time." I held a triangle of toast under her nose.

She looked at me like I had a horn growing out of my forehead.

"I believe in him," I said. "Maybe he won't show up, but I think he will. And if he does, we need to be there. Come on, babe. We'll feel better in motion."

"But what if—"

I shoved the toast into her mouth. "Then we'll deal with that then. One swing at a time."

To my surprise, she got out of bed and made her way into

the shower. No time to take Jojo home. She was riding with us. I called Coach and told him we were on our way.

Fifty minutes later we arrived. It was a scene. The local news had picked up the story. A lot of members and their friends had turned out. Families. Fathers and sons. Staging had been set up. Tall stands for the camera crew. A brand-new Lexus SUV was on display with the name of Dolan's family car dealership stretched across a huge banner. More Colorado-based sponsorships: an energy drink start-up; a big dispensary chain advertising their edibles and smokables; food stalls selling pizza slices, burritos, smoothies, coffee, beer.

It was 7:48 a.m. The match was to begin at nine.

Josh Parker was nowhere to be found.

walk up

Our entire crew was there to represent. Vince and his wife, Rita. My moms. Jamie and Mellow Mike and a dozen other guys we played with. Shyla, TaylorMade, and another cart girl from Twin were all dressed up and working some marketing angle, promoting off-brand golf accessories, handing out free gloves and divot tools. Coach Lowry and a lot of his staff, even the grounds crew, Stevens with his gray buzz and a new white Mizuno polo, plus more guys from the pro shop.

It was overwhelming. Everyone was keyed up, excited to support their local boy in his big debut. There were actual PGA banners strapped to stacks of baled hay, though this was not in any way a PGA-sanctioned event. Our local sports radio station *104.3 The Fan* had a booth, broadcasting live, giving away towels.

"Bro, bro, check it out." Jamie had sneaked up on me. He turned me around and pointed up. "Look what I hooked up for you guys."

There, some two hundred feet above us, was a blimp. Silently floating by in the clear morning sky, it was maybe thirty or forty feet long, the size of a school bus. It was mostly black with some kind of orange stripe down each side.

"What the hell? Is that an actual blimp?"

"It's a drone," Jamie said. "One of my boys got us another sponsor. Five grand to the winner. My dude is controlling that shit from his house in Los Angeles. You see who it is?"

I couldn't make out the sign; then I did. "Are you kidding me? You can't have that here. You're gonna get us all in a huge load of shit."

"It's all good, bro. No one will know who did it."

As if on cue, the blimp turned and headed our way, descending until it loomed over the crowd. People began to notice. Children were running after it. Some of the parents thought it was neat. And then, as the orange-striped logo revealed itself, many of the parents did not find it neat at all.

"Fuck Goodyear." Jamie slapped my back. "We got the Pornhub blimp! It's perfect, right? How G is that!"

There it was. The Pornhub blimp.

"Am I imagining it, or is it shaped like . . ."

Jamie laughed again. "No, you're not imagining it. I tried to get some of the models to go boots on the ground, but all the stepmoms were booked. Dope, right?"

"You're out of your goddamn mind," I said. "But well played."

"Anything for my boys."

More people began to realize what they were seeing. Coach Lowry was watching the blimp. He turned and stared at us and adjusted his sunglasses. I hurried away.

For the next fifteen minutes, I milled around and said hi to everyone and answered the same questions over and over. "No, haven't seen him yet. He's running a little late, but he'll be here. He's ready." I looked around for Morgan. She had not texted us back in almost three hours. I asked the other girls if they had seen her—nope.

I ran into the Swede. He was standing with a tall, handsome older man in khakis and a blue blazer, expensive loafers. "Casey, good to see you, bud!" Dolan exclaimed. "We're super pumped! Our sales team lit things up in the last few days. Sponsorships way above our expectations. Did you meet my father?"

"Hello, Mr. Johanssen," I said, shaking his hand. "Thank you for organizing this. It's a big deal to Josh. To all of us."

Mr. Johanssen's giant white teeth appeared. "We're happy to help the guys making their way up. I've been looking forward to seeing Jimmy play. I hear he's got quite the swing."

"Josh," I corrected. "Yes, he's something."

"Is he here?" Dolan asked. "You guys need anything?"

I could see he was getting anxious. "We're all set, thanks. He's just warming up."

Dolan did not believe me but nodded in acceptance. For now.

I went off to check on Damaris and discovered her sitting in a golf cart, my bulldog panting in the seat beside her. It was Vince's idea, and he had wrangled a cart for Jamie and Shyla, one for himself and Rita, and one for the moms to share.

"Good morning, ladies." I offered the widows Sweet some bottles of water. They wore fancy summer caftans and huge sun hats.

"Hi, Casey!" Janey said. "This is quite the production."

"Where's my grandson?" Linda said, lighting a cigarette. "Why are you so sweaty? Did you stay up late drinking?"

I took a breath. "Mom. I don't drink anymore. So stop asking."

"Then why do you look like shit?"

"I'm nervous. Drink some water. It's going to be brutal out here today."

Janey removed a plastic grocery bag from the cart's basket and handed it to me. "We got a little something for you and Josh. It was Linda's idea, but I found them just in time. That Etsy on the internet is something else!"

I opened the bag. There were two hats. Trucker caps, cheap polyester with red, white, and blue iron-on lettering. One hat said WORLD'S GREATEST GOLFER. The other said WORLD'S GREAT-EST DAD.

"Which one's mine?" I deadpanned.

"Oh, for Christ's sake," my mom said. "Get away from me."

"This was very thoughtful of you both. Thank you."

"Tell Josh to wear his for good luck," Linda said. Janey frowned, knowing better.

"Uh, yeah, we'll see. He might have to wear one from his sponsors."

"Well? Put it on!" my mom belted. "I want to take a picture."

"Can we do that later?" I hurried away. "I have to make sure everything's ready. Back soon!"

We all gathered around the first tee and made small talk. I looked at my phone every few minutes. At eight forty, a group of men and women, mostly Hispanic, approached from the club-house. They all wore uniform colors of red, white, and green, the colors of the Mexican flag. Some had towels around their necks. Dark sunglasses. Serious expressions.

"Dominguez's team," Coach said.

I stayed near Coach for the authority he conveyed, allow-ing us to stand right on the first tee box. Damaris was sitting in the cart, head down, staring at her phone. I began to sweat. The temperature was already in the mid-eighties. Forecast said we'd hit ninety-seven. No clouds. I drank water. *Come on, come on, kiddo. I know you're here somewhere. I can feel it.* Maybe I couldn't. But I had to believe.

Dolan had told us this was an exhibition fundraiser, that they wanted to make it fun for the families, but I wasn't prepared for the theatrics that unfolded. The tower speakers on the public-address system squelched to life with the absurd, car-dealer-commercial voice of Colorado's own Alan Roach.

"Good morning, ladies and gentlemen, golf fans from Mexico and the United States. Welcome to TPC Fort Collins, host of the first-ever Colorado Summer Amateur Showdown, Eighteen for Green and Red. Please be sure to visit our gracious sponsor, Johanssen Lexus and Audi of Northern Colorado, and enter to win a brand-new Lexus TX. Luxury performance to haul the whole family in safety and style. And now, representing the red, white, and green, hailing from Mexico City, Mexico . . ."

Cannons BOOMED. White smoke began to rise. Everyone startled, and the clubhouse maintenance doors blew open. A bombastic reggaeton song began to blare from the speakers. Frankie's wife or girlfriend emerged first—a tall, stunningly beautiful, dark-skinned woman with flowing black hair, wearing a festive dress and huaraches.

Roach continued. ". . . three-time Korn Ferry winner, PGA Tour Latinoamérica Amateur of the Year, and new member of the PGA Tour, Francisco 'Frankie El Guapo' Dominguez!"

He was taller than I expected, probably because I was picturing another version of Josh. Around five feet nine, slender but roped with muscle. He was quite handsome, especially in his red pants, white polo, and bright-green wing tips, as well as a black hat and dark, oversize sunglasses. He strode out with a huge smile and waved his cap at all the fans. There were hundreds now and more by the minute. The crowd cheered, and Coach and I joined in to show respect.

As the music played, El Guapo did a little matador dance, waving a club around like a sword, then twirling his lady to make her dress fly up. She had a large rose behind one ear, and they looked exactly like two young people about to take on the world. Instagram ready, on point, and on brand, ready to play at the elite level. This was a real branding opportunity, I realized. Another thing I had failed to prepare Josh for.

When they reached the tee box, El Guapo twirled his lady once more, dipped her, and gave her a big kiss. The crowd oohed and aahed. The lady blew kisses all around and then took her place with the rest of their team.

Frankie's caddie was an absolutely ripped hombre of sixty-some years wearing jeans and a leather vest, his arms and chest covered with prison tats. He planted the golf bag—alligator skin in the colors of the Mexican flag—with pride and not a small amount of menace.

Frankie took a dramatic bow.

I looked at my phone. Eight fifty-seven. This was it. If Josh did not appear in the next three minutes, the whole thing would fall apart. It would be a terrible look for Josh, a stain on his name. Everyone was watching the clubhouse, waiting.

Dolan approached, no longer anxious but downright pissed. "Dude. Where is he? He's got to step up. And I mean now, baby. What's the story?"

"Two minutes. It's cool. We're good." I couldn't bring myself to admit this was a bust.

"Don't fuck with me, Casey. You've got one minute. *One*."

The announcer looked on, waiting, and then someone pulled him aside. Another official went to the DJ booth and said something to him. The DJ nodded, then pulled up some kind of tablet wired into his system.

"Yo!" Jamie yelled. "There goes Morgan!"

I turned back to the clubhouse. Dressed in a black tracksuit, Morgan ran toward the doors and disappeared inside. My heart kicked into a new gear. Damaris was staring off at a nearby lake. "Damaris!" I pointed to the clubhouse. She got out of the cart. Coach Lowry came to stand with us. The speakers crackled again. The announcer was waiting for his cue. Sweat trickled down my ribs.

The speakers filled with an ominous low keening, a synthesizer drone. Spacey, weird whistling, the first notes of a song I vaguely recognized. An ethereal voice said, "See you on the other side . . ." Then the first guitar chords hit like a series of buzz saws, one-two: DUN-DUN! Sharp, eerie, threatening. My skin began to crawl.

DUN-DUN!

I knew this song. Oh God, did I know it.

DUN-DUN!

"Lunatic Fringe" by Red Rider. From *Vision Quest*.

My boy had heard me at the party talking about *Vision Quest*. Had he watched it? Had he already known it?

Slashing guitars.

DUN-DUN! DUN-DUN! DUN-DUN!

The smoke began to blow. The clubhouse doors banged open.

Morgan stepped out into the sun, sans tracksuit. Now there was only a black spandex jumper-wrap thing that crisscrossed her hips, shredded midriff, and boobs. Her blond hair shimmered beneath a Fidel Castro cap. She looked like a gangster's girlfriend, and she was carrying a black golf bag over her shoulder. She raised one arm and made a fist, punching a rhythm to the sky. ONE-TWO-THREE . . . !

"What the fuck is she doing?" Damaris asked.

I started to tremble. *Yes, yes, yes!*

BOOM! The drums kicked in. The guitars shifted into a slow grinding rhythm. Louder and louder and louder. The crowd was on their toes now. Swaying. Hypnotized.

"Come on, kid. Do it. Do it."

The singer came in. The voice of every eighties rock guy driving a Firebird. Familiar as your bad cousin. Raw, stoned, ready to get down and dirty. Morgan danced through a series of fly-girl moves and stomped down hard, pointing to all of us. *Watch out, bitches—something wicked is coming for you.*

BA-BA-BOOM—the doors blew open again.

And then someone I did not recognize walked out. He wore all black. Black shoes. Black pants. Black polo. Black sunglasses. No hat. He was Josh's size, but instead of long shaggy brown hair, this dude's hair was buzzed tight on the sides, bleached stark white, with three-inch spikes on top. He looked like an albino rooster, a little Swiss assassin. With Morgan at his side, he strode toward the crowd like he was leading an army. He bore no expression at all. He did not turn his head. He did not wave. He was moving in a tunnel. On another planet.

"Is that my son?" Damaris cried, shaking me. "Is that my Josh?"

"There goes my dude!" I raised my arms and shook my fists. "Yeah, boy! There he is! COME ON, JOSH! LET'S GOOOOOOOOO!"

Josh did not acknowledge me, his mother, Coach, the crowd, anyone. Morgan set his bag on the tee box, leaned in, and kissed him full on the lips. He did not acknowledge her either. He was a machine. "Fringe" reached its crescendo with its nasty, filthy, soaring guitar solo. The crowd bobbed and swayed. I saw stars. I was drunk, high, riding a dragon in the sky.

Can you feeeeeel the resistance?

CAN YOU FEEL THE THUNDER!

Josh had been battling his demons his whole life. This was his battle cry. He was riding the fringe as far as he could, and he'd come to win.

The song slammed to its conclusion. Everyone was rockin'

one minute, then left in silence. Josh stood at the back of the tee box, still as a cobra, staring at the fairway. Might have been my imagination, but he seemed thinner. Pale. Not altogether healthy.

"Josh, are you okay, baby?" his mother said. "Josh? Josh!"

Coach took her under one arm and whispered something to calm her down.

Then he turned to me. "He's ready."

I could hardly contain myself while Roach announced him. "And representing the red of Colorado, hailing from Longmont and Twin Peaks Golf, ladies and gentlemen, please give a warm welcome to Josh Parker!"

We all went nuts. If our thirty or forty hardcore fans weren't as loud as Frankie's team and his fans, we were damn close. El Guapo walked over and chinned at Josh. They shook hands briefly, but Josh did not *see* his opponent. He was locked on the course. Some kind of official stepped up between the young men. He had a small mic that didn't work very well.

"Gentlemen, we're here for a single-round match of eighteen holes. All USGA rules apply. The total prize purse is two hundred fifty thousand dollars, winner take all. Should eighteen end in a tie, a playoff will commence, one-hole sudden death until a victor is declared. As our guest amateur, Mr. Parker has honors. When you're ready, Josh."

Everyone cleared the tee box.

Josh stood for a moment, then walked to his bag and withdrew his new magic stick. The Sorcerer. I doubted he had hit it even once. He removed the leather clubhead cover and set it on his bag. Snugged his black glove. Morgan backed off. He was on his own now. She would not be caddying for him. No one would.

Josh planted a tee and set his ball. He took one more look

at the fairway, and I noted that it was a par five playing 607 yards from the pro tees. It rose and fell in the distance, and the little flag seemed a mile away.

Josh set up over his ball. His butt wiggled. The driver's head looked like a *Star Wars* toy hovering over the grass. I stopped breathing.

He went into his backswing. His signature hitch move was gone. His body coiled and unfurled with ferocious speed, downright viciousness, the club whistling through the air like a barely contained scream. There was a black blur, and people gasped. His finish pose was Baryshnikov, balancing on his tiptoes with his spine twisted to an unnatural degree. He held it, held it, then slowly relaxed.

A woman in the crowd said, "Oh my God."

No chance I could follow the ball. It was here, and in less than a blink it had vanished. I looked to Coach. He was staring off into the distance, watching it go. Then he turned to me with a sly smile.

People began to murmur. One of the guys manning the launch monitor said, "Can't be right. Look at this." A few others crowded around a screen. One of them whistled. "Good Lord Almighty."

"Four sixteen?" another man said. "You shittin' me?"

"*¿Qué pasa?*" someone from Frankie's team asked. "*¿Cuán lejos?*"

"Three seven one carry," the guy on the monitor said. "Four sixteen with the rollout."

"What happened?" Damaris asked.

Her son had slipped behind the rest of Frankie's crew.

"Hole plays six hundred and change," Coach said, adjusting his shades. "Josh just drove all but a six iron of it. I think he likes the new stick."

The crowd began to applaud.

Frankie was scowling when he set up over his ball. His team looked unsettled. Frankie backed off, shaking his head. He set up again, became still. Dialed it up and went at it. He released an audible grunt as he connected, and as soon as he looked up, he dropped his driver and spat into the grass.

"Hijo de puta."

This time I was able to follow the ball. It sailed long and began to turn over right, harder right, over some trees into a barren field of waist-high dying native grass, over a rusted tractor. I didn't think they would ever find that one, and they never did.

Josh was already fifty steps ahead, his black bag slung over his shoulder.

Walking alone.

Morgan walked alongside our cart and filled us in on what little she knew. I drove and Damaris held Jojo in her lap as we followed the boy from a hundred yards back. Josh had shown up at Morgan's house about three hours ago. He was shirtless and shoeless, with pine needles in his hair, dirt all over him, cuts on his hands and legs as if he had been wrestling with trees. He had gone into the mountains for somewhere between twenty-four and forty hours, wandering alone. As best she could tell, he had not eaten in at least two days. He made Morgan promise not to tell anyone because he was afraid his mom wouldn't let him play. She had to coax him into drinking water while she cut his hair and dyed it, his idea. When she asked why he had disappeared, why the hair, why the secrecy, he replied with only five words.

"The boy told me to."

When she pressed him—who was this boy?—he said, "My blind friend."

He hadn't seemed happy or sad, stressed or hurried. She asked him if he was really okay to play today, and he only nodded. So Morgan had taken him home, missing us by only half an hour or so, to get dressed and load his clubs into the car. He hadn't talked on the way. Morgan had improvised the opening routine based on the last song on his playlist. And here we were. That's all she knew.

"Something's wrong," Damaris said. "I can tell."

Coach's words came back to me. When he had given Josh the club and told him he could not be his caddie, that everything Josh needed was already inside him.

"And when you walk onto the box Saturday morning," Coach said, *"I want you to tune this world out. It's not real. The real world is inside you. Will you do that for me? Will you play your game, no one else's?"*

"Yes, sir."

"He's here," I said. "Safe. That's the important thing."

Damaris shook her head. "Is he really? Because I don't think he's here *or* safe."

the Blind Boy

Josh is here, and also *there*. On the other side, in his other realm, where the sky is blood red and the fairways shift from sea blue to emerald green to sooty black. In this place, he is known as Jozua, and a round of golf is not a game but another battle in his long-waged war to save the kingdom. Today's campaign is the greatest test he has faced in all his wheels, and he is slashing his way to a terrifying victory.

On hole one, he drove so long he stunned his opponent into silence, then finished with a bird.

On hole two, more of the mind-melting length before he closed with a surgical approach and tap-in for his second bird.

On hole three, his blood warmed like a serpent's, he felt out of body and at one with the grass, the need to think replaced by pure feel, and he slayed with midiron to another one-putt bird.

On hole four, he played low from the tees, using the Sorcerer to deliver a center missile, followed by a tricky approach exposed to unpredictable winds, causing his pearl to miss the green and forcing him to settle for par.

On hole five, with his anger fueling another level of cold

concentration and infusing the Sorcerer with deadly purpose, he annihilated the ugly fairway and danced his way to his fourth bird.

On hole six, his thoughts followed quantum lines to alert him of the ideal lay-up, from which he could spy the perfect feeder within the green, leaving himself another single wave of the flatstick to bird.

On hole seven, he fell so deep into the Rowdy he forgot where he was, who he was, forgot even that there was an opponent chasing him in desperation, and there was nothing but grass and sky and distances to carve in between, until he emerged to thunderous applause and the awareness of another stroke advantage.

By the time he alights from the next tee box in hunt of hole eight, he is approaching something like immortality of the mind, a certainty that he cannot swing wrong and unknown forces are conspiring to hand him a monumental victory. What will it mean? What comes after today? Such ruminations in the midst of battle are dangerous, he knows. But he cannot resist the faces he will see when he returns home from this beautiful and terrible war.

As always, he wages battle for his Queen, who has a curse only Jozua can lift. And for his Captain, who has long been his most valiant counselor but has nothing left to teach. He fights for another now as well: the Lost Man, who mysteriously appeared two moons ago and has become an important figure in the future unknown. It is also a war within himself, against himself, as it has been for all golfers, for centuries.

But losing this day Jozua fears not. He has frightened the lesser Warmaker with his newly earned staggie, the one his Captain claims to have created. But this eerily black instrument is no ordinary staggie. It is something much rarer, the kind of maji stick the Ancient Ones played. Forged in dark fire, laced with prime materials thieved from Fallen Stars and blessed by the Rigor Demons, 'tis not a staggie but the All-Wand itself. A weapon beholden to none but he who wields it, a weapon with the power to destroy all enemies.

He is readying his gappie for a wee bitty approach, yet another so simple a child could make velvet of it, when the intruder Jozua has been dreading announces his arrival. The high-pitched and reedy voice shatters his calm.

"Oi, Jozie! Fair Jozua!" the voice calls with desperate relief. "I missed ye, True Friend! Me's so glad ye come back to sport—I could use the company, so I could."

Reluctantly, Jozua steps off his shot and turns to greet the Blind Boy, the one he used to call Sorcerer. Did he really, then? How silly. The Blind Boy is no longer the real Sorcerer, if he ever was. Jozua's Captain declared as much, and Jozua's acumen today has confirmed it.

"Aye, mate, 'tis true I am returned to wage battle," Jozua answers, concealing a sneer. "I'm in the thick of it now, so spit your business and be gone."

The Blind Boy arrives all out of breeze and lowers the hood of his black cloak, revealing his pale decrepitude. In Jozua's absence, or perhaps because of it, he has become sickly. Much of his fine red hair has departed his balding, sore-infested head, and many of the crooked teeth have toppled in agreement. His eyes—those lifeless white coins that once glowed with warmth but are now yellowed by sickness—drift toward Jozua's new quiver of staggies with naked covetousness.

"All quite splendid. Ye look fine indeed, staggies a-gleamin'," the Blind Boy says, rubbing his dirty hands together. He was always fussing about the new staggies, perhaps because he was not allowed to possess any of his own. "Mightn't I walk along, then? Can keep my eye on yar pearl and read some of the nastier lies for ye, like we did in old times."

"Afraid not today, mate," Jozua says. "Already seven deep into her, so I am, with a massive claim to insurrection. Don't need your tired eyes at this point, thank ye all the same."

The Blind Boy frowns. "But we's True Friends. I always carry for ye and advise upon the wise path in this land. All the way back to the First Walks, back when I found ye lying by the trees, lost and crying up a jag. Have ye forgotten, Jozie? Have ye forgotten all we done together?"

Jozua tries to conceal the anger rising inside. "I have not forgotten, mate. But those were childish games, and I am no longer a child. 'Tis a man's hunt now."

"Ye mean ye don't want to be friendsies no more, Jozie? Would this be the True meanin' of ye words?"

"It's not so simple as what I want," Jozua snaps, seething now. "I come to reap the Crown. I have no time to gabber and no reason to put ye on the bag. My swing has been purified. Spy for yourself."

Jozua returns his attention to the pearl, glances at the black flag yonder, and in his mind draws the golden circle around the cup until it glows like a sun, unmissable. He swings. The gappie feels supple as leather, and the pearl flies true, dropping within the ring of light with a sweet thump before catching hold of the velvet and reeling itself back in like a yo-yo.

Plottle.

"Ye see? A mighty eagle to sit with my growing flock of birds." Jozua allows himself a grim smile. "I own this track. Ga' home now, mate, for your own safety."

"Great golly sweet pigeons," the Blind Boy admires. "Ye've found yar next level, True Friend. But beware the pitfall of arrogance, for she may be your curse over fairways to come. Better I carry yar quiver this day, me thinks."

Somewhere in the distance, as if coming from over a hillock, Jozua can hear the masses applauding, screaming his name.

"Are ye deaf? G'home, imp! I can't be botherin' to argue with ye. Ye'll never be accepted by them, so quit foolin' yourself. Ye are a freak, and where I am destined, freaks are not allowed."

The Blind Boy's shoulders rise and fall in a tense rhythm. His gnarled nose drips. He is crying, wetting his own bib. Slowly he points to the All-Wand, eyes agog. Before Jozua can move to stop him, the Blind Boy rushes forth and seizes the All-Wand in his dirty mitts.

"Put that back!" Jozua cries. "Ye've no business with it, dimwit!"

The Blind Boy moans as if burned by its touch yet does not release the wand. "This is why ye forsake me? Ye comes into a bit of dark maji and be ready to toss me away? After all the times I help ye hunt the flag and calm yar mind when the troubles threaten to break ye apart—'twas I, not yar staggies, not yar Captain, who saved ye!"

Jozua is about to protest, but the Blind Boy has become enchanted by the head of the All-Wand, where the magic compels him deeper as it begins to reveal its secret script.

"Whazzit say here, then?" the lad asks, mouth twisting to form the sounds. "So-sah-sah-sor-sork . . ." Jozua wants to smack him, beat him for his insolence. "Like white smoke, sneaky . . . So-so-sor-sor-sorsk . . ."

"SORCERER!" Jozua bellows. "It's called Sorcerer! I did not name it, but a name's all 'tis. Now can ye leave us in peace? Ye're too dumb and deformed to swing anything so precious, so hand her over before it devours ye."

The Blind Boy lets the All-Wand fall to the grass. Immediately the soil begins to sour, purpling in all directions like the blight on the crops.

"But that's *my name*, Jozie! What ye nicked me, once upon a walk. 'Twas Sorcerer ye called me back when I saved ye life!

'Twas Sorcerer who helped ye capture countless Flags and survive to fight again!"

The rage within Jozua is boundless. He has no choice, he understands now. He must finish the Rowdy on his own, one man. There is but one way to be rid of the belligerent stinker.

The Blind Boy shakes his head slowly, pulling his caul over his cold skull. "I beg ye, do not cast aside yar True Friend for mere covets and glamour. Yar mind be infected, 'tis plain to see, but we can make things True again, so we can. Pray let me walk by ye side."

"'Fraid not," Jozua answers. "I have grown far from this place. I'm done here. Go home and tend your own fair fields."

"*But ye are mine home!*" the Blind Boy cries. "I cannot exist without ye, Jozie, don't ye understand? Please don't leave me, True Friend. Please. *Please. Pleeeeeaaaaasssseeee . . .*"

Jozua retrieves the All-Wand and stands over the Blind Boy, who has fallen to his scabby knees, heaving and slobbering with tears.

"Leave now or own the consequences." Jozua's voice is hoarse.

"I cannot," the Blind Boy whispers. He raises his sagging face to stare up at his master, resigned to his fate. "For I am ye."

"Then it is my right," Jozua says with relief, "to banish ye."

Closing his eyes, squeezing back tears, Jozua raises the mighty Sorcerer above his head and slashes down. The sound is a dull thump. Again, Jozua brings the club down. Again, again, and again, until there is no more Blind Boy, only a wide black-red stain across the grass. Heaving with breath, Jozua shoulders his quiver and walks on.

The Blind Boy's howls echo within him and all around, loud enough to pierce the bleeding sky. Jozua feels a cold stab, the reverbs in his chest rising like a twisting sword up through his spine, spreading in his mind like the wings of a great carrion bird.

When he steps onto the tee box for hole nine, he feels shaken, sickly, but he must not disappoint the crowd, the idiots and mongers who've come to watch him ascend. They sense a new king being forged with every strike, and they long for the spectacle of his violent rising.

He withdraws his mighty Sorcerer, grinning like a fool, drooling from one corner of his mouth as he coils, twisting away, harnessing the winds from All Five Horizons, and releases his charge. There is a great scream, a supernatural peal of thunder and flash of lightning that blinds him and springs blood from his nose. He sees white light, then the Blind Boy's white eyes gone cold gray dead, and then Jozua sees nothing at all.

Darkness reigns.

return of the king

When Josh stepped onto the ninth tee box, the crowd was frothing. There were maybe eight hundred people following the match, but they sounded like five thousand. Josh's only par had come on number four. The rest were birdies, and now he'd eagled number eight. He was on pace to obliterate this young course's record of sixty-two. Not one of his drives had gone less than 340 yards, and he'd yet to miss a fairway. His approach game had become almost an afterthought. His wedges had never been so deadly. He hadn't missed a single putt. But then, he hadn't needed to putt from more than fourteen feet all morning.

Leaderboard:

Parker: −8
Dominguez: +1

But the score was the least of Frankie's woes. The young man who had come in as the clear favorite, with a track record of professional wins, was floundering. His confidence was shaken on the first tee, and he had not recovered. His entourage was pissed.

His wife looked miserable. His caddie, he of the Danny Trejo school of hard knocks, was eyeballing Josh like he was one disrespectful word from getting shanked.

Josh had been brutally efficient, ice cold in his demeanor—but he hadn't done anything wrong, had he? In terms of etiquette, pace, respecting Frankie's lines, he had been a model of professionalism. But something was off, and people were starting to feel it. It wasn't just how brilliantly he was playing or the way he seemed to tune out the crowd, refusing to even nod or take a small bow after the eagle. He moved and reacted as if we were simply not there. For the first few holes, Coach and I admired his focus, his intensity. But as he sliced and diced his way through six, seven, and eight, I began to see a weariness in Coach's face, like he was watching a robot play, not his dear nephew and protégé.

Damaris was also disheartened. The immense fear she had harbored while he was missing had been replaced by a quiet sadness. She clapped without emotion. She was no longer afraid of him leaving home. She was afraid of what he was becoming right before her eyes.

As Josh made his way to number nine, she turned to Coach. "Is he even having fun out there? Does this hold any real joy for him, anything at all?"

"He's definitely on another level," Coach said.

"But is this normal?" Damaris pressed. "Do other pros act like this?"

"Stories about Tiger in the zone," Coach began, but his heart wasn't in it. "The coldness. He could be merciless in his prime."

"But does this fit with anything you know about Josh? Because I've seen him golf alone, in his little world, and even when he was fully in it, he smiled. He celebrated his own shots. This is like an alien abducted him and ripped his heart out."

Coach smiled tightly. "Let's see how the rest goes. Things can change quickly out here."

On the ninth tee box, Josh seemed to be mumbling to himself. We couldn't hear much, but what I could make out did *not* sound like Josh's voice. The words didn't even sound like English. I must have been hallucinating in the heat, but I could swear he was channeling *Trainspotting* in a full Scottish brogue. *Ya daft fookin' ween . . .*

Now as he pulled the Sorcerer from his bag, he grappled with it, yanking it violently as if prying it from a thief. He stomped around, appearing disoriented. His spiked hair was soaked with sweat, matted to his head. He had to replace his ball on the tee three times because his hands were shaking. He set up, then let the club rest against his hip while he rubbed his face. He shook his head like a dog just out of water, then covered his ears, his face a mask of pain, as if he were trying to block out some horrible sound or dampen the world's worst headache.

Damaris had started toward him when suddenly he picked up the driver, set his feet, and unleashed a swing both harder and wilder than all the others. His body contorted, jerked, and spun like a puppet, and I heard or imagined hearing something in his spine go *POP*.

The ball took off like another artillery shell, and a piercing shriek cut through the air. I could not tell if it was the swing or a noise Josh made, but it was awful. The shattering of a glass bell releasing a banshee.

Simultaneously, hundreds of tiny black slivers flew in all directions as the Sorcerer's head turned into a small bomb. We learned later that spectators were still picking shrapnel from their clothes and hair on the way home. The shattering was so swift, so complete, Josh was left reeling with a black stick in his hands.

He stumbled and fell to the ground, face up. His body twitched once, twice, then went limp.

People screamed. Officials rushed in, but Damaris got there first. I followed, elbowing people aside, and when I reached them, Damaris was kneeling beside him, shouting his name, shaking him by the shirt.

Josh's pupils had rolled back. Only the white orbs were visible, streaked with sickly yellow and red veins. Twin threads of blood ran from his nose, dripping into the grass, down his neck, into his collar.

"Help!" Damaris screamed. "Help him! Joshie! Josh, wake up! Ambulance! Oh God, no, baby, no, no, no!"

I put my fingers on his neck. Pulse beating hard. I cupped my palm under his nose, over his open mouth.

"He's breathing," I said. "His pulse is strong."

"Medic, need a medic here!" Coach pushed me aside and somehow pried Damaris away, then knelt, tilting Josh's head back and rolling a towel under his neck. His voice was calm.

"Everyone back up, thank you," Coach said. "Do we have a medical team?"

A man and a woman in first responder uniforms made their way in, their hands sheathed in purple latex gloves. Coach got out of their way but hovered over Josh's head. "Josh, wake up. This is your coach, Josh. Wake up, son. You're okay, but I need you to wake up."

Josh did not respond. The medics were cutting into his polo. They had the clear plastic CPR pump thing ready to go.

"Tee time, boyo, let's go!" Coach clapped his hands hard, loud, right above Josh's face. "Josh, wake up!" He clapped again, and this time it worked.

Josh bolted upright, turned, and coughed blood into the grass. He rolled to his knees and threw up. It was mostly water, some yellow bile, a little more blood from his nose. He raised one hand with a finger pointed up: *Gimme a second here.*

"Oh, thank God!" Damaris said.

Josh coughed again, spat, and then sat back on his butt, arms hanging over his knees. "Wow. That was weird. Someone get me a water? Dying of thirst."

Coach handed him a water bottle. Josh drank, spat, drank more. He tried to get up, and Coach said, "Nope, just stay right there. We got you."

Josh looked around. For the first time that day, he made eye contact with his mother, then me, then Coach. He gave everyone a faint smile. He drank more water. Eventually he got to his feet, and Damaris smothered him. Soon he was laughing, apologizing.

"It's all good, I'm good. I just fainted. Somebody get me a hot dog—I'm starving here."

"You're bleeding, baby," Damaris said, dabbing his face with napkins.

The medics checked him all over, tested his eyes. Coach spoke with him for a few minutes, and it was clear Josh was able to press on. He would not consider forfeiting. I fetched a clean polo from his bag and noted the empty slot where his driver had been stowed.

"Where's the Sorc—my driver?" Josh asked.

Coach held up what remained of the shaft. "In heaven, where all good clubs go. You killed it, boy. But this is on me. Should have never let you put a club in the bag wasn't properly field-tested. I'm sorry."

Josh sighed. "Can I get a replacement? I don't care whose it is."

Coach did not need to consult with the officials. He paraphrased: "USGA rule 4.1. A player is allowed to keep using and/

or repair a damaged club, but they are not allowed to replace a damaged club, except when it is damaged during the round by an outside influence or natural forces or by someone other than the player or their caddie."

Josh said, "Well, technically the Blind . . ." then stopped. He smiled, but there was sadness in it. "Never mind. I guess I'm screwed."

Behind him, El Guapo was grinning.

it's just a game

After the disastrous drive, we expected number nine to be a shit show, and it didn't let us down. Josh's first ball, the one that detonated the Sorcerer, was never found. He reteed and pulled his next-longest club, his four iron. He was loyal to his irons to a fault, never trusted the three wood and didn't carry a hybrid. He snap-hooked into the native grass maybe a hundred yards ahead. He found that one, hit back into the fairway, but then his short sticks went wonky. He ended up carding a seven, triple bogey. Frankie birdied.

Leaderboard:

Parker: −5
Dominguez: 0

By the skin of his teeth, Josh somehow tied number ten for par, but only because Frankie lipped out a twelve-footer and Josh sank his. They pushed.

On number eleven, Josh teed off with his four iron again and sliced again but at least recovered his ball. His wedges and putter were still cold, and Frankie took the hole, birdie to Josh's bogey.

Parker: −4
Dominguez: −1

On number twelve, a par five, Frankie drove his ball just over 310 into the sweet meat of the fairway's left edge. Josh made the fairway but came up well short. He was sitting 320 out. He switched to his five iron but hit fat, flying low and leaving him 175 to the green. Frankie got on with a beautifully striped second but ended up high right, fifty feet or more to putt.

Josh hit one of his signature eight irons to within fifteen feet. Frankie lagged to within three feet. Josh two-putted for par. Frankie closed out with another bird.

Parker: −4
Dominguez: −2

"He's lost without the driver," I said on number thirteen, a little par three playing 156 with an elevation drop of nearly a hundred feet. Coach, Damaris, and I were hovering as close as we could. Jamie and Shyla had taken Jojo in their cart. "But even his wedges have abandoned him. His whole bag's gone cold."

"Six holes to go," Coach said. "Be patient," he added, loud enough for Josh to hear.

The boy glanced at us and nodded.

Frankie was loose, having fun again. He did a little dance and sang "cha-cha-cha" as he circled his tee, and the crowd couldn't help but give him a laugh. "Or maybe Chi-Chi-Chi?" Frankie sang, a nod to the great Chi-Chi Rodríguez, and we had to clap in approval. Even Josh smiled, offering a small bow.

"There you go," I said to Damaris. "See? A little fun. He's coming back."

She smirked. It was something.

Frankie set up with a slight crouch and flung his ball out low, a little flier that hung over the green forever. I was sure it was going to play long, too much roll, but it dented the green and spun back to within six paces of the cup.

Josh pulled his pitching wedge, replaced it, and went with his nine iron instead.

"Good move," Coach said. "He's tired. More club, less swing."

Josh's insanely dialed-up swing was replaced by something that looked like I could have done it. His tempo was Lionel Richie, "Easy." The ball went high, caught a bit of wind, and drifted right, narrowly sticking the very top of the right shoulder. Not on the green but pin high. Okay.

Josh walked down the steeply winding cart path, taking his time, and Coach said, "Good boy. Settle the mind. Calm the breathing."

He used his fifty-eight to flop. The ball went high, and I was sure it was going to stop too far above the cup, but it bounced once before releasing, dribbling downward, curving beautifully, finding its way . . . As it slowed, Josh broke into a silly kind of breakdance routine there on the shoulder, as if he were steering the ball with his blocky movements.

The ball slowed to a crawl. You could see the logo turning over.

"Two more rotations," Coach implored.

One . . . The ball was dying . . . Two.

In.

The crowd cheered, and Josh finished with a dorky pop move. Frankie shook his head in disbelief.

"You started it, amigo!" Josh said.

Frankie smiled. We all smiled. Damaris most of all.

Frankie's putt was a downhill bender, tricky as hell, but he gave it a kiss, and the line was legit. A birdie to match Josh's, if a tad less exciting.

Josh walked onto the green and chinned his opponent, raising his hand. They high-fived and walked off together, talking like new friends.

Parker: −5

Dominguez: −3

Coach marched past us, tucking his shirt in. "He's stopped the bleeding. We got ourselves a match."

The fun continued on number fourteen, a par four. Josh wailed on his four iron and finally unlocked some distance but hit a fairway bunker en route. The ball skidded through and found the fairway, but he was well short, maybe 225 to go. Frankie drove long and safe, leaving himself 155 to get home.

Josh went with the six iron and came up just short of the green, but the low front was the best miss here. Frankie made another green in regulation. Josh bumped on and up, tagging the stick before rolling past it. Frankie two-putted for par. Josh had maybe thirty feet to go, uphill and right, with a nasty knoll in his path. His ball climbed the knoll, came to a dead stop . . . and in typical links-nightmare fashion began to slide back, gaining steam, until it rolled all the way back to where it began at Josh's feet.

"I hate that," Jamie said. "Happens to me all the time at Twin."

But instead of tensing up, Josh threw his hands up at the crowd: *What can you do?*

"Second time's the charm!" he hollered and drilled it for bogey.

Growing applause. He was keeping his composure. I was comforted by this until I realized they were now tied.

Dominguez: −4
Parker: −4

Number fifteen was a short par four playing just 328.

"A gimme hole," Coach said. "I don't like these."

"At least it's something he doesn't need to be so long on," I said.

"They're designed to make you take them for granted," Coach said.

Frankie had honors now. Not only did he drive the green, but he was all but guaranteed a birdie and had an opportunity to eagle. Thirty-some feet was no tap-in, but there wasn't much break in his path.

Josh swung too hard and blocked it into the native grass, out with the prairie dogs. Anything native past the white sticks was out of bounds, so he had to retee and hit a second ball as his third stroke. The great fear here, Coach explained, was that this was now a high-pressure shot, not a simple do-over. Josh displayed no real emotion as he set up again.

His second tee shot pulled left, and I held my breath, fearing he was going out of bounds in the other direction. No one was in the vicinity to immediately spot his ball.

Josh turned to Coach. "Should I play a provisional?"

Coach shook his head. "Let's go look for it. I think you'll be all right."

They spent most of the three minutes allowed to find it, and when they did, neither looked relieved. The ball was not out of bounds but nested pretty good into swirls of green grass. One hundred sixty yards to go, lying four in cooked spaghetti.

Josh chopped out but fell short of the green. He chipped to within twenty feet.

Frankie was away. Dolan had said Frankie putted like Cam Smith, and here was a flash of the Aussie. He jarred his thirty-six-footer for a ridiculous eagle.

Josh canned his sixth for double bogey.

Dominguez: −6
Parker: −2

With just three holes to go, down by four strokes, Josh's chances were slipping away. But the tenor of the match had completely changed. We had moved from creepy domination to goofy fun to neck-and-neck competition. And now, pure desperation. I wondered if Josh had really let go of the pressure or if he still wanted to win.

Did it even matter now?

Number sixteen was a par four doglegging left. Nothing out of the ordinary, except that it featured a pond at the elbow with a long shore stretching nearly to the green, an evil mirror of number sixteen at Twin Peaks. Players with a natural fade could smash their drives without reprisal. Players who depended on a draw had to be extremely careful—lay up or else go for a swim.

Both Josh and Frankie were elite; they knew how to shape any kind of shot they wanted. But every player has tendencies. We have no way to know what Frankie intended, but Coach told me his fade was not automatic. Regardless, he swung too aggressively, as if he were behind, not leading. He hit long and splashed down about 270 yards away. The water was penalty area but not out of bounds.

While Frankie was waiting for a ruling on his drop location, Coach huddled with Josh. I was not able to make out their words, but Coach was flipping through the clubs in Josh's bag. He came to a certain club and urged it on the kid. Josh flinched, turning away with a laugh: *No way, not a chance.*

Damaris caught on and said the obvious. "I know he doesn't like woods, but he's got to have something else in there. Something longer."

"The new clubs we picked out, I know he got the four iron through the pitch. He insisted on keeping his old wedges. Then the new driver and putter, so that's eleven. I figured he was saving room for a couple of his old lost and found clubs, but I didn't get into it with him."

"This is making me insane," she said.

Behind us, the moms got their cart all screwed around and had to reverse, the beeping obnoxiously loud. We turned. My mom was pointing at her head, then at me. *Where's your hat?!* I waved her off. Now was not the time.

Josh went with his four iron again. Nice safe shot, about 220, fairway.

Frankie dropped where the judges told him to. His third stroke flew left of the green but not far enough to doom him. My prayers for real trouble went unanswered.

Josh belted it and made the green, way up on the top end. *Okay, so even with a two-putt he probably makes par*, I thought, *and Frankie will have to hole his chip shot to tie. Josh gets a stroke back, two if we're lucky.*

Frankie chipped out of the swale he'd rolled into, taking a beaver pelt with it because the turf was so wet down there. His divot spun through the air, separating into thirds like a space rocket, and a big chunk twirled onward and landed not an inch below Josh's ball. Part of it may have grazed the ball. Some people swore the ball moved. A long debate on the ruling commenced. Everyone had a theory, a prediction.

As always, Coach had the answer. "We're not on TV replay here. There's no evidence the ball moved. The ball is where it is. They can sweep the green around it, but they're not moving it."

While the officials dithered, Josh picked up a hunk of Frankie's pelt and showed it to the crowd. "Someday this is going to be worth a fortune. My man's gonna go light it up, and after he wins his third major, I'm selling this baby on eBay to pay for my new driver!"

Everybody had a good laugh.

Frankie turned serious and began stomping around the green. He found another piece of his own divot and looked around suspiciously, as if he were making sure no one was watching, then stuffed the hunk of grass into the pocket of his clean pants and scurried away.

The crowd laughed harder. Applause.

Then it was time to get back to the business of putting. With the distraction of the divot and the antics around it, I hadn't even noticed where Frankie's ball ended up. He was still well short, at least twenty, maybe twenty-five feet out.

Josh was away, and his next stroke was a bad miscalculation of distance, pulling up short. He had a reasonable seven to eight feet remaining for par, but I didn't like this at all.

Frankie studied his line for a long time, straddling it, walking around the cup, reading things with his hands in ways I had never seen before. He settled over it and became so still I found myself studying his chest for a sign he was still breathing. His fingers looked delicate, without an ounce of tension, as if he were holding a long feather. The pendulum went back and forth, and the ball went in a recklessly fast curving line, then jarred with a bang. Someone in the gallery said, "Jay-sus Kee-rist, this kid can putt!" and everyone applauded.

Josh's seven-footer now seemed like thirty. He walked to the opposite side of the cup, knelt, then returned to set up. He exhaled and tapped. The ball inscribed a perfect arrow to the center of the cup, until the last three inches, where some invisible evil shoved it off course. He finished two inches left and tapped in for his bogey.

Dominguez: −6
Parker: −1

I consulted a scorecard to remind myself what we had left. Not nearly enough.

Number seventeen was a strange par four. Average length around 395, but it played uphill for about 170 yards before the fairway split around a rocky, manmade water feature surrounded by beautiful flowers and small brush trees. You couldn't see the fairway beyond the water until you were standing up on the hill, and I hoped Josh remembered that it played to the right and back downhill after. There were two common strategies: You could play straight but not too long, just clear the waterfall and set yourself up for a long approach. Or you could cut the corner, avoid the waterfall altogether, and take at least 80 yards off the hole. If you chose that route, you had to cut it perfectly and send one at least 235 to 250 but not more than 280, or else risk exiting the fairway left for more misery in the native. On his best day, Josh might be able to hit a five iron 250, but that would be extremely rare.

Frankie took the safer long route and landed the fairway some 270 out, the uphill sucking the wind out of his sails. But he was carrying a five-stroke lead, so no need to mess around.

Josh looked at me, and I made a cutting motion to the right. He nodded, and I was confident he not only remembered the hole but agreed with my vote. He teed the ball high as if he were using a wood and let the four iron eat. The flight seemed spot on, but we wouldn't know until we crested the hill.

We drove ahead to spot him, and we found his ball holding the last of the fairway's right edge. It was a great shot; he'd gotten some of the downhill roll, but he still had a good 180 to go. Downhill plus wind was a distance benefit but could easily throw him off target or cause him to fly the green. I don't know what club he chose, and it didn't much matter.

He tossed a few blades of grass, then set up. Found his target. Go.

The ball launched high and hung up there in peak wind for a while. I thought he was way long, but the ball came down on the back left of the green. It was a huge green, and he was at least fifty feet from the cup. Maybe sixty.

Frankie's second went low but climbed, hit the front edge, bounced on, and bit down. His putt for bird would be thirty feet at most.

Josh walked around the green and carefully eyed his line. He set up, backed off, set up, backed off. Maybe this was a good thing, being so careful. But it was not what I was used to seeing. Usually, he found his line quickly and putted on instinct.

When he finally gave it a rap, the ball took off wide left, rode a wave, and then began turning back to the hole. The speed seemed too fast, but there must have been a slope near the end. The ball slowed dramatically and came to a stop.

"Six?" I asked.

"Ten at least," Coach answered.

I closed my eyes. Par. Maybe.

Frankie sank his third monster of the day. It was a twister.

A ride. And he'd read it perfectly. You had to give it up for the young man. He was a rock star.

"That's it," Damaris said. "I'm gonna be sick. Take me home."

Josh made his par putt—admirable given the pressure. A few people clapped politely.

Dominguez: −7
Parker: −1

Number seventeen had been his last chance. That was where Frankie slammed the door. But here's the thing. No one would ever remember what happened on number seventeen, for one simple reason:

What happened on number eighteen.

1950

Number eighteen was a par four, a miserably long one. Today it was playing 465, and when you factored in the wind on any given day, you could make a reasonable argument it should have been a par five.

The hole played west, directly toward the Rocky Mountains, and the wind was rolling off those big hills and fanning down across the plains in curly, temperamental gusts. Sometimes blowing left, sometimes right, but it was all headwind. The worst of conditions for someone who did not have a driver and needed every damn yard he could get just to keep up.

Our only hope was that Frankie misfired and sliced hard into trouble.

Josh watched as Frankie stepped up, driver in hand. All the fun and showmanship were over. While Frankie held a commanding lead and this had been billed as an exhibition, he was not here just to smile and sign autographs for the kids. He was also here to make one final statement, to remind the world he was ready for the PGA Tour. And Tour guys, they don't play nice. They don't let up, ever. They are trained to close out tournaments by driving the dagger into the heart of the opponent before stepping on his throat.

Because you never know until it's over.

Frankie drove low into the wind. A lovely little hummer that turned a bit left at the end, missing the fairway by a few feet but settling in some very manageable rough. Probably 265, maybe 275.

A death blow.

Before Josh teed off, he and Coach conferred. It was the last time they would talk until it was over. This time there was no debate. Just a short minute of whispering, during which Coach used his hands to pantomime a particular grip. He mimed half a backswing and repeated it twice. I could almost hear him saying, *Like this, you got it?*

Josh nodded. *I got it, Coach.*

"There's no chance," Damaris said to Coach as he returned to stand with us. "He's too far back. He can't make up six strokes on one hole, can he? Can anyone?"

I did not want to be the one to tell her.

"Josh has not controlled his own destiny for a while now, so he'd need a lot of help from Dominguez," Coach said. "But I have seen crazier things in golf. Things that defy all logic and the laws of nature. Guys melting down. Four-putting the last hole. It's taught me to never say never. Never give up. Play every stroke until it's really, truly over. And that's something I always tried to teach the kid. I don't know if he heard me, but it's as true today as it's ever been."

I couldn't help feeling a ray of hope at these words.

"But no," Coach said. "Josh has played a phenomenal round. He has much to build on. He has a future. But winning? He has no chance to win today."

I was crushed to hear that, especially coming from Coach.

Because it meant it was true, and because even Coach had lost all hope. I wanted to go home now. I was finished, but this wasn't about me. It was about Josh.

And Josh—he wasn't ready to go home. Not by a long shot.

Josh did what he could with his four iron. He looked relieved to put the damn thing away for the day when he saw his ball make the fairway some 200 out, maybe 210 with the roll. I wouldn't say he looked tired. Nor frustrated. But he did look like he was holding back another hard emotion. The kind that hits any golfer on the eighteenth hole when we realize we're out of time, that we failed to bring our best and left glory somewhere far behind.

The walk to Josh's ball seemed to take forever. Much of the crowd had peeled off. The day was hot and dry. With the match's outcome no longer in question, it was time to take the kids to the pool, go for lunch, mow the lawn, knock back a cold beer, and maybe catch a couple of hours of a real PGA tourney on the tube.

I came to pity the ones who left.

There were no ropes lining the fairways that day, and the gallery had done a good job of staying out of the way so far. When we pulled even with Josh's ball, Coach, Damaris, and I edged our way as close to the fairway as we could. The marshals had gotten a little lax. No one was going to tell us to stand back unless we really abused the privilege.

Josh arrived, set his bag down, and glanced around at what was left of the gallery. We gave him signs of support. I threw him a strong arm. Damaris blew him a kiss. Coach made a tomahawk motion with the flat of his hand and chopped it forward, just once, in the direction of the flag.

Josh went over his clubs as if unsure what to pull here. After a minute, he licked his index finger and raised it above his head. Well, no shit, the wind was coming at him hard. Probably thirty miles per hour, with gusts even stronger. Felt like an insult on top of everything else. Josh licked his finger again and raised it. This time he turned in a slow circle, that lone digit raised, as if he wanted everyone to take note.

"What's he doing?" Damaris asked.

"Measuring the wind?"

But that wasn't all. Josh licked his finger a third time and raised it again, this time stabbing at the sky. His face was serious. He scowled and stabbed the air. People were starting to wake up a little.

"What's he trying to say?" Damaris asked.

"I don't know."

But when I glanced at Coach, the old dog was deeply focused. Watching every move. Nodding solemnly. He raised his own finger in salute, the pointer finger, and stabbed it at the sky just like Josh.

What the hell. I followed suit. One finger up.

Josh kept pointing up, up, up.

"Come on," I said to Damaris. "Get it up there."

She did. So did the rest of our crew. Then the crowd started to follow along. All the while, Josh kept turning in a slow circle, stabbing his finger at the sky, in a rhythm now. Once every two or three seconds, until he had a whole bunch of us pointing to the sky.

And that's when I started to get it. He wasn't testing the wind, never had been.

Number one.

The one?

I am number one?

But no, he wouldn't do that now, not when he was soundly beaten. And yet he smiled on, throwing that salute to the sky.

Number one.

Number one.

Number one.

He lowered his hand. Slowly, ever so slowly, he began to pull a club from the bag. He teased it out, making us wait. We moved closer. I could barely make out the club. It was not one of the irons we had purchased three days ago. I didn't know what the hell it was, but it looked old, shitty, boring.

Beside us, Coach cupped his hands over his mouth like he was blowing into a conch and bellowed with everything he had in his lungs.

"HOOOOOOOOOOOOGGGGGAAAANNN!"

Josh held the club in his fist for all to see, turning in that slow circle one last time.

And then I remembered that day just last week, the round that felt like an entire summer ago, when Josh and Dolan had been duking it out on number eighteen at Twin, arguing over whether Josh's ball had flown OB. Coach yelling at us. Little Amanda on the range, in the midst of her lesson.

"Why on earth is he making that poor little girl use a two iron?" Dolan asked.

"Oh, he's not making her," Josh said, and went on to explain how Coach used the two to instill fear, then mystery, then longing.

Dolan smiled. "Jesus, he really messed you up, huh?"

"You don't know the half of it," Josh answered. "But it wasn't the two iron for me."

"What was it?"

Josh held up his index finger.

The one iron. The one iron was old; it wasn't going to give him the distance the advanced tech in a new four iron could. No, it was a dare, a dream, a message. Josh was returning to Hogan's playbook. Taking this moment to deliver the Irish bulldog a symbol of respect. To show his coach how much it had all meant. That he was a good student of the game, that he cared about tradition. And to do that the best way he knew how, Josh was returning to the 1950 United States Open, when Hogan had used the one iron on the eighteenth hole to seal his comeback win.

Did Damaris understand? I leaned in to explain, and she said, "I know the story. This is insane, but what the hell. Let's go, Josh! We love you!"

A goddamn one iron.

A relic. An abomination. Trying to hit the moon with a slingshot.

All Josh did then was step up and swing. He made his arms long and fluid, put ball bearings in his hips, and ended swift. He laid the pure butter on that battered old stick and delivered a stinger whose like you just won't see ever again. If the term *piss missile* had not been invented before this day, here was the blueprint.

The ball went through that hot Colorado wind like a scythe, never rising more than fifty feet off the grass as it bored a hole in the horizon, and you'd have thought more than once she was going to die short, way the hell short, but that beautiful ball just went and went and became a tiny speck and went some more.

The green was but a manhole cover some 280 yards up ahead, the hole sitting 298. Like a single-prop Cessna in a hurricane being shoved this way and that, the ball kept reclaiming its intended line and powered on, steaming ahead until it was floating, hovering, touching down twenty yards shy, right there across the apron, right there in the throat, right up eighteen's dirty gullet. She bounced once, twice, a third time off the collar, and may we all be damned if that ball didn't accelerate up the green, chasing after the cup like it was starving for cover.

It rolled up, up . . .

Fifteen feet away . . .

Ten feet away . . .

Eight . . .

Four . . .

One . . .

Then no feet at all.

She came to rest one inch, 1 inch, under her home.

So it was that that day Josh Parker, age twenty-two, of Long-mont, Colorado, hit the finest golf shot I've ever seen or ever will see.

An ancient one iron. Into a gnarly headwind. Two hundred ninety-seven yards, eleven inches.

The cheers built and built as we walked after it. Frankie must have hit his second somewhere along the way, but no one watched. I'm sorry to say it, but no one cared.

By the time we reached the green and confirmed it, the crowd was in an ecstasy. Jamie was screaming like a madman. Vince was crying, hugging Rita, and she was bawling too. So were the moms. The cart girls. Coach and his staff. Complete strangers. Jojo was pogoing her way around, barking at everything in sight. Everybody was dancing and screaming and laughing and crying.

I hugged Damaris, and she wasn't crying. She had cried enough lately. She was beaming, relieved to have her son back. As proud as a mama could be.

Frankie, maybe more than anyone besides Coach, under-stood the immortal moment this no-name kid had just carved into golf lore, and he and his crew were clapping along to cele-brate. Even scary old Johnny Cell Block #9 was grinning. Josh tried to clear the green on his way to apologize to Frankie. He felt bad everyone was stealing the moment, but El Guapo stopped him and spun him right back around.

"Just go, go tap it in," Frankie said, pushing him on. "Finish out, amigo."

We all cleared away just enough for Josh to step up. He used the one iron to finish his round, and then he turned and hushed everyone.

"I concede today's match. Ladies and gentlemen, give it up for your champion, the one and only Francisco 'El Guapo' Dominguez!"

Frankie came in and gave Josh a big hug. They laughed, and Josh offered Frankie the one iron. As a gift? To take a shot? I don't know, but Frankie was having none of it. He backed away: *No, no way, amigo.*

The final leaderboard had Dominguez on top, of course. He won by six or seven, maybe eight. We never saw him finish. Didn't matter, not one bit. Coach had been wrong on the last hole when he said Josh had no chance of winning. Frankie won the match. Josh won the day. The summer.

He won the real battle inside, and it was a right Rowdy.

I got turned around for a minute, and when I found Josh again, he was running toward me with two caps in his hands. Behind him, my mother, Linda, and my second mother, Janey, were cautiously approaching on foot, waving at us. Josh put his hat on, the one that said WORLD'S GREATEST GOLFER.

He turned and posed for some photos, and the moms clapped.

Then Josh turned, looked down at the other hat, and pulled it over my head. This one said WORLD'S GREATEST DAD.

We posed for more photos, arms around each other.

"Thank you," I said. "You just made two moms extremely happy."

I was dizzy from it all. Lost. Until there was a tug at my sleeve. I glanced down to see Josh's hand out. In his palm was the miracle ball, on which he had used a marker to draw a big green *#1.*

"No, sir. No way," I said. "That goes in your Hall of Fame trophy case."

"I want you to have it," he said. "Please?"

"What for? I haven't done anything."

Damaris had joined the moms, Coach, and our friends, all of them watching us.

"You showed up," Josh said. "You always show up." He peered into my eyes. "And I don't know if you're him. But I do know if I was gonna have a dad, you're the kind I'd be lucky to have as mine."

And that's where my round ended. I was all out of words.

I held him.

I held him.

And he held me back.

player handicap -11.6

My tee time is six forty. I used to set four different alarms just to be safe, but that's no longer necessary, because I've been sober for almost a year and I wake up well before sunrise. I know what's coming. The pain. The game. My next chance at glory.

It's early April, and every day is a little longer, brighter, filling with the promise of greener grass, a fresh start, my new personal best. The Masters is nearly upon us. Once more I am summoned, ready to take the next step in my game. In life.

During the offseason closures, I swung the orange ball, I hit Topgolf, I dabbled in yoga, free weights, swimming laps, whatever I could to stay loose. This year it included a trip to Scottsdale and another to Myrtle. Arizona was with Damaris, Josh and Morgan, and Vince and Rita. Myrtle was just us boys, Josh and me, the last real father-and-son time we would have before he left.

Morgan put her marketing degree to work, creating a business plan and running his social platforms to make sure the world would be ready to meet Josh Parker when his real debut arrived. The two of them took possession of the Sprinter van—the one Dolan sold Josh for $107,400, 3 percent below invoice—just after New Year's Day.

I still see the Diabolical Dr. Lisa every two weeks, even when I'm not in the midst of a crisis or even really messed up about something. She took me in when no other headjobbers would. She's been pushy, honest, real, and for that I've come to respect her very much.

"But before I agree to keep seeing you as a client," she said at the end of last summer, "I need you to tell me one thing. And you need to be honest, Casey, no more games."

"Sure, Doc, we're soulmates. You're on a first-name basis with all my demons."

"Why in God's name do you know that *Forrest Gump* scene in four languages?"

"More than that," I said. "My favorite is the Punjabi. *Mai koi bahuta tez aadmi nahin haan, par mai jaan da Haan ke pyar ki hunda hai.*"

She sighed. I caved in. "Big Halloween party contest in my twenties. I was trying to impress this girl, so I memorized it in ten languages and stayed in character for a month just to prepare. I won first place."

"I think you're still in character. See you next Tuesday."

I don't have to be at work until ten a.m. My partners understand because they golf too. My partners are Vince and Dave—yep, that Dave, the big Van Halen fan, my former boss from Flagstaff Solutions. When I went back to tell him I was ready to give him one more year, one year to make up for wasting the company's time being too drunk or hungover to do the job they were paying me for, Dave really appreciated that. He asked what would come after the year, and I told him about the golf app I was designing. He was intrigued.

"I was right about you," Dave said. "You were never going

to make it as a complete bag of shit. You just needed some time to clear your head. Now tell me more about this golf app."

After I told him about Vince and introduced the two of them, Dave became an investor too. They decided I should devote myself to working on BioLinks full-time. The seed round had come through in January, higher than we expected, $3.1 million. Enough for the three of us to hire some staff and give this thing two years, full tilt.

Tee time says six forty, but I'm forty-five minutes early, delivering bagels for the Twin Peaks crew. Coach is off today, but the guys in the clubhouse appreciate it.

"Just you and Vince today?" Stevens asks.

"Just me and my woman today."

Stevens smiles. "She's finally getting the itch. Good to have her out here again."

"I think she likes the air more than anything," I say. "But she keeps my scorecard honest."

"I bet she does." Stevens winks and slides me a token for the range balls. "Enjoy your round, Casey."

"Thank you, good sir."

I hit the range, get that eight working on a tight line, imagining a gold ring. I work on the things Coach has been teaching me, until she texts me from the lot. I drive the cart up to meet her. We live in my house. She rents hers to McKenzie and her son. The rental income means she doesn't have to work at CVS anymore, and she can focus on her health. I would have driven us both, but she needed more time to get ready. She's dressed in golf apparel, the pink skort, plus some layers. A cute little hat. Rainbow fingerless gloves.

"Does all this make me look ridiculous?" she asks, plopping down into the cart.

"Makes you look sexy," I say. "Gimme a kiss."

She does, then hands me a fresh coffee. We motor over to the first tee.

"Want to hit a few today?"

"Maybe on the back. When I can feel my fingers."

I stick the tee. "You hear from the boy this morning?"

"He was busy warming up. Morgan says he's feeling golfy. He's in twelfth place as we speak."

"Could be his week." I perch my orange Vice ball on the tee. "I like his odds."

"Are you finally going to break eighty? Or are you gonna drag me out here all summer?"

"You never know," I say. "But I like having you in the gallery."

I pick my target. See the shot in my mind. But I can't bring myself to swing just yet. The morning is so quiet. The sky is tinted rose, the fairways dark and moist. A hundred feet south, the geese are coasting in their pond like Viking longships. A blue heron waits for his breakfast. And I can't help but think about Josh and the day we bade farewell.

The day he and Morgan loaded the van with all their clothes, his gear, and a month's worth of Costco groceries, I felt a pang of longing for the past twenty-two years and tried to console myself with what lay ahead. Josh promised to call and text and hugged his mom for the twentieth time. When there was nothing left to say, the kids got in the van and slowly made their way down the block.

Then the brake lights glowed, and the van made a U-turn. They came back, and I figured they must have forgotten something. Josh parked and said a few words to Morgan before he hopped out.

He walked toward us with something in his hands, a thick book of some sort. When he got closer, he was staring at me, not his mom. It was a heavy three-ring binder, black vinyl, the kind used for storing files. Without saying anything more, Damaris turned away and walked back to the house, leaving the two of us alone.

"You forget something?"

"I meant to give it to you yesterday, but with everything happening . . ." He handed me the binder. "This belongs to you now."

I opened it. The first page was thick card stock, on which had been printed some official-looking words.

PATIENT HISTORY
Damaris K. Parker

As I began to flip the pages, I noted the color-coded tabs, with section titles.

DIAGNOSIS—TEST RESULTS—DOCTORS—FACILITIES— SPECIALISTS—MEDICATIONS—ALLERGIES—DIET—INSURANCE— RESOURCES—INDEX

And as I thumbed deeper through all these pages, I began to understand. It was Damaris's entire medical history, meticulously organized, with helpful notes scribbled in many of the margins, and I recognized the writing from the few golf scorecards Josh and I had kept. Josh had written all this. Josh had put this together. Josh had maintained it for years and years, going back to when he was no more than a boy of eight.

"I did the best I could," he said. "She has a hard time keeping track of everything, especially when she's fighting through another episode. If you need anything clarified, just call. I've memorized most of it, but I kept the records just in case. Oh, and this." He removed a thumb drive from his pocket and handed it to me. "It's all digitized, and there's another copy in my cloud. I'll email you the link."

I had to swallow twice before I spoke. "It's her green book."

"Exactly."

Just as my father had done with his green book for Twin Peaks, the one that had made its way from his hands to Coach to Josh, now my father's grandson was passing an even more important green book to me.

"I know you'll do fine with everything," he said. "She can be a handful, but well, I guess you know that by now."

"I will take care of her." I tried to compose myself. "You never stop amazing me, Josh. This is something no kid should ever . . . but you're not like any other kid, so I shouldn't be surprised."

"That's how we do in this family. Right?"

"Yes, sir."

I tucked the binder under my arm. I shook his hand. We shared one more hug. And then he was off to conquer the world.

"The hell are you waiting for?" Damaris asks. I am still posted up on the tee box, lost in thought. "An invitation?"

I turn to her. "It's too perfect. I don't want to spoil it."

"What are you talking about? It's just one more swing."

She's right. It's just one more swing. And whichever way it goes, I can live with that. I did my time in the rough. Everything else, this right here, is a gift.

I swing. The ball goes pretty good, maybe 240 up the right edge before turning back, coming to rest in the fairway. I walk back to the cart and holster the driver.

"Somebody feelin' Black Mamba today," Damaris says.

I kiss her cheek. "If I birdie this one, you gonna give me some of that sweet stuff over on thirteen? Those trees make a pretty good cover."

"I came all the way out here to wait until the thirteenth hole? Sometimes I don't think you know me at all, Casey Sweet."

I give her another kiss. Her tongue finds mine, and we linger for a bit, handsy.

The PA system from the clubhouse squelches to life. "Move it along, you goddamn kids," Steven says. "This isn't a swingers' club."

Damaris pats my leg. "All right, all right. Let's roll."

"We're rolling." We drive toward the Rockies with the morning sun at our backs. "We're definitely rollin' now."

acknowledgments

Life is a round of good swings and bad swings, bogeys and doubles, sometimes a par or birdie, and inevitably the occasional double-digit blow-up holes. *The Turn* was conceived and written over a period of five years that saw this golfer go from the absolute shitsville of loss and addiction to one of the happiest, most balanced periods of my entire life. Maybe as close to scratch as I will ever get.

Some important people helped me get through these years and deserve my deepest thanks for their unwavering friendship, love, and faith that I would complete my own difficult turn and learn to play better on the back nine.

In no particular order, huge love and gratitude to:

My dear friend and phenomenal agent, Scott Miller, who launched my career as a horror writer and didn't flinch when I gave him a golf comedy to reboot it. Rick Bleiweiss, for believing we had something here and bringing me into the Blackstone family. William Boggess, who did a superb job editing *The Turn* and helped me find that extra something special in so many scenes. Riam Griswold, copyediting ace who handled a million little things without a single complaint. And the entire Blackstone team, thank you for backing my underdog story like World Champs.

The moms, Kathy and Sandy, for loving and supporting me as only moms can. My brother, Mike, who's been blocking for me since I was old enough to walk. My dad, who didn't leave me his golf clubs, only the whole damn house.

Paul Bolinger, who showed me how incredibly "simple" it was to stop drinking and gave me a peanut butter and jelly sandwich when I needed it most. James Gardner, who was there with me for hundreds of rounds, witnessed the two aces I shot within thirty-three days, and far more importantly, strongly encouraged my best while relentlessly reminding me I could always do better. Christopher Lay, who gave me the blimp and other big laughs and kept reminding me to return to the green book. Jordan Mullins, who cheered my every shot, from a decent drive to our twelfth Fireball, and who defended me the same way he defends our country—selflessly and with full heart.

Huge love to Keith Martin, my real-life Coach Lowry, whose lessons were instrumental in bringing my handicap down from minus thirty to minus eleven and instilled in me a deeper respect and love for the game that's not just a game. Thank you for teaching me about load efficiency and reminding me over and over again that two-thirds of a full swing is enough for a supremely athletic specimen like me.

And of course our gangster cart girls, who made Twin Peaks the most beautiful place to golf in all of Colorado—Zoe, Shea, Cecily, and especially Megan, who kept me smiling while we grew up together over those five special summers. And so many other friends I connected or reconnected with through golf— Spanky, Ed, Darnell, Jose, and too many more to list—you are all extraordinary gentlemen, even when you're smoking, drinking, cussing, and pissing your way through a miserable round. And to the entire staff at Twin Peaks, who made the place so much more than a damn nice municipal course—you made me feel at home.